Praise for
EXPENDABLE

"This is a good read, and a very good first novel."
Locus

"An auspicious debut: the best first novel
I've read this decade."
Robert J. Sawyer, Nebula award-winning author of *Starplex*

COMMITMENT HOUR

"*Commitment Hour* has something for everyone."
SF Site Featured Review

"A quirky SF riddle and diverting small town murder
mystery, with some truly unusual characters."
Locus

VIGILANT

"Features a quick-witted heroine whose self-
deprecating narrative adds a personal touch to this
blend of mystery and high-tech thriller."
Library Journal

"Another thought-provoker . . . I promise that
you'll enjoy the reading."
San Diego Union-Tribune

"Action-packed . . . a fun read . . .
an enjoyable, fast-moving, off-planet adventure."
SF Site

Books by
James Alan Gardner

EXPENDABLE
COMMITMENT HOUR
VIGILANT
HUNTED
ASCENDING
TRAPPED

JAMES ALAN GARDNER

HUNTED

James Alan Gardner

An Imprint of HarperCollins*Publishers*

This is a work of fiction. Names, characters, places, and incidents are products of the author's imagination or are used fictitiously and are not to be construed as real. Any resemblance to actual events, locales, organizations, or persons, living or dead, is entirely coincidental.

EOS
An Imprint of HarperCollins*Publishers*
10 East 53rd Street
New York, New York 10022-5299

Copyright © 2000 by James Alan Gardner
Library of Congress Catalog Card Number: 00-90032
ISBN: 0-380-80209-0
www.eosbooks.com

First Eos paperback printing: July 2000

Eos Trademark Reg. U.S. Pat. Off. and in Other Countries, Marca Registrada, Hecho en U.S.A.
HarperCollins® is a trademark of HarperCollins Publishers Inc.

Printed in the U.S.A.

10 9 8 7 6 5 4 3

To Rob and Carolyn,
for getting me started in the Show,
then continuing to cheer from the stands

THANKS

Thanks to the usual crew: Linda Carson, Richard Curtis, and Jennifer Brehl. For continuing support, a big thank-you too to Andy Heidel and Lou Aronica.

Since I'm writing this in 1999, I'd like to thank the developers of Microsoft Word for DOS 5.0, still the most useful word processor for a fiction writer; and then I'd like to whack those same developers upside the head for not making the software Y2K-compliant. Come December 31, I'll have to switch to some elephantine replacement that thinks it knows what I want . . . when what I want is a decent thesaurus, intelligent use of style sheets, and a user interface that doesn't keep making me take my hands off the keyboard. (Gardner's Third Law: When a particular computer operation requires you to use the mouse, you will never get faster at that operation than your very first day of using the software. In other words, hunt-and-peck beats point-and-click. Grumble, grumble, grumble . . .)

Part 1

CROSSING THE LINE

1

GOING TO A PARTY

The first day of the flight, I was so happy to be heading home that I went to *Willow*'s cafeteria for supper with the crew . . . and it seemed as if every woman on the starship wanted me to try the Angoddi mushrooms, or did I listen to razzah poetry, or would I like a look at the engine-room service tunnels when the next shift was over?

I'd forgotten how bored folks get on long tours of duty. Bored with their jobs, bored with each other. One glimpse of a new face, and people go into feeding frenzy. Or breeding frenzy. Maybe I should have been flattered, but all that eager attention sort of got me terrified—I'd been stuck on a three-person moonbase for twenty whole years, so I felt way out of my depth when a dozen women wanted to make conversation with me.

"You're so cute for an Explorer!"

"And you don't smell bad!"

"Do you have a funny voice? I bet you have a funny voice. Say something."

"Um," I said. "Um."

"Look, he's *shy*!" One of the women giggled. "Can they stick you in the Explorer Corps just because you're shy? With a guy this built, I could cure his shyness real fast. Overnight!"

"He must be one of the *new* Explorers," another woman

said. "The volunteers. The ones who don't have anything wrong with them."

"Anyone who volunteers to be an Explorer has something wrong with them. Him. Whatever." A bald-headed woman laid both hands on my wrist and stared straight into my eyes. "Come on, handsome, you can be honest with us. You're an Explorer, and Explorers are never normal. What's wrong with you?"

I took a deep breath and told them all, "I'm stupid, okay? I'm stupid." Then I went back to my cabin and locked myself in.

The whole next day I kept getting comm-messages saying, "Sorry," or "We were just teasing," or "That invitation is still on for getting together in the service tunnels." Three women actually came to apologize at my door . . . and later, a man who said, "The women here are such bitches, aren't they? Forget 'em. Why don't you come down to my cabin for some sudsy VR?" I said thanks anyway, but maybe another time.

After that, when somebody knocked I pretended I wasn't home.

Just before noon on the third day, I got another visitor . . . and the peep-monitor showed it was a woman wearing an admiral's gray uniform. I couldn't very well keep an admiral shut out, so I ran my fingers through my hair, then told the door to open.

The admiral woman was short and brown and young, with a big purply blotch on her cheek; I couldn't tell what the blotch was, and didn't know if I was supposed to compliment it or pretend it didn't exist. My twin sister Samantha used to yell at me, "Edward, when you see a woman has done something special with her face, for God's sake say she looks pretty." It was easy to tell Sam she looked pretty, because she was always as beautiful as sunshine on a lake. With other women though, either I sat there tongue-tied, or I'd try a compliment and the woman would just stare at me . . . like maybe I was trying to be funny or something. I sure didn't want an admiral to think I was making fun of her face; so I just ignored her blotchy cheek and gave her my best salute.

It's hard to go wrong saluting. Especially with an admiral.

The woman at my door introduced herself as Lieutenant Admiral Festina Ramos, and said I had to come to the party. "What party?" I asked. Back when Samantha and I had been on active duty, I couldn't remember navy starships ever having parties. At least, none that I'd been invited to.

"We're crossing the line in fifteen minutes," the admiral woman said. "You should be there."

I didn't know what she meant, crossing the line; I was pretty sure there were no lines in outer space. When I said that, she laughed and pinched my cheek. "You're an angel." Then she took me by the arm and leaned against me all warm and a bit perfumed while she led me to the *Willow*'s recreation lounge.

The perfume was in her hair.

I wasn't so used to having perfumey women take me by the arm. Part of it was just being away from human things for so long—what with escorting Samantha on her big diplomatic mission, then the long awful time after, it'd been a whole thirty-five years since I'd gone out in human company. (That made me middle-aged, I guess: fifty-seven . . . though with YouthBoost treatments, I hadn't changed a whit since my twenties.)

But even when I was a teenager on New Earth, I didn't spend much time with women. My father didn't like me being seen by anyone off our estate. Dad was rich and important—Alexander York, Admiral of the Gold in the Outward Fleet—and he treated me like a big smeary stain on his personal reputation. Even though it wasn't my fault.

Back before I was born, Dad paid a doctor lots of money to make my sister and me more perfect than perfect: athletic and dazzling and smart, smart, smart. It didn't matter that gene engineering was illegal in the Technocracy—my father went to an independent world where the laws were different . . . or where the police were cheaper to buy off.

The gene-splicing worked real well for Samantha, but with me it only did part of the job. I can do hundreds of push-ups without stopping, and Sam always called me devilishly handsome, but my brain chemistry didn't come out so good. Too much of some things, too little of others. So Dad kept me at home for fear his "retarded idiot son" would embarrass him in public.

I didn't mind so much. He kept Samantha at home too, with all kinds of private tutors. Sam became *my* private tutor, so it worked out pretty well. She taught me to be polite and brave and honest, and to think really hard about being good to people. Later, when we were teenagers, she'd take me on pretend-dates so I wouldn't feel left out: to the gazebo on the south lawn near the reflecting pool, where we'd dance and dance and dance.

Sometimes I wished I had someone else to dance with—someone who liked me, who wasn't my twin sister. But I never said that to Sam; I didn't want to hurt her feelings.

On our way to the party, the perfumey admiral woman explained that "crossing the line" meant leaving the Troyen star system for interstellar space. It was a big moment in any starship flight, the point where you cross out of your starting system . . . because the League of Peoples has a law, if you've been a bad person, you aren't allowed to go from one star system to another. If you try it, they kill you. Not messily or anything like that—you just die the second you leave the system where you did the bad things. It's like magic; except that there is no magic, just superadvanced science from races millions of years older than us humans. To the League, we were as stupid as worms on a plate, and no matter how smart we thought we were, the League was a billion times smarter. No one *ever* fooled them.

Samantha told me the same thing years ago. "Edward, if

you ever do something really awful, you'd better stay put after that. Don't go running off into space, thinking you can just sneak away without anyone knowing; because the League always knows. Always." I'd followed my sister's advice ever since . . . till now.

Now I was headed for a party to celebrate leaving the Troyen system. If it weren't for the admiral pulling me along with her, I might have gone back to my cabin and tried not to cry.

The lounge was decked out like one of those old masquerade carnivals in Venice or Rome—all the walls set to starry night, with fountains and cobblestones and fancy bridges over canals that stretched far back into the distance. Now and then, the moving pictures showed people in masks and patchwork costumes, running through the streets with torches or gathering in courtyards for medieval dances.

Very pretty and classical. Unlike the *real* party.

Nearly everybody in *Willow*'s crew was there . . . and they sure weren't acting like sober navy personnel. Only the woman and I were in uniform, her in admiral's gray, me in Explorer Corps black. The rest were all costumed up, either in strange clothes or body paints or holo-surrounds. I couldn't tell what half of them were supposed to be—like the man just inside the door, wearing pink-silk pajamas and a big putty nose. He gave me a sloppy wet kiss on the cheek, and said, "Ooo, aren't you the fetching whelp!" . . . in a high voice with an odd accent, like he was imitating a character on some broadcast. The woman on my arm laughed, and glanced to see if I'd laugh too; but it'd been so long since I'd seen any shows, I didn't know why this was supposed to be funny.

After a moment, the admiral woman gave my arm a squeeze, and said, "Come on, angel, relax, okay? You want to dance?"

I hadn't even realized there was music playing. It was soft as rainfall but tinkly-jangly, with no beat I could make out. "I don't know how to dance to this," I said. It wasn't anything like the music Sam and I listened to, back in the darkened gazebo.

"This is just Coy-Grip," the admiral woman told me. "You don't have to do anything special." Which wasn't true at all. Apparently, she and I had to wrap our arms tight together in something like a *chin na* submission hold I'd learned once. (Over the years, Dad's security guards gave me a heap of free martial-arts training.) I ended up hunched over like a bear, while the woman was practically on tiptoe; but she told me we fitted together perfectly, my shoulders touching hers, our arms all twined around each other, holding hands, our faces very close.

The woman murmured I could move my feet any way I wanted—the dance was the position, not the steps. She started an inch-by-inch shuffle and I followed along, doing my best to match her every motion; I was terrified if I went the wrong direction, I might accidentally snap her thin little wrists. After a few seconds, she gave a twittery laugh and whispered, "Relax, angel, relax. You look like you're at a funeral."

She gave me a quick kiss on the nose. I could smell wine on her breath: really strong. She must have been partying a fair while before she fetched me from my cabin.

In fact, everyone on the dance floor seemed tipsy. We kept getting bumped by a wobbly slobbery man wearing the holo of an alien species I didn't recognize—something brown and cockroachy with six of everything, legs, arms, eyes. The man was too drunk to care about staying inside his hologram "costume" . . . so I could see bare human legs kicking out from the edges of the cockroach image, and once, a hairy human rump.

Yes, it was *that* kind of party: where people went naked under their holos. Here and there, I could see couples squashed together against the wall. Right in front of me, a larger-than-life holo of a Roman soldier had his breastplate buried in the face of a holo-alien who looked like a walking thistle bush. The two holograms broke into jagged interference patterns where they overlapped each other, so now and then I could see through to the people underneath. It was a nude woman and a nude man; she had her legs scissored around his waist.

In the middle of the day. On a navy ship. And they all had to be crew members, because I was the only passenger.

"Is something wrong here?" I whispered to the woman Coy-Gripping my arms.

"Nothing's wrong, angel. You're fucking gorgeous. Relax." She pressed herself harder against me. It had to be hurting her wrists, but she didn't seem to care.

Maybe she'd been taking more than just wine.

The music stopped. I got ready to untangle myself, but the woman held on tight. "Wait," she whispered. "Wait. It's time."

"Time for what?"

Before she could answer, a gong sounded over the ship's speaker system: like a clock bell tolling the hour in some fairy tale. The woman whispered, "It'll strike thirteen . . . melodramatic bastards. We cross the line on the last stroke. Hold me till then, angel, would you? Please?"

All around the room, lots of other people were pairing off too—the drunk in the cockroach hologram stumbled up against the man in pink pajamas and they grabbed each other in a tight hug, the drunk's arms reaching out of the roach's chest, the pajama man's head disappearing through the roach's mandibles. He must have been leaning in to rest his cheek on the drunk's shoulder.

Gong.

Four seconds of silence.

Gong.

Everyone had stopped talking, but I could hear somebody sniffling back tears. And somebody else praying. And somebody whispering, "Please, please, please . . ."

Gong.

Then I gasped as someone new came through the door: someone wearing the holo of a Mandasar hive-queen, sulphur yellow, four meters long, built like a four-clawed lobster with a huge brain-hump on her back. Her venom glands were fat and inflamed—days past the time she should have been milked. Even though I could tell it was only a holo, the sight still made me flinch.

Remembering what happened to Samantha.

The man in silk pajamas saw the queen and screamed. He wasn't the only one: people shouted and wailed all over the room, till a voice inside the queen said, "At ease, damn it, it's only me."

"Christ Almighty!" the man in pajamas said, pressing a hand against his chest. "You nearly gave us a heart attack, Captain."

"He should have worn something different," whispered the woman in my arms. "He's the captain; he should know better."

Gong.

"What's the count?" she asked suddenly.

"I don't know." My mind had shut down for a moment when I saw the hive-queen. I might have missed a gong or two.

"What's the count?" my admiral called to the room.

No one answered. Faces looked wildly at each other, some of them going pale . . . as if no one had kept track of the tolling.

Gong.

"Shit," the woman muttered to no one in particular. Then she looked up into my eyes, and said, "Kiss me. Now."

"What?"

She didn't answer; she just bent her elbows, twisting my wrists so I was levered down close to her. Pushing up hard on tiptoe, she jammed her mouth against mine. Open. And her tongue swept inside urgently, moving fast, her eyes closed tight.

I closed my eyes too. Feeling strange and fizzy, as if I'd been drinking myself: the taste of the woman who tasted like wine, the touch of her pressing against me. I knew this wasn't a love kiss, or even a sex kiss—it was fear, pure fear, some awful terror that made her want to be holding someone as tight as her arms and heart could squeeze. Like a little girl who felt better for hugging her brother, when the lightning and thunder rattled outside. I held the woman and let her kiss me as desperately as she wanted, while the clock continued toward thirteen.

Gong.

Gong.

Gong.

Gong.

The woman's tongue stopped. Her grip on my arms loosened and her lips eased back. When I opened my eyes, I saw her head loll to one side. A string of saliva trailed across the purple-red splotch on her cheek.

Her eyes hadn't opened.

As I unwrapped myself from the Coy-Grip position, the woman's weight slumped away from me. Trying to hold her up, I called to the rest of the room, "Can somebody help here? I think . . ."

But by then, I'd had time to look around.

The man in pink pajamas had fallen on his face. The drunk he'd been holding was on the floor too, lying half-in/half-out of his hologram. The hologram was tilted at an odd angle.

Over against the wall, the soldier and the thistle bush had sagged straight down, still connected to each other. Their holos had gone askew, so that the head of the longest thistle stuck out of the Roman's back like the hilt of a sword.

People all around the room sprawled limply over the furniture or spread-eagled on the carpet. Even the captain. One of his hands lay on the ground, poking out through the edge of the hive-queen's shell.

Silence. No more gongs.

We had crossed the line, and the whole crew was dead. Even the woman who called me angel.

It made my eyes sting: that she died kissing a complete stranger.

I laid her body onto the floor as gently as I could. "I'm

sorry," I said. "If the League of Peoples wanted to kill someone for being bad..." I looked around the room at the corpses. "Sorry," I told them all. "I thought it would be me."

2

INSPECTING MY COMMAND

I couldn't think of what to do next, so I just sat down on the floor beside the admiral woman. People look so helpless when they're dead—like they're expecting you to make it all better. Any other time, I might have tried CPR to start the woman's heart again; but it wouldn't work now. When the League of Peoples kills you, you stay dead.

Dead forever, the woman who kissed me. And everyone else. So quiet: the music had stopped when the gonging began, and now there was no one to tell the sound system, "Resume play." The lounge walls continued to show Italian masqueraders laughing and dancing in feathered masks, but they were just silent pictures.

No sound.

No breathing.

You don't know how much you miss the sound of breathing till it's not there.

In all that silence, I desperately wanted to *do* something. Help these poor people. But all I could think of was wiping the little saliva string from the admiral woman's cheek. So that's the useless stupid thing I did.

When I looked at my finger, some of the purple splotch had come off on my skin. I rubbed the woman's face again; the splotch was a waxy sort of makeup she must have put on for the party. Was it the popular fashion now to wear big garish blobs? Or was the admiral woman like the man in pink pajamas, dressed up to imitate somebody I didn't know?

The woman might not be an admiral at all. Maybe this was just another costume.

I wanted to wash her face: scrub off the gunk so she'd look like herself. Underneath, she might have been pretty. But when people died, you weren't supposed to touch them. *Contact Security and leave the site undisturbed*—that's what they always said in VR stories when things went terribly wrong.

"Ship-soul, attend," I called out . . . hoping that was still the phrase you used when you wanted to talk to a starship's central computer. "Can you please call the security officer who's on watch?"

A sexless metallic voice answered from the ceiling: "There are no security officers available."

Uh-oh.

"Ship-soul," I said, "please connect me with . . ." Who? The captain? No, he was dead inside the hive-queen. (I avoided looking that direction; even if the queen was just a hologram, she still gave me the jitters.) "Please connect me with the ship's commanding officer."

"The commanding officer is Explorer Second Class Edward York."

"Me?"

"You are the highest-ranking officer aboard *Willow*."

I swallowed. "Is anyone else alive at all?"

"No, Captain. Awaiting your instructions."

Nobody had ever put me in charge of anything before. That was fine with me; I knew I wasn't captain material.

If you want the honest truth, I wasn't Explorer material either. When Samantha joined the navy's Diplomatic Corps, she absolutely insisted I go with her on her first assignment. She wanted me for her bodyguard—the only person in the universe she could trust one hundred percent. I figured Dad would make a big fuss, but he gave in almost immediately; Sam knew all the ways to make him say yes, and he never found a single way to tell her no.

Being an admiral and all, Dad pulled strings to slip me around the entrance qualification board and straight into the navy. He didn't want me going Diplomatic like Sam—Dad had been a diplomat himself before becoming an admiral, and he refused to let me "sully" the Diplomacy Corps's gold uniform. For a while he was set on me being a Security officer, since the Security Corps was officially in charge of protecting Outward Fleet dignitaries . . . but that fell through when the senior Security admiral got pissy about Dad forcing "a totally inadequate imbecile" into her command. (The Security admiral had never set eyes on me; I guess she'd heard Dad bad-mouth me for so long, she pictured someone all gibbering and drooling.) Dad tried three more service corps without any luck, then he finally just made me an Explorer. I never went to Explorer Academy—you can't get past the door there unless you have *real* brains—but Dad said I'd still fit in just fine with the other Explorers. "None of them are normal either."

I wondered if my father might possibly feel proud of me now, seeing as I'd become a sort of a kind of a captain. No. Not likely. From the day Sam and I were born, she was the precious jewel and me the steaming mound of dog turd. Just look at what happened when things fell apart on Troyen, with the riots and war and all. The surviving diplomats got evacuated all the way back to New Earth, but I only made it as far as a stifling little observation post on Troyen's larger moon.

Twenty whole years Dad left me stuck there; dumped into exile and isolation. Twenty years without a break, while the other observers got rotated off in six-month shifts. Dad left me on that moonbase like something stuffed into the far back corner of the attic, something he couldn't get rid of but never wanted to see again.

Because of what had happened to Sam.

Because I hadn't been a good enough bodyguard.

If Dad found out I'd become acting captain of *Willow*,

he'd probably say, "Get that moron out of there before he wrecks the ship."

It took me a while to learn anything helpful from the ship-soul. I didn't know which questions to ask, or the keywords real captains used when they wanted a status report. Eventually though, I found out this much: *Willow* was locked on autopilot, heading toward a navy base near the free planet Celestia. Regulations wouldn't let the ship dock unless we had a competent human pilot at the helm; but we could hang off at a distance till the base sent over someone who knew how to drive. Barring accidents or breakdowns, I'd be sitting in port within a week.

That wasn't so bad—nothing for me to do but wait and stay out of trouble.

I decided my one and only order would be to have the ship-soul lower the temperature in the lounge: make it a big walk-in refrigerator. There were dozens of dead people lying around, and I didn't want them starting to rot.

My first inclination was to sit out the week in my cabin . . . but soon I couldn't stand moping there, wallowing all morose. The crazy thing was, I wasn't really mourning; I was feeling bad for not feeling worse. All those people dead—people who'd talked with me and flirted with me, and even one who'd kissed me—but now that they were out of sight, I felt more alone than sad. Pitying my live healthy self rather than all those blank corpses.

What was wrong with me? Shouldn't I be crying and grieving and all? But the most I could do was touch my lips over and over, like maybe if I remembered the kiss *exactly*, I would melt into some decent sorrow, the way a normal person would feel.

No. I just felt dull. Deadened and distant and dumb.

After a while, I decided this was no way for a captain to act. A good captain doesn't hang about sulking, trying to prod himself into emotion; a good captain looks after his ship. Maybe when the crew members died, one of them had left the water running, or a pressure pot boiling up coffee. In my years at the Troyen moonbase, it'd been my job to watch for things like that. So I decided to walk around *Willow*, every square centimeter, hoping maybe I'd find something productive to do instead of brooding all by myself.

That's how I found the hive-queen. A real one. Except she was just as dead as the crew.

The venom sacs on the queen were inflamed bright green, just like the holo I'd seen in the lounge. I guess that's where the hologram came from—the captain had taken a picture of the queen as she sat in the ship's hold.

From the look of the hold, the queen had done more than just sit there: she'd tried to rip straight through the walls with her claws. You wouldn't think a creature of flesh and blood would be strong enough to gouge out whole chunks of steel-plast . . . but the far bulkhead was ribboned with huge ragged furrows, so deep I could stick my hand in up to the wrist.

If the walls looked bad, the queen's claws looked worse. With all that smashing and bashing, her claws had got their points hammered down blunt and their armor plate fractured like peanut brittle. Sticky brown blood was still oozing up through the cracks in her shell.

It made me go sick in the stomach to see a queen all damaged and smashed. Injured. *Broken*. But it was a good thing she'd hurt herself too much to keep whacking on the walls; otherwise, she would have bashed through the hull and let hard vacuum into the ship.

Why was *Willow* transporting her here on her own, without attendants? Queens go mad if they aren't milked every day. Her poor venom sacs were like two swollen balloons bulging up where her tail met her torso: both sacs had turned grass green against her yellow body, so you couldn't possibly miss how full they were. Queen Verity once told me it hurt like daggers to go unmilked for even a few hours past ripeness, and this queen . . .

This queen wasn't Queen Verity. And at the moment, I

didn't want to think about Verity, not with one of her royal sisters lying dead in front of me. Which one was this, I wondered. Queen Fortitude? Clemency? Honor? Or one of the queens-in-waiting who escaped from deep freeze while Troyen was spinning into civil war?

Me, I couldn't tell; Verity was the only queen I really knew. The palace's chief of protocol claimed that Verity would feel grossly insulted if I ever set eyes on another queen.

High Queen Verity had been fiercely, deeply jealous about me . . . but then, she'd been fiercely, deeply jealous about all her husbands.

3

WATCHING THE QUEEN

That night I had bad dreams: a woman dying in my arms, but I couldn't tell whether she was the blotchy-faced admiral or Samantha. Her death left something black and oily on my hands—everything I touched got smudged all over with the grease. I looked up, and floating overhead was a mirror showing that the stuff covered my face too, smeared thick everywhere . . . till suddenly, the oily gunk went one way and I went the other, so there were two of us standing side by side. Me, and then a second me made of sludge.

The sludge-me screamed and screamed and screamed.

Then a different dream: being chased by a queen in venom-frenzy, down the long promenade that swept along the side of Verity's palace. All kinds of people cluttered the pavement, humans, Mandasars, Fasskisters, Divians, everyone hanging about, getting in the way; and I had to dodge around them or knock them over, which drove me frantic with frustration even though the queen never seemed to close the gap behind me. She ran like she could catch me anytime, but was toying with me, letting me tire myself out. Now and then she'd aim her stingers at me, and they'd spray me down with venom, like fire hoses. Eventually, the promenade got so slimy with bright green poison, I slipped and fell down hard. Before I could get up again, the queen was bending over me . . . only it wasn't a real queen, but

Samantha, with her head on a queen's body . . .

I woke in the darkness, all prickled with sweat. Alone in my cabin. Alone on the ship. Trembling with cold night terrors.

That's when it finally hit home: just how alone I really was. Nobody else on *Willow* but corpses. Maybe no living thing within light-years.

As alone as a human could get.

The realization spooked me. Gave me the rabid creeps. I suddenly got the idea that any second I'd hear a scratch at the door: the dead woman wanting another kiss, except now she was some withered skeletal thing, moaning with hunger. Or maybe it would be the queen with her blood-cracked claws, trying to break down the door and stab me with her stingers, just to ease the pain in her venom sacs.

I held my breath, waiting for the scratching noise. Scared stiff to move for fear something outside would hear me. But nothing happened. The dead don't really get up and walk . . . even when you panic yourself into thinking it's possible.

After a while, I thought of turning on a light. I did it fast, before I had a chance to get the creeps about that too. With the light on, it wasn't so hard to get out of bed and get dressed; maybe it would be a good idea to go to the cafeteria for something to drink. Not alcohol—I was acting captain. But in stories, people talk about warm milk making you feel better. I couldn't remember ever drinking warm milk, but I thought why not give it a try.

The corridors were quiet. And empty. And dimmed down to twilight because this was *Willow*'s sleep shift. I could have ordered the ship-soul to power everything to daytime brightness or to play bouncy music wherever I went, but that wouldn't fool me. The manuals pretend that night and day are just arbitrary conventions on a starship, that you can flip them back to front and no one will know the difference. Me, I *felt* the difference. Deep in my bones, I felt pure night smothering all around me—like it'd been waiting for years and years to catch me alone, and finally had its chance to grab me by the throat.

Samantha would have slapped me for imagining those kind of things. She used to roll her eyes and laugh: "You're such a *child*, Edward." Usually I'd laugh too and say *she* was the child—younger than me by a whole ten minutes.

But I knew I was acting like a kid, letting myself get scared of nothing. Fifty-seven years old; I should know better. Halfway to the cafeteria, I turned around and headed for the captain's quarters instead. I was supposed to be master and commander, not some puss-puppy trying to make it all better with warm milk. As of now, I'd devote myself to captainly things instead of hiding back in my cabin.

Besides, it'd be harder to have bad dreams in a captain's bunk, wouldn't it? Captains don't let themselves get carried away by imagination.

"Ship-soul, attend," I called out loudly as I entered the captain's room. "Vidscreen on, forward view."

The room had a nice big monitor, filling up a whole half of one wall. The screen flicked on, showing a calm empty starscape. Nothing out there but nothingness.

"Aft view," I said.

More stars in the infinite black. No nightmares chasing us.

I took a breath. "Interior view, recreation lounge."

The screen changed to show the lounge and all the bodies, still exactly where they'd fallen. Most of the holograms were gone: their battery power had run down. Instead of the Roman soldier and the alien thistle bush, an ordinary man and woman lay crumpled against each other, both of them naked except for the harnesses that held their holo-projectors.

The dead people looked so sad and pointless. Even the admiral woman, lying where I'd set her down . . . she wasn't going to turn into a kiss-hungry demon who came slobbering at my door. She was just going to lie there and lie there and lie there, never getting up again.

"Interior view," I told the ship-soul, trying not to let my voice crack. "The hold with the Mandasar queen."

The image on the screen shifted to show the hold . . . and nothing had changed there either. The queen lay dead, her claws smashed bloody, her stingers dangling limp, her venom sacs . . .

Her venom sacs . . .

They weren't bulging quite so full. They had a tiny sag to them now. And their grass green color had faded a bit.

That wasn't right.

"Ship-soul," I said, walking up to the screen, "can you zoom in on this area here?" I pointed to the closest sac.

The image expanded, so big I had to step back from the screen to see it properly: a huge looming close-up of the sac, and even as I watched I could see the outer membrane deflate a bit more.

What was going on?

On Troyen, one of Verity's attendants told me queens kept making venom for two days after death . . . like hair and fingernails growing on human corpses. The sacs on the screen should be swelling even larger, not shrinking. I guess one of the sacs might have built up so much pressure it sprang a leak; but both sacs? Anyway, the magnified view didn't show any spills on the floor or the queen's body.

For a second, I had another nudge of the cold creeps. Something was happening, something I didn't understand . . . and whatever it was, I had to deal with it on my own. No one would warn me if I was about to do something so brainlessly stupid any normal person would laugh out loud.

"Just move," I said to myself. "Just get moving."

I forced my feet toward the door; and soon after that I was running for the hold.

There was no one there; of course there wasn't. The hold had looked empty on the ship's cameras, and it looked empty when I entered in person. But just in the time I took to sprint down from the captain's quarters, the queen's venom sacs had sagged another few millimeters.

I approached as cautious as a mouse, keeping my eyes on the floor—if venom was spilling down, I didn't want to step in it. For all I knew, it might eat a hole straight through my boot. Not that venom is usually acidic, but you can never tell for sure.

It's strange, dangerous stuff, queen's venom, especially to humans. Sometimes a teeny droplet on your skin is enough to kill you . . . like when it contains nerve toxins that garble up signals going to and from your brain. Your heart stops beating because it isn't getting the right instructions anymore. Other times, though, venom isn't lethal after all; it just gives you hallucinations . . . or a rash . . . or a crusty patch on your wrist, at which point the doctors cut off your whole arm.

(That happened once to a human maid at the palace. Queen Verity said the spill was just a terrible accident.)

The thing about venom is it runs through a cycle, over a full Troyen year. Queens are milked every day, and each batch has slightly different properties. The local biochemists have filled up dozens of confidential databases, keeping track of what you get at each point in the cycle, not to mention what happens if you milk a few hours early or late. It's all gigantically complicated, and the scientists were always struggling over the fine details; during my time as consort, they were constantly finding new trace chemicals that turned up for maybe half a day in the cycle, then vanished for the rest of year.

But everyone on Troyen understood the basic principle of what venom did: it made queens.

If a Mandasar female of six years old started suckling on a queen during the right week in spring—and if she was allowed to suckle whenever she wanted, day or night, big sips or small, throughout the year—by the next spring the little girl lobster would be a junior queen. The constantly changing mix of chemicals mutated her body; one day's feeding multiplied her brain cells, the next day stimulated a gland, the next made her muscles grow. Soon she'd be bigger, smarter, stronger, and lots more *regal* than other girls her age. (Provided she didn't die or go mad. Things like that happened now and then. There's a reason it's called venom.)

So walking across *Willow*'s hold, where there might be venom on the floor, I watched my step real carefully. But even when I got close to the queen's carcass, I couldn't see any leaks—not a drop on her lobstery tail, no wetness on the sacs themselves, no dribbles down her carapace or puddles on the steel-plast beneath her. Still, the sacs kept shrinking: very very slowly, but over the course of a minute, I could definitely see the difference.

So where was the stuff going? Seeping back into her corpse? I guess she had to have ducts or tubes connecting the sacs to the inside part of her body. Maybe the tubes got damaged as the queen tried to bash her way through the hull. Or maybe, when the League of Peoples wanted the queen to die, they'd just broken open a valve and let the venom slop back into her insides. Maybe that was considered poetic justice, having the queen poisoned by her own juices.

The League folks were aliens. Who knew how their minds worked?

As gingerly as a feather, I reached toward the nearest sac . . . and just before my hand touched the surface tissue, I felt a funny sort of fuzzy sensation on my palm.

Fuzz? There shouldn't be any fuzz. The outside of the sac was as smooth as a balloon.

Then the truth struck me. "Ship-soul," I yelled, "nano scan! Here, now, centered on my hand."

Two seconds later, a rackety choir of alarms started wailing their brains out.

Lucky for me I'd left the hatch open. I dived out the door just before the automatic computer defenses slammed it shut with a great whacking clang. That didn't mean I was safe, but at least I wouldn't be locked in the hold when a full-scale nanotech war broke out.

I rolled to my feet and wondered if I had time to get

back to the captain's quarters. No—a black cloud was already roaring down the corridor toward me, like a dust devil whirling on the desert wind. I dropped to the deck again, squeezing my eyes shut, covering my mouth and nose with my left hand while holding my right far out from my body. That was the hand that had touched the venom sac; that was the hand that needed to be sanitized.

The cloud swept over me like a tornado. Each tiny black-dust particle was a microscopic robot, a hunter-killer built to destroy the equally small nanites that had been buzzing about the queen. Yes—the fuzz I'd felt had been little machines, the size of bacteria or maybe even viruses; and they'd been crowding around the venom sacs so thick I could actually detect them with my fingers.

Fuzzy air.

There was only one thing the nanites could be doing: sneaking their microscopic way through the membrane of the venom sac, scooping up minidrops of venom like bees sipping nectar, then crawling out again. That's why the venom sacs had been deflating—weeny little robots were draining them in a miniscule bucket brigade.

And now *Willow* had sent a cloud of its own nanites to wipe out the intruders.

I could feel the defense nano scouring my skin—not just the hand that had touched the enemy, but everywhere: my face, my scalp, all under my clothes. The defenders would rip apart everything they found . . . even natural skin bacteria, because the people who built nano invaders often tried to disguise the tiny little monsters as ordinary microbes. When something is the same shape and size as an everyday bread mold, it's easier to sneak past an antinano scan.

Every ship in the navy was constantly running defense scans. When crew members came aboard, they all got the once-over. So did cargo and supplies and equipment. The ship-soul also took down-to-the-atom audits of selected cubic centimeters of air, checking out every microscopic thingy to make sure it wasn't a nanite in paramecium's clothing. Even so, with all those precautions, a camouflaged swarm of invaders could usually avoid being noticed unless the computerized detectors knew exactly where to look. Most times you didn't know you'd been boarded till the nanites actually attacked.

The only good news was that the League of Peoples killed bad nanotech the same way they killed bad humans: instant death as soon as the host ship crossed the line. So those of us in the Outward Fleet didn't have to worry much about lethal attacks to ourselves or essential life-support systems. Microrobot invaders could be programmed for vandalism, like cracking ship security or gumming up fuel lines, but they were never allowed to out-and-out kill you.

They could, however, steal stuff. Valuable stuff. Like hive-queen venom.

Willow's defense cloud chafed me hard for twenty seconds. Then it swept away, heading for the hold and the bigger battle. I was left on the deck, feeling as if a whole layer of my skin had been chewed clean off.

It had. My right hand was covered with stinging pin-pricks of blood, like I'd scraped it full strength against rough concrete. As for my clothes . . . well, the little hunter-killers had ripped furiously into the fabric, chewing it to tatters wherever they found the least little microbe lurking in the weave. Natural microbes or otherwise. Considering how many microbes there are everywhere, I scarcely had an intact stitch left on my body.

Good thing there was no one on board to see me.

I hurried back to my cabin for new clothes. And to wash off my blood-specked hand. While I was dressing, I asked the ship-soul what was happening down in the hold.

"Our defenses are engaging the enemy," the ship-soul answered. "There is ongoing opposition."

"So the nanites are fighting back?"

"Some are providing cover while their fellows retreat. Our defenses have numerical superiority, but are encountering difficulties."

"Show me."

The vidscreen in my cabin wasn't nearly as big as the captain's, but it still gave a decent view of the hold. Not that I had much to see: the black cloud of *Willow*'s defenders were bunched up close to the door and trying to push farther into the room. Something unseen was pushing back, bottling up the cloud in a pocket around the hatch.

Our forces and the enemy, fighting nano-a-nano.

"Can you magnify the shot?" I asked the ship-soul. "I want to see what they're actually doing."

The picture switched to microscopic resolution: four black hunter-killers, each with a blobby body, a whiplike tail, and a jaggedy pincer claw, had surrounded a much smaller enemy. The enemy looked like it was made from jelly, and shaped like a ripped-out eyeball—a juice-filled balloon with a little bulge on the front and a stringy tail out the back. The tail was for propulsion, so the little beastie could swim through air like a tadpole through pond water; the bulgy bit up top probably held the nanite's tiny brain. As for the main balloon body, it was full of grass green fluid . . . Mandasar venom, stolen from the dead queen.

The hunter-killers closed in fast, whipping their own tails and driving forward till the enemy was within pincer range. They all grabbed on at the same second: four claws scissoring into the enemy's jelly body and slicing right through. The eyeball didn't try to defend itself . . . and it didn't have to. As soon as its body got cut open, venom splooged out onto all four attackers, beading up on their claws and slopping back onto their bodies. The hunter-killers suddenly started jerking their tails as if they were having fits, two of them flying right off the screen while the other pair jittered like crazy till their claws broke off.

That venom was wicked stuff. Especially against hunter-killers who weren't built for chemical warfare.

I sat back from the vidscreen and chewed a bit on one of my knuckles. Our hunter-killers were programmed to attack four-on-one, I knew that much . . . so for each enemy eyeball destroyed, four of our guys would be taken out by the venom spill. Not such a great ratio for our side. We'd still win in the end, by sheer force of numbers—*Willow* carried at least three full defense clouds, and could manufacture more pretty quick—but by the time we fought through the nanites who were trying to delay us, the other invaders would have retreated to other parts of the ship. Finding them would be a real needle-in-the-haystack.

Of course, the computers would handle the search. Nothing for me but to sit back wondering what it all meant.

Who in the world could smuggle nano onto a navy ship? Who knew the queen would be on *Willow*? And who would ever want to steal queen's venom?

Drug pirates? Supposedly the big crime lords were always looking for new chemicals that did strange things to people. So were legitimate drug companies. Those databases on Troyen, the ones that listed the ingredients of venom at each point in the cycle . . . they were locked up top-secret, passworded and encrypted. Samantha once called the databanks "the high queen's golden trust fund"— formulas that could be sold for tons of money if Verity ever needed the cash.

Of course, Verity was dead now. Maybe all the people who knew the passwords were dead too. Troyen's civil war had been going on for twenty years.

I wondered if one of the rebel factions on Troyen might want to steal venom to manufacture a whole bunch of new queens. But that was crazy—even if they milked this dead queen dry, they'd only get juice from one point in the year-long cycle. You couldn't use that on some poor little girl. Today's venom might kick a gland into high gear, and tomorrow's shut it off again. If you gave a girl one day's dose without giving her the next day's too, you'd completely throw off her body's chemical balance. Like the gene treatments that were supposed to make Sam and me extra special, you might end up with someone better than average . . . but you might also make the little girl "a hopeless retarded idiot."

Would anyone take such an awful risk with a child?

Well, yes—who knew that better than me? But it still didn't make sense. Sending nano onto a navy ship would make the Admiralty as mad as a swarm of hornets. There had to be easier ways to get a sip of venom than taking on the entire Outward Fleet.

So why did someone do it?

For a second, I wished there was a special venom to make *humans* smarter. I knew I'd never be smart-smart; but I hated the way so many things went straight over my head.

If Samantha were here, *she'd* know what was going on.

4

SHIVERING A LOT

The pinpricks on my hand kept stinging. I soaked the sore parts in cold water and thought about going to sick bay for ointment . . . but the doctors were dead, and I wouldn't know what to look for on my own. Instead, I headed for the captain's quarters again, to keep tabs on the search for the nanites.

An hour later, the computer reported the hold was clean. That didn't mean we'd killed the intruders—they'd just managed to get away to other parts of the ship. The ship-soul had found a teeny hole chewed through one of the lock hatches in the vent shafts between the hold and hydroponics next door. No surprise there; even if most of the nanites were miniature tankers loading up venom, they'd have an escort of sappers for digging in and out of wherever they wanted to go.

By now, the nanites might be spread like dust through the whole of *Willow*, or hiding in little bunches, tucked into crawl spaces where no one would notice them. The ship's scans might trip over a few invaders, but a Security officer once told me such scans missed at least 95 percent of the bugs that were out there. It's just monumentally difficult to search every particle of air for something the size of a virus, especially when the things you're trying to find are programmed to avoid being caught.

The best I could do was tell the ship-soul to station a

defense cloud around the queen's venom sacs in case the invaders came back. I didn't expect the cloud would have any luck—the rotten little thieves knew we were onto them. But you have to do something, don't you?

I fell asleep in front of the captain's vidscreen, just as ship's day was dawning. When I woke again, my right hand *really* hurt—the pinprick marks were redder than before, and turning hot. So I went to sick bay after all, where I spent half an hour holding up one medicine after another and asking the ship-soul, "What does this do?" (It's no good reading the packages; they're all written in doctorese. Big complicated words that are intentionally invented so people can't understand them.)

Eventually I found something to smear on: an anti-inflammatory, the ship-soul said, and that sounded like just what I wanted. By then, I was worried the swelling might be more than a simple infection; there might be eyeball nanites under my skin, or hunter-killers that had got carried away when they were cleaning me off. Supposedly the hunter-killers knew enough not to chop up human tissue . . . but if they noticed an eyeball burrowing its way into me, they might decide to claw in after it.

That's not something you want to think about too long.

The infection got worse over the next day. My hand swelled up; I tried icing it, but after a while I couldn't stand the pain of anything touching my skin. The red flush of inflammation started creeping past my wrist and slowly up my arm. I wondered if I should put on a tourniquet or something . . . but that seemed like a lot of work, and I was deep-to-the-bone tired. No energy to care about stupid red flushes. I felt freezing cold, too—now and then I'd get so shivery, my teeth would chatter. Eventually I pulled myself over to the captain's bed, dialed up the heat to maximum, and wondered why I still wasn't warm enough.

Sick and dizzy, jumbled and confused. Sometimes I thought I was back on Troyen again, where I'd spent a year in and out of my head with a disease called the Coughing Jaundice. My sister had come by every day—wasting time on me when she should have been solving the little crises that were piling up into one big disaster. For years after, I wondered if *I* was the one to blame for the civil war: keeping Sam from her work, because I'd caught some alien flu. Me, lying in a special royal infirmary, woozy and out of touch, while the streets filled up with mutineers . . .

I tried to keep my mind off the bad times. Soon, I couldn't think of anything else.

Every so often, I'd hallucinate there was someone else in the captain's cabin, trying to talk to me. For a while it sounded like Samantha and Queen Verity, asking why I hadn't saved them. Then it turned into a male voice I didn't recognize, telling me it was time to wake up, that I'd slept long enough and people would suffer if I didn't come to my senses soon. I decided it must be the ship-soul trying to snap me out of the shivers . . . except for one little snippet of pleading that must have been completely inside my head.

"Please, Edward. Innocence needs us. Both of us."

That's what the voice said. And it wasn't the ship-soul speaking, because *Willow*'s computer couldn't possibly know about Innocence. Nobody did, except me and Verity and a few other people who were bloodily murdered twenty years ago. So it must have been my own brain talking, babbling all mixed-up and bleary.

Well . . . yes and no.

Two days of that, all spinning and confused. Then I woke and it was over. My head clear. My shivers gone. Even a bit of energy and appetite.

But I'd sure made a mess of the captain's bed.

While I cleaned up the sheets, the ship-soul gave me an official report on the status of *Willow*. Most of the words just bounced off my brain—there was a big long recitation of statistics, fuel, battery power, and what all, which I guess the captain was supposed to listen to every few days. The ship-soul absolutely refused to talk about anything else till I'd heard the whole checklist.

I nodded and said, "Oh, is that right?" now and then, the way my sister taught me when I didn't understand much of what someone was saying. You'd be surprised how seldom you get into trouble that way. Most times, when people go on and on, they aren't talking about things you have to *do* anything with, they're just emptying their heads.

After the ship-soul finished its spiel, I wanted to say, "How much of that is normal, and is there anything that's really broken?" But if something was broken I wouldn't know how to fix it, so there wasn't much point in asking. Samantha always claimed it was a golden rule of diplomacy, *Never ask a question when you don't want to hear the answer.*

So instead I got the ship-soul to tell me about the search for invader nano. In the three days since the fight in the hold, our defense clouds had apparently destroyed 143 definites, 587 probables. Those were pathetic numbers, even if the probables were all real nanites, which they likely weren't—just unidentified bacteria that the hunter-killers ripped apart on the theory of better-safe-than-sorry. Seeing as there must have been millions of nanites in that fuzz I'd felt, *Willow*'s defenses were doing a pretty lousy job.

Maybe if there'd been a *real* captain running the search, we would have found the invaders by now. Of course, I'd been sick with that infection . . .

I stopped, and thought about that. Had it really been an infection? No—now that I wasn't dizzy or delirious, my head was clear enough to understand what had happened. There'd been a whole bunch of eyeball nanites on my hand: nanites filled with venom. The hunter-killers had ripped those nanites apart, spilling venom droplets all over me. Even worse, the hunter-killers had clawed up my skin pretty good during the fight. The pinpricks they'd chewed into me had given the venom a way into my bloodstream. What I'd thought was infection had actually been a microscopic dose of venom poisoning. I figured it was a good thing I'd only absorbed a tiny bit of the stuff—anything more might have killed me.

But I was all right now. Wasn't I?

5

ARRIVING AT
STARBASE IRIS

Three days later, *Willow* reached the Celestia system. I'd
spent most of that time wandering around the ship, hoping I'd find something useful to do. It wasn't much fun
walking through the lounge and the hold, or the bridge
either, where there were three more corpses: people who'd
stayed on duty instead of going to the party. But I went
through every room anyway, because I was the captain. I
even asked the ship-soul if there were logs I should be
keeping, or paperwork or something. But the computers
handled stuff like that automatically, so they didn't need
me getting in the way.

A few times I checked over computer files, just to see if
there was stuff I ought to be taking care of. Mission stuff . . .
you know. But every database I tried to look at, records
and logs and all, turned out to be passworded or encrypted
or just plain inaccessible to lowly Explorers Second Class,
even if they'd become acting captain. Maybe that was normal; keeping everything locked away just on general prin-
ciples. Then again, maybe *Willow* had been doing something
extra-specially secret, and outsiders like me were supposed
to mind our own business.

I found out there was only one thing I absolutely had to
do as captain of *Willow*. Apparently, captains are supposed

to get at least half an hour of exercise every day, to keep themselves fit for command. So my only mandatory duty was going down to the gym when the ship-soul told me, and working up a sweat.

Weights. Jogging. Bagwork. It made me laugh, that my one compulsory chore was the only thing I'd ever been good at. I went to the gym twice a day and stayed a lot longer than just half an hour—thinking maybe I'd turn out to be captain material after all.

I made a point of being on the bridge as we drew near Celestia. Not that I actually sat in the captain's command chair—there was a sweet-looking red-haired woman slumped dead in it, and I didn't want to disturb her. (She seemed too young to be officer of the watch. Nineteen or twenty, tops. All the senior officers must have wanted to go to the party, so they'd given the bridge to the most junior lieutenant-cadet on board. Poor kid: I wondered what she could have done that was so bad the League needed to kill her.)

"Starbase Iris is hailing us," the ship-soul announced.

"Okay," I said. My breath came out steamy—I'd asked for the bridge to be cooled like the lounge so the bodies didn't go bad. "Do I just talk or what?"

"Connecting now."

The vidscreen on the command chair lit up with a young man who started to say, "Greetings, *Willow*, this is—" Then he broke off and gawped at his own screen, staring at the face of the dead woman in the chair.

I should have thought of that. Now I'd gone and scared the poor boy on the other end of the line.

"Sorry," I said, as I nudged the woman aside and pushed my own head in front of the vidscreen. "I didn't mean to startle you," I told the boy, "but we've got a problem up here."

"Is she . . ." The boy stopped himself, gave his head a shake, and went all professional. "State your problem, *Willow*."

I told him about everybody being dead. Then I told the same thing to his commanding officer. Then I told the base's Commander of Security. After that I spoke to a doctor who kept talking like the people on *Willow* had died of a disease. To me that was just plain foolish—if several dozen humans and a hive-queen die in the same second while crossing the line, you don't need to be a genius to figure out why. But next thing I knew, everyone at the base had latched onto the disease idea, and they told me I'd have to stay quarantined where I was till the Admiralty could fly in an Outbreak Team. Whenever I tried to point out what really happened, the base personnel cut me off, saying maybe I was delirious with the plague myself.

"No," I told a Security captain, "I was delirious for a while but now I'm better."

"What do you mean you were delirious?" she snapped in surprise. Then suddenly, she said, "Oh. Right. You were *delirious*. Thank you, Explorer York, that confirms our disease hypothesis. Thank you." She gave me a relieved smile before she cut the connection.

After chewing my knuckle a bit, I figured out why she'd acted that way. People at the base wanted to *pretend* there'd been an outbreak, because otherwise they'd have to admit the truth: a whole navy ship had done something so horribly bad, the League decided to execute everybody. And when I'd talked about getting delirious myself, the Security captain thought I was helpfully playing along.

It was so strange. Something important had happened, and the whole starbase staff just wanted to hide their heads in the sand.

I wasn't too happy being part of the lie, but Samantha used to tell me, "If everyone else is denying an obvious truth, you go along with them, Edward, okay? Because the Admiralty sometimes plays games, and if you spoil the game, they'll be mad at you."

I didn't want anyone mad at me. Even if this particular game seemed stupid. And dishonest. And cowardly.

Maybe it all made sense if you had the big picture.

*   *   *

While I waited for the Outbreak Team to arrive from some other starbase, I used the captain's vidscreen to watch outside the ship. I didn't see much—nothing came or went at Starbase Iris, not even in-system shuttles. Once I noticed a merchant vessel passing within range of *Willow*'s hull cameras, but it didn't come very close; it was aiming for the planet Celestia, a light-minute nearer the local sun.

After two more days of waiting, another navy ship popped into view with that gorgeous FTL effect: the ship appears without warning and then you see a streak trail out behind it. That's light from where the ship used to be, catching up with where the ship *is*.

Through a nearby speaker, my ship-soul announced, "Heavy cruiser *Jacaranda* of the Outward Fleet."

"Is it hailing us?" I asked.

"No. It's communicating privately with the starbase."

Jacaranda chatted with Starbase Iris for half an hour . . . and according to my ship-soul, they were using higher-than-normal levels of encryption to keep anyone from eavesdropping. I wondered if they were worried about being overheard by civilians on Celestia, or if they were just keeping secrets from me. Maybe both.

So I sat and stewed, staring at the *Jacaranda* as it floated in the blackness. The ship was shaped like a long baton, with a big round knob on the front end; that was where they kept the Sperm-tail generator. The tail itself rippled all milky around the ship's hull and far back into space until it dwindled away to nothing. Mostly the free end of the tail just drifted . . . but every now and then it gave a flick, the way a fish in a quiet river sometimes comes awake for a second to dart at something too small to see.

My sister once told me the Sperm-field created a separate little universe around the ship, and the little universe could slide through the big outside universe faster than light, without worrying about inertial effects of acceleration. I got lost when she tried to explain how it worked. Samantha was usually pretty good at avoiding subjects that confused

me, but sometimes she got extra fired-up like she was absolutely certain she could make everything clear, no matter
how slow I was. "I'm a *communicator*, Edward," she would
say. "It's my *gift*. If I can communicate with alien races, I
can damned well communicate with you."

Well . . . sometimes it didn't work with me; and I thought
to myself, *There at the end, it didn't work with the aliens
either.*

At last I got a call from *Jacaranda*'s captain, a woman
named Prope. In all the days to come, she never let on
whether that was her first or last name. Maybe she came
from one of those colonies where people only have one
name, because they think it sounds more dramatic.

Prope certainly was the dramatic type. Whenever you
talked to her, she always made you think she was half listening for something that was *really* worth her attention—
like assassins sneaking up behind her back, or a Mayday
from a luxury liner struck by a meteorite. Now and then
she'd suddenly pause, as if she'd thought of some important
point that went over the head of everybody else in the room
. . . except she never told us what these great insights were,
and after a while, I wondered if maybe she was just playacting.

As my sister's bodyguard, I'd met a lot of diplomats. I'd
seen *tons* of playacting.

So Prope's face appeared on my vidscreen. She was lit
from only one side, which meant the left part of her face
was swallowed up in deep dark shadow—the captain's attempt at dazzling me with a dramatic first impression. As
far as I knew, the only way she could get that effect was
turning off the lights on one whole side of her ship's bridge.

"Captain Prope of the *Jacaranda*, calling for Acting Captain Edward York of *Willow*. Are you Explorer York?"

"Yes, Captain." I couldn't help noticing how fast I got
switched from acting captain to Explorer. Maybe Prope
didn't like treating me anywhere close to an equal.

"How are you feeling, Explorer?" the captain asked. "No ill effects from the disease?"

"I'm okay," I said. "Are you going to send someone to help dock this ship?"

"Sorry, not yet. Because of the risk of contagion, standard operating procedure says we start by sending an Explorer team to assess the situation."

"There's not much risk of contagion," I answered. "Really."

"Even so, you can never go wrong following the proper protocols. Don't you agree?"

"Um." In my years with the Outward Fleet, I'd seen things go wrong all over the place, protocols or no. "So after your Explorers check things out," I said, "then can I go home?"

"One thing at a time," Prope replied. "Please go to your transport bay and let my people in through the main airlock. They should be there in fifteen minutes."

She nodded a vague good-bye and waved her hand in the general neighborhood of her forehead. Ship captains are supposed to exchange full salutes after talking to each other . . . even if one of you is only a lowly acting captain. I guess Prope couldn't bring herself to give me a real salute, seeing as I was only an Explorer.

Lots of regular navy people are embarrassed by Explorers. Or scared of them. Even fake Explorers like me. Everybody knows Explorers aren't normal.

Before I could show Prope what a real salute looked like, she cut her end of the connection. I saluted anyway, to the blank screen. As long as I was sort of a kind of a captain, I wanted to do the right thing.

6

MEETING THE EXPLORERS

Fifteen minutes later I sat at the transport bay's control console, watching two Explorers float weightless outside the ship. These were *real* Explorers, not just fakes like me. Their suits were as glinty white as washed stucco, with cords of black piping along the sleeves and pant legs. As they drew close to *Willow*, little jets puffed out from their hips and shoulders to slow their approach.

From my point of view, the two people looked like they were completely upside down: flying along with their feet poking up in the air, because that was the angle they'd happened to come in on. But as soon as they touched the ship's hull, they grabbed the handbar railings that surrounded the airlock entrance and pulled themselves right way up. I'd already told the ship-soul to open the outer hatch, so they slipped straight inside.

It took a minute for the airlock to cycle—and that minute felt like forever, I was so eager to see people again. These two were both humans, I could tell that from the shape of their outfits . . . but looking at their tinted visors and their lumpy tightsuits (with pockets and pouches and electronic attachments front and back) I couldn't tell if the Explorers were young or old, male or female, bulky or slim. They hadn't talked to me by radio either; there'd been no need, and Explorers aren't the sort to chat for the sake of chatting. Not to strangers, anyway.

Finally, the inside airlock door opened and the two Explorers stepped out. A big thick observation window separated me from the transport bay, but I banged on the glass and waved. After a few seconds staring at me, both Explorers waved back. Pretty halfhearted waves, if you ask me.

"York?" a growly man's voice asked. The Explorers had patched their helmet radios into *Willow*'s speaker system. "The name's Tobit—Phylar Tobit." One of the white-suited figures gave a slight bow. "And my know-nothing greenhorn partner is Benny Dade."

"Benjamin!" the other snapped in a peevish high-pitched voice. "But everybody just calls me Dade."

Tobit gave a loud snort. "Dade? Who the hell calls you Dade? Everyone *I* know calls you the Sissy-boy Whiner . . . but I thought I'd be polite in front of company."

Dade (or Benny or Benjamin) gave a hissy sniff that may or may not have been good-natured. I tried to keep a straight face. Explorers make a point of never addressing each other by title—it's tradition. But without titles to go by, the young cadets sometimes get hung up on what they should or shouldn't be called. Carefully I said, "Hello, Tobit. And, um, Benjamin. Welcome aboard the *Willow*."

"Yeah, yeah, swell," Tobit answered, waving his arm dismissively. I tried to lock down in my head which Explorer was which, but knew I'd get mixed up as soon as they started moving. The two tightsuits looked exactly like each other on the outside, no names or insignia or anything.

"So what do you want to do first?" I called down. "Would you like a tour?"

"We're supposed to follow a specific search pattern," Benjamin replied, still a bit miffed and huffy. "You're an Explorer, aren't you, York? You should know there are procedures for this sort of thing."

His voice sounded as young as wet paint. All full-fledged Explorers had to be at least twenty-two, but I didn't think the boy could possibly be that old. It made me feel dry-dust ancient, the way I kept coming across recruits who were practically babies. "All right," I told him, "you do what you have to do. I'll tag along and watch."

"Yeah," Tobit muttered, "we love spectators." The tint on his visor had started to fade now that he was inside the ship; I could see his eyes, puffy and a little bloodshot. He stared at me a moment longer, then said, "Oh all right, you can come along. Professional courtesy to a fellow Explorer. Although if I were you, I'd just mix myself a drink and let other people do the work. You've been sick, haven't you?"

"I'm fine now," I told him. Then I whispered, "You know there isn't really a disease, right? Everyone at the starbase is just pretending."

He made a phlegmy noise in his throat, then said, "If everyone else is pretending, pal, I wouldn't want to be the odd man out. The Admiralty High Council are rabid old bastards on the subject of solidarity."

Benjamin looked at him in surprise. Before the boy could speak, Tobit went on quickly, "Okay, time to get our asses in gear. We got some damned important standard procedures to follow." He belched loudly, then headed for the door.

It was too bad the Explorers couldn't take off their tight-suits. As it was, I still felt kind of alone, even with them walking right beside me. They were all bundled up so I couldn't see more than their eyes, and their voices came from the ship's overhead speakers instead of from the people themselves.

Not that they talked to me much; Explorers really *focus* on their jobs. From the moment they left the transport bay, Tobit and Benjamin were so busy giving their home ship a running commentary of what they saw, they scarcely tossed a word in my direction. I tagged behind like baggage, through machinery rooms with automatic systems doing automatic things . . . till we got to the hold.

When Benjamin saw the queen he nearly jumped out of his suit. "Shit!" he squeaked. "I mean, shoot! Look at the size of that thing! I had no idea they were that big!"

Tobit didn't take his eyes off the queen's corpse, but he gave a deep sigh. "Benny. Buddy. My dear bright spark. Didn't you study the goddamned Mandasar castes in Explorer Academy?"

"Yeah, sure," Benjamin answered, "but it's one thing to watch them on chip and another to see one up close."

"Christ on a crutch," Tobit muttered. "If you don't have enough imagination to learn from normal pictures, run yourself a VR sim. The first time you meet a real alien in the flesh, I don't want my partner gibbering, '*Mercy me, look at the size of that thing!*'"

Benjamin mumbled something I couldn't make out. If Tobit had belonged to any other branch of the navy, he'd yell, "What was that, mister?" then shout in the boy's face for ten minutes about subordinates keeping their mouths to themselves. But Explorers hated acting authoritarian, especially if it meant browbeating their partners. Instead, Tobit turned to me. "What's with the defense clouds around the venom sacs?"

"Oh those. Um." I dropped my gaze. "The ship had uninvited nanites show up a few days ago . . ."

"What?" Tobit snapped. "No one told *us* about nanites."

"The folks at Starbase Iris never let me get that far," I answered. "As soon as I reported the whole crew dying, they just stopped talking to me. When I tried to tell them other stuff, they cut me off sharp."

"Bloody hell. Those morons at Iris have their heads up their candy-coated asses." Tobit took a deep breath. "All right, York, we're listening now. Tell us everything. The truth, not what you think we want to hear."

So I went through the story, right from the start—which shocked young Benjamin, let me tell you. He couldn't believe the kind of party *Willow* held for crossing the line. Tobit told him not to be naive. "Just goes to show," he said, "the crew knew they'd pissed off the League. They were all in on it, they were all guilty . . . and they were all whacked out with fear as they came up to crossing the line. In a way, you have to admire these bastards; most Vac-heads would just sit around moaning if they knew they were going to die. At least this group had the good taste to hold an orgy." He sighed, then glanced at me. "I don't suppose you know what gruesome deed they'd done?"

I shook my head. "No one told me anything."

"You were just a passenger. Getting rotated back to New Earth, right?"

"Right. I was stationed on the moonbase near Troyen, but it was getting too dangerous to stay. You know Troyen's having a big civil war? Most of the time they just fight among themselves, but a few weeks ago someone took a potshot at us—a missile came close to landing on top of our station. The blast disrupted our outer dome field and nearly knocked down the inner one . . . so our base commander decided we had to evacuate. The other personnel got away in a two-person scoutship, but I was assigned to stay behind till everything shut down properly."

"They left you on your own?" Benjamin said. "While Mandasars were shooting missiles at your base?"

"There was only the one missile," I told him, "and I volunteered to stay. Somebody had to make sure the computers finished locking everything down. Anyway, *Willow* came to get me, so it was all right."

Tobit asked, "When did *Willow* show up in the Troyen system?"

"Right after the others left in the scoutship. *Willow*'s name just appeared on the base's list of in-system ships. They hung around for five days, then picked me up to go home."

"Sounds like they were on a secret mission," Benjamin said with sudden interest. "The way they didn't come out till everyone else had gone. Orbiting the planet five days even when they might get shot at. Not telling you what they were up to . . ."

"Of course, they were on a secret mission, toad-breath!" Tobit rolled his eyes. "For one thing, they were ferrying this queen from Troyen to Celestia . . . which was probably what got the poor buggers killed. The League takes a dim view of folks transporting dangerous non-sentients from one star system to another. And I'll lay you good odds this queen qualified as non-sentient—ready and willing to commit murder. You said Troyen's been at war for twenty years?"

I nodded.

"Well then," Tobit went on, "she'd have her own army, wouldn't she?" He patted the queen's chitinous flank. "How long d'you think this old gal could play warlord and still keep her mandibles clean . . . never taking a single wee life except in direct self-defense?" He snorted. "When I studied hive-queens at the academy, no one ever described them as saints."

"So," I said, "the League killed the queen because she'd killed other people. And they killed *Willow*'s crew for trying to transport a dangerous creature to another world?"

Tobit nodded. "It's the League's own version of disease control: never let uncivilized organisms leave their home system. This queen must have claimed to be a perfect angel, and *Willow*'s crew gambled she was telling the truth. They lost the bet."

It made me feel bad, how I'd been puzzling over things for more than a week without getting anywhere, then someone like Tobit could walk in, take one look, and explain why everybody died. "So," I said, worried this would be obvious too, "who sent the nanites? What did they want?"

"Fucked if I know," Tobit answered. "What good is stolen venom? And how did the nanites get smuggled onto the ship? Who knew *Willow* would be transporting a hive-queen? Someone on Troyen? Or maybe someone on Celestia?"

"Why Celestia?" Benjamin asked.

"Jesus, boy," Tobit groaned, "didn't you learn *anything* at the Academy? Celestia has a Mandasar population too—ten million children were evacuated just before the shit hit the fan on Troyen. Everyone thought it was only a temporary measure; a happy-sappy field trip. But the war's dragged on for two decades, and the brats have all grown up."

He turned suddenly toward the queen's corpse and stared for a few seconds. "Hey... when the Outward Fleet shipped the kids to Celestia, I don't remember the Admiralty including any queens."

"They didn't," I said. "My sister belonged to the Diplomacy Corps back then; the High Council wanted her to check with all the queens to see if any wanted to evacuate with the children. Samantha just laughed—a queen would never abandon her home territory to baby-sit a bunch of kids. It wouldn't be regal.".

"So Celestia has ten million junior Mandasars," Tobit murmured, "and nary a queen. Then again, who gives a shit? The lower castes are as smart as humans. They can take care of themselves."

"But they have all these instincts," I said. "They want guidance. They need to be ruled by a proper queen."

Tobit made a face. "I bet a queen told you that. *The poor dear peasants couldn't possibly survive without kissing my royal heinie.*" He grunted. "But whether or not it's true, some of the damned lobsters probably believe it. Especially on Celestia, where they don't remember life under a queen's thumb. If they arrived as kids, what are they now, in their twenties? There's bound to be some who think their lives are fucked up—at that age, you're *supposed* to think your life is fucked up—keep your trap shut, Benny—so it wouldn't surprise me if a chunk of the population thought a queen would make everything better. Somehow they persuaded the Admiralty to bring them one... or else the Admiralty is running a scam of its own and wanted a queen to whip the baby lobsters into line."

"The Admiralty doesn't run scams anymore," Benjamin protested. "They cleaned house three years ago."

Tobit reached out and pretended to whack the boy on the helmet. "Every time you say pig-ignorant things like that," Tobit said, "I dock another point off your performance evaluation." He turned to me and rolled his eyes. "Fucking useless cadets."

7

GETTING WARNED
ABOUT MY FUTURE

We kept poking our way forward through the ship. The closer we came to the lounge, the more nervous I got that the Explorers would think I was a terrible captain for not cleaning up. The refrigeration had stopped people from rotting too much, but they'd still messed themselves when all their muscles went limp; the place smelled like a toilet no one had scoured for a long time. I kept apologizing in advance, saying I'd wanted to tidy up but knew I wasn't supposed to touch anything no matter how bad it got. Just as we went through the door, it finally occurred to me Tobit and Benjamin wouldn't smell a thing—they were closed up in their suits, with their own air and all, so I was the only one who had to hold his nose.

Even so, young Benjamin went stone quiet when he saw dead people lying around—a lot of them naked and none nice to look at anymore. Tobit seemed okay till he caught sight of the admiral woman who'd kissed me; then he stormed straight to the corpse and stared down at it.

"What's wrong?" I asked. "Do you know her?"

"I know the original," Tobit answered, "and I guess there's a slight resemblance. Explains why Ms. Deadmeat here thought it would be a good costume for the party. But it's not the real Admiral Ramos. Just some chippie dressed up." He turned away quickly. "Do me a favor, York, and scrub that crap off her face."

"I can clean up now?"

"As if anyone ever cared. It's not like there's a question about cause of death. Right, Benny?"

Benjamin was staring at the *Willow*'s captain. The captain's holo-surround had used up its battery power days ago, so you could see the man himself now. He was wearing his uniform shirt, but from the waist down, all he had on were white socks. It was a pretty undignified look for someone of his rank. If I were a captain and thought I might die, I'd aim at leaving a more presentable corpse.

"Benny," Tobit said. "Partner mine. Prospective pride of the Explorer Corps. Are you with us?"

"What? Oh. Sorry. Do you want to move on?"

"No," Tobit answered, "I want to go home for a bubble bath. We've wasted enough time on goddamned standard procedures." He glowered at the boy for a moment, then said, "For novelty's sake, how 'bout I give you a direct order? Head back to the hold, cut off the queen's venom sacs, and pack 'em for transport back to *Jacaranda*."

"What?" The boy's voice sounded like a yelp. I felt kind of yelpy myself. Mutilate a queen? Even if she was dead, that was nigh-on sacrilege. "Why?" Benjamin asked.

"Because somewhere on *Willow*," Tobit replied, "there are nasty wee nanites who want to steal her venom. Christ knows why they want it, but I can't imagine it's for the blissful good of the universe. Besides, it pisses me off when people sneak nano onto a navy ship; just on general principle, I don't want the bastards to get what they're after. Best way to do that is haul the venom back to *Jacaranda*— empty the place so the nanites are shit out of luck." He held his hand up quickly, to stop me from saying anything. "And before you ask, we'll have *Jacaranda* triple-check to make sure we aren't carrying nanites ourselves. Our micro-defenses aren't half-bad . . . on the rare occasions we're willing to cool our heels six hours in quarantine getting a full nano scan."

Benjamin's eyes were wide. "You really want me to hack the sacs off?"

"Not hack, you lunkhead. Perform a delicate surgical excision. With all due care and safety. Use a scalpel instead of a chainsaw. You know—finesse. Now get your scrawny butt moving."

The boy sounded sick but he started off. I called after him, "Be careful, okay? Venom is dangerous stuff."

"He'll do fine," Tobit said. "Benny trained for Medical Corps before he transferred to exploring. He has great hands with a scalpel."

"Thank you," Benjamin called back over his shoulder. He could still hear Tobit's words over the ship's speaker system.

"But you're a piss-awful Explorer!" Tobit shouted as the boy disappeared.

I think Benjamin gave Tobit the finger, but it's hard to tell with a tightsuit's bulgy gloves.

As soon as the boy was out of sight, Tobit popped off his helmet. That surprised me; Explorers are supposed to stay suited up whenever they're on a mission, even if it's just over to another navy ship. For another surprise, he reached up to the bulge on his throat—his communications implant—and gave it a double-tap. "There," he said. "I'm not transmitting anymore." He took a deep breath. "Christ, it reeks in here, doesn't it?"

"Sorry."

"Not your fault, pal. You wanted to leave everything as is because you thought there'd be a real investigation. Which there won't."

He gave me a long look as if trying to decide something. Me, I was just trying not to stare. Tobit's face had a ravaged flush to it, pockmarked, red and veiny. An old soak's face, though I couldn't smell booze on him. Maybe he'd been an alcoholic but had lately gone on the wagon; or maybe he had some genetic condition that made him *look* like a lush. Sure, that had to be it—Explorers always had things wrong with them, whether they looked funny or smelled funny or sounded funny. Phylar Tobit's problem was just a whiskey-ish face. The navy surely wouldn't let drunks be Explorers.

"We don't have much time," Tobit told me, "so just shut up and listen, okay? It turns out, York, you're in a shitload of trouble."

"I'm sorry," I said. Apologizing was always a good first step, even if I didn't understand what I'd done.

"Nothing to feel sorry about," Tobit replied. "This crapfest isn't your fault. But the Admiralty is plotting a cover-up, I positively guarantee it. They've lost an entire ship because navy personnel acted non-sentient: all of *Willow's* crew, and maybe the admiral who gave them their orders. That's the sort of thing the High Council dearly wants to keep secret. Makes the whole fleet look bad."

"I can keep secrets," I said.

He patted my shoulder. "Yeah. Sure. But the Admiralty won't take the chance. They only trust certain types of people—assholes who want to be admirals themselves and will do anything to get into the inner circle. Our beloved Captain Prope is like that, and a lot of other folks on our ship. High Admiral Vincence has stacked *Jacaranda* with scumbags who don't mind taking orders that would disturb normal navy personnel."

"Orders like what?" I asked.

"Like making you disappear, so you can't spill the beans. Prope already has reassignment papers for you; I read them when I accidentally logged onto her computer and decrypted all her files. You're headed for some godforsaken outpost in the back of beyond, where contact ships only show up once a decade. A one-man station. *Jacaranda* will take you straight there without a chance to talk to anyone, then they'll fly away without looking back." Tobit gritted his teeth. "You won't be the first person our shite of a captain has marooned."

For a second I didn't say anything. You can't imagine what it's like, to be going home after twenty years—twenty years on a moon with nothing but vacuum outside, like a prison except no one has the decency to call it that—and just when you think it's all over, that you'll soon see grass and sky and lakes again, someone decides you're going to be dumped on some new lonely dung heap. And why? Because a boneheaded *admiral* wants to hide you away from everyone else, for fear you'll make him look bad.

The story of my life.

"So what should I do?" I whispered to Tobit. Whispering because if I didn't whisper, I'd scream. "I'm stuck out in space," I said. "I can't run away."

"Yes, you can," Tobit answered, "but you have to make your move while you're still acting captain of *Willow*. Hop into one of the evac modules and declare an immediate forced landing emergency. Use those exact words: immediate forced landing emergency. The ship-soul will launch all the escape pods straight toward Celestia, because it's the optimal site for a forced landing right now: close by and habitable. You hit it lucky there, York—Celestia is a free planet, not part of the Technocracy. Once you touch down, the navy has no legal right to drag you back."

"But won't *Jacaranda* stop me from getting away?"

"They'll try. But they can only catch one pod at a time. Even if they're lucky, they'll only grab four of the eight pods before you reach Celestia's atmosphere. You've got a fifty-fifty chance of making it to the ground."

"And a fifty-fifty chance of getting caught."

"So what?" Tobit asked. "The worst they can do is banish you to some asswipe of a planet, and they plan on doing that anyway." He gave me a yellow-toothed grin. "You have dick-all to lose, York. And Celestia is reportedly a cream-puff world: all tame and terraformed. If you lie low for a while, you can head back for the Technocracy eventually. Within six months, some new crisis will make the High Council forget all about you. Admirals have the attention span of lobotomized gnats."

Tobit obviously didn't know who my father was . . . or he'd know Dad wouldn't be so quick to forget. On the other hand, I figured my old man wouldn't waste energy chasing me if I stayed out of his way—more than anything, he just wanted to pretend I didn't exist.

I asked Tobit, "Will you get in trouble for telling me this?"

He shook his head. "Nah—they won't have any evidence. I'm not transmitting back to *Jacaranda*, and you can erase *Willow*'s records of this conversation. You're the captain; you have authority to wipe all the memory banks here if you feel like it." Tobit grinned. "I also have a friend in high places: the real Admiral Ramos. She was the one who drafted me for First Explorer on the *Jacaranda* . . . to counterbalance whatever shitwork Prope is up to. Eventually the council will find an excuse to get me reassigned; and Ramos will send another of her favorite Explorers to keep *Jacaranda* honest. Even a dirty-tricks ship needs Explorers. Otherwise, the lily-fingered crew members would be the ones marching into stink holes full of rotting corpses."

Tobit gave a sour look at the nearest dead bodies . . . and at that very moment, *Willow*'s alarm bells started blaring out RED ALERT.

8

EVACUATING *WILLOW*

The lounge's vidscreen lit up on its own, showing the view through *Willow*'s hull cameras. "Danger status one," the ship-soul announced. "Awaiting captain's orders." Its computer voice sounded sharper than usual. That wasn't good—voice synthesizers don't simulate emotion unless it's really important for people to pay attention.

On the vidscreen, a new ship had popped up between the *Jacaranda* and Starbase Iris: a ship shaped exactly like *Jacaranda* itself but painted black with starlike speckles. The paint job looked prettier than the navy's boring old white, but it sure wouldn't work as camouflage . . . especially not at the moment, when the black ship was surrounded by the milky swim of a Sperm-field.

"What the hell's going on?" Tobit asked. "Civilian vessels shouldn't come anywhere near . . . holy shit!"

The strange black ship had just shot two missiles at *Jacaranda*.

The ships were less than a kilometer apart, so it didn't take long for the missiles to cross the gap: two flashes of flame and vapor racing toward their target in less than a second. I caught my breath, wondering what would happen when the rockets struck home . . . but instead of banging straight into *Jacaranda*'s hull, they angled off to swish close by on either side.

The missiles missed the ship, but snagged *Jacaranda*'s Sperm-field.

Oh. Now I understood.

The missiles plowed on into empty space, and the Sperm-tail bagged out to stay with them, as if the milky field had got caught on the missiles' noses. Probably, it had; I guessed that both missiles were using Sperm anchors to latch onto the field and drag it with them. They continued angling off in opposite directions, spreading *Jacaranda*'s sperm envelope wide, like two hands inside a plastic bag, pushing out hard to make the bag stretch.

At the last second, the milky color of the Sperm-field broke into an unstable glitter of green and blue and gold; then the field popped like a soap bubble, stressed beyond its limits.

The missiles continued on their courses, disappearing into the darkness of space.

So much for *Jacaranda*'s ability to go FTL. The crew would need twelve hours to generate a new field and get it aligned properly around the hull. That gave the black ship loads of time to do whatever it wanted and still escape without pursuit.

The stranger ship swiveled its nose toward *Willow*. "Uh-oh," Tobit and I said in unison.

Tobit slammed his helmet back onto his head. Even before he'd locked it in place, he was yelling into the radio, "Benny, evacuate the ship. Don't ask questions. Now, now, now!"

"Do you think they're going to board us?" I asked.

"Maybe," he said. "Or they might take *Willow* in tow and run off with the whole damned ship."

Steal the ship? While I was acting captain? I didn't want to think what Dad would say about that.

"No more lollygagging," Tobit shouted, grabbing my arm. "We have to get out of here."

He dragged me from the lounge and down the corridor to the nearest evac module. It wasn't far—in a navy ship, you're never more than ten seconds from an escape pod. "Get in," he said. "Next stop, Celestia."

"What about you?"

"As soon as you're gone, I'll jump out an emergency airlock. There's one just . . ."

The floor heaved beneath our feet. I grabbed at something to keep my balance; the "something" was Tobit, who was grabbing me too. "No more time," he growled, shoving me toward the pod. "They're grappling the ship with tractors."

"They're really going to steal my ship?"

"York," he said, "it's not your ship and it's not your fault. You're just caught in a High Council fuck-up. Bad enough that this whole crew died . . . but the Admiralty must have opened itself a whopping security hole that let all the wrong people hear about *Willow*. Someone smuggled nano aboard. Someone else heard there's a crewless ship here, ripe for the taking. It's a grade A extra large chrome-plated cluster fuck, but you aren't the one responsible. You've stepped in someone else's dog shit, York; scrape it off your shoe and just walk away."

"Can't I do anything?"

The ship lurched again; I barely managed to stay on my feet. Tobit stumbled and went down on one knee, but scrambled up again fast.

"Yeah, one thing you can do," he said, pushing me all the way into the pod. "Ship-soul, attend," he called. "Captain is abandoning ship and invoking Captain's Last Act."

The computer voice came over the speakers outside the pod. "Captain York confirms Captain's Last Act?"

"Say 'confirm,' " Tobit whispered to me.

"Confirm," I said.

"Captain repeats confirmation?" the computer asked.

"Repeat confirmation," I said. "Confirm, confirm, confirm. And, umm . . . immediate forced landing emergency."

The corridor snapped completely black. I couldn't even see Tobit in front of me in his bright white tightsuit.

"What did I just do?" I asked him.

"The ship-soul EMP'd itself," he replied. His voice wasn't piped over the speakers now; it came out unamplified and muffled, straight from his tightsuit. "Every data storage on board just got fried with a massive electric pulse," he said. "As of now, *Willow* is a brainless chunk of scrap metal. The people stealing this baby won't get any navy codes or records . . ."

Something went clang in front of me. The next second, lights came on inside the escape pod and I could see the hatch had slammed closed, shutting me off from Tobit back in the corridor. The pod had computers of its own, and I guess they'd detected the main ship-soul dropping off-line. The evac module had decided to go automatic.

"Ejecting in ten seconds," a computer voice announced.

There were no seats or controls. The interior of the pod was just a room-sized cube, five meters on each edge, with grab-bars stuck into the walls, the floor, and even the ceiling. You could jam all of *Willow*'s crew into a single one of the modules . . . and now that I thought of it, the whole crew *was* here. Me.

I dropped to the floor, wrapped my arms around the two nearest bars and tucked my feet under two more. "Five seconds," the computer voice said.

Overhead, a vidscreen turned on: it covered half the ceiling and showed the outside of the ship. The idea must have been to let people in the pod watch what was happening, rather than making them wait blindly in a closed capsule. That was fine if you wanted to see what was coming for you. Me, I was more inclined to close my eyes; but that would be uncaptainly, so I kept watching the screen.

The black ship had lined itself straight in front of *Willow*, shooting a snaky red beam back at the bulb on our prow. The beam was just starting to pull our ship forward, drawing us up toward the stranger's long Sperm-tail. It wouldn't take long to get us inside; once something starts entering a Sperm-field, it gets sucked in really fast.

Meanwhile, a few klicks away, *Jacaranda* was just beginning to move in our direction. The crew over there must have been caught totally off guard; they didn't even have their real-space engines warmed up. Most ships don't, not when they're inside their Sperm envelope—no point burning fuel if you don't have to. So *Jacaranda* was going to be slow, slow, slow for a few more minutes. By the time they got up to speed, *Willow* would probably be nabbed.

Even if *Jacaranda* got to us in time, I didn't know what they could do. Navy ships don't have weapons—the League of Peoples won't let any ship in the galaxy sail around armed, not with the teeniest bit of killing power. Ships could carry nonlethal things like those missiles that ripped away the Sperm-field; but I doubted if *Jacaranda* had anything like that ready to hand.

At most, *Jacaranda* could latch onto us with its own tractors and try a tug-of-war . . . but even that was a waste of time till they got nearer. Tractor beams are strong close up but weak farther off. Seeing as the black ship had grabbed *Willow* at point-blank range, *Jacaranda* would have to get nearly that close before they had a chance of holding onto us.

Willow shuddered. Up ahead, I could see the open mouth of the stranger's Sperm-tail, like a milky ghost-worm about to swallow us. Any second, we'd be slurped inside . . .

The evac module blew straight up into space, strong as an explosion. My body was squashed hard against the floor, all my bones and muscles pressed down like something wanted to roll me flat. I couldn't breathe; I couldn't move a finger. My eyes were watering, but I could still see enough of the vidscreen to make out *Willow*, far away already. There was the black ship, there was *Jacaranda* lumbering up slowly, there were the seven other escape pods soaring all around me.

And there was something fuzzy pushing hard on my face.

Uh-oh.

Eyeball nano, here in the escape pod; that's where the nanites had been hiding all along. Maybe the defense clouds didn't search much inside the evac modules, because the modules weren't critical to ship's operation. Our defenders were busy watching *Willow*'s life support and engines and all; why worry about the escape pods, when they were hardly ever used?

Now I could feel the fuzz of little bugs, dragged down by the force of acceleration and squishing against my cheeks. Little jelly eyeballs pressed hard onto my skin. How much squish could a microscopic eyeball take before it mushed open?

My face felt damp. Was that hive-queen venom or just cold sweat? On my forehead. My lips. Around my eyes.

A computer voice said, "Confirm immediate forced landing emergency."

I didn't want to open my mouth. But if I didn't, the escape pod would never land on Celestia; it would just hang around the ejection site to make it easier for rescuers to find. Sooner or later I'd get picked up by the black ship . . . or *Jacaranda* . . . or just hang out in space forever, me, the nano, and the venom.

"Confirm," I said, keeping my lips closed as tight as I could and still let the word out. Even so, I didn't want to think how many nanites got driven down my throat through my clenched teeth.

"Maximum acceleration in five seconds," the computer said. "Placing passenger cube into safety stasis." That meant the escape pod was going to freeze time for me, so I wouldn't get mashed to pulp when the propulsion kicked in. It was the same principle as getting put into a Spermfield's pocket universe, except that a stasis field's universe didn't have a time dimension. It just sat there, a dumb old $\mathcal{R}^3$ with no ambition or progress.

"Five," the computer counted, "four, three, two, one . . ."

There was a soft sound, like a BINK. Then suddenly, the vidscreen showed a blue sky with stringy clouds wisping high above me. The escape module had completely stopped moving—nothing but an easy rocking, and the sound of water lapping at the outside of the pod.

"Time in stasis, forty-six minutes, twenty-one seconds,"

the computer voice said. "Successful forced landing."

Sure, successful. Except that I had a tinny pickly taste in my mouth. When I wiped my face with my shirt cuff, the sleeve came away green with venom.

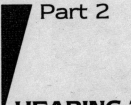

Part 2

HEARING THE CALL

9

RETURNING TO
SOLID GROUND

Venom on my face and in my mouth. It didn't burn or
sting, but it terrified me. How long till I started shivering
again? How long before I went frothing crazy-sick with
poison?

Maybe this time it'd be better; maybe I'd built up resistance. But it could just as easily go the other way, with me
all weakened and sensitized from the last dose. The effect
could hit me ten times harder than before.

You can never be sure with venom.

Out loud I said, "If I get sick, I get sick; there's nothing
I can do." Which sounded noble and stoic and all, but didn't
untie the knot of fear in my stomach. My mouth was still
puckered with the pickly aftertaste of poison . . . and that
was more real than any brave words.

I went to the exit hatch and hiked up the OPEN lever. That
got me into the airlock, which had a peep-monitor showing
the world outside the pod. I could see a stretch of water so
muddy it looked like creamed coffee . . . but the shore was
only a stone's throw away, a low dirt bank supporting a
scraggly line of trees. The trees looked shining wet, as if
they'd just got doused with rain. Considering how blue
clear the sky was, I figured all that drip-off had actually

come from my module smacking the water. Escape pods make relatively gentle landings—they don't come in like fireballs, and they always aim for water to avoid smushing houses or people—but even a soft landing splashes down like a kid doing a cannonball. A good slap. Much spillage.

Too bad I missed seeing it. I bet it would have been great.

When I looked again at those trees on shore, I noticed their leaves weren't the nice chlorophyll green of New Earth and Troyen. Their colors ran a lot more funereal. Purply black. Bluish black. Orangey black. Yellow with black spottles. Gloss black on matte black with ebony accents.

But it'd take more than dark leaves to make me feel gloomy. After twenty years of living inside a lunar dome, never seeing a tree except in VR sims, I was kiss-the-ground happy to be this close to the real thing. I pushed the EXIT button; the interior airlock door closed, the door to the outside opened . . . and I jumped into the muddy water, doing a cannonball of my own.

Okay. Maybe the water was bone-shaking cold. And I'd swum halfway to shore before it occurred to me Celestia might have its own types of piranha or anacondas, not to mention swarms of alien germs. But nothing sank its teeth into my leg, and a short swim was exactly what I needed to wash the venom off my face. I even considered taking a glug of water to rinse the venom out of my mouth; but there was all that mud, and maybe the water did have germs, and anyway, some of the venom must have already gone down my throat. Keeping my eyes and mouth closed, treading water, I ducked my head under a few times, then wiped off my face with my hands. At least that rinsed the venom from my skin . . . and it made me feel cleaner in general, even if I could still taste the stuff I'd swallowed.

When I clambered onto the bank, I was muddy, wet, and cold. It felt good. I found a spot where the sun shone through a gap in the trees and sat down to wring the damp from my uniform. While I squeezed out water, I looked around to take stock of my situation.

Escape pods try not to put you down in a desert or an icecap or the middle of an ocean. They pick a spot with nice weather and plenty of plant life, preferably with signs of intelligent civilization.

Me, I'd landed in a thirty-meter-wide canal. You could tell it wasn't a natural river by how straight it ran, a perfect line in both directions. The water showed almost no current: the escape pod was floating free, but it'd barely budged since I'd left it. I wouldn't have to worry about it drifting out of sight downstream anytime soon.

If need be, I could swim back out and ask the pod's computer for food rations when I got hungry—I hadn't noticed any storage bins, but it'd be a pathetic excuse for an evac module if it didn't carry basic supplies. On the other hand, I didn't think I'd have to settle for bland protein bars and squeeze tubes of fiber paste . . . because behind me were fields full of vegetables as far as the eye could see.

The canal ran along one edge of a valley whose soil was almost jet-black. That meant the dirt was as rich as gravy . . . and it was covered with crops planted in neat rows forming neat squares—a checkerboard in shades of green stretching from the canal all the way to some distant hills. The plants looked young, like this was only late spring or early summer, but I could already recognize onions and lettuce and carrots in the fields closest to me. Honest-to-goodness Earth food growing in a big gorgeous garden that smelled of humus and greenery.

A paved road ran close in front of me, parallel to the canal and separated from the water by the scrawny trees growing on the bank. Here and there along the road stood little environment domes in clusters of two or three—living spaces for the families who worked these farms. At the moment, I couldn't see anyone out in the fields . . . but the strong orange sun was straight overhead, and toasty hot even with my clothes soaked to the skin, so I guessed everybody had gone inside for siesta.

I got up, brushed the worst-caked mud off my uniform, and started down the road toward the nearest domes. No one would want me showing up unannounced in the middle of lunch; but I'd wait till people went back out to work, and I'd say hello then. On a day like this, there was no need to hurry. It was heaven just to breathe real air, away from the nanites and the black ship and Troyen . . .

A doorway dilated in the side of the closest dome. Out stepped a Mandasar—warrior caste, big and red. The instant he caught sight of me, he screamed a battle cry and charged.

Mandasar warriors are only half as big as queens, but they're still the size of Brahma bulls. They've got the basic lobsterish look, but bulked-up and stocky, from their flat wide faces to their strong blunt tails. If a warrior props his tail good and solid on the ground behind him, you can hit him with a truck and he won't be knocked backward; in fact, once he gets his eight legs on solid footing, he can push that truck back the other way, over rough terrain, for hour after hour. Put a bunch of warriors together and you get a line of foot soldiers who can steamroll over anything in their path . . . except another line of Mandasars driving the opposite way.

Don't get the idea warriors are slow-moving hulks; they can storm forward on those eight strong legs as fast as horse cavalry. When they're running they look like old Greek centaurs, because the front part of their body is angled up vertically as tall as a human. Upright front, lobstery behind.

Like queens, every warrior has pincer claws, but only two of them, on stubby arms down at the waist. The claws are sharp and nasty enough to lop clean through a human's leg, bones and all, if you're careless enough to let your ankle come within reach. At shoulder level, warriors have another set of arms, called the *Cheejreth* or "clever twigs": spindly six-fingered things used for fine manipulation. *Cheejreth* are nearly as long as human arms, but skinny and fragile—so weak, a human five-year-old could wrist-wrestle a warrior ten wins out of ten. During a serious fight, the *Cheejreth* stay folded against the chest, tucked into arm-sized niches in the warrior's carapace; those niches evolved to keep *Cheejreth* safely out of the way, rather than flopping around and getting snapped off.

Topping the body is a head like a cannonball, its carapace armor twice as thick as any other part of the warrior's shell. The head has a few delicate parts—huge feathery ears like moth antennas, and cat-style whiskers around the snout to serve as extra scent receptors, waving about to catch odor molecules from the air—but the flimsy bits aren't at all vital. If they break or get mangled during a fight, it scarcely hurts a bit. The warrior just can't hear or smell as well for a few days, until the damaged part grows back.

The one indispensable part of a warrior's face is the spike on his pointy snout. It's sharp and bony, only as big as a human thumb, but perfect for use as a bayonet—in an emergency, the warrior can use his spike to stab an enemy in the eye. Of course, it has to be a *big* emergency. All Mandasar castes have a finicky sense of smell, and they absolutely hate the stink of someone's blood gucking up the tip of their noses.

The warrior charging toward me had a shell so fiery red, I knew he had to be young, in his twenties—the color fades as warriors get older, not to mention that they learn not to attack people at first sight. You never know when you'll meet someone who spent years on the Mandasar home-world, learning all kinds of tricks to show overeager youngsters that humans aren't as soft as they look.

All the same, I didn't want to hurt an impetuous kid just because he was short on common sense. Fast as I could, I crossed my hands over my chest in the high-court submission posture and hollered, "*Naizó!*" . . . short for *Nai hala-bad tajjef su rellid puzó*, which means *I yield to your queen and her rightful hegemony over these, her duly apportioned lands*. (A thousand years ago, old-time Mandasar warriors got their kicks by trying to recite the long form of the phrase before they got a pincer rammed through their guts.

They did it as a test of nerve—to show how cool-headed they could be, speaking calm and slow while an opponent raced straight at them. The flowery words got collapsed to *Naizó* about the time firearms were invented, when it suddenly became important for surrenders to be short and snappy.)

Of course, if someone barrels down on you, either with guns or with pincers, there's always a chance he won't stop, even when you yell uncle. The warrior charging toward me didn't slow a bit when I *Naizó'd* him—he pounded on like a thoroughbred stallion, intending to gallop down my throat at trampling speed.

I'd have been pee-in-the-pants scared if he were a real horse; horses have hammer-hard hooves, and real good instincts when it comes to kicking. Lucky for me, Mandasar warriors are built all wrong for horsy maneuvers like rearing up, and they can't kick worth a darn unless they practice for years. Nature designed them for using their waist pincers and nose spikes; get around those, and they don't have much left to throw at you.

I kept shouting, "*Naizó!*" as long as I could, in case the warrior was just putting on a show to impress the rest of his family—four other Mandasars, three workers and a gentle, had come out of the dome behind him and were watching his every move, all excited and worshipful. But when the warrior got so close I could see he really planned to run me over, I dropped the submission stance and faked a move to my left, as if I were dodging out of the way. The warrior swerved in the same direction . . . which showed he had zero training in actual fights. He spread his waist arms wide to prevent me from going around, and opened his claws to catch me; but I was already slipping back to the right, outside the reach of his pincers.

The warrior charged straight past me, with way too much momentum to stop. If he'd had any experience fighting humans, he would have kept going; but he dropped his lobstery tail as a brake, dragging it along the ground like Mandasars always do when they want to slow down fast.

For sure, he intended to swing around and take another grab at me . . . but I was right behind him now and his tail was close in front of my feet.

So I ran up his tail and threw myself flat onto his back.

Mandasar warriors can jump, but not nearly as much as a bucking bronco. Like I said, they're built wrong for horse tricks—eight legs just can't hop as wildly as four. I held on just fine by wrapping my arm around his throat in a neck-bar . . . not tight enough to crush his windpipe, but every time he bounced, my arm dragged across the little sections of carapace that covered his neck. My combat instructors on Troyen said that applying pressure there made the plates of the outer shell grind into the soft flesh beneath, smushing it and pinching it. Apparently you dig into three nerves at once: major nerves that feel fierce stabbing pain but don't suffer any real damage.

So I kept my hold jammed in strong while the rest of my body flopped about on the warrior's back. I got bruises and bumps galore, but from the sound of it, I wasn't suffering half as much as the kid I was squeezing. He screamed blue murder and scrabbled with his *Cheejreth* arms trying to pull me off, while his waist pincers clacked sharp and angry, not able to reach any part of me.

I could smell the battle musk rising thick off his skin: Battle Musk C, the one that smells like strong sweet caramel. It meant he was scared and starting to lose his head. The scent glands for Musk C only kick in when a warrior is feeling desperate—a signal telling his comrades-in-arms he needs help, even if he's too stubborn to admit it. Lucky for me, there weren't other warriors around . . . and the Mandasars back at the dome, the workers and the gentle, would never dream of joining the fight. It would be a horrible insult to this warrior's honor, the tiniest suggestion that he'd need help from other castes in dealing with an unarmed human.

After ten seconds of trying to toss me off, the warrior settled down a bit: either trying to think of new tactics, or just not keen on scrunching up his throat anymore. While he considered his next move, I left my one arm in place around his neck, but reached out with the other hand and wrapped it around the end of his snout.

A Mandasar's muscles for opening his mouth aren't very strong—if you hook your thumb on his nose spike and your fingers under his jaw, you can easily hold his mouth shut. Work it right, and you can even press your palm up against his nostrils. You never get a perfect seal, but he still has serious trouble taking in air . . . especially when he's panting from trying to buck you off. It's a good way to impress a sparring partner that you're in control, but not so life-threatening that he thinks you want to smother him dead.

Another few seconds of that and the kid under me stopped struggling. He said something out the side of his mouth, but with his jaw held shut, the words were too muffled to understand. I loosened my grip and let him try again.

"Give," he said.

"What?" I asked, letting go completely.

"Give up." He shook his head and snorted to clear his nose. "I." He shook his head again, then sneezed full force, spraying out a hurricane of spit and mucus. "Surrender, I. Yield, I. Grovel I, you stinky hume."

The warrior flapped one of his *Cheejreth* arms across the tip of his snout, like wiping his nose on his sleeve. "No fight wanted I but all, save you with nonwords made mock of me." He swung his head around till he could glare me full in the face with his beady black eyes. "What in hot hell means *Naizó*?"

10

SMELLING SOMETHING AWFUL

I slid off the warrior's back, making sure to keep clear of his pincers. He didn't even look in my direction—too busy cleaning his nose with his hands, fussing and blowing and sniffling.

"*Naizó* is a short form," I said, then waited for him to finish an especially liquidish round of snorting. "It stands for *Nai halabad tajjef su rellid puzó*. Have you ever heard that?"

His whiskers gave an angry flick; for a second I thought he was going to attack. I hopped back fast into a defense position, but he contented himself with a bristly glare. "Contemptible your accent. Twist the words sideways, almost to mockery . . . yet choose I to think it is mere hume ignorance."

"How would you say it then?"

The warrior stared at me a second more, then intoned his own version of *Nai halabad tajjef su rellid puzó*. He recited it in a deep reverent voice, like he might be saying a prayer . . . but his pronunciation was halfway between gutterspeak and baby talk. A Mandasar from Troyen would break up laughing at the very sound; either that, or slap the boy on the nose.

"Um," I said. Which obviously wasn't the worshipful

praise the warrior expected, so I added, "Interesting. Very interesting."

I shouldn't have been surprised at the warrior's horrible accent. The Mandasar children had come to Celestia a whole twenty years ago; back then, this warrior must have been a mere hatchling . . . baby talk only. On the other hand, a baby wouldn't know big formal sentences like *Nai halabad tajjef su rellid puzó*. The warrior must have learned that later on—either from an older Mandasar kid, or from a human who'd picked up the words but not how to pronounce them properly.

Why didn't the warrior have a better teacher for his own language? I knew the answer, and it didn't reflect too well on my own family. If you want the honest truth, the evacuation had been my father's idea—his pet project, planned and executed by him from start to finish.

No one had even considered the possibility of getting the kids out till Dad suggested it to Sam. I actually read the message he sent from New Earth. Sam was supposed to take credit for the notion, so she could win brownie points with grateful parents on Troyen . . . but it was Dad who organized the big navy airlift to ferry youngsters to the nearest safe planet.

"Just a temporary thing," Sam told me. I was sick in the palace infirmary by then, with a big isolation room all to myself. Humans weren't supposed to visit unless they wore rubbery orange isolation suits, but Sam never followed the rules. She'd handpicked my doctors and nurses; they let her do whatever she wanted, almost as if she were an honorary queen. So she held my hand like she couldn't possibly catch Coughing Jaundice herself, and she said, "The evacuation is only for a few weeks. Till I get the situation here back under control. Dad made a lot of important friends when he was a bright young diplomat on Troyen; now he's keen to keep them happy. If a few Mandasar nobles want to send their kids to safety, Dad's glad to arrange it."

Don't ask me how helping a few friends turned into the

full-scale removal of ten million young Mandasars; but things have a way of snowballing. When word gets out rich and powerful people want their kids offplanet, folks who aren't so well heeled start clamoring for the same thing. Dad refused to take any adults—just a bare minimum of Mandasar nursemaids—but he found a place for every child who was brought to the transport depots.

When anyone asked who'd look after the kids, Dad promised he was sending "trained caregivers" to Celestia. "What a scam!" my sister had said, rolling her eyes. "People on Celestia will never know what hit them. The thing is, Edward, Celestia is an independent world sitting right in the path of Technocracy expansion. They're undeveloped and underpopulated, not to mention their environment is nicely compatible with Terran life. Everyone knows the planet is a juicy prize the Technocracy wants to scoop up . . . and the Celestian government is sweating its tits off, trying to attract nonhuman immigrants to fill up all that inviting empty space."

Sam laughed. "At this very second, folks on Celestia are congratulating themselves how lucky they are to get ten million Mandasars. Warm bodies to add to the census so they can tell the Technocracy, 'Hey, you can't take us over, we've got a thriving population here.' What the Celestians don't understand is that the ten million kids are going to get *twenty* million humans to take care of them . . . courtesy of the High Council of Admirals. Celestia will find itself inundated with *Homo sap* guardians, and if anyone complains to the League, we'll say we're only acting from compassion for the poor wee lobsters."

"But," I said, "if the kids are only going to Celestia for a few weeks . . ."

"When the kids go home," Sam replied, "the baby-sitters will stay. What can Celestia do? It's one thing to run off a few dozen squatters . . . but not twenty million. Especially not twenty million cranky pioneers who've been waiting impatiently for land of their own. This time next week, Celestia will be a de facto human settlement, answering only to Alexander York, Admiral of the Gold. Colonization by fait accompli."

So the people supposed to tend the kids weren't trained caregivers at all; they were a bunch of get-rich-quickers who'd been waiting for colony homes to open up anywhere in frontier space. I guess they had visions of marching down to Celestia and owning the place within a year, while the current nonhuman inhabitants got shunted into reservations and scut jobs. Most of the would-be land-grabbers had no idea how hard they'd have to work to establish any kind of homestead . . . and they definitely didn't have a clue how to raise Mandasar hatchlings.

That wouldn't have mattered much if the children had really only stayed a few weeks. But then the war broke out full bloom back on Troyen and the Technocracy pronounced a quarantine: Troyen was off-limits, nobody in or out. The kids on Celestia couldn't go home; they couldn't even get teachers of their own species, except for the tiny number of Mandasars who'd been offplanet when Troyen fell under blockade.

I can imagine my dad cursing a blue streak about the situation. He'd taken responsibility for the kids, and now he had no choice but to raise them. Somehow. Even if it cut into the "colonization and settlement fees" he'd collected from those Celestia homesteaders. Worse than that, the Admiralty demanded he educate the Mandasar kids in their own history and geography and all; otherwise, civilians would go crazy, throwing around words like "imperialism" and "oppression" and "cultural genocide." Still cursing, my father put out a call for people who knew anything at all about Troyen, so they could teach Mandasar children about themselves.

Ten million kids need an awful lot of teachers. Dad couldn't find nearly enough people who actually knew what they were talking about; up till the war, no one in the Technocracy paid much attention to Troyen. So the kids had had to get by with folks who didn't know as much about hive culture as they pretended: who'd learned from books or ten-day tourist visits. Twenty years later, all that ignorance showed—I was no Troyen expert, but I'd spent fifteen years there with the diplomatic mission, plus another twenty years watching from the moonbase. I knew the difference between a decent accent, and one that sounded like a toddler with his mouth full of porridge.

"My name's Edward," I said, deciding it was safer to speak English rather than Mandasar. "I don't mean any trouble to you or your hive. It's just . . ." I stopped and waved at the evac module, still floating calmly in the canal behind us. "There was trouble with my ship. Up in space. And the escape pod just happened to land here."

"Am Zeeleepull, I," the warrior answered. *Zeeleepull* was a Mandasar word meaning "dauntless" and "undefeated" and "stubborn" . . . a really popular birth name for warriors. He looked glumly at the escape pod for a few seconds, then asked, "More humes will come? Navy humes to find and reclaim you?"

"I guess so. Maybe."

The pod's onboard computer was surely broadcasting "Come and get me" on the fleet's emergency band. *Jacaranda* and Starbase Iris might have their hands full dealing with the black ship, but when they got free time they'd send someone to make a pickup. I wondered if they'd bother to search for me; none of *Willow*'s other evac modules had anyone inside, so the retrieval team might think this one had been empty too. Maybe the retrieval team would just load up the pod and leave, without asking anyone questions.

I could always hope.

So far, Zeeleepull and his hive-mates were the only ones who knew I was here. If I got out of sight before other people came out from siesta . . . and if I could persuade these Mandasar kids not to tell the navy they'd seen me . . .

"Um," I said to Zeeleepull. "Could I maybe talk to your family a minute? Inside, in private somewhere?"

He gave me a mistrustful look. At least, I think that's what it was; on Troyen, I'd got the hang of reading Man-

dasar facial expressions, but I was twenty years out of practice. Zeeleepull stared at me a few more seconds, his
breathing all huffy and puffy. Then, he turned away and
headed for home, muttering over his shoulder, "Come then,
you stinky hume."

I followed behind him, wondering what he meant. Twice
now, he'd called me "stinky"; was that just a sulky-kid
insult, or did I really smell bad? Mandasars had tremen-
dously more sensitive noses than humans, but they were
also pretty broad-minded when it came to odors. A few
things they hated, like the scent of their own race's blood,
but mostly they snuffled around, happy as dogs: interested
in all sorts of smells, even ones humans thought were rude.
Queen Verity once told me she thought *Homo sapiens*
smelled "delicious" . . . which was kind of terrifying, coming from an alien the size of an elephant, but it definitely
wasn't "stinky."

The only stink I could think of was the corpses back on
Willow. I'd walked through the lounge often enough;
maybe the smell of folks rotting had soaked into my
clothes.

As usual, I was wrong.

Zeeleepull's hive-mates didn't look happy to meet me, but
at least they showed good manners. "Hello, good day, good
afternoon, you're wet."

Standoffish politeness was okay. I'd been afraid the Mandasars on Celestia might really be hostile toward humans;
otherwise, why had Zeeleepull attacked me on sight? But
as far as I could tell, these people just thought I was a
nuisance—an unwanted stranger who'd dropped by at
lunch.

Besides Zeeleepull, the hive had four other members:
three white workers, Hib & Nib & Pib (all neuter, of
course); and a brown gentle (female) named Counselor. At
least that's how she introduced herself . . . she must have
had a hidden name, but she'd never reveal it to someone
she'd just met. The only surprise was how she used an

English word for her public title instead of something in her own language. Then again, maybe English *was* her own language—she spoke it a lot better than Zeeleepull, and immediately took over the conversation.

"You claim you're with the navy?" she asked, looking hard at my uniform. It made me realize how bad I must look, all muddy and wet.

"I had to swim," I said, pointing back to the canal.

"No," she replied, her whiskers twitching. "You didn't have to swim. You could have stayed in your capsule till someone came for you."

"Ahh," the three workers said in unison, as if they were tickled pink by Counselor's logic. Workers tend to adore gentles the way grandparents adore grandchildren: fond and admiring, but along the lines of, "Oh how clever the little one is." In a hive like this, Hib & Nib & Pib would do just about anything Counselor asked, but always as if they were indulging the cute little whims of a five-year-old. "You want us to spend twelve hours in the blazing sun, digging up carrots? Well, dear, if that's what you really think we should do, I guess we could manage."

If I were a gentle, it would make me tired and sad and angry—all those people treating me like I was childish and just a bit crazy. But I guess that's the way gentles expect things to be.

"I could have stayed in the escape pod," I told Counselor, "but I've been out in space for a long time and I felt like breathing fresh air."

"More air you need even now," Zeeleepull muttered. "Dirty stink on your fingers."

He made a great show of wiping his nose where I'd put my palm over his snout. All four of his hive-mates immediately poked their muzzles in to sniff me. Mandasars are like that: "You say it smells bad? Really, really bad? Really, really, really bad? Ooo, let me check." Hib and Pib aimed for my armpits while Nib took my crotch—I guess they knew the places where humans usually smelled strongest. Counselor, however, had paid attention to what Zeeleepull actually said; she pushed her nose toward my hands. One deep snort, then she jerked her head up and stepped back fast.

"What *is* that?" she demanded.

"Umm." I couldn't help notice it was my right hand she'd been smelling. The same hand I put around Zeelee-pull's nose.

The same hand that'd got queen's venom spilled on it.

But the venom was only a tiny dose days ago. I'd taken plenty of showers since then . . . not to mention bathing in fever sweat while I was sick. Could Counselor really smell venom after all that? Or was it just dirty water and mud, maybe something I'd put my hand into without noticing as I pulled myself onto the canal bank?

One way to find out: I'd just had a lot fresher dose of venom squish onto my cheeks in the escape pod. "Um," I said, "do you, uhh, smell the same thing on my face?"

All five Mandasars leaned their muzzles toward me. Their whiskers quivered as they drew nearer, looking nervous and eager, both at once . . .

The workers jumped back like I'd whacked them in the snouts. Zeeleepull held his ground but whipped his head away, nearly gouging me with his nose spike by accident. As for Counselor, she just dropped in a dead faint, planting her face into the deep dark soil.

11

MEETING THE HIVE

Fast as I could, I knelt and lifted Counselor out of the dirt. Gentles are the smallest caste of Mandasars; they look frail and fragile in comparison to warriors or workers, but they still weigh as much as a hefty human adult. And they're all floppy-awkward to pick up.

"Let's get her inside," I said to her hive-mates. They didn't answer. They were still all gaping in shock—fresh venom must pack quite a wallop to the Mandasar nose. Struggling on my own, I lugged Counselor through the door of the nearest environment dome, then set her on one of the lounging pallets around the dining-room table.

The communal water bowl was still half-full from lunch. I started to splash Counselor's face and neck, mostly because I didn't know a truly useful way to help her recover. When a gentle faints, it isn't from shock or anything like that—it's actually more of a trance, when she's come up against something that needs a whole lot of thought. Her conscious mind shuts down so her unconscious can go into overdrive . . . kind of like a computer letting its external interface go blank so it can use all its processing power internally. Counselor would wake up when her brain had come to grips with the venom she smelled; but I still kept splashing, because I had to do *something*.

While I splashed, I had time to peek around the dome's interior. More than anything, it looked like one of the "heritage chambers" at Queen Verity's palace: a room where you stored stuff that was too historical to throw out, but too many centuries out of fashion to actually use. The dining table was a perfect example. Laminated on its surface was a glossy reproduction of a two-hundred-year-old Troyenese painting: the one of old Queen Wisdom rising from the sea after sporting with the first envoy from the League of Peoples. It's as famous to Mandasars as the *Mona Lisa* is to humans . . . and that means it's a great whopping cliché you'd never want to show in your home.

At least, that's how people felt on Troyen. Things might be different on Celestia. I could imagine a hive buying the Queen Wisdom table as a joke, the way kids in their twenties get a kick out of kitschy old treasures; but maybe these kids didn't *know* the Queen Wisdom painting was corny and old-fashioned. As one of the few works of Mandasar art known to the outside world, maybe they thought it was special and important—a connection to their lost home planet.

The same could go for the mish-mosh of other knick-knacks around the dome: a cheap little rain-stick from Queen Honor's continent, Rupplish; a pair of sharp iron tips that bolted onto a warrior's pincers . . . something no one on Troyen had used since preindustrial days; a little needlepoint sampler with words written in one of the ancient pictograph languages. I didn't know which language, which continent, or how long ago these particular pictographs had been edged out by the unromantic efficiency of an alphabet.

The nobles back in Queen Verity's palace would have flicked their whiskers at such a rummage of decorations clumped in one room. The stuff didn't *go* together: antiquey things from a dozen different ages and regions, all dating back at least a hundred years. But the pieces weren't real antiques; they weren't even good fakes. Every hunk of bric-a-brac looked gleaming and modern, as if Celestia had a hundred factories knocking off shiny-bright copies of old

Troyenese things . . . whatever artwork and gewgaws the outside world happened to have pictures of.

I couldn't help feeling sorry for these kids, how they were ready to buy anything that was sort of a kind of a teeny bit like mementos from Troyen. They didn't mind mixing stuff together from all three continents and heaven knows how many eras of history, so long as it brought back memories of their birth world.

So lonely. So homesick.

But as much as I felt sorry for them, I felt pretty proud too . . . the way they hung on, trying to stay connected to a planet they only half remembered. Big red Zeeleepull had never heard the word *Naizó*, even though it'd been standard for centuries . . . but he knew the longer phrase, the original, like some cherished hand-me-down from the medieval warriors who'd invented it.

The more I thought about it, the more I saw what was really going on: the Mandasars here weren't just twenty-year-old kids, they were *children*. No matter how grown-up their bodies had got, their house was like a tree fort filled with a hodgepodge of valuable junk they'd pulled out of trash heaps or bought for a penny. None of this was sad and pathetic, or even noble; it was just what youngsters did while they were rehearsing to own adult things.

Even if a Queen Wisdom table was still tacky, tacky, tacky.

The other four hive-mates trooped in from outside just as Counselor started to wake. From the looks on their faces, Zeeleepull and the workers had mumbled and grumbled about what to do with me but hadn't come to any conclusion. All Mandasars can make decisions when they have to, but if there's a gentle handy, the other castes give her the deciding vote. I don't know if that's instinct or just habit; the gentles all swear it's biologically hardwired, how other castes defer to them . . . but warriors and workers claim they only do it because gentles whine when they don't get their own way.

Counselor blinked and twitched her whiskers a few times, shaking off the water I'd splashed on her face. Suddenly, she sat bolt-upright, staring at me in horror. "You smell . . ."

She couldn't finish the sentence. Zeeleepull muttered, "Stinky hume," while the workers crowded in to see if Counselor was okay. They did all the standard things worried Mandasar moms do with children: patting Counselor's face to check for fever; examining the color of her fingertips; sniffing the tiny musk glands at the base of her tail to make sure she didn't smell injured.

I looked down at those button-sized glands myself. If Counselor had become a queen when she was little, those glands would have ballooned into huge green sacs.

"The smell on my face," I said to them all. "It's venom. From a Mandasar queen."

That sent the five of them into another bout of whisker-twitching shock. With Zeeleepull, the shock only took half a second to swoop into outrage. "Dare you to pretend—"

"I'm not pretending," I interrupted. "It's the truth."

"Then worse!" Zeeleepull yelled.

The burning-wood odor of Battle Musk B began to pour off him like smoke. Thirty seconds of that and he'd go berserk . . . especially in the dining room's enclosed space, where his own musk would fill the air and whip him to frenzy. Counselor put her hand to his cheek, and whispered, "Calm, calm," but Zeeleepull just kept yelling.

"If a hume, dirty awful you, dares to wear sacred venom like . . . like *perfume* . . ."

Uh-oh. It's too complicated to explain now, but one of the causes of Troyen's civil war was snooty-pants aliens riling the populace by dousing themselves with Mandasar pheromones. Zeeleepull obviously knew that . . . and in his mind, he'd suddenly identified me with the troublemakers who drove Troyen over the edge.

The workers were snorting and trembling now, half-scared to death by the Musk B in the air. That particular type of musk always terrifies nonwarrior castes. *A scent specifically evolved to stimulate the fear response*, a Mandasar scientist once told me. Counselor hollered, "*Nai halabad tajjef su rellid puzó*," but Zeeleepull was too far gone for that to have an effect. The words only work when everyone's cool-headed, not when a warrior desperately *wants* to run riot.

Any second, there was going to be a fight . . . and a real fight this time, not just a warrior feeling testy, deciding to drive off an unwanted visitor. Now Zeeleepull had a reason to really hurt me: because he thought I'd committed the deliberate sacrilege of wearing venom as cologne.

I had no room to maneuver inside the house. Even worse, the dome had closed and sealed itself shut after everyone came inside; I couldn't find the door to get out. Zeeleepull would try to kill me, and the only way to prevent that was to hurt him . . . bash him unconscious or cripple him so badly he couldn't pincer me in half. I didn't want to do it; I didn't even know if I *could* do it, because there was so little space for ducking and dodging.

Then . . . while I was thinking and worrying and trying to figure out what to do, my hands reached out of their own accord. I wasn't moving them, I swear. I had no idea what they were going to do. But they grabbed Zeeleepull's snout like I was as strong as a tiger, and dragged his nose around till it was a hair breadth from my face.

He tried to yank away, but couldn't. I remember thinking, *I shouldn't be able to hold him. In a straight tug-of-war, he outweighs me three to one.* But I wrestled him close so that all he could smell was the fresh venom on my face; and I heard my own voice saying, "I am Blood-Consort Edward York, last and rightful husband of Verity the Second, High Queen and Supreme Ruler of all those who tread the Blessed Land. If you fear her name, you will yield; if not, be named her enemy and pay the price of your folly."

The words came out in a dream. I couldn't tell if I was talking English or Troyenese; I'd never said such things before, never once tried to bully people by using my position. For all I knew, these Mandasars had no idea Queen

Verity ever married a human husband . . . and even if they'd heard the story, why would they believe I was that man?

But Zeeleepull's nostrils were full of the odor of queen's venom: the venom on my face, stronger than the scent of battle musk, or the aroma of fear rising from Counselor and the workers.

Slowly, the warrior crossed his *Cheejreth* over his chest and closed his eyes. When I let go of his snout, he lowered it to the ground till his whole body was flat on the floor.

"*Nai halabad tajjef su rellid puzó,*" he whispered.

Counselor was already lying down. Hib & Nib & Pib dropped prostrate too, pressing their faces tight against the chipped-wood rug. For a second I was standing high above their heads . . . and I could feel an unfamiliar expression twisting up my face. I didn't know how it looked, but it scared me. Something out of nowhere was making me act like a stranger.

I pushed and pushed, trying to shift my face, my arms, anything. Suddenly, everything holding me back let go and I was in control again, able to move my body however I wanted. I dropped to my knees and nearly blurted out, *I'm sorry, I didn't mean it* . . . but I stopped myself in time. Warriors are quick to recognize signs of weakness; if I started apologizing, we might head back where we started, Zeeleepull going berserk and no way to avoid an all-out bonecrushing.

"Um, rise," I said. Which didn't sound very regal. I tried to remember how Queen Verity talked to her subjects when she held court. "Rise," I said again with my deepest, most gracious voice. "Rise and let us converse."

Counselor was the first to perk up. She'd only caught a slight whiff of the venom . . . not like Zeeleepull, who'd practically had his nose rubbed in it while I held his snout to my face. No wonder he was slow getting up off the floor. The workers, of course, were busy being cowed—opening one eyelid for a quick peek at me, then closing the eye fast

if they saw I was looking their way. You can never tell
with workers whether they're really as intimidated as they
seem, or if they're just putting on a show of being menial.
Maybe the workers don't know either.

"Were you really the high queen's blood-consort?"
Counselor asked in a hushed voice.

"Yes. I really was." For eight whole years, till Verity got
killed and the war began . . . but I didn't say that. I also
didn't mention she'd had six other consorts at the same
time.

"What are you doing here?" Counselor asked.

"I told you: my escape pod landed in your canal."

"So you didn't . . . seek us out?"

Counselor suddenly had a hopeful look on her face,
enough to break my heart. I could imagine the kids on
Celestia, cut off from their home for twenty years and looking to the sky every night, wondering if anyone would ever
come to tell them, "We love you and want you back."
They'd have a terrible time if they actually *did* go back to
Troyen—with their gutter-baby accents and their attach-
ment to dreadful fake antiques—but they didn't know
they'd be out of place.

As out of place as they were now.

"Things are still bad back home," I said. "When I left a
week and a half ago, the war was as fierce as ever." Not
that I paid much attention to the fighting . . . but the other
observers on the moonbase would have told me if the war
had ended.

"Yet you recently had contact with . . . a royal person,"
Counselor said. "The smell on your face is fresh."

"Yes," I nodded, "but that queen is dead now." When I
realized how bad that sounded, I quickly added, "Someone
else killed her. It's really complicated. A ship was trying
to bring her here, but things went wrong."

"So you've come in her stead?" Counselor asked, all
shining eager. "To save us from the recruiters?"

"Um. Hmm."

Counselor sounded so beamingly hopeful, I didn't want

to ask, "What recruiters?" That would dash her down hard,
like I'd come all this way, then didn't know the first thing
about her troubles. From the sound of her voice, I could
tell she wanted me to be a great savior, fallen out of the
sky to rescue her hive from danger. So I didn't open my
mouth till I'd picked my words carefully. "Talk to me about
these recruiters," I said. "Tell me everything."

And she did.

Counselor started with something I already knew: despite
all those human settlers twenty years ago, Celestia still
didn't belong to the Technocracy. Then she told me a secret: over the past two decades, Celestia had become one
of the Technocracy's most valuable assets, precisely because it'd never signed the Technocracy charter.

It turned out the humans Dad brought to Celestia weren't
interested in clearing a few grubby acres and trying to grow
butternut squash. Instead, they wanted to grow huge acres
of cash: for example, by establishing big secretive banks
outside the Technocracy regulatory system. Places where
wealthy Tech-citizens could store money without worrying
about taxes or subpoenas. Celestia also became a meeting
ground for folks making shady deals . . . especially under-
the-table arrangements with alien species. One group of
newly arrived entrepreneurs took up catering to tourists
with tastes that would be illegal elsewhere; others built factories that spewed pollution or exploited workers in ways
the Technocracy would never allow.

In other words, Counselor said, Celestia had become a
place where big rich important people could do sneaky
slimy things—all the things they couldn't get away with
inside the boring old Technocracy. (Of course, those big
rich important people still *lived* in the Technocracy, where
life was safe and civilized. What's the point of being rich
if you can't milk the system, then avoid its inconven-
iences?)

So Celestia was a nice little planet, but also your basic
swill hole. People and things got dumped here. The Man-

dasars were a prime example: brought in as a ruse for colonization, then kept here because the place didn't have fuddy-duddy laws about raising kids properly. Folks in this star system wouldn't demand you build "quality orphanages" or find teachers who knew what they were talking about.

The kids had grown up without a lot of attention . . . but that wasn't so bad, Counselor said, when they were raised in big schools that crammed a lot of children into one place. Mandasars don't mind being crammed. In fact, I knew it was good for them to be chucked in tight together, warriors and workers and gentles.

If you want the honest truth, they thrive on each other's smell.

This is something I learned in Queen Verity's palace: a crucial fact of Mandasar biology. They need to be surrounded by people of other castes. Every waking second, for instance, a warrior gives off a vinegary perfume (Musk A) that stimulates workers and gentles to be a bit . . . well, aggressive isn't the right word. Sharp. Keen. Alert and ambitious.

It's a pheromone that works directly on receptors in the Mandasar brain. It's not psychological, it's purely physical; for Mandasars, inhaling that aroma is like snorting a psychoactive drug. Only it's more like absorbing a vitamin their brains need to work properly—without regular exposure to warrior musk, workers and gentles start to go funny in the head.

It's the same for other castes. Workers give off a scent that keeps warriors and gentles more stable, more patient; and the fragrance of a gentle makes warriors and workers more thoughtful in both senses of the word—they reflect more on what they're doing, and are more considerate about how their actions affect other people.

Separate the castes from each other, and their brain chemicals skitter out of balance. If you keep warriors stuck in barracks with other warriors day after day, the buildup of warrior musk keeps them hair-trigger ready for a fight . . .

but they have no patience, and they don't think much about what they're asked to do. That's great if you want blood-thirsty killing machines who don't question their orders. In the long run, though, it doesn't make for a smart depend-able army. Or for productive law-abiding citizens.

The same with other castes. Make a segregated camp that only contains workers, and you get a drove of plodding drudges. Verity told me you could make them work long hours for zero pay, but they had no initiative and never used their wits to deal with unexpected problems.

Ditto for gentles. If they only hung around with other gentles, they ended up all brains and no common sense: ivory-tower types who were great at coming up with ideas, inventions and theories, but lousy at judging priorities. They'd be just as happy brainstorming new ways to kill people as they would be inventing medicines or things to make life better. Basically, they turned into amoral gen-iuses, ready to tackle any problem so long as it was inter-esting, and to hell with the long-term consequences.

Counselor said the kids on Celestia knew about phero-mones too. They wouldn't be whole people unless they lived in hives with all three castes in close quarters; it was the only way to keep every part of their brains wide-awake and functioning. But this bit of biology wasn't common knowledge amongst outside races . . . not till those "trained human caregivers" on Celestia began tending Mandasar children. That's when the secret got out, and the human world started contemplating the possibilities.

Remember: Celestia had become home to sleazy profi-teers. Even I could see how things might take a nasty turn.

Given a choice, the Mandasar children dearly loved to live in hives like this one: workers taking care of regular chores inside the house and around the farm; a warrior for heavy lifting and for protecting the others; a gentle to act as manager, to keep the books, to deal with customers and suppliers. They fit together as a family. The next time Counselor came into egg-heat, she and Zeeleepull would likely make a big happy clutch of hatchlings to carry on the tradition. (Egg-heat only happens once every nine years; the rest of the time, Mandasars are pretty mind-bogglingly platonic.)

But Counselor told me the sneaky slimy wheeler-dealers on Celestia didn't care about Mandasars living balanced lives. Did warriors turn into mad dogs when you kept them apart from gentles and workers? Then they'd be perfect for guards at sweatshops and at factories that made illegal nano. Did workers turn into easy-to-control drones? That made them great for sixteen-hour shifts on assembly lines. Did gentles turn into brilliant intellectuals who didn't fret about the effects of what they did? Then why not use them in disreputable think tanks or research institutes?

That's what started the practice of "recruiting" on Celestia. According to Counselor, Mandasars were offered good money and benefits to sign on with various outfits, whereupon they'd be bundled off into single-caste units until their brains turned to one-track minds. The kids caught onto this pretty quick, and stopped signing up voluntarily. That's when the recruitment process started to work more like old-time press-gangs: if you didn't say yes to the soft sell, thugs would break into your house, gas the whole hive into unconsciousness, and take everyone away to "reorientation centers."

A month in isolation, Counselor said, and the poor Mandasars weren't themselves anymore—the warriors would be spoiling for a fight, the workers would turn into zombies, and the gentles would be reduced to spoiled brats eager to show off how bright they were. Sure, they'd all remember the more balanced people they'd once been . . . but their pheromone-deprived brains just didn't care. They were either too riled-up, too sluggish, or too giddy to be interested in changing back. Definitely, they'd never *dream* of complaining they were kidnapped and forced to become degenerate versions of their former selves.

In a way, they were like human adults who look back on childhood and say, "Sure, it was nice to be open and imaginative and alive, but we all have to grow up, don't we?" Soon enough, the Mandasars stopped believing there'd ever been an alternative to their walled-up tunnel-vision lives.

But Counselor swore there *were* alternatives. This farming area, for instance, the Hollen Marsh: a big swath of reclaimed swampland, full of Mandasar kids living in small integrated hives. They watched out for each other with volunteer sentry patrols. The second that humans showed up, a militia of warriors would run off the intruders. That's why Zeeleepull had charged me—he thought I was a recruiter, coming around with a bright smile and a pocketful of promises, but really spying out the territory for midnight press-gangs.

Counselor said there were other communities like theirs around Celestia: small-scale places where Mandasars could be themselves, farming or fishing or building useful things. But rumor had it that one by one, the communities were being wiped out . . . blitzed by recruitment gangs, families broken up and carted off to segregated isolation camps in wilderness parts of the planet. The local authorities were no help; a few took bribes from the recruiters, while the rest had been fooled by the stories Mandasars told after they'd been *acclimatized*: "Oh, it's all a big fuss over nothing. We were stupid kids who wanted to live lazy unattached lives, but I feel so much better, now that I have a sense of *purpose*."

Well . . . Counselor had a sense of purpose too: to avoid the recruiters and live the way she wanted, with a healthy balanced brain. For a long time, the hive had been praying for someone to come and help them. They'd always pictured their savior as a grand and glorious queen, straight from Troyen . . . but maybe a blood-consort would do just as well.

Um.

12

TALKING OVER OUR PROBLEMS

When Counselor finished her story, all five of the kids sat smiling expectantly at me. Not human smiles, of course; Mandasars smile with their ears and whiskers, both sort of relaxing down in calm droops.

Pity I couldn't smile too.

The truth is I'd never been so great as a blood-consort. Queen Verity said she married me mostly because of my delicious smell. Samantha claimed it was also a political thing, sending a message to Verity's enemies that the queen was backed by my father and the full force of the Outward Fleet.

But once I became Verity's husband, it turned out I didn't have much to do. Smelling delicious doesn't qualify you for being a general or cabinet minister or important jobs like that. Mostly I just hung around the palace being Verity's bodyguard. (By then, sister Sam didn't need me to be her bodyguard anymore. She'd assembled her own security team of warriors, humans, and even some Fasskisters. Anyway, she was getting busier and busier with secret diplomat stuff, "and it's better, Edward, if you don't know about that.")

As for me being Verity's consort/husband/bodyguard, the queen once said, "You may not be a genius, Edward, but you're the only honest creature I've ever known. I keep you around for inspiration. And curiosity value." It made me feel good when she talked like that . . . but being an inspiration doesn't mean you're good for much else. Definitely I wasn't cut out for saving people.

(Memories of corpses flashed through my mind: Verity herself, head laid out on a platter. Samantha in a pool of blood. All the people on *Willow*, dressed up for their last party.)

But Counselor and the others still wore those big trusting smiles. Five minutes before, they had been cheering for Zeeleepull to snip me bloody. Now their black eyes gleamed as if I were topped off with a halo.

Or maybe, as if I were topped off with a crown. I'd been sitting in their midst, giving off the scent of queen's venom, so why *wouldn't* they start responding to me like royalty? If you smell like a queen, all their instincts tell them to treat you like you're three-quarters divine. (Mandasars are a smart species, they really are, but they're way too much at the mercy of their noses. Then again, they laugh at us humans and say we're way too much at the mercy of our gonads . . . so maybe it balances out.)

"What do you think I can do?" I asked Counselor.

She looked at me in surprise, maybe wondering why I didn't instantly have a plan to save all ten million kids on Celestia. "Do what is required," Counselor told me.

"Yes, but in the high queen's court," I said, "Verity never started anything without consulting her privy council. Even a queen knows it's smart to talk things over with people who've studied the situation."

Everyone smiled and nodded. Counselor went all bashful to be compared to a royal advisor, the workers beamed as if their darling grandchild had won a prize, and even Zeeleepull showed some real approval . . . like maybe I wasn't just a stupid thug with queen-spill on my face.

"Well," said Counselor, "you're with the navy, are you not? This is not a Technocracy world, but the fleet still wields great influence. If you summoned a dozen cruisers with tractor beams to stop ships from docking at our orbitals, the Celestian authorities would soon do whatever you asked. Even if the navy just took the name of everyone coming and going, there'd be great pressure on our government to remedy the situation immediately. Powerful people often don't want it known when and why they come to this world. They value secrecy much more than they care about a few Mandasar employees."

She wiggled her whiskers the way gentles do when they're pleased with themselves. I guess I was supposed to say, "Tremendous idea, I'll do it." But the Admiralty wasn't going to annoy influential people just on the request of a lowly Explorer Second Class—especially not an Explorer Second Class they intended to strand on some lonely outpost as soon as they caught him. Now that I thought about it, maybe it was kind of risky doing *anything* for these kids: if I attracted attention, people might come to snatch *me* in the middle of the night, and they wouldn't just be recruiters for some factory that didn't pay overtime.

On the other hand . . . when I'd married Queen Verity, I'd taken an oath to protect her people forever and ever. Verity's reign was over, but "forever and ever" wasn't.

"Sorry," I told Counselor, "we can't look for help from the navy. So let's think what else we can do . . ."

We kicked around ideas for an hour. Everyone got in on the act—even Hib & Nib & Pib. Usually workers just sit back and smile when other people are discussing plans, as if they already know the right answer and are just waiting for everyone else to reach the same conclusion . . . but maybe the smell of queen's venom had stirred them enough that they just couldn't keep quiet. All three workers actually got involved, tossing in suggestions and comments and nitpicks.

Too bad we never decided anything.

The ideas basically fell into two classes: big fancy schemes that would only work if I was a colossally important person (which I wasn't); and small practical ways to resist the recruiters, which were already being done. For example, Hib suggested I should bring all the Mandasars together in a special shelter where they'd be safe from recruiters. But who would build the shelter? Me? The navy? The League? And who would protect us how, when we didn't have money to pay for security guards or equipment? On the other hand, if we were talking about making our own special shelters, and protecting ourselves . . . weren't the Mandasars doing that right now? There in the Hollen Marsh and elsewhere? They'd banded together all on their own, without needing me as a figurehead. What more could *I* do? If they were looking for a great military leader to improve their organization or tactics, I was the last person to put in charge.

Hib and the others didn't understand that. No matter how much I told them I wasn't generalissimo material, they thought I was just being modest.

So the talk went around and around, the kids thrashing through the pros and cons, while I listened . . . and listened . . . and kept on listening till it dawned on me I'd stopped taking anything in. I was watching the way their mouths moved as they spoke. The bobbing of their whiskers. The spike at the end of Zeeleepull's snout as it swished through the air.

I'm dizzy, I thought. *I've gone all dizzy.* It was the kind of dizziness that seems absolutely fascinating, so you start rotating your neck slowly just to feel the world blur: to see exactly how much you can control the spaciness inside your skull . . .

Someone gave me a shake. Counselor was holding onto my shoulders with her upper arms and saying, "Are you all right?"—really loud as if she'd already asked the question a whole bunch of times.

"I'm sick," I said. "The little eyeballs poisoned me." Which struck me as funny, so I laughed and laughed . . . way too hard. The dizziness whooshed down over me like ice water, starting cold at the roots of my hair and draining bleak down my face. I remember thinking, *This isn't regal at all.*

Then, very unregally, I passed out.

It was hard to tell when I was awake and when I wasn't. Sometimes I thought I was dreaming about a little Mandasar girl with her arms wrapped around my neck and both of us crying; but sometimes I had the idea maybe Counselor was the one holding me, and she was trying to keep me down on a bed pallet as I thrashed about half-crazy. It all blended together, so confused and light-headed that I couldn't tell the borderline between dream and delirium.

Still . . . Counselor, the real Counselor, was a deep gentle brown. The little girl who came weeping into my hallucinations was a bright queenly yellow. "Oh Father Prince," she whispered, "wake and save us all. Please, please wake."

Which had to be Counselor talking, or one of her hivemates. Someone so naive, she thought I was smart enough to save people.

When I woke for real, the dining room was dark and quiet. I just lay there woozy for a while, trying to collect my thoughts. The Mandasar kids had left me on my own . . . but probably they were lying close by in the next room. If I made the slightest noise, they'd come running to tend their "prince."

Not that I'd acted like a prince so far. All I'd done was rough up Zeeleepull, tell the others why I couldn't help against the recruiters, then pass out on their dining-room floor. Pretty pathetically awful, even by my normal useless-dummy standards.

But at least the kids hadn't tossed me out of the house. I was lying almost exactly where I'd fallen—they'd just shifted me onto a dining pallet. When I reached out, I could touch the table . . . with its big glossy picture of Queen Wisdom . . .

That reminded me of the water bowl, the one I'd used for splashing Counselor's face. My mouth was dust-dry, probably because I'd been sweating buckets while I was unconscious. (You don't want to know how soaked and sodden my clothes were.) I sat up and edged my way over to the table, hoping maybe the kids had left the bowl full overnight. On Troyen, a lot of families did that in case someone wanted a drink.

The bowl was still there, but flipped upside down. The glossy table surface had puddles everywhere, as if someone had knocked the bowl over and not bothered to mop up the wet.

Odd.

The room was almost coal-mine black, just a tiny bit of starshine coming through the ceiling; the kids had adjusted the environment dome so a wee patch of roof was transparent like a skylight. I could just barely see the outlines of things close up . . . nothing distinct, nothing that would tell me what was wrong.

"House-soul, attend," I whispered. "Can you give me some light?"

Nothing happened: the dome's computer didn't want to take commands from me. No big surprise; why would the kids reprogram their house so I could boss it around? But in a lot of homes, the computer lets *anyone* turn on the lights. Most house-souls have a set of instructions considered safe to obey, even from strangers. Flushing the toilet. Telling what time it is. Letting you wash your hands. But maybe the Mandasars were so worried about recruiters, they'd adjusted their system to "total noncooperation" mode.

I leaned against the table, wondering what to do. One thing about venom poisoning: both times after the delirium broke, I felt pretty good. Relatively speaking, anyway—I was thirsty and hungry, and not even Queen Verity would think I smelled delicious, but I was strong enough to stand without wobbling too much. After being unconscious so long, I felt wide-awake too. The polite thing might be to go back to bed till the Mandasars got up in the morning, but at the moment I wasn't sleepy.

What to do? If I wandered around in the dark, I'd probably break something. On the other hand . . . I thought about that knocked-over water bowl. There must be plenty of harmless explanations, but it still made me edgy.

I was standing there, thinking hard and chewing my knuckle in the dark, when my wrist started squealing.

13

RUNNING AROUND
IN THE DARK

It had been twenty years since I'd heard that squeal: a
personal Mayday from someone close by. A navyish
someone. When you joined the fleet, you got a tiny beeper
embedded under the skin of your wrist, so if you got caught
in some terrible disaster, you could call for help. The beeper
sent out a radio beam that activated everyone else's beeper
within a few kilometers—a shrieky shrill signal that said,
"Come running, shipmate in trouble."

The last time my beeper went off was on Troyen: Sam
desperately trying to reach me.

I'd got there too late.

"Counselor!" I yelled into the darkness. "Sorry to disturb
you, but this is important. Can you turn on the lights and
open the door? Counselor? Counselor?"

No answer.

"Hey!" I shouted louder. "Hey!"

Nothing.

"Can anybody hear me? Anybody there?"

It was only a small dome: two rooms. And Mandasars
are light sleepers. In fact, experts get into arguments
whether Mandasars ever truly sleep, or just go into a resting
doze where they're always half-conscious. Either way,

Counselor and the others would never snooze through me calling, let alone the squealing from my wrist.

That squeal was making me jumpy. I told the implant, "Shut off," and the beeper stopped its noise, leaving behind a thick stuffy silence. No sound of moving or breathing anywhere close by; I was all alone in the dome.

Why did that worry me? There'd been two other domes beside this one. The kids probably ate here, and slept next door. Nothing strange about that . . . but it was surprising they'd left me alone, me being sick and all. Before I'd passed out, they were giving me the royal treatment. Did they change their minds once I went delirious? Or had they been watching over me, till something big and important drew everybody away?

I could imagine Counselor dozing on a pallet beside me when suddenly some crisis struck. Maybe one of her hive-mates yelled from outside. Counselor ran to help, knocking over the water bowl and not even stopping to clean up.

But what could cause such a fuss? Recruiters on a raid?

I thought about my wrist beeper again . . . and suddenly, it all made sense. Someone had come from the navy. A recovery team had picked up the escape pod's homing beacon and followed the signal here. Maybe they'd decided to look around a bit, to see if anyone had been inside the pod.

What would the Mandasars think when they spotted humans wandering about in the dark? Every warrior in the valley would come howling for blood, believing recruiters were on the march.

No wonder the poor navy people fired off a Mayday.

I blundered across the room and banged my fist against the wall. The dome field didn't budge. "House-soul, attend!" I yelled. "Can you open a door? Please."

The house-soul ignored me. For all it knew, I could be a burglar trying to make a getaway. The computer would keep me locked in here, unable to help the navy folks till some recognized member of the hive came to let me out.

"House-soul!" I yelled again. "This is an emergency. The warriors might kill someone innocent."

No response. I took a breath, then drove my heel into the wall with a hard side-kick. The impact knocked me backward, but it didn't make any impression on the dome. A typical dome field is strong enough to withstand a hurricane or lightning bolt; my strongest kick just wasn't an irresistible force of nature.

"House-soul, come on! Listen to me! It's a matter of life and death. Don't you have any overrides for when sentient lives are threatened?"

Still nothing. I could be speaking a foreign language for all this computer cared about me . . .

Oh.

Three seconds later, the house-soul had popped open a door right in front of my face. Counselor must have authorized the computer to take orders from me. All I had to do was ask in Mandasar.

The weather had turned spring-night cool, with a starry sky and three yellow moons the size of confetti. I lifted my wrist, and whispered to the implant, "Find Mayday source." Then I held out my arm and turned in a slow circle till the implant gave a beep. At that second, my arm pointed up the road and along the canal, in the direction the escape pod had been floating when I left it.

That made sense. If the Mayday had come from a navy recovery team, the team would be close to the evac module.

I told my wrist implant to switch to silent mode, so it wouldn't squeal no matter what. You don't want your beeper going off when you're trying to sneak around in the dark . . . especially not within earshot of Mandasar warriors, ready to gut any human they met.

For a second, I wondered if I was crazy to be out here at all. How did I think I could help? It was one thing to take on a single untrained warrior in full daylight; but if a navy recovery team was under attack by a whole militia of warriors, with every Mandasar believing the team was a

desperate threat to their hives . . . it would take more than
a few fighting tricks to get anyone out in one piece.

Including me.

On top of that, these navy folks likely came from the
Jacaranda. They may have been sent to capture me and
drag me off to some awful place halfway across the galaxy.
If they were as nasty as Tobit said, they might even have
set off a fake Mayday to flush me out of hiding.

But . . . it was stupid to worry over what-ifs when there
was only one right thing to do.

Help the best I could. Hope the rest worked out.

I started running up the road beside the silent dark waters
of the canal.

The first thing I found was an unconscious worker. It could
have been Hib, Nib, or Pib . . . but it could also have been
any other worker in the valley. Even with the moonlight,
it was too dark to make out the teeny facial features that
distinguish one worker from another.

As far as I could tell, the worker wasn't hurt, just unconscious. Breathing peacefully. That made me think it'd
been shot by a hypersonic stunner—a standard navy-issue
weapon, mostly used by Explorers who encounter unknown
alien lifeforms. It's handy to have a little pistol that knocks
out attackers without killing them . . . especially when
you're on an unexplored planet and don't know whether
you're shooting at a big dumb predator or a sentient being
who's just mad at you for trampling its sweet potatoes.

If the navy team had stunners, they might not be in such
trouble . . . as long as the guns' batteries held out. Stun-
pistols were good for twenty shots or so. That wasn't nearly
enough to take down every Mandasar in the marsh, but it
was better than nothing. I'd have to be careful myself. If
the team was looking to capture me, one shot from a stunner could lay me out cold for six hours.

I left the worker where it was and moved forward again,
this time keeping under the shadow of the trees between
the road and canal. Soon after, I found an unconscious gen-

tle, then an unconscious warrior. During our discussions that afternoon, Counselor had said all three castes took turns at sentry duty . . . and if an alert came in, the whole community fanned out over the marsh to find the intruders. Lucky for me, the searchers in this area had already got stunned; otherwise, they might be shouting, "He's here, he's here," and bringing the militia down on my head.

That would be very bad.

Half a kilometer and six more unconscious bodies later, I came to the escape pod. It was still floating in the middle of the canal, barely moving on the slow current. A scatter of Mandasar bodies lay flumped unconscious at the edge of the water, all of them warriors . . . as if there'd been a pitched battle here, not just sentries caught off guard in the dark.

No human bodies in sight. So far, the navy folks were holding their own.

I used my wrist implant to take another direction reading on the Mayday. Now, the signal was coming from the far side of the canal. The recovery team must have decided it was crazy to go farther into the marsh; instead, they'd headed across the water, where the land wasn't cleared for crops. Nothing over there but scruffy black forest, and the ground sloping upward into low hills. The navy people were obviously running for cover and getting the heck out of Hollen valley.

Good, I thought, *they'll be okay now.* The recovery folks were retreating, and they didn't have far to go till they'd be safe; Counselor had said there was no Mandasar population once you got to higher ground. I could go back the way I'd come, without having to worry about the navy team . . . and I'd better do that fast, before I ran into someone who wanted to slice first and ask questions later.

When I turned around, the starlit marsh was alive with warriors galloping in my direction.

*   *   *

The Mandasars hadn't seen me yet: I was standing in dark shadows under trees. One of the unconscious warriors lying in the mud must have got off a signal before he was stunned—it only made sense that someone would be carrying a radio. Now the whole militia was charging toward the battle site . . . and I wanted to be long gone before they arrived.

As quietly as I could, staying in shadow, I knelt and slipped into the canal. The water was just as cold as at lunchtime; just as muddy too, with the stagnant smell of algae right under my nose. I took a deep breath, then slipped beneath the surface, swimming with my eyes shut because I wouldn't be able to see in the black muddiness anyway.

My plan was to reach the trees on the other bank and just hide in the woods. I wasn't one of those stealthy stalker-types who could slip silently past a horde of warriors on the hunt. My only hope was that they wouldn't bother to search the far side; none of their people lived over there, so the warriors would likely concentrate their efforts on patrolling the main valley rather than making forays across the canal.

I slid onto the opposite shore just before the first warriors arrived. When they saw the heaps of unconscious bodies, they broke into an angry chatter that covered any noise I made creeping into the woods. I kept going, crouched low and moving as fast as I could, trying to put distance between me and the Mandasars. Any second, I expected someone to shout, "Look over there!" But they were all too busy gabbling over their fallen comrades, and pointing toward the evac module bobbing quietly in the water.

As I moved, things squished softly under my feet. I didn't know what they were: insects, or puffballs, or jellyish Celestian lifeforms, I couldn't tell. Fleeing through the dark doesn't give you much chance to appreciate alien ecologies. I just hoped I wouldn't disturb any teeny critters with venomous bites. The Mandasars would've cleared out all larger predators—their race has no guilt about endangering species they don't like—but they wouldn't bother to deal with anything whose teeth were too small to go through carapace. Black widow spiders, for instance. The closest real black widow was surely forty light-years away, but I still managed to make myself nervous about them as I slunk through the pitch-dark forest.

Every now and then, a puff of breeze brought the burning-wood smell of Musk B. The warriors behind me were keyed up, just itching to fight something. If I were a worker or gentle, I'd be heading for home real fast—warriors would soon be swiping at trees just to work off their tension. It wouldn't surprise me if they hauled the escape pod out of the canal and tin-snipped it to ribbons; with so much musk in the air, they'd be looking for *anything* to attack.

The land under my feet angled upward in fits and starts: a little slope, then a level patch, then another slanty climb. The sound of angry voices faded behind me. I was just thinking it might be safe to rest when I came across a heavy slash of damage to the forest's undergrowth.

It looked like someone had driven a bulldozer through here, on a big swath leading backward to the canal and forward up the wooded hillslope. That could only mean one thing: a warrior had come to this side of the canal and was plowing his way after the navy team. He must have spotted them running away from the scene of the battle . . . and like a typical musk-mad lunatic, he'd charged after them on his own instead of waiting for reinforcements.

That was good news for the recovery team—if the warrior had stayed behind to tell the militia what was happening, the whole forest would be crawling with berserker Mandasars. As it was, the warrior probably got himself stunned cold as soon as he got close to the navy folks.

Still . . . I decided to follow the smashed-down trail. If nothing else, I could make better time taking the flattened path than trying to pick my way through the brush.

*   *   *

Three minutes later, I heard noises ahead of me. Crashing. Something going WHUMP. Branches breaking.

I ran forward without thinking. The noises got louder: grunts and the clack of pincers closing on empty air. A warrior had just missed grabbing hold of somebody.

My eye caught a silvery glint on the trail in front of me: a stun-pistol tossed away. Usually, the guns have a green light telling when there's enough juice in their batteries for another shot . . . but as I sprinted past, the light didn't show the tiniest flicker. The stunner was completely tapped out, while up ahead some poor unarmed someone was trying to fight an angry warrior bare-handed.

The trail broke into a level clearing; and that was where the unarmed someone had decided to make a stand. It wasn't a full navy recovery team—there was only one person, ducking away from a warrior even bigger than Zee-leepull. In the dark I could only see silhouettes, but that was enough to tell me the target under attack was a woman. She moved fast and dodgy, as if she'd done a fair bit of martial arts. Still, general combat training doesn't teach you the specific ways to take down a Mandasar warrior . . . and a fight to the death isn't the best time to start experimenting.

The warrior hadn't noticed me yet. Even better, he had his back to me; and that meant his tail pointed in my direction. Since it worked so well before, I launched myself forward with a run and a dive, landing on the warrior's shell and cinching my arm around his neck.

My move took both the warrior and the woman by surprise. She gasped, then dived to one side, out of my field of vision. I hoped she was going to put some distance between herself and the Mandasar's feet, because he started to buck and bounce like crazy; if the woman didn't get clear, she'd be trampled to paste.

"Keep back," I told her, half-whispering for fear of being heard by someone back at the canal . . . which was crazy because the warrior was shouting his head off. "Don't worry," I said to the woman, "it'll be okay."

I hoped that was true. This ride was ten times worse than

my scuffle with Zeeleepull; the warrior beneath me had worked himself into frothing battle frenzy, not to mention he thought I wanted to kidnap his family. His neck may have pinched as my arm rubbed up and down the shell plates on his throat, but it would take more than a little chafing to make him surrender.

As the warrior hopped and heaved, I did too: flopping about on his back, waiting for him to get tired enough to siow down. It took a long, long time; at least it felt long, though maybe it was only a minute. At last I could feel him weaken, to the point where he might actually be using his brain to think of new tactics . . . so I leaned forward again like I did with Zeeleepull, held the warrior's snout shut and pushed my palm to seal over his nose.

Speaking in Mandasar, I whispered, "I am Blood-Consort Edward York, last and rightful husband of Verity the Second, High Queen and Supreme Ruler of all those who tread the Blessed Land. If you fear her name, you will yield; if not, be named her enemy and pay the price of your folly."

They were the same words that came out of my mouth earlier in the day. This time, though, I was just reciting from memory—it wasn't like before, when I felt like something had possessed me. Still, if the speech worked once, it might work again . . . and with luck, the warrior would catch a faint whiff of queen's venom on my hand.

Slowly, the Mandasar stopped struggling. I couldn't tell if he was just tired, or if maybe my words and smell had cut through the battle rage. Whatever it was, he finally eased to a standstill. I kept my arm around his throat but let go of his nose so he could breathe. For a few seconds, both of us did nothing but suck in air.

Close by my side, a soft voice whispered, "Damn, it's good to see that black uniform. Thank God there's always an Explorer when you need one."

I turned my head . . . and nearly screamed. There in the shadows was the admiral woman who'd died kissing me— face splotch and all.

14

TAKING ON THE LARRY

The dead woman had come back, wrapped in thick midnight blackness—as if the only thing I could see was that smudge on her cheek. Terror jolted through me, and I hurled myself off the warrior onto the ground . . . anything to get away from some withered-up corpse who wanted to kiss me.

"What's wrong?" the woman whispered.

I couldn't answer—my whole body had clenched tight with fear. I might have just lain there, gibbering and quivering, if the warrior hadn't given his pincers an angry clack. He heaved himself up to full height, giving the woman a sneer before turning toward me. I was the one who'd hurt him. The look in his eye said he wanted to hurt me back.

"Hold on," the woman told the warrior. "Stop fighting and let's talk."

The warrior ignored her. "Bleed you, recruiter," he growled at me in English. "Suffer you, as our people have suffered."

One second I was sprawled on the ground, still trembling at the thought of ghosts; the next, I was on my feet, with my hands wrapped around the warrior's nose-spike. The move wasn't my doing—something had taken charge of my body again, making my legs leap forward without orders from my brain. My arms had gone all strong too, strong enough to drag the warrior's nose toward me the way I'd dragged Zeeleepull . . . except that I pulled him toward my chest instead of my face.

That was crazy. I'd never got venom on my chest. There was just my shirt, wet from my swim across the canal and sweaty from the hours of fever.

"You know who I am," my mouth said in Mandasar. "You know *what* I am. You know."

The warrior's eyes narrowed, as if he was about to ram his snout forward—stab his nose-spike through my ribs. Then his whole face changed, opening wide with wonderment. "*Teelu*," he whispered.

Your Majesty.

If I'd had control over my body, I would have blurted out, "No, no, no." You never use the word *Teelu* for anyone but a Mandasar queen—*Teelu* is way too worshipful to waste on a mere consort. But the poor kid was so ignorant about his own culture, he didn't know better.

The moment I let go of him, he dropped his body to the ground, pressing his nose into the dirt. "*Teelu . . . Teelu . . . Teelu . . .*"

Which was a whole lot better than trying to kill me. Maybe it wasn't the best time to correct his vocabulary.

"I'm impressed," the admiral woman said.

Fright chilled me again, and I retreated a step—I was back in command of my body, and feeling a strong urge to bolt into the dark. But I swallowed hard and made myself say something half-intelligible. "Who are you?"

"Lieutenant Admiral Festina Ramos," she said. The same name she'd used before we crossed the line. "What's your name?"

"Edward." Talking to an admiral, I should have been way more military: *Explorer Second Class Edward York, reporting for duty!* But my mouth was too dry with fear. "I saw you die," I said. "On the *Willow*."

The admiral shook her head. "I've never been on the *Willow*. And I've never died—I'd remember something like that." She stared at me a moment. "Was that your ship then? The *Willow*?"

I nodded.

"Why did you have to evacuate?"

"Someone was stealing it," I said. "I hated just to run, but Explorer Tobit told me—"

"Tobit?" the admiral interrupted "Phylar Tobit?"

"Yes."

"Which means *Jacaranda* is in this system?"

"It was for a while," I answered. "It might have gone chasing the black ship."

"Bloody hell," the admiral muttered, "I hate it when Prope's in the neighborhood. She takes her orders from Admiral Vincence; and Vincence is the slipperiest schemer on the whole High Council."

Even in the dark, I could see the admiral make a face like she'd bitten into an apple and found a worm. Or maybe just the back half of a worm.

"You'll have to tell me everything," she said, "like why Prope is chasing a black ship, and why you thought I was dead. But for now, let's just get out of here. Give me a second to grab my Bumbler . . ."

She started across the clearing toward a shadowy blob lying in the grass. Bumblers were small machines with all kinds of data sensors—standard equipment for Explorers, though no one ever gave me one. Halfway to the Bumbler, the admiral stopped. "I'd better turn off my emergency signal," she muttered. "It just tells Prope where to find me." She lifted her wrist and told the implant, "Terminate Mayday." Lowering her wrist, she added, "For all I know, it might have told recruiters where to find me too."

"You know about the recruiters?" I asked.

"That's why I'm on Celestia," she replied. "Trying to shut down the bastards. I was watching their main offices on the other side of the planet when I picked up your escape pod's homing signal. Considering how tedious stakeouts are, I decided it would be more interesting to make sure you were okay."

"Well," I said, feeling all awkward, "thanks for coming. I'm sorry to drag an admiral so far from her . . ."

"Don't apologize." She smiled, her teeth white in the dark. "And don't think of me as an admiral. I may wear the gray, but I'm an Explorer, first, last, and always. So you have to call me Festina, all right? I don't want to hear any more . . ."

She never finished her sentence. In the darkness, something started to laugh.

The sound was like a pack of hyenas, but breathier: piercing and whistly, echoing off the hillside. The noise seemed intentionally designed to carry long distances . . . and to scare the heebie-jeebies out of anyone who heard it. The crazy cackle never stopped for air, on and on, digging its fingernails into my nerves; and it was coming toward us.

"Holy shit," the admiral, Festina, whispered. "It's a Laughing Larry."

She looked across at me, seeing if I knew what she meant. I nodded. In my years as a bodyguard, I worked real hard to read up on every weapon in human space . . . not to use the weapons myself, but to know how to defend against them if Sam or Verity ever came under attack.

The best way to defend against a Laughing Larry was to surround yourself with steel-plast walls. Not very likely in the middle of a forest.

I was trying to think of other defenses when something spun into the far side of the clearing. It was a golden metal ball, a meter wide: hovering a little way off the ground and rotating fast like a kid's top. All around its outside, the thing had little slit openings that caught the air, making that whistle-ish laughing sound. Inside, I knew it had electric amplifiers to make the whistles louder—the person who invented this thing thought the cackly hyena laugh would be great for intimidation.

Absolutely right. I was shaking in my boots, hearing that sound chuckling in the darkness—and it didn't help that I knew how Laughing Larries worked. Each of those whistly slit openings could shoot a hundred razor-sharp fléchettes, tiny boomerang-shaped darts that could slice through skin like an ax through jelly. They could even pierce a Mandasar warrior's carapace, spiking through the shell and deep into the flesh beneath. If this Larry opened fire, it would spray out a full 360 degrees of shrapnel, cutting us open like a hail of knives.

The golden ball whirled to the Bumbler where the little machine still lay in the grass. More hyena laughing. The Larry circled the Bumbler like a cat that's found a dying mouse and wants to poke at it a bit. Or maybe it was more like a dog: a bloodhound that's been following a trail and has sniffed out something that smells like prey.

Around and around the Larry hummed, prowling near the Bumbler as if trying to pick up someone's scent.

"What is it?" a voice whispered. The warrior had lifted his head off the dirt and was staring at the spinning ball. His ear antennas had flattened straight back against his skull; he didn't like the hyena cackle either.

"It's a weapon," I answered softly. "It shoots sharp things that can hurt even you."

"Run, *Teelu*," he said immediately. "Hold it I, whilst you escape."

"Stay still!" Festina snapped. "Maybe it's looking for someone else."

At that moment, the thin whistly sound coming from the ball shaped itself into a single word.

"Ramoss . . . osss . . . osss . . . osss."

"Okay," Admiral Ramos muttered, "maybe it's *not* looking for someone else."

"Ramoss . . . osss . . . osss . . . osss . . ."

The whispery sound whistled through the clearing as the ball continued to spin. Fifty revolutions a second . . . I remembered that was their top speed. Then again, that was twenty years ago; they were probably better now.

I held my breath for almost a minute . . . and still the

Larry didn't attack. "Maybe it's just trying to scare you," I whispered to the admiral.

"Or maybe it isn't sure who I am," she whispered back. "I'll bet it was tracking my Mayday. Now that I've shut down the signal, it can't identify me."

"I thought Laughing Larrys had visual sensors too."

"They do," the admiral replied, "but Larries aren't smart, and it's hard to recognize people in the dark. In the normal visual range we're just black blobs; on IR, we're still blobs, only brighter. So it's straining its tiny computer brain, trying to figure out who we are. It doesn't want to waste a thousand rounds of ammunition killing us if we aren't its programmed target."

"Ramosss . . . osss . . . osss . . ."

The ghostly voice was getting on my nerves. "Why is it after you?" I whispered. There was no harm talking—when a Larry's making noise, it can't hear anything else.

"It must have been sent by the recruiters," Festina said. The warrior's ears perked up and he turned, as if seeing her for the first time. "They know I'm investigating them," Festina continued, "and I've already had threats to stay out of their business. One of them must have followed me here . . . and decided this was the perfect time to take me out of the picture. All alone on Mandasar territory. If people find my body sliced to ribbons, they'll blame it on local warriors, not the recruiters."

"Villains they," the warrior growled. "Black black villains . . ."

The smell of burning wood poured off his hide.

"Stay still," Festina warned. "It looks like Friend Larry is stuck in a decision loop. Let confused dogs lie."

"But if it's confused," I said, "won't it radio its controller for further instructions?"

Suddenly, the laughter increased to deafening volume and the Larry whizzed toward us.

All three of us jumped. Festina and I leapt toward the woods, hoping we could get behind a good solid tree trunk before the Larry opened fire. The only reason we succeeded was because the warrior jumped the other direction— straight on top of the golden ball, like throwing himself on a grenade.

The next two seconds weren't pretty. It took that long for the barrage of fléchettes to flense the carapace off him and slash his insides to pulp. The Larry's laughter was overridden with a scream, then a gooey slurp of organs getting splattered in every direction. When I looked back, I couldn't see the gold ball at all; just the warrior's shell lying over the ball like a lid, and underneath, the whirling butcher-thing was still as loud as hyenas, spinning inside the warrior's husk. The Larry had completely cored its way into the warrior's belly . . . and soon enough, the occasional fléchette was able to pierce out the warrior's side, blowing away little chips of armor. I ducked my head behind my tree trunk just as the Larry giggled into view again, carving out through the last bits of shell like a buzz saw.

My heart was pounding as I listened to the Larry laughing just a few paces away. If it wanted to come after us, there was nothing to stop it from chopping the admiral and me to gobbets; Larries could fly upward of eighty kilometers an hour, way faster than a human could run. I decided if it started toward us, I'd hit my Mayday implant and take to my heels, hoping the signal would draw the Larry after me. It might give the admiral a chance to get away.

But when I looked over at Festina, propped up behind another tree, she had her fingers resting lightly on her own wrist implant. Planning exactly the same thing, to sacrifice herself for *me*.

I didn't want to think what my dad would say if I let an admiral die in my place. When I was little, Dad called me "Jetsam," saying I'd be the first thing he threw out if he ever had to lighten his ship. It made me mad, how something like that flashed through my mind at a time like this. But I really had no choice—given the trade-off between

Admiral Ramos and me, I had to trigger my Mayday first. So I did.

A high-pitched squeal filled the air: my Mayday sounding on the admiral's implant. Except that my implant was squealing too—Festina must have set off her own Mayday at the same instant.

Both of us playing the self-sacrifice sweepstakes. It would have made me smile . . . if I wasn't sure I was going to be sliced to ribbons.

But the Larry wasn't moving. Maydays or not, it remained out in the clearing, spinning in place on top of the warrior's puréed carcass. Why wasn't it coming after our signals? Had it used all its ammunition digging out through the poor warrior's body? Or was it confused because it had two separate Maydays, and didn't know whether to come after Festina or me?

I held my breath and started to count the seconds. As I reached twenty-three, the Larry suddenly lifted into the air and swooshed away above the trees, heading back toward the canal. A trick to draw us out? I counted another thirty as the hyena laughter receded . . . and then only let myself move because the admiral called, "Edward, are you all right?"

"Sure."

We both turned off our Maydays and eased out of our hiding places—where we'd cowered while a brave warrior gave his life for people he didn't know. Looking at the blood-spattered grass, I told myself the poor kid might have died happy, knowing it was a warrior's most honorable death: killed in righteous battle, protecting others. In the last millisecond before he was shredded, he might have felt . . . what, fulfilled? Validated? Triumphant?

But he was still dead. And I'd never even learned his name.

Admiral Ramos walked stiffly into the clearing. She paused over the remains of her Bumbler . . . but the little machine looked like it had been whacked a thousand times with a meat cleaver. Another casualty of the fléchette barrage. Festina nudged the mechanical remains with her toe, then ground the debris angrily under her heel.

Fragments of circuit boards went crunch. I didn't like listening to the sound, so I asked, "Why did the Larry leave?"

The admiral shook her head in the darkness. "Who knows?" Slowly, she walked over scattered scraps of the warrior's body and knelt beside the largest piece of carcass. "Thanks," she said, laying her hand lightly on the boy's blood-drenched shell. "Thanks, whoever you were." Then in a soft gentle voice: "That's what 'expendable' means."

It was a thing Explorers said to each other when somebody died—like a little prayer. I'd never heard an admiral use it before. Most of the admirals I'd met were the sort to say, "Good riddance."

Festina stood up again. "I'd better follow the Larry," she said. "See where it's going. With luck, the bad guys will come to fetch it, and I can see who they are."

"Then let's go," I told her.

She gave me a look. "This isn't really your business, Edward . . ." She stopped. "You wouldn't be Edward *York*, would you? The Explorer who married the Mandasar high queen?"

"Um. Yes. That's me." I didn't think the outside world had heard about that, but admirals must be pretty well informed.

Festina let her breath come out in a whoosh. "Sometime real soon, you'll have to tell me how you're mixed up in this . . . but for now, tag along with me. If I leave you alone, the wrong people might find you."

I wondered who she thought were the wrong people. Recruiters? Captain Prope? Battle-mad Mandasars? But I didn't ask, and the admiral didn't explain. She just waved for me to follow as she headed into the trees.

* * *

The Larry was no longer in sight, but the laughter still rattled through the forest, occasionally hitting a note that made the trees buzz with resonance. We plunged after the cackling as fast as we could, thrashing through the undergrowth on a general downhill slant, back toward the canal.

Soon we reached an area where the brush was trampled flat. A lot of warriors had stormed past this way—maybe the whole militia. They must have heard the Larry too; they'd swum across the water, then started to search the woods, trying to figure out what was making the howl.

I winced—the warriors' trail led in the same direction as the Larry's laughter. Were they following it, or was it following them?

With the undergrowth all squashed, Festina and I could move through the woods more quickly, angling downhill toward the Larry's cackle. Laughter wasn't the only thing on the night breeze; I could smell the crusty burning-wood whiff of Musk B as thick as the smoke from a forest fire. It was the odor of disaster waiting to happen—a whole pack of warriors aching to crush recruiter bones, and a single Laughing Larry that could hover high overhead, spraying down death.

Half a minute later, we were closing in on the hyena chatter ... and also on the choking musk. Up ahead, a bright light suddenly beamed from the sky, reflecting crimson off the shells of two dozen warriors gathered in a marshy clearing. The warriors had drawn into a wide ring, circling the edge of the open area. In the middle stood a human man, and straight over his head the Laughing Larry hovered in the air like a gold-glinting sun. The light came from higher in the night sky where a skimmer floated, searchlights in its belly and a rope ladder dangling down to ground level.

Festina put her hand on my arm and held me back out of the light. No one in the clearing noticed us; the man in the center had his gaze glued on the warriors, and they were too busy eyeing the Larry. One of the Mandasars must have recognized the gold ball as a weapon and told the others to keep back.

"It's a standoff," Festina whispered. "That man's right in the Larry's eye. You know about that?"

I nodded. Straight under a Larry's spin-axis, there's a spot that isn't covered by any firing slits. Stand there, and it's like the eye of a hurricane—things get destroyed all around you, but you're safe. Larries are intentionally built that way; I'd once seen an underground advertisement showing a smug business exec walking down the street with a Larry over his head, while thugs fled out of his path. THE ULTIMATE IN PROTECTION, the ad said. SLAUGHTER EVERYTHING AROUND YOU FOR A 50-METER RADIUS, THEN WAIT FOR THE BLOOD TO STOP DRIPPING.

Just one problem for the man in the middle: to escape with his skin intact, he had to climb the ladder up to the skimmer. The easiest way to do that was clambering past the Larry; but that meant leaving the safety of the eye. For a few seconds, he'd be smack in the Larry's kill zone . . . and during those moments when he couldn't let the Larry fire, the Mandasars would race forward and shake him off the ladder. He'd be dead by the time he hit the ground— not from the fall, but from dozens of claws lopping him into giblets.

I could see one other way for the man to try his escape: ordering the Larry to rise with him as he climbed, always keeping a meter or so above his head. Staying safe in the weapon's eye, he wouldn't have to worry about it shooting him . . . but there was still the problem of the Larry shooting the *ladder*. It was a skimmer's standard emergency rope ladder; if the warriors charged forward and the man told the Larry to let loose, a razor storm of fléchettes would slice clean through the rope. Once again, he'd fall straight into the warriors' waiting claws.

As Festina said, it was a standoff: the militia holding back from the Larry's death radius, the man unable to move from his only place of safety.

I squinted to see the man more clearly. With the search-beams coming from straight over his head, I couldn't make out his face; but he was tall and thin, with a great ball of wispy-fine hair that caught the light like a halo. He wore no shirt, just a leather vest . . . and as my eyes adjusted to the brightness, I saw that the front of his body was transparent, like he'd had his skin peeled off and replaced with glass. You could see his ribs, stark and white, covering a shadowy lot of internal organs. I was too far away to make out his heart beating, but it was easy to watch his lungs expand and deflate with every breath.

He was breathing fast, like he was nervous. I'd be nervous too if I could look down and see my stomach churn.

Maybe if you came across a sight like this man at a museum, it would be an interesting way to learn about anatomy. Here in the dark night forest, it made my skin crawl. Whether Mr. Clear Chest was a recruiter or just someone wandering through the woods with illegal weapons, the guy was clearly a mean piece of work. He'd let the Larry kill that poor warrior . . . and he would have slaughtered Festina and me, except that he must have heard the militia thundering their way through the forest. That's when he called the Larry off hunting us and brought it back to protect his own transparent hide. The little gold ball must have got to him just in time to keep the warriors at bay.

But it wouldn't hold them off forever—not with so much Musk B rippling through the night. I could hear a dozen pincers clacking fiercely, blood-eager to rip into an enemy. Pretty soon, the kids would be so riled they wouldn't care about getting shredded by razor fléchettes. Someone would do something stupid, and then they'd all rush in: charging into the slashing flurry, as if the Larry couldn't kill them all.

Maybe it couldn't. Maybe a few ragged survivors would make it to Mr. Clear Chest and tear him apart. That had to be why he hadn't used the Larry already; he couldn't be sure it would kill every warrior there. But it would spill a lot of blood . . . and I knew that at any second, the warriors just wouldn't be able to hold themselves back any longer.

"What should we do?" I whispered to Festina.

"I don't know," she answered. "If you're a blood-consort, can you order the Mandasars to pull back? Tell them to let the guy go and fight another day?"

With so much musk in the air, I didn't know whether *anything* could make the warriors retreat . . . certainly not some stinky-hume stranger they'd never seen before. But if this was the only chance to avoid a ton of carnage, I had to give it a try.

Swallowing my fear, I stepped out from the cover of the forest. "Hello," I called in a loud voice. Better to speak English than Troyenese—the warriors should understand, and so would Mr. Clear Chest. I didn't want him panicking and ordering the Larry to fire . . . which he might, if he thought I was talking in Mandasar and giving the warriors a battle strategy.

"You don't know me," I said as I walked toward the circle, "but you might know my name. I'm . . ." *Edward York*, I thought. But the words that came out of my mouth were, "*Teeshpodin Ridd ha Wahlisteen*." The Little Father Without Blame. Queen Verity had given me that title a long time ago; I hadn't thought about it in years. But in the split second before I spoke the phrase, I'd lost control of my tongue again: back to being a helpless spectator while an unknown something walked around in my skin.

If you want the honest truth, getting possessed was a relief—I didn't have a clue what I would have said next. Whichever spook or spirit kept slipping into my shoes, it was sure better at bossing around Mandasars than I was.

"Gentlemen," my mouth said, sounding all of a sudden more confident, breezy, and in control. "Pleasant though it would be to dance on a recruiter's entrails, the price would be too high. At least for tonight. Don't you agree?"

I glanced around the circle of warriors. The way they glared at me wasn't much friendlier than their fury at Mr. Clear Chest; but they'd been too surprised to rip me apart in the first second, and now the spirit possessing me had momentum on his side.

Calmly, I stepped into the circle of the skimmer's spot-lights. The warriors looked back and forth between me and Mr. Clear Chest, their pincers whisking angrily. The threat didn't faze the spirit possessing me; I kept walking forward, right up the tail of the nearest warrior until I was standing high on his back. The sheer nerve of doing that froze him in place—otherwise, he would have bucked me straight to the moon.

"There'll be other nights and other recruiters," I told the Mandasars . . . but I kept my eye on the glass-chest man and his Larry. "If you all die now, who'll protect your hives? No matter how much you want to spill this re-cruiter's blood—and no matter how much he deserves it—as of this moment, you gentlemen are at war. War to save your homes, your hives, and your personal honor as war-riors, keeping your heads clear to defend what is truly pre-cious rather than becoming some recruiter's brainwashed thugs."

The Mandasars growled at that. I took that as a good sign. "And when you're at war," I said, "you don't fight stupid battles. You pick your time and you pick your place, because you're fighting for something that must not be lost. You act like true warriors serving an honorable cause, not fools who get into pointless brawls because you can't con-trol your tempers."

Off to my right, one of the Mandasars growled, "Fools? Fools we? Fools?"

Uh-oh, I thought. The spirit possessing me had gone too far. I could sense it in the face of every warrior there: fiery indignation at what had come out of my mouth. Musk surged up from the warrior beneath me, so thick I swear I could see it—a thin pheromone mist oozing out of his pores. It scared the willies out of me, but obviously not the spirit in command of my body. I could feel my head shak-ing sadly, as if I pitied the huge hulking warriors around me . . .

. . . then I ripped off my shirt and threw it in the face of the kid who didn't want to be called a fool.

It surprised me as much as anyone else. Out of the corner of my eye, I saw Mr. Clear Chest tense up, but he didn't tell the Larry to shoot; by now, he realized I was his best chance for getting out alive. His gaze flicked from me to the warrior with the shirt over his face. The youngster was snorting angrily, pawing at the fabric with his weak upper arms ... but by the time he'd pulled his snout clear, he wasn't snorting so much as sniffing.

Sniffing at my sweaty shirt.

I jumped lightly forward, straight in front of more warriors—within easy reach of their claws. Calmly, cockily, the spirit moving my legs made me walk bare-chested around the circle of Mandasars, passing before each one in turn. They were all sniffing me now, jutting out their snouts, almost touching me with their nose spikes. None of them tried to get a whiff of my face, where there might still be queen's venom; they were snuffling at my body, as if it had some amazing perfume they'd never smelled before.

I couldn't smell it myself. Just the burning-wood odor everywhere, covering the natural stink of the stagnant canal, the trees all around, even my own sweat.

Like taking a walk in the park, I went around the whole circle. Zeeleepull was part of the crowd, on the far side of the clearing where I hadn't recognized him before. Even he seemed surprised by whatever he smelled on me; I couldn't understand that, considering that he'd got a snootful of queen's venom when it was several hours fresher. But the spirit possessing me didn't think anything was unusual—I walked past Zeeleepull no faster or slower than any of the others, till I'd finished a complete circuit of the assembled militia.

"Now," I said to them all. "Back up and let this shit of a recruiter go. He's not worth any of our lives. This is the first action in a war ... and it's our enemy who's running with his tail in the air."

I looked at Mr. Clear Chest. With the light coming from straight over his head, I still had trouble making out his features . . . but I could tell he was glaring at me in hate. His heart jerked fast beneath his plastic skin; his lungs heaved tight against his ribs.

Let him huff and puff, I thought. *As long as he realizes there's only one way to get out alive.*

"Back up," I said again to the warriors. "Let the bastard leave."

Eyes glittering fiercely in the searchlights, every warrior slowly pulled back out of the clearing. I retreated with them, feeling shaky relief once I'd been swallowed by the shadows of the forest.

We all watched the recruiter grab hold of the rope ladder and climb quickly to the waiting skimmer. The Larry held its position, hovering three meters above the clearing till the man was safely inside the vehicle. That was the moment that scared me most—when the recruiter might send the Larry swooshing at us for a strafing run, just as a parting shot.

But it didn't happen. The Larry spun its way laughing up to the skimmer, and disappeared inside.

For another moment, the clear-chested man stood in the skimmer's dark hatchway: a shadowy figure peering out from the blackness. In that instant I saw a pinpoint of crimson burning in his belly, like the tip of a ruby laser shining deep within his guts. I blinked, not believing my eyes . . . and when I looked again, the light was gone.

With a soft hiss of engines the skimmer zipped away, speeding off into the night.

All quiet in the forest—no sound but the night breeze rustling through the branches, starting to thin out the fumes of musk in the air. Then softly, in a whisper, one of the warriors murmured, *"Teelu."*

"Um," I said. Suddenly I was unpossessed again. Wondering how to tell a bunch of Mandasar kids they had the wrong idea what *Teelu* meant.

"Teelu," whispered someone else.

"Teelu." From the opposite side of the clearing.

"*Teelu. Teelu. Teelu.*"

They were all chanting now, the whole militia, prostrate on the ground. "*Teelu. Teelu. Teelu.*"

Getting louder. Getting stronger. "*Teelu. Teelu. Teelu.*" Till they were roaring the word, fierce and proud, their voices ripping through the trees, echoing across the valley, rising to the hills.

"*Teelu! Teelu! Teelu!*"

Your Majesty. Your Majesty. Your Majesty.

Part 3

DONNING THE ERMINE

15

IDENTIFYING WIFTIM

The thing about chants is you need a signal when to stop. People want some leader to call out "Amen!" or a choir to start singing, or lights coming on, or curtains going down, or something. Otherwise, the chanters get to feeling awkward, and wondering when it would be polite to shut up, but not really comfortable just letting things dwindle and die off, because that takes away from the great uplifting solidarity.

After three minutes of *"Teelu, Teelu, Teelu,"* I could tell the warriors were trying to find a graceful way to give it up. They'd chanted enough; they wanted to move onto the next glorious thing, whatever it would be. I guess they expected me to wave my hands, call for quiet, then give some rousing speech that would channel their excitement into something useful. Trouble was, I didn't have a clue what to say . . . and it would be horrible having two dozen kids waiting for me to speak when my mind was a total blank. They wouldn't turn violent or anything; they'd just sit and stare, thinking, *Well, he may be a blood-consort, but he can't be very smart.*

Desperately I peered into the darkness, hoping to catch sight of Admiral Ramos. It would be great if I could thank the warriors for their nice adulation, then turn everything over to Festina. She was an admiral; she had to be good at public speaking, even if she didn't have a specific plan of

action. While Festina talked I could stand back listening,
all serene and placid ... the way Queen Verity always
posed on her silver dais as she let some cabinet minister
read the latest speech from the throne.

But Admiral Ramos was nowhere to be seen. Either
she'd left or was hiding, both of which were good ideas
considering what the warriors might do if they noticed an
unknown human lurking in the dark.

Without thinking, I lifted my hand to chew on my
knuckle ... and that's all it took to stop the chanting dead
silent. Shows you how eager the kids were to hear me pon-
tificate. "Um," I said. "Well. Hi." Then I remembered a
standard thing the protocol ministers had taught me to say
years and years ago: in Troyenese, "Greetings to you all
from the court of the high queen. You are valued; you are
worthy. Just as you give your hearts to her service, so the
queen gives her heart to you."

That brought on a big cheer ... even though these kids
had to realize the court of the high queen was twenty years
dead. Maybe they thought the war was over: that Troyen
had a new high queen who'd sent me to solve their problems. All of a sudden I got myself tongue-tied, worried I'd
just given them false hopes and terrified I'd keep putting
my foot in my mouth whatever I tried to say.

"Um. Don't get all ... I'm not ..."

There were so many things I wasn't, I didn't know how
to finish that sentence. I'm not what you think. I'm not
what you *need*. "Okay," I said, taking a deep breath,
"there's a lot of stuff you don't understand ..."

That's when the police skimmer buzzed in overhead and
a loudspeaker blared, "Nobody move!"

The best way to get a Mandasar moving is to tell him,
"Keep still." In a split second, the kids had scrambled to
their feet and were gearing up for an outraged display of
claws and shouts and stamping ... but I yelled, "At ease!
Parade rest!" and that got their attention. None of them had
a clue how to stand at parade rest, but they all stiffened

into postures that were unnatural enough to come across as military. I hissed to a few who looked outright hostile ("Close your claws!" "All feet on the ground!" "Why are you waving your hands over your head?") but it didn't take long to get them settled into poses that wouldn't scare the police too badly.

"You there!" blared the loudspeaker . . . and a searchlight stabbed down on me from the skimmer's belly. "Are you in charge?"

"Yes!" shouted the whole militia. Thanks a lot, guys.

"Are you Admiral Ramos?" the loudspeaker asked.

"No," I answered—thinking to myself these cops didn't know much about the navy. Admirals wear gray; my uniform was black. Then again, after I'd swum the canal and run through the forest and hit the dirt I don't know how many times, maybe it wasn't so easy to tell. "I'm Explorer Second Class Edward York," I told the police. "Admiral Ramos is around someplace, but I'm not sure where."

"Here," Festina said, stepping out of the forest. I must have stared in her direction three or four times but never spotted her. She must know some really good tricks for hiding.

"Are you all right, Admiral?" the police asked.

"I'm fine," she replied, "but there's been a murder. One of these warriors was killed in cold blood with a banned weapon."

There was a pause. I got the impression whoever was using the loudspeaker had turned off the microphone and was having a quick conference with other people in the skimmer. Finally, the speaker clicked on again, and a different voice, deep and male, said, "Are you sure it was murder?"

"I saw it myself," the admiral said, as I nodded too. All the warriors looked around the clearing, their expressions going grim. They must have been trying to figure out which one of them wasn't there.

The policeman gave a heavy sigh, loud enough to carry over the loudspeaker. "All right," he said, "I want the Mandasars to return to their homes while Admiral Ramos and Explorer York stay to give us details. We'll get statements from the rest of you later on, but for now, just disperse." Pause. "Please."

The warriors didn't budge. They looked toward me, like they didn't care a snifter for the police unless I said it was okay. "You can go," I said, "we'll be fine."

But the warriors still seemed reluctant to head out . . . as if they didn't trust the cops, or maybe they just wanted to hang around to see what happened next. Before anyone else could move, Zeeleepull stepped forward from the pack. He bulled his way up to me, then lowered himself till his head touched my foot. "Leave cannot I, Edward York," he said. "Sworn to protect, sworn to guard, sworn to defend."

"All right," I told him . . . and because every other warrior was a split second away from rushing forward to vow loyalty too, I held up my hands and waved the crowd back. "One bodyguard is all I need. It doesn't look right for a consort to hide in the middle of an army."

Samantha had come up with that line for me, long ago when Verity wanted to assign a whole platoon of guards to keep me safe. The excuse had worked back then, and it worked now; warriors go all bashfully guylike when you suggest they're undermining your honor.

Slowly, reluctantly, the militia slunk off into the woods till only three of us were left: Festina, Zeeleepull and I. We drew back to the edge of the clearing so the police had plenty of room to land. Despite that, their skimmer took its time . . . scanning its searchlights around the area, checking there weren't big rocks on the landing site, and waiting till the warriors were really gone.

When the skimmer finally touched down, a gaggle of armored folks jumped out—most with truncheons but a few carrying rifles or pistols, and even a shotgun. You never saw police brandishing firearms on a Technocracy world . . . not unless they knew they were dealing with dangerous non-sentient criminals who had lethal weapons of their own. Then again, maybe this response team had heard about the Laughing Larry, in which case bringing out the big guns made perfect sense.

In the middle of the armored people, one hawk-nosed man stood out. He wore the same gear as the others, but on him it looked slapdash: his helmet was shifted way back on his head, with the visor dangling open; his bulletproof jacket was unfastened at the side seam; his boots weren't strapped tight, so they slopped around his ankles as he walked. I couldn't see any insignia on his uniform, but the man had CAPTAIN written all over him. No one else could look so disheveled and get away with it.

The man sloshed forward toward us and nodded a millimeter to Festina. "Admiral Ramos." His eyes flicked over that blotch on her face; the bright police lights heightened the angry purple against the brown of the rest of her skin.

I tried not to stare at the birthmark myself.

"Greetings," Festina told the policeman, bowing the same tiny millimeter. "You are?"

"Captain Adam Tekkahawnee, Greater Bradford Regionals. Where's the murder victim?"

"Follow me," the admiral told him.

She started back the way we'd come, and the whole company tagged along. Tekkahawnee matched our pace while the other cops tried to set up a moving perimeter around us. Since they didn't know which way we'd go from one second to the next, there was a fair bit of jockeying every time Festina shifted a different direction: suddenly, the folks who were trying to stay in front of us had to jog sideways, trying not to trip on undergrowth or smack into trees. Once or twice it seemed the admiral turned deliberately away from the murder scene, just to give the cops more of a run ... but she was probably taking shortcuts around bogs or something.

As we walked, Festina spoke to Tekkahawnee in a low voice. "So, Captain—not that I'm sorry you showed up, but who called you?"

"Who *didn't* call us?" Tekkahawnee growled. He looked

like the sort of man who growled a lot: still young, maybe
in his forties, but already his face had set into permanent
frown lines. "Every damned Mandasar from here to Orore
rang up our station, screaming about recruiters . . . but we
get calls like that five times a month, and they're all false
alarms. A stray dog wanders into the fields, a skimmer flies
too low, or the wind makes a funny noise, and the stupid
lobsters start wailing that someone wants to kidnap them."

Zeeleepull's whiskers twitched angrily. Before the boy
went all hotheaded on us, I told Tekkahawnee, "It wasn't
a false alarm tonight."

"Mmm." The captain didn't sound convinced. "Then,"
he said, "we got a call from someone else, a woman named
Kaisho. She claimed to be a retired Explorer, and said her
exalted friend, Admiral Festina Ramos, was broadcasting
an emergency Mayday from this area. Word is, this Kaisho
threatened our police chief your navy would blockade the
whole planet if we didn't give you every possible assistance."

Festina rolled her eyes. "Kaisho, Kaisho, Kaisho," she
muttered under her breath. To Tekkahawnee she said, "Kaisho is indeed an ex-Explorer now living on Celestia—
she's the one who tipped me off about the recruiter problem, and she's been helping me investigate . . . says it's the
most fun she's had since she retired. But I gave her strict
orders to stay on the other side of the planet; she's confined
to a hoverchair these days and completely unfit to go waltz-
ing into trouble." Festina made a face. "As if Kaisho ever
obeys my orders. She must have followed me here in her
own skimmer. If Kaisho heard my Mayday, she couldn't
run to my rescue herself; so she bullied the cops into doing
it."

Tekkahawnee glanced in the admiral's direction. "That
talk about blockades was exaggeration?"

"You can never tell with the Admiralty," Festina replied.
"Their idea of deterrence is being irrationally unpredictable.
When outsiders endanger an admiral, sometimes the High
Council just blows hot air. Other times they overreact spec-

tacularly, blockading star systems, seizing ships, imposing sanctions on everyone who twitches. As far as I can tell, it's deliberately random—if you annoy the navy, you never know if you'll get away with it or be clobbered by an extravagant show of force."

"But," Tekkahawnee said, "you're bottom of the barrel when it comes to admirals, right?" He wasn't taunting her; it sounded like he was stating a widely known fact. Even so, it shocked me how anyone could say such a thing to an admiral's face. No one would *ever* talk like that to my dad.

"Celestia may not be part of the Technocracy," Tekkahawnee went on, "but we hear rumors, Ramos. Word is, the High Council invented the rank of Lieutenant Admiral for you and you alone, as a sign you didn't have a chance in hell of making it to the inner circle."

"Absolutely right," Festina agreed, "but the High Council might still go bugfuck if someone managed to kill me. It would be good PR to make a lavish show of grief. *Poor Festina—she never saw eye to eye with us, but we still respected her.* I can just picture them professing how dearly they loved me. And inner circle or not, I *do* wear the sacred gray uniform. It's in the council's best interest to send a message to Celestia and every other two-bit parasite world clinging to the Technocracy's shirttails: 'Thou shalt not allow *any* admiral to come to harm.'"

Tekkahawnee grunted in reply. With only dim starlight, I couldn't see the captain's face clearly, but I could tell his mood was turning glowery. He had to be wondering if Festina was just trying to intimidate him or if there was really a chance the fleet would mount a serious crackdown.

Me, I was wondering the same thing. Back on Troyen, Samantha constantly used fudged-up threats as leverage. She would tell Queen Verity the navy demanded this or insisted on that, and nobody ever knew if Sam was actually relaying a message from the High Council or just spouting personal whims off the top of her head. A lot of times, she'd whisper afterward, "Of *course*, that wasn't official,

Edward; but it's fun to see how much you can get away
with."

That tells you something about my sister, doesn't it?

Zeeleepull got the growls long before we reached the murder site. From the way he snuffled—loudly, with a lot of
nose-wiping—I knew he could smell the dead warrior's
blood. I put my arm around his shoulder, and whispered,
"Can you tell who it is?"

He shook his head. "Guts too much the stink. Know I
my friends by skin scent, not by intestines."

Even when we got to the clearing, he couldn't identify
the other warrior by smell. He had to walk straight up to
the corpse and stare into the dead face, while one of the
policefolk held a flashlight. "Wiftim is," Zeeleepull said at
last. "Wiftim of Hive Seeliwon."

"Wiftim" meant "ever-prepared" and Seeliwon was a
pretty little lake district where Verity had kept a manor
house. That might have been why Wiftim's hive adopted
the name—because of its connection with the long-lost
high queen.

I wanted to explain that to the policewoman who recorded Zeeleepull's statement. Someone should have told
her the names meant something: not just empty facts about
some dead stranger. But I was afraid she'd just look at me,
the way they always do, blankly puzzled about what was
going on inside my head—what was wrong with me, that
I thought such things were important?

I should have told her anyway. I should have.

16

MEETING THE BALROG

The police got busy with murder-scene stuff: putting up big bright lights, taking VR snaps, all that. Captain Tekkahawnee edged us noncops off to the side, then started making calls on a portacomm. I don't know who all he talked to—he went to the far end of the clearing so we couldn't hear what he said—but sometimes he hunched over, almost shouting into the vidscreen, and sometimes he leaned way back with a very neutral expression on his face . . . like he was contacting lower-downs and higher-ups, telling all kinds of people about Wiftim's death.

"Fuss and nothing," Zeeleepull grumbled. "Care they not of recruiters before. Bet I, still nothing but show."

Admiral Ramos shook her head. "There's one big difference tonight, Zeeleepull. This time the recruiters killed someone."

The warrior's whiskers twitched. "Stealing Mandasars, killing as good as."

"No," Festina told him. "Kidnapping and brainwashing are ugly, but the damage is reversible—bring everyone back into mixed-caste hives and they'll return to more balanced personalities. Even if that weren't true, murder is still more serious than anything else the recruiters have done. Murder catches the attention of the League of Peoples."

"The League!" Zeeleepull's voice was full of bitterness. "Nothing, nothing, nothing they do."

Festina shook her head again. "They do one thing, and they do it flawlessly—they stop dangerous non-sentient lifeforms who try to travel from one star system to another. To the most advanced races of the League, humans and Mandasars are no more than bacteria; ignorable unless we start turning nasty, like a disease. Even then, the League doesn't bother to exterminate us . . . they just don't let us spread."

Zeeleepull looked like he was going to argue some more, but I put my finger to his snout and shushed him. I didn't want him raising a ruckus in front of the police; the cops already thought Mandasars were whiny troublemakers, and we didn't want to show them they were right.

"Trust me," Festina told Zeeleepull in a low voice, "the League doesn't give a damn if lesser species kidnap, brainwash, and enslave each other. The upper echelons of the League are too lofty, and too damned alien in their thought patterns, to care about such minor mischief. But murder is something different. Deliberately killing a sentient being automatically brands you as non-sentient . . . and if a government is negligent in controlling dangerous non-sentient creatures, the government gets declared non-sentient too."

She waved her hands toward the police, dutifully picking up bloody fléchettes from the dirt. "The Celestian authorities might have looked the other way when recruiters just took slaves, but no government can ignore intentional homicide. The League won't let them. If the police don't make a sincere effort to catch that glass-chest guy, all of Celestia may be declared non-sentient . . . which means no traffic in or out till the civil system is cleaned up. And I'm not talking about a pissy little blockade by the Outward Fleet, where ships are simply impounded; this will be the League flexing its muscles, killing whole crews till everyone gets the message."

I nodded. "The way they killed everyone on *Willow*."

"They did *what*?" Festina said, spinning to face me. "Something happened to *Willow*?"

She made me tell the story, all of it: the party and the

queen and the nanites and the black ship . . . even how the
woman in admiral costume died kissing me. Now that the
cops had lit up the clearing, I could see the real Admiral
Ramos didn't look much like the *Willow* woman; it was
only the dark that made me think I was seeing a ghost.
Still, I got plenty embarrassed talking about that kiss to the
admiral's face—as if I were one of those folks who use
VR to do dirty stuff with famous people. I kept stammering
and apologizing, saying the kiss hadn't been my idea but
the woman was so sad and desperate . . .

The admiral stopped me: lifted her hand and patted me
on the cheek. "It's all right, Edward—really it is. If I'd
been in your position, I probably would have kissed her
too." She smiled. "Besides, with a sweet handsome face
like yours, people must be dying to kiss you all the time."

Um. I decided that last bit was a joke.

Just as I was finishing my story, I heard a *whoosh* coming
up behind me. I spun around fast, thinking it might be the
Larry back for another run . . . and Festina spun tight in
unison with me, her fists up in guard position. Even Zeeleepull clicked his pincers to the ready, all three of us jumping like we'd heard a ghost.

Which made it embarrassing when the noise turned out
to be a lady in a wheelchair.

Of course, regular wheelchairs don't go *whoosh;* but this
one had a tiny skimmer engine under the seat, strong
enough to lift it to knee height off the ground so it could
fly over sticks and tangles. The chair traveled slowly, half
as fast as a baby's crawl, keeping straight and upright so
the passenger wouldn't get jostled . . . but as stately as a
bride inching down the aisle, the wheelchair-woman drifted
up the hillside toward us.

Because of the shadows under the trees, I couldn't see
the woman clearly . . . except for her legs. They glowed
dim red, like embers in a campfire: one leg shone all the
way to the hip, the other from her toes to the knee. The
glow had a fuzzy look to it; as she got closer I realized she

had luminescent moss slathered thick as carpet on her skin.

Was that the fashion now, wearing patches of scarlet mold from ankle to thigh? Or could it be some medical treatment? The woman *was* in a wheelchair; maybe the moss was a sort of medicine, a nanotech foam working to repair whatever damage kept her from walking.

You never know what crazy stuff doctors will come up with.

The woman floated into the spill from the floodlights, but I still couldn't see her face; it was hidden behind streamers of long straight hair, like maybe she was so ugly she didn't want to be looked at. The hair itself wasn't ugly at all—jet-black threaded through with silver, that gorgeously dignified effect you see with some folks as they start to turn gray. The woman's clothes were black mixed with silver too . . . skintight and seamless, as if someone had sprayed coal-pitch ink over her whole body from the throat down: over her hands and fingers, over her arms, her chest, her stomach, right to the very edge of the glowing red moss. Then, while all that ink was still wet, bits of silver glitter had been sprinkled everywhere so she'd glint in the starlight.

Probably her clothes weren't fabric at all . . . just a sweat sheen of nano paint, programmed to cling snugly to her body. (Also to lift what needed lifting, corset what needed corseting, and so on—my dad always wore tuck-and-tidy nano under his clothes to make himself look trim and muscular. This woman did the same, but without the clothes on top.)

"Gentlemen," Festina said softly to Zeeleepull and me, "this is Kaisho . . . who supposedly works for me as an informant, but is piss-poor at remembering who signs her paycheck." The admiral had lowered her fists, but her jaw was still clenched tight. "Are you out of your mind?" she asked the wheelchair-woman. "Didn't I give you a direct order to stay someplace safe?"

"Dear simple Festina," Kaisho answered in a whisper, "we don't do orders anymore. It's not in the Balrog nature.

We had a feeling you were heading for trouble . . ."

"You had a feeling, but you didn't tell me?"

"One must never speak of feelings until they come true. The Mother of Time will pull out your tongue."

Zeeleepull nudged me. "Mad crazy hume," he muttered, in a voice he probably thought was too soft for the woman to hear.

"Wrong on all counts, young warrior," Kaisho said. "Not mad, not crazy, not hume. Very much not hume." I could see a brief smile flash under the cover of her long long hair: the whiteness of teeth in the darkness, disappearing quickly. Then she shook her head so the hair fell in and hid even more of her face—both eyes concealed completely, nothing more than a thin open strip down the middle, showing her nose and a tiny peek of lips. She probably couldn't see much; I got the feeling she didn't have to.

"Kaisho has an unusual condition," Festina murmured to Zeeleepull and me. "Twenty-five years ago, when she was an Explorer, she, uhh, had the honor to be chosen as the host for an advanced lifeform."

"To be precise," the woman said in her whispery voice, "I stepped on something I shouldn't have. Simple red moss. Which immediately corroded through the soles of my boots and implanted itself in both feet." Her smile flashed again. "I have since christened it the Balrog—a creature of glowing flame that has locked me in its grapple. Which is to say, it's slowly eating me."

I gulped hard. "Can't doctors do anything?"

"No," Festina replied. "Detaching the Balrog would kill it. That's not allowed because . . . well, the moss is sentient. Several rungs up the evolutionary ladder from both humans and Mandasars. Grossly intelligent . . . marginally tele-pathic and telekinetic . . . possibly precognitive . . ."

"Oh no," Kaisho whispered, "we avoid peering directly under Mother Time's skirts. But compared to your species, we *are* more astute at guessing where things will lead."

I stared at her . . . which means I stared at the thick black hair covering her face. Was there moss on her face too:

thick clots of red, fuzzed all over her cheeks . . . her forehead . . . her eyes? Was that why she used her hair as a
veil? And was her voice stuck in that soft whisper because
she had moss on her vocal cords, a layer of glowing red
velvet coating all down her throat? I wanted to ask, but was
afraid the answer would turn my stomach. Instead, I said,
"How can this moss stuff be sentient if it's eating you?
Sentient beings don't hurt other people."

"Sentient beings don't *murder* other people," Kaisho corrected, "and the Balrog takes care not to threaten my life.
At its current rate of digestion, I will happily live my al-
lotted span . . . which alas is only another eighteen years,
twenty-three days, six hours, and forty-two minutes. I have
an untreatable liver condition. Or I will have by then. Or
you could say I've been sick since the moment of my conception, and it will just take a hundred and thirty years for
the disease to get down to business."

"You know that for sure?" I asked.

"The Balrog knows," Kaisho told me, "and therefore I
do too."

"Stupid hume," Zeeleepull muttered, "believing true a
parasite."

"*Other* people have parasites," Kaisho answered. "*I* have
a highly beneficial symbiont." She chuckled softly. "Or
rather, we have each other. We are now a human-Balrog
synthesis. Not completely integrated yet, but we're gradually coming to . . . a meeting of the minds."

"Eating you," Zeeleepull growled, "and corrupting your
brain."

"Say rather, *improving* my brain."

Zeeleepull gave a dismissive sniff. "Heard I the same tale
from recruiters: *Smarter you happy when we get done*."

Kaisho shrugged. "I recognize the parallels. If you'd
asked me, 'Would you like to have your mind and body
mutated by an alien organism for its own secret ends, while
it slowly consumes your flesh?'—well, tempting though the
offer sounds, I once might have said no. Now, it's what I
am. My identity, even if I never asked for it."

"Stupid identity then," Zeeleepull muttered.

"Are you any different?" Kaisho asked. "You think your brain is fine; but I've talked to warriors living in single-caste barracks, and they're convinced *you're* the one who's been brainwashed. They *like* having hair-trigger tempers; they appreciate the simplicity of always following orders, without suffering pangs of conscience; and they claim you've been brainwashed by an unnatural human-biased upbringing that's kept you a self-centered little boy instead of an honest-to-God warrior. You, naturally, disagree. Your current identity is precious to you, and you'll fight any son-of-a-bitch recruiters who try to make you change.

"And what about you, dear Festina?" Kaisho said, turning to the admiral. "You've made no secret how much you despise the Admiralty: how they prevented you from leading a normal life and forced you into the Explorer Corps. You were methodically indoctrinated by behavior-mod programming into the permanent paranoia required for xeno-exploration . . . yet knowing all this, you're still profoundly proud to be an Explorer. Isn't that odd? When you were a girl, I'm sure you were furious at the people who were taking away your choices—I know I was—but now that you *are* an Explorer, it's the very heart of your identity. You never wanted to be this, and now you can't imagine being anything else. Just like me."

Festina turned slightly so her face was out of the light. Even Zeeleepull was sensitive enough not to stare at Festina while she . . . I don't know, I wasn't looking either, whether she was crying or angry or wistful or what. The silence got strained real fast, and Zeeleepull leapt in to break it. "*Teelu* then?" he growled, glaring at Kaisho. "Is just fine, *Teelu*. No brainwash him, no question his mind."

Kaisho turned to me. "What about it, *Teelu*?" she asked in a teasing whisper. "No one ever tampered with your head? You got to choose what you are, without anyone forcing an identity down your throat?"

Her hair hid her face, but I could imagine her eyes glittering—as if she'd just told a joke that only the two of us got, and only *she* found funny. Did she know I was a gene-engineering mistake with mixed-up chemicals in my brain? Could she read my mind and see my past? Or maybe, was the precognitive part of her seeing my future?

Kaisho's lips opened, and for a second I got the feeling she was going to answer the questions I hadn't spoken. The dull red glow on her legs flared brighter, like a warning, and she closed her mouth again.

"What?" I asked.

Kaisho shook her head. "Mother Time says it isn't my secret to tell."

No matter how much I asked her to say more, her mouth stayed shut in a mysterious little smile.

17

INVESTIGATING THE BANDOLIER

Kaisho soon got tired of being badgered for answers. She pointedly turned her chair away from me and glided over to the admiral. "Festina dear," Kaisho said in her whisper, "if you're finished your little cry . . ."

Festina lifted her head immediately, and it sure didn't look like she'd been crying. "What do you want?" she said, all tightly controlled.

"Just to tell you I noticed something back in the woods. Or perhaps the Balrog noticed it—it's hard to tell where I stop and the Balrog begins. I'm not sure I remember what it's like to see with ordinary eyes."

Zeeleepull squinched up his whiskers the way Mandasars do when something turns their stomachs. He was clearly squeamish about the Balrog-brainmeld thing . . . and I think Kaisho got a kick out of making him squirm.

Festina didn't have an ounce of squirm in her. With a no-nonsense voice, she asked Kaisho, "What did you see?"

Kaisho gave a meaningful glance toward the police, still puttering nearby. "Maybe I'd just better show you."

After a moment, Festina nodded. "All right. Lead on."

The police paid no attention as we headed off through the trees. Maybe they were happy to get rid of us: easier for

143

them to get their work done without noncop observers.

Kaisho took the lead, her chair moving slow as molasses. I found myself looking down at her glowing legs, all limp and useless under that moss. Were they moss clear through? Was that how the Balrog ate her, replacing human muscle and bone with its own fuzzy self? Or was the moss just a coating and there was still a woman underneath, maybe all paralyzed and sucked dry of nutrients, but recognizable as flesh and blood no matter how withered? I imagined putting my fingertips against her glowing thigh and pushing down, my nails squishing through the damp fuzz, deeper and deeper till they touched raw bone . . . or maybe going all the way through to the leather seat of the chair without touching anything solid . . .

A hand patted my own thigh, right where I'd imagined touching Kaisho. I nearly jumped out of my skin. When I looked up, Kaisho was obviously staring at me from behind her veil of hair. "Don't be embarrassed," she whispered. "I don't mind people looking at my legs. I know they're magnificent."

"Oh," I said. "Um."

"And," she went on, "many people have an irresistible urge to touch."

"Does the stuff rub off on them?"

She shook her head. "I stepped on the Balrog when it was in a dispersal phase—actively looking for a new host. Now, it's happily bonded to me and reproductively dormant. Entirely. Almost. It would only spread to someone else if the chance was too promising to pass up: a host so superior, the Balrog had to seize the opportunity, for the greater good of the universe." Her smile flashed under the cover of her hair. "Do you consider yourself that superior, *Teelu*?"

"No," I said. But I kept well clear of the moss. Kaisho was kind of daring me to touch her . . . and Samantha trained me when we were kids, never ever ever take a dare.

*   *   *

Kaisho's wheelchair stopped beside a clump of scrawny trees. The trees didn't look much different from any others we'd passed—almost like Earth trees, except for the blackish leaves and a light puffiness to their trunks, as if their bark was wooden foam—but Kaisho cut her chair's skimmer engine so the chair settled down on its big solid wheels.

Apart from the starlight and those three confetti moons, we only had the glow of Kaisho's legs to see by. Still, it was easy to tell the soil had been trampled half to mire by the Mandasar militia; they'd come through here chasing Mr. Clear Chest.

"There," Kaisho said, pointing to the ground between four close-growing trees. Festina and I leaned our heads in; Zeeleepull tried to look too, but the trees were rooted too near each other for him to get his wide shoulders into the gap. I guess that's why the dirt here didn't get mucked up as the warriors stampeded past—they had to go around the trees instead of between.

Imprinted in the soft mud was a sharp-edged circular outline . . . like a big heavy can had been set down long enough for it to settle its weight into the soil. As far as I could tell, there was nothing else to see; but Festina made a soft, "Hah!" sound and grabbed a little thread caught on one of the tree trunks.

"What is it?" I asked.

"Black fiber," the admiral answered. "Probably off that recruiter's pants. They were black, right?"

I couldn't remember. I'd been so busy gawking at his exposed heaving lungs, I hadn't noticed much else. "You think he was doing something here?" I asked.

"He tucked himself between these trees for a while," Kaisho said. "A good place to hide—his shadow would blend in with the tree trunks." She turned to Festina. "Do you recognize that outline on the ground?"

The admiral nodded. "It's exactly the size of a Bumbler."

"Bumbler?" Zeeleepull asked. "Bumbler what is?"

"Equipment from the navy's Explorer Corps," I told him. Too bad Festina's Bumbler had been destroyed, or I could have showed him. "It's like a medium-sized cooking pot," I said, "only the lid is a vidscreen. It's got cameras and sensors and things, so it can show you an IR scan of the area, or work like a telescope or microscope . . ."

"Not to mention reading and recording the entire EM spectrum from gamma waves to radio," Kaisho put in.

"So the recruiter . . . Explorer is? Navy hume Explorer?" His voice was going huffy with outrage.

"Of course not," Festina answered, just as huffy. "I've read the files on every Explorer in the fleet, and not one has a see-through thorax. That recruiter might have carried Explorer equipment, but he doesn't belong to the corps." She turned to Kaisho. "Do you think it really was a Bumbler? All we've got is a circle in the mud . . ."

"The Balrog assures me it was a genuine Bumbler," Kaisho replied. "It left a characteristic metallic taste on the dirt. As distinctive as a fingerprint."

I stared at her a moment, trying to think how the Balrog could *taste* the soil. Had Kaisho touched her mossy legs against the ground? Or could Balrogs taste things from long distance, the way you can sometimes taste campfire smoke, or the vinegar in strong pickles before you actually lift them to your mouth?

"My guess," Kaisho said, "is the recruiter set down his Bumbler while he was busy with something else. Probably he had some gadget for monitoring the Laughing Larry as it homed in on our dear Festina. He stayed till he heard the Mandasar militia coming toward him . . ." She looked at Zeeleepull. "Following his scent, correct?"

"Smelled him we," Zeeleepull agreed proudly. "First the loud laugh-laugh that drew us across the water. Then the stink of hume on the ground. Chased him we. Harried him we."

Kaisho nodded. "The recruiter snatched up his Bumbler and ran, with the warriors on his heels. He headed for that other clearing, where his skimmer waited to pick him up."

Festina frowned. "I saw him on the rope ladder," she said. "No Bumbler then. Which means," she went on, suddenly eager, "he must have lost it as he ran from the warriors. Either he dumped it deliberately so he could sprint faster, or he got the carrying strap snagged on something and he didn't have time to work it free." She gave a wry smile. "When I think how often I've caught my own Bumbler on bushes . . . well, finally, some poetic justice."

"You really were an Explorer?" I asked. "With a Bumbler and everything?" The first time Festina had mentioned being an Explorer, the Larry showed up before I could ask any questions. Now . . . I still found it hard to believe an Explorer could ever make admiral. When I was young, the Explorer Corps was stuck off to one side, out of the chain of promotion for the regular navy. Explorers couldn't become ship captains or admirals or anything. That was one reason Dad made me wear the black uniform—to be sure I'd never get put in charge of anything. (Or maybe just because the High Council had no Admiral of the Black to tell Dad I wasn't wanted.)

The navy must have changed a lot in the twenty years I'd been out of touch. An admiral who'd been an Explorer—pretty amazing. But when I studied Festina's face for a moment, that big purple blotch sure made her *look* like an Explorer.

"Yes, Edward," Festina said, "once upon a time, I was a full-fledged ECM." (ECM means Expendable Crew Member . . . what Explorers call themselves.) "But I'll tell you my life story later," she went on. "Right now, we have more pressing business. If we find that recruiter's Bumbler, its memory may contain useful evidence."

She struck off forward, tracing the recruiter's path as he'd run from the militia. Soon she called for Kaisho to take the lead; a Balrog's spooky senses were better than human eyes following a track in the dark. That didn't sit well with Zeeleepull—he couldn't stand waiting for the wheelchair's snail-slow progress, so he put his nose to the ground, caught the scent, and barged his way forward as fast as he could sniff. You'd think the trail would be hard for him to make out, considering how a horde of warriors had trampled over the original scent . . . but Zeeleepull never seemed to hesitate. Of course, he'd gone this way before: only half an hour ago, when the militia followed the same spoor through the trees.

Mr. Clear Chest must have had a rough time of it, racing on the slant of a hillside through the deep night dark . . . trying not to trip over logs or get tangled in patches of brush. Of course, this forest was alien, not like the nice Terran woodlands on my father's estate; but the undergrowth here knew all the Earth tricks, with bristles and prickers and nettly bits to jab you as you dashed by.

It also had those puffbally things I'd felt popping under my feet ever since I came into these woods. Festina said they were insect eggs and got a crinkly fond look in her eyes; she even scraped up a few and put them in a test-tubey thing she had in her pocket. Me, I just saw those eggs as slimy gunk that made it easy to fall if you didn't watch your step. That recruiter must have got whipped and ripped by branches pretty thoroughly on his run . . . till finally he hit a major hitch.

"Bandolier," Festina said, crouching to peer at something in the mud: a big leather sash with all kinds of clips, the sort of thing you sling from your shoulder and hang doo-dads on. It was tangled into a shrub with thorns the size of knitting needles, nasty sharp things that stuck out in all directions. Mr. Clear Chest must have brushed too close to the plant and got himself snagged; in the dark, with all those thorns, he wouldn't have a chance of getting the sash unstuck without gouging up his hands. Especially not with a horde of musk-crazed warriors on his heels. All he could do was unbuckle the strap and abandon his gear.

Which may have given us all kinds of good evidence, like stuff from the Bumbler's memory . . . except that right after Mr. Clear Chest ditched his equipment, it got trampled to topsoil by two dozen stampeding Mandasars.

The shrub with the thorns was crushed into the dirt. So was the Bumbler—nothing but scrap metal now, hammered as flat as a waffle. Now, the only data you could read on it was a whopping bunch of dents from warrior feet.

Festina kept poking at the ground, prying up the squashed remains of everything from the recruiter's bandolier. A lot of it looked like navy equipment—not just the Bumbler, but a service communicator, a deluxe multitool, and even a universal map. (The map was a flexible vidscreen that could fold down to palm-size or out to a meter square. Its memory didn't really have charts of the whole universe, but it could display top-sheets for every planet known to the Outward Fleet.)

The map and everything else was smashed and dirty . . . not even good for fingerprints, though the admiral did her best not to smear the surfaces more than they were already. I knelt beside her for a closer look at the wrecked equipment. The plastic case of the multitool had split open, showing its broken insides, all folded neatly in place: a jackknife, some scissors, a whisk brush, several electronic skeleton keys . . .

Those keys sparked a memory. "That tool," I said to the admiral. "It's the kind used by Security Corps." All the Security officers who guarded Dad and Samantha had carried little gizmos like this one.

Festina grabbed a pair of nearby twigs and used them like chopsticks to pick up the tool. When she brought the casing close to the glow of Kaisho's legs, we could see the plastic was olive green—the color of navy Security. "A Security Corps tool," Festina murmured, "but an Explorer's Bumbler. And universal maps are only carried by the Diplomacy Corps."

"They're all navy issue," Kaisho agreed. "Can you see any serial numbers?"

The admiral used her chopsticks to flip through the debris. Despite dents and damage, it wasn't hard to find ID codes notched into every piece of equipment. The navy was always real thorough about labeling fleet property. "You've got your communicator?" Festina asked Kaisho.

"Of course."

"Then call Starbase Iris and check the ordnance database. I'll give you my own access codes. Find out who's registered as the owner of this stuff."

Kaisho's legs flared a little brighter. "Is that an order, dear admiral?" she asked, all innocence.

Festina rolled her eyes. "I know—the Balrog doesn't take orders from lesser species. Consider it a humble request."

"We love to serve," Kaisho said with a smile.

18

THINKING ABOUT ADMIRALS

Kaisho got to work, whispering into her communicator: reading off serial numbers, issuing search instructions to the computers on Starbase Iris. Meanwhile, the rest of us prowled around, looking for anything else that might be in the neighborhood. Zeeleepull snuffled in the mud; Festina tracked forward a bit, still following the recruiter's path through the woods; and since I couldn't think of anything else to do, I tagged along behind her.

When she saw I was following, she waited for me to join her . . . and even smiled a bit as I came up. I couldn't remember an admiral ever smiling at me—laughing, yes, but not smiling. When I was young, Dad mostly kept me out of sight when other admirals came to call . . . but if someone stayed for several days, I couldn't be hidden forever. My father had this trick of staging "family" breakfasts, as if he and Sam and I ate together every morning; he thought it would make a good impression on visitors. When my sister and I were old enough not to give away the game, he even put a photo of our "late mother" above the dining table.

I don't know who the woman in the picture was—someone blond and pretty. Our real mother had been a paid surrogate, chosen for her healthy medical profile and ability to keep a secret. Dad never took a photo of *her*.

So I'd met a fair number of admirals at those contrived

151

little meals: men and women, humans and Divians, but all of them with the same sort of look in their eyes. Staring at me when no one else was watching, as if I were a mystery they were keen to figure out. Exactly how stupid was I? Was it a miracle I could even handle a knife and fork, or had Dad exaggerated how dumb I was? Could I be some kind of secret weapon—that Dad wanted them to think I was a total idiot, when really it was part of some devious plan?

The admirals I'd met were very keen on devious plans.

But Festina Ramos was different. A real smile for me. Not a grin, like someone amused at the way I got tongue-tied in front of strangers, or a leer, like those women on *Willow* who offered to show me the service tunnels. Just a smile, a nice smile.

"How are you feeling?" she asked, as we walked side by side through the woods.

"I'm all right," I said.

"No aftereffects from the venom?"

"Not that I can tell."

"Good." She glanced my way. "You should still see a doctor, as soon as you can."

"Oh." I didn't like doctors so much; I decided to change the subject. "That recruiter guy—Mr. Clear Chest. He sure had a lot of navy equipment."

"He did, didn't he?" She was looking away from me now: making a show of examining the ground, though there was nothing down there but trampled mud.

"How do you think he got it?" I asked.

She didn't answer for a moment. We were entering the clearing where the recruiter had faced off with the militia; ridges of stone poked up through the soil, which must have been why the trees hadn't grown in to fill the gap.

"What do you know about admirals?" Festina suddenly asked.

"Um," I said. "One or two things, I guess." She must not know who my father was . . . and I didn't want to tell her, not right now—for fear she started looking at me like those admirals at the breakfast table, sizing me up to see if I could be used as political leverage.

"Do you know the difference," she asked, "between the High Council and the lower admirals?"

I thought, *Lower admirals never got invited to breakfast.* But out loud, I said, "The High Council is the inner circle. One for each corps in the service."

"Except the Explorer Corps," she told me in something close to a growl. "Officially, Explorers fall under the jurisdiction of the council president. Which mean they mostly fall between the cracks."

"But if *you* used to be an Explorer," I said, "and now you're an admiral, couldn't you sort of be the admiral in charge of the Explorer Corps?"

She turned to me and smiled. Another nice, real smile. And pretty, too. Even with just the starlight, I could see the splotch on her face, but I was getting used to it. It wasn't so bad, especially when her eyes were so alive . . . and the way she moved, very easy and graceful, sure on her feet. I even liked her voice—it was sweet and kind, without the teeniest bit of talking down to me. Just for a second, I wondered if she ever put perfume in her hair; then I nearly smacked my own face for being so stupid.

Thank heavens Festina couldn't read my mind the way Kaisho seemed to. Still smiling, the admiral sat down on a small stone outjut in the middle of the clearing and patted the rock beside her, like I should sit too. She was just being friendly, I knew that; ready to have a talk with a fellow Explorer. Feeling shy and awkward, I took a seat but made darned sure I wasn't so close I might accidentally brush against her.

"Edward," she murmured quietly, "I'm never going to be the admiral in charge of the Explorer Corps. Like I said, that job goes to the council president—Admiral Vincence. Vincence would never surrender a shred of his power to someone else . . . which means he won't let anyone take over the Explorers, even if he doesn't give a damn about the corps."

She sighed and stared out into the darkness. "The High Council is like that, Edward. Admirals lower on the totem pole are mostly decent competent professionals: the ones who make sure ships are where they're supposed to be with the supplies they need. But the bastards who claw their way to the top—and stay there for decade after decade—sometimes I think they're all clones of a single Machiavellian bastard who seized power four hundred . . . what's wrong?"

I'd nearly jumped to my feet and run off into the night. Talk about clones always did that to me—flooding me with guilt. "Sorry," I said, trying not to sound like a terrible liar, "I just saw a shadow . . . like a wolf or something."

"There *are* no wolves on Celestia," she answered. "The planet's still in its Devonian period; the only native life-forms on land are insects." Festina rolled to her feet. "Maybe we'd better look around, in case the recruiters have come back."

"No, no," I said, "it was nothing. Just a shadow. A tree moving in the wind. Sorry."

She peered off into the woods for another moment, then slowly sat down. "Where was I?" she asked.

"Um." I remembered very clearly but didn't want to remind her. "You were talking about admirals, but I'm not sure why."

"Oh. Well." She thought for a moment. "You asked how that recruiter got hold of navy equipment. I was getting around to that." She eased back onto her elbows, staring idly up at the stars. "For the past twenty years, the High Council has taken a great interest in Celestia. And when I say great interest, I mean on the order of eighteen percent interest per annum."

"Money?"

"Money. The Admiralty funded a lot of people to come to Celestia two decades ago, and they've been reaping dividends ever since. Solid returns on investment." She glanced at me. "Does that surprise you?"

"Um. No." When Sam described how Dad had sneaked twenty million humans onto Celestia, she hadn't described all the financial arrangements; but of course the Admiralty would have worked out some way to take a percentage of whatever the settlers earned.

"So," Festina went on, "members of the High Council have a strong incentive to ensure that Celestian business stays profitable. Lately, the biggest profits have been coming from . . ."

She looked at me as if she was sure I could finish the sentence. "From recruiting Mandasars?" I guessed.

"That's right," she nodded. "Cheap blue-collar workers, brilliant white-collar workers, and fanatic security guards to keep everybody in line."

"So the High Council is on the recruiters' side?" I asked, outraged.

"The recruiters put money in the High Council's pockets, but I doubt if they're backed by the council as a whole. My guess is the recruiters are sponsored by a single admiral."

"Who?"

"I don't know," Festina replied. "But it's someone who's decided to equip the recruiters with navy gear."

"That's awful!" I said.

"Business as usual for High Council admirals," she sighed. "But that's not the worst part."

I didn't want to hear the worst part. But I swallowed and said, "Tell me."

She didn't speak for a moment; she was staring up at the stars over her head. "There it is," she said suddenly. "See that constellation that looks like a big X? Second star from the middle on the upper right arm—that's Troyen's sun."

I looked up quickly. The X was easy enough to see; but the star she'd pointed out was nothing special. Somehow I thought it should be brighter than any other object in the sky, not an ordinary little pinpoint like everything else. I lay on my back beside Festina to get a better look.

"Edward," she said softly, "why did someone order *Willow* to transport a queen from Troyen to Celestia?"

"I don't know." My voice sounded distant in my own

ears; I was staring up at the star, wanting to feel some connection with it. That was Troyen. The closest thing I had to a home. But my heart didn't beat a millisecond faster. Nothing.

"It's getting harder for the recruiters to find more victims," Festina murmured. Her voice was quiet, right there on the ground beside me. "Mandasar communities like this one have organized for their own protection: militias, sentry patrols, security systems. And the Mandasars are starting to find sympathetic ears among humans and other races on Celestia: people who will lobby politicians or raise a stink in the media. So the recruiter press gangs have found it harder and harder to meet their quotas."

She lifted up on one elbow and looked down at me. "Now think, Edward. How would that change if the recruiters had a queen on their side?"

"You mean . . . *Willow* was bringing the queen to help the *recruiters*?"

"*Willow* was following orders from someone in the High Council—no one else would dare send a ship to a planet that's having a war. And someone in the High Council is probably channeling navy equipment to the recruiters. Odds are it's the same person."

I thought about that a second. "If this bad admiral gave orders to *Willow*, wouldn't there be records or something? I mean, if it's an official order . . ."

My voice trailed off as Festina shook her head. "Sorry, Edward," she told me. "Our navy computer systems are so full of back doors and secret access codes and intentional security loopholes . . ." She sighed. "An inner-circle admiral can issue instructions, then erase any trace that it happened. I'll check, of course, just in case someone got sloppy covering up tracks; but in all likelihood, not even the admirals on the High Council can figure out which of them sent *Willow* to Troyen."

"But you're sure," I said, "that *Willow* was bringing that queen for the recruiters?"

"That's my guess," Festina answered. Her face was dark

with shadows. "Now tell me: what would happen if the recruiters had a queen working with them?"

I winced. Mandasars have fanatically strong instincts to follow a queen's orders. Even if the queen said something ridiculous like, "Surrender to the recruiters," a good chunk of the population would start thinking, "If a queen wants us recruited, maybe that's the way things should be. Maybe we just don't understand, and it's selfish trying to stay the way we are."

More likely though, the queen wouldn't be so blatant. The recruiters would use her to trick a few kids at a time, luring warriors into traps, thinning out numbers gradually, till the hives weren't strong enough to defend themselves. These kids were so innocent, one queen could make suckers of them all. Look how eagerly the warriors listened to me, just because I smelled of week-old venom and once had a fancy title.

Yes, a queen would be a godsend to the recruiters . . . if she felt like cooperating with them. "But why would a queen do it?" I asked. "Why would she help humans do bad things to her own kind?"

"Maybe just to get off Troyen," Festina said. "Suppose a queen was doing badly in the war—surrounded by enemies, low on troops and supplies. Then *Willow* shows up with a proposition: free passage to Celestia and a chance to start fresh on a new planet. All she has to do is help the recruiters a bit. Would the queen take the deal?"

"Yes," I said. "Then double-cross the recruiters as soon as she got the chance."

"They wouldn't give her the chance," Festina told me. "They'd keep a gun to her head the rest of her life. Except the League killed her and the whole of *Willow* before any of that could happen."

Festina eased off her elbow and rolled onto her back again—side by side with me in the darkness, staring up at Troyen's sun. "That's what makes me think it's just one admiral, rather than the whole council. The council are power-mad sleazebags, but they aren't collectively stupid.

Transporting a queen from one star system to another? When the queen had been waging a war for twenty years? That's an insane risk. The League was almost sure to consider the queen a dangerous non-sentient . . . so any fool could see they'd kill her and the *Willow*'s crew. If the council jointly agreed to give *Willow* its orders, then the council would be branded non-sentient too. Next thing you know, the League might ground our whole navy till the admirals were thrown out on their asses. That's a very real threat, and the inner circle knows it."

She shook her head. "No, Edward, our noble leaders have a finely honed sense of self-preservation; they'd never go far enough to bring the League down on their heads. But a single admiral might—if he or she had a big stake, keeping the recruiters in business."

"Which admiral?" I asked.

"I don't know. One who can't leave New Earth anymore—he or she is definitely non-sentient. But that doesn't narrow down the possibilities. None of the high admirals leave New Earth; they're all afraid of people conspiring against them while they're gone."

"So you can't even make a guess who it is?" I was up on my elbow now, leaning in over her. Her eyes opened wider, maybe surprised I was so concerned who it might be. She just stared at me for a moment . . .

. . . and that's when I realized I was lying beside an admiral, a young woman admiral, a very pretty young woman admiral, in the middle of a forest, in the middle of the night. More than lying *beside* her, I was practically on top of her, for heaven's sake.

That's also when Zeeleepull walked into the clearing. "Oh, you humes! Always the sex, sex, sex."

19

FIGURING OUT
WHO DID WHAT

I bounded to my feet, afraid my face was burning as red as Kaisho's legs. Festina didn't look bothered at all; with an impish little smile, she actually held out her hand for me to help her up.

She didn't need help getting up—she probably could have done a backflip straight to her feet. But she'd reached out her hand, and I had no choice except taking it. Her skin felt so warm against mine . . . I had to force myself not to give her a huge yank up, jerking her arm out of its socket or tossing her halfway across the clearing. But I went very easy: pulled her up, then let go of her hand fast. She smiled again, amused by my flusterment. "Thank you," she said, then turned to Zeeleepull. "Yes?"

Zeeleepull's ears were twitching in the Mandasar version of a you-randy-old-humans laugh. But all he said was, "Tracked serial numbers Kaisho has. Come. Come."

Festina gave me a look—a mischievous sort of look, and for a second I thought she might try to fluster me more, by taking my arm or something. But I guess she decided teasing me would be mean. She told Zeeleepull, "All right. Let's see what Kaisho's got." Then the three of us walked back in silence, little puffbally things going pop under our feet.

*   *   *

While we were gone, Kaisho had rearranged her hair. Now it completely covered her face, not the tiniest gap down the middle; in fact, she'd grabbed the long straight strands that'd been hanging down her back and flipped them up over her forehead, so they covered her nose, chin, throat, all the way to her chest. I didn't know how she could see a thing . . . but as we trudged up to her, she said, "Festina dear, you're looking amused."

"Enjoying the fresh night air," Festina replied. "What have you found?"

Kaisho lifted her hand and ticked off points on her fingers. "The communicator: still supposedly present and accounted for in a storehouse on New Earth. The universal map: present and accounted for on Moglin. The Bumbler: present and accounted for on He'Barr."

Festina wrinkled her forehead. "Three different storehouses, dozens of light-years from each other. And dozens of light-years from Celestia too."

The two women nodded to each other, like it was obvious what was going on. I tried to think it through myself. If the computer records said the Bumbler was still on He'Barr, but it was right here crushed into the mud . . . then someone had stolen the Bumbler and rigged the inventory computers to overlook the discrepancy. That might mean a thief in the local Supply Corps; but you wouldn't have three thieves at three different supply depots, all sending stuff to one recruiter. Easier to assume a single thief: someone so high up in the navy, he or she had access to *any* depot. And also had computer permission codes to cover up the thefts.

In other words, an admiral.

"So who?" Kaisho asked . . . looking straight at me for some reason instead of at Festina.

"What who?" Zeeleepull demanded. He glared around at the rest of us, like we were intentionally hiding some secret from him.

"Who provided the recruiters with navy equipment?"

Festina told him. "And who ordered *Willow* to fetch a queen from Troyen? It can only be an admiral on the High Council. Someone who's sponsoring the recruiters . . . for cash or for power, or for some scheme we don't know about yet."

"An admiral?" Zeeleepull growled. "Humes never trust be can." He glared at Festina, then caught sight of me right beside her. "*Teelu* exception is," he mumbled. "Not really hume at all."

Kaisho giggled at that. You wouldn't think an advanced human-Balrog synthesis could giggle. Festina stared at her in surprise for a moment, then said sternly, "Let's get a grip, shall we? A rogue admiral is helping the recruiters!"

"Ah, dear Festina," Kaisho sighed, "always business, business, business." Her head suddenly cocked on an angle; when she spoke again, her voice had the sly smug tone of someone who's realized something you haven't. "Pity no one from *Willow* survived," she said. "They might have known which admiral ordered them to Troyen."

Festina looked back at her. "You have an idea? Or should I say, the Balrog has some brilliant alien insight?"

The moss on Kaisho's legs flared brighter for a second, almost as if it was taking a bow. "Who were the Explorers on *Willow*?" Kaisho asked.

"Plebon and Olympia Mell," the admiral answered.

"Ever meet them?"

"I knew Plebon," Festina replied. "He was one of the Explorers marooned with me on Melaquin. After we got back, I made a point of spending time with him because he was a friend of my old partner Yarrun; they'd considered themselves kindred spirits because they both had the same . . ."

The admiral stopped, lowering her eyes as if she was suddenly embarrassed. Vaguely, she waved her hand under her chin. I had no idea what she meant but Kaisho did. She turned straight to me and said, "Among the bodies on *Willow*, did you see a man with a deformed jaw?"

I stared stupidly at her while my brain tried to catch up

with the question. Festina was way ahead of me. She gawped at Kaisho, then whirled and grabbed my arm. "Edward, please . . . think back. Was there a man, an African man, very tall and dark, but missing the lower half of his face? If you saw it, you wouldn't forget it. He had practically no jaw at all."

Still not quite understanding, I cast my mind back over the crumpled bodies in the lounge. "No," I said, "there wasn't anyone with a funny jaw on the ship." Not in the lounge, not on the bridge, not in any possible hidey-hole. "I'm certain."

Festina let out a sigh of relief. "Hallelujah."

Kaisho held up her hands in a "What would you expect?" gesture. All smug and proud, she said, "The Explorer Corps vindicates itself again."

"Cryptic and mysterious and annoying humes," Zeeleepull grumped. "What, what, what this means?"

"*Willow* carried two Explorers," Festina answered, "and at least one of them wasn't aboard when they headed back to Celestia."

"Probably both," Kaisho put in. "If Plebon stayed on Troyen, his partner would too."

"Why would they stay on Troyen?" I asked.

"Because Explorers are smart," Kaisho said. "Because they believed the queen was non-sentient. They knew the League would kill the queen and everyone who helped transport her. Plebon and Olympia wanted no part of it."

Zeeleepull sniffed, all disapproving. "Desertion is," he said. "If orders say, no cowarding out."

"Not true," Festina told him. "The Admiralty can give orders that skate to the edge of non-sentience, but if they ever go over the line, you don't have to obey. In fact, official policy says you must *not* obey. Of course, the High Council really wants subordinates to shut up and do as they're told; but the council has to keep the League of Peoples happy, and that means allowing folks to follow their consciences. NAVY PERSONNEL WILL AT ALL TIMES CONFORM TO THE STRICTEST STANDARDS OF SENTIENCE,

EVEN WHEN THIS NECESSITATES DEFIANCE OF A DIRECT COMMAND. That's right in the Outward Fleet's charter— the League wouldn't accept anything less. So if Plebon and Olympia believed the queen committed atrocities during the war, they had every right to say, 'Count us out.'" Festina paused. "I wonder if others from *Willow*'s crew stayed behind."

"No way to tell," Kaisho said. "Not with the ship missing and its records EMP'd."

I stared at her a second. How did Kaisho know that? She hadn't showed up till *after* I'd told my story. But before I could say anything, Festina was talking—all excitement and glee. "Plebon and Olympia must know which admiral controlled *Willow*," she said. "Any good Explorer would demand to know who ordered such a lunatic mission. Hell, they'd break into the captain's quarters if they had to, just to peek at the signature on the official dispatches."

"So," Kaisho murmured, "if we find Plebon and Olympia, we learn which admiral is backing the recruiters."

"Whereupon we raise a big stink with the High Council," Festina said, "condemning the bastard for stealing navy property. And for routing that property to a group who murdered poor Wiftim and tried to kill me. The council will not be pleased. The council will, in fact, howl for blood . . . if only because one of their own was playing fast and loose behind their backs. Next thing you know, they'll squeeze the guilty party to spill his or her guts: demand name, rank, and serial number for every recruiter on Celestia. Anything else would be harboring a murderer, and not even the Admiralty would be stupid enough to do that."

Kaisho gave a whispery chuckle. "Knowing the High Council, they'll make a show of arresting the recruiters personally. Demonstrate their good intentions by sending a Security force straight to the recruiters' base. Once you back the council into a corner, they have a knack for turning a hundred eighty degrees, snatching the limelight, and taking credit for defending the weak."

"Just their style," Festina nodded. She made a face, like

she'd seen it happen plenty of times before. "On the other hand, our first concern is stopping the recruiters. Doesn't matter who gets their pictures in *Mind Spurs Weekly*."

"But, um," I said, "you have to get the name of the guilty admiral, right? And the only people who might know that are stuck on Troyen."

"True," Festina agreed. "You understand the situation admirably."

Her eyes glittered in the glow from Kaisho's legs. Both women were looking at me now. Even though I couldn't see Kaisho's face, I could tell she was grinning. "Um," I said. "So I guess you're going to Troyen?"

"Not just me," Festina answered. She put her hand on my arm. "I'll need a native guide, won't I?"

Kaisho laughed and laughed. The sound of it made me dizzy.

20

LYING BESIDE COUNSELOR

I don't remember much from there on—all of a sudden my body got so tired I couldn't think straight. It felt like Kaisho's laughter was going all hyena-ish like the Laughing Larry, getting so loud it drowned out everything else in my head. I had time to think, *It's the venom again.* Then things turned into a fuddled-up blur where time seemed to get the hiccups.

First I was lying facedown in the mud, while insects no bigger than pepper scuttled under my nose; then suddenly I was neck deep in water, with Zeeleepull and the admiral dragging me across the canal; then whoops, I was back where I started, in the hive's dome, lying on a pallet beside the Queen Wisdom table. After that, I might have slept, or just passed out for an hour or two . . . but not the whole night. When I woke with a clearer head, it was still dark, and Counselor had snuggled in beside me.

Several of her legs draped lightly over my body. One of her upper hands was cupped against my cheek: six delicate fingers covered in soft walnut brown skin. The fingers were too long to be human, and they had no nails, but they didn't look strange to me; they looked like home. Night after night in Verity's palace, the queen would assign a maidservant to stay next to me as I slept, in case I might wake and want something.

"Are you well now, *Teelu*?" Counselor whispered.

There was no light in the room where we lay, but a dim glow came from next door—just enough for Counselor to watch me as I slept. Mandasars love to do that . . . I guess because they don't sleep deeply themselves. They're curious about it; the way humans go totally unconscious is kind of eerie to them, creepy but magical. Some of the maid-servants back on Troyen actually took anaesthetics before sliding into bed beside me: they wanted to knock them-selves out cold, to see what it was like, "sleeping together."

Of course, they didn't understand what that phrase means to humans . . . any more than Counselor understood what a man gets to feeling when he wakes up and there's someone stroking his face. Mandasars never think about sex stuff at all, except during egg-heat. They know humans work dif-ferently, but Mandasars don't realize how much . . . um . . . how *often* . . . how *persistently* certain urges keep poking their way into a *Homo sapiens'* imagination.

(Close your eyes, and a gentle's voice sounds pretty much like a human woman's. Her hand feels the same too. And so soft.)

Looking at Counselor, feeling her hand on my cheek, I found myself remembering that kiss aboard *Willow*—the woman pulling me in tight, the perfume in her hair . . . a woman who was exactly like Admiral Ramos except she wasn't . . . and Festina herself, lying beside me in the dark forest, looking up at the stars . . .

Crazy, I thought to myself. *My brain must still be jum-bled, going all swimmy with what-ifs.* Festina was pretty and kind, but she was an admiral; as for Counselor, she was just in my bed because I'd been sick. Why was I so eager to get dumb ideas about every female around me: an admiral and an *alien* for heaven's sake . . . and I was even having thoughts about Kaisho, with her skintight clothes and her dangerous glowing thighs . . .

"*Teelu*," Counselor whispered. "Are you troubled?"

I reached up and took her hand, pulling it gingerly away from my face. "Maybe you shouldn't call me *Teelu*, okay? It's kind of . . ." I wanted to say "sacrilegious," but that would upset her. "You shouldn't overuse the word," I mumbled.

"Very well," she said. "Is there anything else I should or shouldn't do?" She asked it in a soft sweet whisper, still holding my hand—all innocently intimate, not knowing how complicated things can get inside a human's head. When you're tired and lonely, you can catch yourself thinking, maybe, maybe, she really meant . . .

No. She didn't.

But I couldn't get my thoughts aimed any other direction. I told myself, *Don't be stupid, she's a big brown lobster.* It didn't help. I'd had more kindness in my life from Mandasars than I ever got from humans. Lying beside one again brought back the golden days when the war hadn't started and Sam was alive and we were all twenty years younger . . .

I slipped my hand out of Counselor's grasp and eased down on my pallet: rolling away from her, flat on my back, feeling lumpish and rude. "Where's Admiral Ramos?" I asked.

"She left with the other human—the one with frightening legs."

"Are they coming back?"

"In the morning. But the admiral had to arrange a journey. To Troyen."

Counselor leaned in close to my face, her whiskers trembling. Her snout brushed lightly against my cheek, delicate and cool. Gentles have no nose-spike; just soft skin that smells faintly of ginger. "Are you really going to the homeworld?"

"Admiral Ramos wants me to. She thinks I know the lay of the land."

"You do," Counselor said. "You were the high queen's consort."

"That was twenty years ago. Before the war." I closed my eyes. "All the time I stayed at the moonbase, I did my best not to hear what was happening on the planet. The observers couldn't tell much anyway—with all the rogue nano on Troyen, nobody can use radios or computers or anything, so there's nothing to listen in on. Our satellites kept track of troop movements, but when you don't know who's in charge of which army . . . half the time, the observers just made stuff up so their reports wouldn't look too skimpy. Nobody really knows what's happening."

Counselor lay silent for a few seconds. I wanted to see the expression on her face, but decided eye contact would be a mistake: she'd take my hand again or go back to stroking my cheek. "Admiral Ramos has been investigating the recruiters," Counselor murmured at last. "The woman with the red legs said the admiral tries to prevent regrettable things. Admiral Ramos is what you call a *watchdog* and a *troubleshooter*."

I didn't know the navy had such things, but I was glad they put someone like Festina in the position. "She thinks another admiral is helping the recruiters," I said. "It makes her mad, and she's trying to set things right."

"Then Admiral Ramos is a good hume," Counselor murmured. "Even if she wants to take you away from us."

"Um."

When I looked at Counselor, her face was sad—the terrible kind of sad where someone is trying hard not to show it, and it spills through anyway.

"Do you *want* to go away?" Counselor asked.

"No," I told her. "But Admiral Ramos thinks people on Troyen might know who's behind the recruiters. She said it could solve your problems."

"She told me the same," Counselor said. "But it's painful to gain you and lose you in the same day."

Suddenly, she bent in and pressed the soft end of her snout against my lips. A kiss. I'd never seen a gentle do that on Troyen. It must have been something she'd learned on Celestia, a gesture picked up from the humans who took care of her in childhood. So awkward and clumsy, like a little girl imitating adult things—she wrapped one arm around my neck and kept her nose against me . . . not moving her mouth, just holding it tight to my face as if she didn't know a kiss could be anything else.

I pulled back away from her, feeling awkward and clumsy myself. "It's all right," I whispered. "Really. It'll be all right."

She lowered her chin so she could look me in the eye. Her eyes were solid black, blinking slightly—Mandasars don't cry when they're sad, but their faces can still be heart-breaking. "Troyen is at war. You could be killed . . . and then where would we be?"

What could I say? That I wasn't the savior she thought? I didn't want to go back to Troyen, but I wasn't worth much on Celestia. People would soon see I didn't have a head for organization, or strategy, or rousing speeches, or anything that could help anyone. I said, "If Admiral Ramos thinks I'd be useful on Troyen—"

"This Admiral Ramos," Counselor interrupted. "Is she your lover?"

I winced. Zeeleepull must have blabbed how he'd found Festina and me in the forest. "No," I said. "She's not my lover."

"Do you intend to make her your lover?"

"No. She's an admiral. Anyway, I can't *make* anyone my lover—people don't work that way."

"*Teelu*," Counselor whispered, "*Teelu, Teelu, Teelu*, don't you know you can make anyone into anything you want?" She cupped my chin in her weak upper hands, holding me so she could stare straight into my eyes. "Don't you know," she whispered, "you can stir any heart and make it yours?"

If she'd been human, her words would have been an invitation. Maybe even a plea. Over the years, other women had come to me with that kind of offer . . . because they liked the way I looked, because they were bored, or because they'd been hurt by someone else and thought, *Oh, Edward, at least he won't be cruel*. They told me that to my face—I was "pretty" and "safe" and "decent."

And plenty of times, I'd said yes. In my twenty years on

the moonbase, new personnel would arrive and even though I knew they'd just leave again after six months, sometimes you tell yourself six months is six months. (Forgetting how lonely it is when they go away . . . the awful point where they start pulling back from you, even before they ship out . . . how sometimes they're never there with you at all, just treating you like medicine that'll keep them from getting cranky.)

So yes, there'd been human women; but not Mandasars. Gentles didn't make come-ons, ever. Not to their own species and certainly not to humans. Even in egg-heat, gentles didn't act amorous—it was all pheromone signals, not direct attempts at seduction. "I'm available," not "Now, now, now!" Whatever Counselor wanted to tell me, it was just my one-track human mind misinterpreting it as . . . the sort of proposition you yearn for when things are going all lonesome.

"Counselor." I wrapped my arms around her shoulders, feeling her thin carapace yield: fragile as eggshell compared to a warrior's armor. She put her arms around my shoulders and my waist, then pressed her snout against my neck . . . maybe another kiss, maybe just where her nose ended up. "I'm not as special as you think," I told her. "Verity married me for politics, not because I was some hero. And the way you kids react to me—it's just the smell of venom, that's all. Sooner or later, you'll get mad at me for not being what you hope."

She pulled back a bit from my neck so she could look me in the eye. "You are the Little Father Without Blame," she said. "You're more than we hoped, and more than you know. Just for tonight, I wish I were your own species . . . so you'd stop treating me like some child you mustn't corrupt. I was raised by humans, *Teelu*; I'm not as naive as you think."

Once more she leaned in for a kiss: light, quick, on my cheek, then she slipped softly out of my arms. I let her go, stunned by what she was suggesting. I couldn't, I couldn't, I couldn't—for all that she was a grown-up of her species, she didn't know . . . she was confused by the smell of venom, that had to be it. And by her human upbringing. After years of hume stories like "Snow White" and "Cinderella," Counselor might fantasize about offering herself to some Prince Charming; but Mandasars didn't really *feel* . . . they didn't really *want* . . .

Did they?

She was still very close, near enough that I could smell her soft ginger scent; and she was waiting for me to call her back. To reach for her hand or her kiss. But it wouldn't be right. Whatever she thought she wanted, it truly wasn't in her nature. I couldn't take advantage of her, no matter how soothing it would be just to give in, surrender, get lost in the dark.

Counselor must have seen the decision on my face because she sighed quietly—a human sigh, yet another mannerism she must have picked up from the people who raised her. "*Teelu*," she murmured, "may I at least accompany you on your journey? To Troyen?"

"It'll be dangerous," I said. "They're still at war."

"All the more reason for me to go. You humans will be conspicuous and perhaps treated as enemies. I won't attract as much attention."

"Yes, you will," I told her. "There are so many things you were never taught. Ways to behave. And habits you've picked up that just aren't Mandasar. You'd stand out as badly as any human."

"Not if you teach me. The voyage to Troyen takes ten days—I can learn quickly. I'll study with you every waking second."

"But if I let you come," I said, "then Zeeleepull would want to go too. And Hib & Nib & Pib."

"Well, of course," she answered, as if that had never been in doubt. "We all have to go." She fluttered her whiskers teasingly. "You wouldn't want to recruit me off by myself, would you?" The fluttering stopped. "Would you?"

Her last "would you?" was so wistful—as if she still hoped I might take her seriously. I couldn't possibly . . .

not because she was an alien, but because she was so young and innocent.

And because in my head I might be thinking of other women besides her.

If I told that to Counselor straight out, it would hurt her feelings; so I decided to give her one thing when I couldn't give the other.

"All right," I said. "I'll talk to Admiral Ramos about taking your hive to Troyen."

Immediately there was a cheer—not from Counselor but from four other voices. Zeeleepull and the workers tumbled out of the next room, all glee and triumph. "Troyen!" Zeeleepull yelled. "Troyen going, Troyen seeing, Troyen going, Troyen seeing . . ."

He might have been singing. And dancing. It's hard to tell with Mandasars.

"I told you she could make *Teelu* say yes," Hib whispered, elbowing Nib proudly. "And she didn't even have to sleep with him."

"Don't you know anything?" Nib answered. "She *wanted* to sleep with him."

"After all," Pib added, "he's a king."

21

TAKING OUR LEAVE

Festina came back the next day at noon. By then the workers had packed, Counselor had arranged for neighboring hives to look after the vegetable fields, and Zeeleepull had made a complete nuisance of himself, getting in everybody else's way.

Of all of the kids, he was the most excited—telling me things he wanted to see on Troyen, places he wanted to go, stuff he wanted to do. After a while I just had to say, "You realize if we're lucky, we'll never set foot on the planet. Radio the missing Explorers, pick them up, fly away. No going down ourselves unless there's a problem."

"But Troyen is," he insisted. "Is *Troyen*. Is home."

"*Was* home," I said. "Nobody knows what-all's been destroyed in the past twenty years. Buildings bombed. Famous art burned or stolen. Even natural scenery gets wrecked or covered with ugly-looking bunkers. Whatever you think you'll see, it's not there anymore."

He refused to listen. Of all the people in his hive, Zeeleepull had the most romantic notions about the planet he'd left as a hatchling. He told me he'd been brought up by elderly human sisters, Willa and Walda, who'd devoted themselves to raising the boy in accordance with his sacred heritage. The way he spoke of them, I just knew the women didn't have a clue what they were talking about—their heads had got crammed with off-kilter ideas about Troyen,

173

sparked by a ten-day trip they'd made in their thirties. That trip must have been the one impulsive thing the sisters had ever done, and they'd built their lives around it ever after . . . which explains why they leapt at the chance to take a baby Mandasar under their roof and acquaint him with his fabulous culture.

No wonder Zeeleepull spoke such bad Troyenese. And worse English. He'd come to human language very late, because the sisters didn't want to "pollute his mental development with contaminating influences." When they finally realized he had to learn English to communicate with his fellow Mandasars—the other kids spoke English 99 percent of the time—Willa and Walda encouraged Zeeleepull to use English words but Troyenese syntax, so he wouldn't "warp his brain's neural connections" with an alien grammar.

I got the feeling Zeeleepull could speak normal English if he wanted to, but now he was making a political point. He'd even persuaded his fellow warriors to speak the same way, especially when they were out on maneuvers together. Like a secret code that proved you belonged to the club.

It didn't hurt that Counselor and the workers loved Zeeleepull to pieces for the bullheaded way he stuck to his twisted-up word structures. Us guys—even when we're big red platonic lobsters—we put on silly poses to impress the girls.

No rutabagas got weeded that day—when Festina's skimmer set down on the road, every Mandasar in the valley was there to watch. A big colorful horde of them, reds and whites and browns, all jostled each other for the best view. It reminded me of something Sam said as we watched a riot from my palace balcony: "Like a water tank in a seafood restaurant: lobsters crammed in shoulder to shoulder."

When I thought about it now, it'd been a cruel, mean thing for Sam to say . . . but she had a point. Mandasars cram together a lot; they like it. They're the sort of species who snuggle together all the time—who bed down in a huddle, and who press into a single corner of a room rather than spacing themselves evenly around. Even these kids raised by humans . . . you'd think they'd be taught to maintain some personal distance, but there they were on the road, practically crawling on top of each other as the skimmer settled down to the pavement. Even so, they managed to skootch together a little more to clear a path for me up to the side hatch.

The hatch opened. Festina hopped out and smiled when she saw me. "Edward! You're looking better. Good. Great. Very fine." She was eyeing me up and down. "You had us worried when you passed out last night."

"*I* wasn't worried," said a voice inside the skimmer. "He was just exhausted." Kaisho's wheelchair floated into the sunlight and lowered itself to the road. Her hair looked beautifully combed this morning—combed so it covered her face like a silver-black veil, very neat and glossy. Even the Balrog looked well-groomed. Under the bright orange sun, you couldn't tell Kaisho's legs glowed on their own; they just looked like thick beds of moss, as unthreatening as red pillows.

"Well," Festina said, still giving me the once-over (the twice-over by now), "you look damned terrific for a man who was poisoned yesterday. Are you ready to go?"

"Um." I leaned in, and whispered, "Is it okay if I bring some company?"

"Who?"

I pointed behind me. Counselor, Zeeleepull, and the workers were lined up looking freshly scrubbed and gleamy bright themselves . . . all except Nib, who'd tried to paint a BON VOYAGE sign and got smears of green paint all over its just-washed white hands. (Workers!) Naturally, Zeeleepull carried the luggage; most of the hive's worldly possessions were strapped to his back, boxed up in a wooden crate labeled ONIONS.

Festina sighed deeply. "How many of them do you plan on bringing?"

"Five."

Counselor and the others waved gleefully—antennas as well as hands.

"Told you," Kaisho whispered to Festina.

"I could have guessed myself," Festina muttered back. "Are they all right?"

"They won't cause trouble," I promised.

"That's not what I meant." Festina motioned to Kaisho. "You and the Balrog check them out."

Kaisho's wheelchair glided toward the five Mandasars . . . and all of a sudden, the rest of the crowd scrambled back, putting a good healthy distance between themselves and the woman's mossy legs. I don't know if they'd heard gossip about the Balrog since last night, or if they all just spontaneously decided they didn't like the moss's smell. Either way, they were doing their best to keep clear; and from the looks on their faces, Counselor and the others would have been turning tail too, if they didn't think they'd hurt their chance of seeing Troyen.

"What's Kaisho doing?" I whispered to Festina.

"The Balrog can supposedly determine whether a being is sentient. Don't ask me how it works—maybe a killer gives off non-sentient psychic vibrations. The damned moss isn't perfectly telepathic, thank God, but it can sometimes do an uncanny job of peeking into someone's mind."

No kidding, I thought. Out loud, I said, "You really think the Mandasars are dangerous non-sentients?"

"No." Festina gave me an apologetic look. "But we have to make sure, Edward. Otherwise, we could end up like *Willow*—killed for not being careful enough. The League expects us to make our best efforts not to violate the law."

"So you don't trust the kids, but you trust the Balrog?"

"In this particular instance, I trust the Balrog's judgment. It doesn't mean I trust the Balrog in general—that fuzzy-assed bastard scares the piss out of me. But on our upcoming trip, the Balrog's life is at stake too."

"Why?"

"Kaisho's coming with us to Troyen," Festina replied. "If one of your Mandasars is non-sentient and the Balrog lies to us about that, it's the Balrog who'll die when our ship crosses the line. We mere humans will be blameless; the League won't fault us for being deceived by a superior species."

As she spoke, Festina had a grim little smile on her face . . . and for a second, I thought she might be hoping the Balrog *would* get executed by the League. If there was no other way to get rid of the creature—if you couldn't scrape it off its host—then maybe you'd look for situations that'd kill the Balrog without hurting the human underneath.

A few seconds before, I was going to ask Festina why she wanted Kaisho to come with us to Troyen . . . but I decided I didn't want to know.

The wheelchair drifted around each Mandasar in turn—Counselor trying to look composed, Zeeleepull trying to look tough, the workers trying to look so meekly unimportant they wouldn't be worth eating—while Kaisho barely turned her head to give the kids a glance. Why would she? She couldn't see for all the hair in front of her face, so why pretend to stare at anyone?

"Why does she wear her hair like that?" I asked Festina. "Does she have moss on her face? Is she really really . . ." I stopped. Considering the blotch on the admiral's own cheek, there was no polite way to finish my question.

But Festina guessed what I was going to say. "Is she really really ugly?" Festina suggested. "Is she *disfigured*?"

"Um. Sorry."

"No," the admiral said, "it's a valid question. Especially since Kaisho used to be an Explorer. You know she must have had *something* wrong with her."

I felt myself blush. I couldn't even look in the admiral's direction.

"Kaisho did have . . . a facial condition," Festina said. "You don't need to know the details. But when she got infected with the Balrog, the condition cleared up. The Balrog actually tinkered with Kaisho's genes and hormones to cure the problem. I suppose the Balrog was trying to be

nice; it could read Kaisho's surface thoughts well enough
to know how she hated the . . . blemishes. In a way, clearing up Kaisho's face was like a wedding gift—a demon-
stration that being bonded to a Balrog wasn't all bad.

"But from Kaisho's point of view," Festina continued,
"her face and its flaws were key parts of her life. Her identity. To have that identity casually erased by an alien parasite . . . well, imagine being subjected to cosmetic surgery
till you didn't look like yourself. It wouldn't matter if you
ended up more beautiful than you'd ever dared hope; you'd
feel violated. Especially if your hideous old face was what
made you feel like an Explorer, and that was the one thing
in your life you felt proud of."

Festina suddenly sucked in a sharp breath and turned
away from me. "Anyway," she muttered, "I'm sure that's
what Kaisho feels. Her mind gets more and more integrated
with the Balrog every day, but still there's a part of her,
outraged and bitter over what the damned moss did to her
face. Making her look 'normal' instead of like herself. So
she hides behind her hair in shame—she doesn't want to
be seen as she is now."

Odd. Someone hiding and ashamed for being made better
than she was to start with. Of course, "better" is always in
the eye of the beholder . . . but if I were Kaisho, I'd cover
my legs, not my face.

The Balrog's inspection didn't take long. One circuit
around each Mandasar, then Kaisho announced, "They're
acceptable. No more homicidal than the rest of you."

Festina grimaced. "Not what I'd call an effusive rec-
ommendation."

"What do you expect?" Kaisho asked. "Humans and
Mandasars are borderline at best. With luck in the gene
lottery, and no crisis that stresses you past the breaking
point, you can stay sentient all your life. If luck goes the
other way . . . you flunk the sentience test. Nothing to be
embarrassed about—both your species are still evolving in
the right direction. You just have farther to go before you

reach the exalted level of . . . oh, a certain mossy race that modesty forbids me to mention."

Zeeleepull muttered, "Evolve, evolve, evolve, and end up as moss? Stupid universe."

"Now you know how the dinosaurs felt," Festina told him.

"All right," the admiral announced, raising her voice to the assembled Mandasars, "as you probably know, my name is Festina Ramos and I . . . I'm heading for Troyen, where I hope I'll find information to solve your recruiter problem."

The kids gave a cheer, but short and polite . . . like they wanted to hear more before they got really enthusiastic.

"In the meantime," Festina said, "the recruiters should be lying low. Last night, they murdered one of your people as he bravely protected Consort Edward and me; as a result of Wiftim's sacrifice, the police can't ignore your problems the way they've done in the past. With luck, Mandasars all over Celestia will be able to demand better protection . . . and the cops will have to take them seriously."

That got a slightly bigger cheer. I could imagine how frustrated these kids must be, getting dismissed every time they complained to the Civilian Protection Office. Now, as Festina said, the police had no choice but to put the squeeze on recruiters.

"So I hope," the admiral continued, "you won't have trouble while we're gone. Just in case though, I'm leaving this skimmer which I rigged last night with a Mandasar-shaped control seat. You can fly patrols over the valley and keep watch for anyone suspicious—this baby has the navy's best sensor equipment, able to pick up human heat signatures ten kilometers away. Nobody will be able to sneak up on you."

Everyone in the crowd was beaming now—especially the gentles, who'd probably get into a big fight about who should drive the skimmer. All gentles love to operate expensive machinery . . . and each one is absolutely convinced she's the best driver in the universe.

Maybe it wasn't such a bad thing I was heading off to Troyen; for the next little while, Celestia might get pretty dangerous.

Particularly Celestian airspace.

"That's settled then," Festina said. "I hope we won't be gone more than three weeks, but you never know. Whatever happens, we'll be back as soon as we can." She smiled. "In the meantime, cooperate with the police but don't let down your guard. The recruiters hurt themselves badly last night when they resorted to murder; they've suddenly lost a lot of friends. Even companies that buy employees from slavers will think twice about dealing with killers. So there's a chance the recruiters will grow stupid and desperate in the coming days."

"If that's true," said a gentle in the crowd, "why are you taking *Teelu* away from us?"

Festina glanced at me. "You want to answer, or shall I?"

"Um," I said. Then I found words coming out of my mouth, with no direction from my brain—taken over again by whatever had grabbed me before. That worried me; I'd hoped that getting possessed was just some weirdness from being poisoned. Why was it happening now, when I felt okay and healthy?

"Children of Troyen," my mouth said, "the next few weeks may be hard for everybody; but if we succeed, you'll never need to fear recruiters again. Just as important, good people have been abandoned on the homeworld and they deserve to be rescued . . . if they're still alive. They've been forced to fend for themselves a long long while. It's time we did something to help them."

"*Teelu*," Kaisho whispered, "are you speaking of our poor lost Explorers . . . or someone else?"

Festina looked at her curiously. Kaisho just chuckled. Her legs flickered, as if the Balrog were laughing too.

The crowd let themselves be shooed back, clearing a patch of ground beside the skimmer. Festina walked to the center of the area and set down a small black box covered with horseshoe-shaped inlays of gold. I'd seen such a box before; it was a Sperm-field anchor, designed to attract and snag the tail from a starship. Festina flicked a switch on the box's lid and immediately skipped back a pace.

For three seconds nothing happened; then, fluttering out of the sky like the funnel of a tornado, a milky white tube swept down and slapped silently against one of the anchor's gold horseshoes. The tube was filmy and unsolid, with sparkles of blue and green twinkling deep in its creamy body— like a glittery sleeve of smoke rippling up and up into the blue. It was transparent enough that I could look straight through the tail and see boggled Mandasar faces on the other side.

"Don't worry," I whispered to Counselor. Which meant I was back in control of my body again—I'd been so busy gawking at the tail, I hadn't noticed getting unpossessed. "Don't worry," I repeated, "it's just a sort of elevator up to a starship."

"A starship in orbit?" she asked.

"Yes."

"But the starship must be hundreds of kilometers above us!"

I nodded. "Sperm-tails are really elastic. You can pull them out thousands of kilometers long."

Counselor swallowed hard. "What do we do?"

"Um. If you stick your hand into the tube's open end, you get . . . drawn up. All the way through the tail and into the spaceship overhead."

"*Teelu,*" Counselor said, "if someone dragged me by my arm for several hundred kilometers . . ."

"It won't hurt you," I promised her. "As soon as you put a single finger into the tube, the outside universe kind of shoves you in the rest of the way. You don't get pulled, you get pushed. And once you're inside the tube . . . well, it feels very strange, but it doesn't do actual damage."

Counselor winced. "You're not filling me with confidence, *Teelu.*"

"Then watch."

I walked over to the Sperm-tail. Before reaching down to the mouth, I asked Festina, "Shall I go first?"

"Be my guest," she replied. "I'll go last to make sure everyone else is all right."

I nodded and knelt. If you want the honest truth, I'd never gone through a Sperm-tail before either. Real Explorers shot the chute all the time, but me, I'd always traveled in the company of diplomats. "Diplomats," Sam once told me, "do not subject themselves to indignities. It's called a Sperm-tail, for heaven's sake. The name alone is enough to demolish your credibility. And I understand that riding one is appallingly visceral. Diplomats hate that; we like to remain detached from physical reality at all times."

Maybe part of that was joking, but Sam still meant it. She and the rest of the diplomats took shuttles from ship to surface, not the slippery white way.

At the last second, just as I was sticking my hand into the Sperm's mouth, I wondered what my sister meant by "appallingly visceral." Then I found out.

22

SQUIRTING THROUGH
THE TUBE

Gulp.

That was the Sperm-tube swallowing me. Out of the real universe, into an artificial one that fluttered and fish-tailed, taking me with it. My whole body turned to water, pumping through a pipe that twisted, turned, narrowed, expanded, did loop-the-loops. I had no bones; I had no solid parts at all, just liquid and steam, spurting up the Sperm-tail at high pressure.

One other thing: I wasn't alone.

I could feel another presence squirting along with me, a blaze of intelligence burning right next to my skin, as if it was only separated from me by a tissue-thin membrane. It had to be the thing that'd been possessing me: a spirit, a ghost, an alien parasite, some entity that hitchhiked in my body and occasionally shoved me aside so it could drive.

What are you? I thought. *What do you want? Why me?*

The answer was a blast of fiery emotions—angers and sorrows, regrets and resolutions, all knotted up in a package of memories.

My *own* memories.

Samantha's body, her clothes sodden with the blood that kept gushing from her punctured chest. A red pool spreading over the floor. Smears of red on my fingers.

Queen Verity's head plunked on a platter and placed on the royal dinner table ... while the rest of her corpse lay ten paces away, both venom sacs sliced open and spilling dribbles of green.

Me running through the night with a heavy black sack over my shoulder, while shooting echoed in the palace behind me. Racing to a garden shed, lifting up a floorboard, seeing the little black box with the gold horseshoe inlays, and the narrow mouth of a Sperm-tail threading off through an underground conduit. Feeding one end of the sack into that mouth and holding my breath as the bulky load disappeared through the impossibly tiny opening, zipping off heaven knows where. Smashing my heel down on the anchor box, breaking it, releasing the Sperm-tail to slither off on its own so no one could follow ...

Could follow ...

Innocence. My daughter.

Whom I hadn't seen in twenty years.

Whom I'd abandoned on a planet at war.

And I was supposed to be "The Little Father Without Blame"? If I hadn't been riding the Sperm-tail at that second—if I'd had a solid body—I would have thrown up everything in my stomach.

Second after second, my own memories pounded into my mind like a repeating loop. Sam soaked with blood; Verity dead; carrying young Innocence in that bag; Sam and her blood again. As if the thing riding with me up the Sperm-tail was trying to make me *see* something, but I wasn't smart enough to understand.

Sam's blood. Me, reaching down to touch the red stickiness. Lifting my fingers to my nose ...

A voice screamed *No!* inside my head: fighting the memory, fighting the thing that was trying to make me remember. The screaming voice didn't seem part of me, any more than the force pummeling me with my own memories; but I was eager to shout *No!* myself. Anything to escape ugly replays of the most awful night of my life.

So I yelled, *No, go away, stop it, stop it, stop it!* I could feel the memory-thing howl in despair, burning with frustration at my refusal to watch. It pounded away on the thready thin barrier that separated its consciousness from mine; but before it could bash through, I hurtled back into normal space and collided with a mound of soft padding.

I don't know how long I lay there, trying to clear my head. Not long—the padding was jelly bagged up in rubbery plastic, nice and yielding on impact but cold and wobbly the longer you stayed on top of it. They must have made it that way on purpose, so you wouldn't sprawl there forever . . . especially when other people were coming through the Sperm-tube right behind you.

Other people. Kaisho.

With a surge of adrenaline, I tried to heave myself off the landing pad. The jelly beneath me gurgled and sloshed, absorbing my motion; when I pushed harder, my hand just sank into the folds of the bag. *Like trying to fight a tar baby,* I thought. Forcing myself to be calm, I pulled my hands tight to my chest and simply rolled sideways . . . off the bag just as Kaisho barreled out of the tube behind me.

Her mossy legs missed me by a whisker. I was sure that's why she'd come right after me—in hopes of an accidental collision. The Balrog would slam into me, then a splurge of hungry red spores would ooze across my skin . . .

No, I told myself. *Don't be stupid.* The Balrog couldn't want to possess a person with screwed-up chemicals in his brain. Especially not when I was already half-possessed by something else.

"Help me up," Kaisho whispered as she sprawled on the jelly pad. "Please."

On her trip through the Sperm-tail, Kaisho's hair had got all mussed . . . which means it'd fallen off her face enough to show what she really looked like. I found her striking in an elegant, weathered way—what people usually call "handsome," because they won't call women beautiful after the first wrinkle appears. Kaisho had her share of wrinkles around her soft brown eyes . . . but the wrinkles had such a well-aged grace, maybe they deserved to be called crinkles instead. Serene and amused, both at once. Strong cheekbones, wide half-smiling lips . . .

She saw me staring. The half smile froze on her face—not a sudden jolt, but a clamp-down of control, keeping her expression exactly as it was till she could cover up. I could tell she was forcing herself not to hurry; oh so slowly, she shook her hair down over her eyes, then brushed her fingers through a few times to make sure there were no gaps in the veil.

"Maybe someday you should stop hiding," I said.

"Maybe someday I will," she answered in her usual whisper. "When the Balrog has 'elevated' my consciousness to such heights I can't feel childish emotions." For a moment, the fingers she was combing through her hair clenched into fists—gripped by some sudden emotion, rage, shame, I don't know. She trembled with the power of it; I could imagine her face scrunched in on itself under that hair, her eyes squeezed shut, the serenely crinkled skin bunched up into ridges and hollows.

A long ten seconds passed before she relaxed. Then she shook her head and flung her arms wide toward me, crying, "Help me, *Teelu*." Not a whisper—a desperate plea.

But in the next instant, a shudder went through her; and though her position scarcely changed, all the pleading passion vanished. Got squashed down. "Help me, *Teelu*," she said, back to her old staid whisper. "Help me up, if you please. Festina promised me time to get clear, but soon that Sperm-tube will spit out a three-hundred-kilo lobster with big sharp claws."

I stared at her a moment. What had just happened? The woman herself speaking, "Help me," then the Balrog choking her off? Or was it all playacting: the Balrog amusing itself by making me worry, or trying to trick me into something I'd regret?

No way to know. But Kaisho was right about one thing—if Zeeleepull flew out of the tube while she was still in the line of fire, his pincers could spear straight through her. I hurried over to pull her away ... but realized in the nick of time that if I picked her up face-to-face the way her arms were outstretched, her legs would flop into mine when I lifted her. Instead, I slipped behind her, hiked my hands under her armpits, and dragged her backward off the padding.

"This is a damned undignified position for an advanced lifeform," she muttered.

I didn't answer. I was marveling at how light she was ... like a child. Whatever was under the moss on her legs, it didn't weigh half as much as human flesh and bone. Still, it had to be pretty strong—it'd withstood the sploosh into the jelly pad, not to mention me dragging it across the floor. Normal moss would have crumbled to pieces with all that knocking around. Then again, the Balrog wasn't normal moss, was it?

As I set her down, well clear of the landing pillow, Kai-sho reached up and pressed her hand warm against my cheek. "Thank you, *Teelu*," she whispered.

"You shouldn't really call me that," I said. "It's only for queens."

"Ah," she said, kissing her fingers, then brushing them against my lips. "Thank you for clearing that up. *Teelu*."

As we waited for the next person to shoot through the Sperm-tube, I had a chance to check out our surroundings. We'd arrived in the transport bay of a navy starship: a big empty room with an irising entry mouth at one end. The mouth was wide-open, showing the ghostly white Sperm-field outside as it stretched off into the distance—all the way down to the planet. At the moment, the starship would be orbiting tail down; if you pictured the Sperm-tube as a big tornado sucking up things from Celestia's surface, the transport bay was like a bucket at the top of the funnel, ready to catch anything the wind brought us.

The upper part of the bay's back wall was transparent pink-tinted plastic, a window into the control room where someone would be monitoring the transport process. From my angle down on the floor, I couldn't see if anyone was actually up in the room; but safety regs required a qualified operator at the console whenever people Spermed in or out.

It kind of surprised me the person in charge hadn't said a word: no hello, not even a warning for us to get off the landing pad and clear the way for others. I told myself it must take lots of concentration, keeping track of technical details—aligning the Sperm-tube properly so folks flew straight into the ship, maintaining the proper air pressure in the bay so that it was balanced with Celestia's surface— but still, a simple welcome would be nice.

For one thing, I wanted to know what ship this was. There were rainbow-colored trees painted on the walls of the transport bay, but I didn't recognize the trees' species. Something tropical and flowery. At least they weren't willows; and this wasn't one of the conifer ships (*Jackpine*, *Sequoia*, *Golden Cedar*) used as flagships for admirals. That was good. If this'd turned out to be my father's ship, the *Royal Hemlock*, I would have stood in the entry mouth, just praying for Zeeleepull to come through and skewer me.

"Wondering where we are?" Kaisho whispered. Either she'd read my mind, or noticed me staring at the trees painted on the wall. "It's Festina's old ship," she said. "The *Jacaranda*."

Jacaranda? Where Prope was captain? With orders to dump me someplace forgettable? For a second, I wondered if this had all been a giant trick, a way to make me disappear. If they'd decided they couldn't just kidnap me because the Mandasars would make a fuss, why not engineer an excuse for taking me away? Pretend I was going on an important mission, wait a while, then tell the kids on Celestia, "Sorry, your poor *Teelu* had an accident on Troyen, and he's never coming back."

My father would have considered it a neat strategy—get the results you want without causing a public hubbub. But Festina was a different sort of admiral, wasn't she? Someone who'd be honest with a fellow Explorer?

"You don't look so good," Kaisho whispered. "What's wrong?"

"Twenty-four hours ago, the *Jacaranda*'s captain had orders to get rid of me. Do you think anything's changed since then?"

"Yes," Kaisho said. "Festina has taken charge. She's commandeered the ship using an admiral's Powers of Emergency—*pursuing the vital interests of the Outward Fleet*. Which means she's bailing the council's ass out of hot water. Basically, if Festina thinks the top dogs have screwed up so badly they're risking a League crackdown, she has the authority to do *anything* to put things right."

"The other admirals don't mind?"

"The other admirals practically chew out their own livers, but they can't stop her. The League of Peoples demands that our navy behave in a sentient manner. That doesn't mean acting good or moral or decent in human terms; your average high admiral is a loathsome criminal bastard." She looked straight at me. "As you well know, little Jetsam."

My father's not-so-pet name for me. Which meant the Balrog knew exactly who I was. Not that Kaisho seemed to care; she went straight back to telling me what was what.

"The point is," Kaisho said, "the High Council has to obey the letter of the League's law . . . and that includes policing themselves for non-sentient behavior. Last night, Festina contacted Admiral Vincence and said, 'I have reason to believe an inner-circle admiral has condoned cold-blooded murder, and I require the immediate services of a ship to investigate the matter.' In such a situation, the council simply can't stand in her way. If they block her or silence her or even try to slow her down, it's deliberately abetting a possible non-sentient."

Kaisho shrugged. "The most the council can do is work their tails off to prove Festina wrong. If they conscientiously look into the matter and decide her fears are unfounded, they can pull the plug on her. Maybe even demote her or throw her out of the service. But until that happens, they have to let her follow her conscience . . . and they even have to cooperate with her. Festina wants a ship? She gets the closest one available. *Jacaranda*. And to hell with any previous orders that get in the way." She turned her head toward the pink-tinted window high above us. "Isn't that right, Captain?"

There was a three-second silence. Then a voice came over the transport bay's speakers: a voice I'd heard before. "My orders are to cooperate with Admiral Ramos for the duration of the emergency," Captain Prope said frostily. "If those orders cease to be operative, I can't speculate what new instructions I might receive. Or what old instructions might be reactivated."

In other words, I could still get chucked onto an uninhabited planet if Festina got overruled. I was thinking about that when Hib came flying through the Sperm-tail.

23

MAKING OURSELVES
AT HOME

One by one, the Mandasars came up the tube, each in his, her, or its special way.

The workers enjoyed it. They buzzed excitedly among themselves, probably comparing how much they loved getting turned inside out and pulled through a tube five hundred klicks long. (I couldn't tell for sure what they said; they were speaking their own personal patois, made from English and Troyenese, plus words that were likely invented out of the blue. Workers who are raised together always develop private languages that no one else can understand. It drives warriors and gentles crazy.)

Counselor couldn't decide what to make of her trip up the tube. It obviously disturbed the heck out of her, but she wanted to see it as a religious experience: zipping through a universe where her carapace bent like rubber. Gentles have a sort of mystic fear of getting their shells stripped off. If a gentle loses a sizable chunk of armor through disease or injury, she's considered "blessed by the stars" and treated as a prophet . . . the terrifying kind of prophet who's nine-tenths crazy and one-tenth cosmic bliss. (The Troyenese word for "blessed," *ullee*, also means "naked" and "dangerous.") So when Counselor got herself twisted every which way, as if her husk had turned to taffy . . . well, she must have felt scarily, vulnerably open to the Five Gods. I think she believed they'd planted some great revelation inside her, if only she searched her soul hard enough.

No such spark of divine truth for Zeeleepull—he just hated the sensation, pure and simple. A split second after he hit the landing pad, he launched into a long tirade of Mandasar cursing . . . and on those words, his accent was *perfect*. Next thing you know, he'd ripped open the landing pad and there was jelly slurped all over the transport bay. Zeeleepull got real huffy about it being an accident—his claws had spiked through the rubber bag when he landed, and it wasn't his fault how the Sperm-tail spat him out. Me, I think he might have given the bag a deliberate snip during his blue-streak tantrum; but considering Zeeleepull's temper, I kept my opinion to myself.

Festina was the only one left on Celestia . . . and now instead of a nice soft landing pad, she had a wobbly blob of cold wet jelly to smack into. Not a dignified entrance for an admiral, getting buried and glopped up with goo. I hurried forward to clean things, trying to push the slop back into the torn bag; but Kaisho told me not to bother. "Wait," she said. "You underestimate our noble leader."

"But she's going to fly straight into the—"

"No," Kaisho promised. "Not with Prope watching."

And she didn't. The rest of us had come out of the Sperm-tail like people shot from a cannon, no control at all; but Festina emerged like a gymnast nailing a perfect dismount. Two feet slammed on the floor without the tiniest stumble: Festina Ramos, standing straight and calm and balanced, well short of the guck that trembled with the thunk of her impact.

She lifted her eyes to the pinkish window at the back of the transport bay. "Captain Prope," she said evenly. "Admiral on the deck."

"Yes, Admiral," came back Prope's voice. I couldn't see the captain, but I could tell she was gritting her teeth.

*   *   *

The entry mouth of the transport bay irised shut. Moments later, a door in the back wall opened and Phylar Tobit thudded forward, pouchy face beaming. He was half a second away from giving Festina a bear hug when Prope's voice snapped over the speakers. "Explorer Tobit! At attention for greeting an admiral."

Tobit didn't exactly stop, but he slowed down. Then he did a passable job of faking a trip—catching his right foot behind his left leg—so he could tumble into Festina anyway, wrapping his arms around her shoulders as if to break his fall. She laughed and whispered, "Happy birthday, you dirty old man," before giving him a light kiss on the cheek.

"Never the kisses for aliens," Zeeleepull muttered.

I tried to give him a peck on the forehead, but he ducked.

Over the next hour, we got settled in. The two Explorers, Tobit and Benjamin, showed us to our rooms; Captain Prope and an oily lieutenant named Harque put in a token appearance ("Welcome to *Jacaranda*, always an honor to host an admiral, a consort, and a sentient parasite . . ."), but the captain and lieutenant disappeared again almost immediately. ("Needed on the bridge, have to get started for Troyen.") After they were gone, I think Festina murmured, "Good riddance," but I might have misheard.

So the Mandasars got five separate cabins, and left four of the rooms empty so they could all squash into the fifth; Tobit and Festina went off to talk about unspecified old times; Kaisho got a new hoverchair, and amused herself discussing intimate details of her condition, while a terrified Benjamin tried to lift her into place without touching her legs. ("A hundred and ten years old, but I've started menstruating again! I suppose it means I could have a baby . . . if I found the right man. Dear lovely Benjamin, what would you think of having a fuzzy-haired child whose head glowed in the dark?")

Me, I found myself in an exact twin of the room I'd occupied on *Willow*. No big coincidence since cabin design was standardized throughout the fleet, but it still felt a little creepy. As I sat there alone, wondering why I'd agreed to all this, Prope's face appeared on my vidscreen with that half-light half-shadow trick she'd used before. "Attention, all passengers and crew. Now leaving Celestia orbit. Next stop . . ." (dramatic pause) ". . . Troyen."

I was such a bundle of nerves, even such cheap theatrics could give me the chills.

There's a routine you're supposed to follow when you're stationed on a new ship. I wouldn't have remembered it, except that I'd gone through the same thing recently on *Willow*—two women from Communications Corps had walked me through the whole procedure, taking every possible chance to brush against me accidentally on purpose. (The more I thought about it, the more I realized how everyone on *Willow* had been keyed-up to the point of craziness: ten times more wild and impulsive than you got from mere boredom.)

So I went to the cabin's terminal and introduced myself to the ship-soul. Gave my name, rank, and access code so the computer could fetch my records from Navy Central— not that I had much in the way of records, but at least there'd be stuff about the Coughing Jaundice and my allergy to apples. (That ran in the family—my father and sister too. The doctor who engineered Sam and me offered to fix the problem, but Dad ordered it left in. He didn't want his kids snacking down on a nice juicy apple when he couldn't. That tells you something about my dad . . . and it tells you something more that he *told* us what he'd done: "I could have made you perfect, but I didn't want you little brats enjoying yourselves in a way I can't.")

Once I'd given my ID to the ship-soul, I figured it would take a while to get any response—the closest copy of the navy archives was Starbase Iris, a full light-minute away. But the instant I finished the identification process, the ship-soul announced I had a personal, confidential, eyes-only recorded message.

Um.

"Eyes-only" meant no one could read this message before I did . . . despite the long-standing fleet tradition that if *you* belonged to the navy, so did your mail. The only people authorized to send eyes-only messages were admirals; and there were only two admirals likely to care about Explorer Second Class Edward York:

1. Lieutenant Admiral Festina Ramos. But if she wanted to pass me a note, she could just walk down to my room.

2. Admiral of the Gold, Alexander York. My father.

If *Jacaranda* carried a recorded message from Dad, when had he sent it? Probably a while ago . . . when *Jacaranda*'s mission was to make me disappear. I wondered if the message could possibly be an apology: "Sorry we're forced to do this, son, but the Admiralty can't let you go home." No, not much chance of that. More likely, he wanted to call me a disappointment one last time—his final chance before I got dumped somewhere cold and airless.

Well, only one way to find out. "Ship-soul, attend," I muttered. "I'm alone, so you can display the message."

When the video flicked on, I found there was another possible sender I hadn't considered. "Surprise!" said Samantha from the screen.

"Hold!" I shouted. The picture froze.

Sam. It was Sam.

The honey brown hair, the giggly blue eyes, the spatter of freckles across her nose . . . twenty years and she'd hardly aged a day. Heaven knows how she managed to get hold of YouthBoost on a planet at war; but if anyone could manage, it would be Sam.

My twin sister was alive. And that picture of her in my memory, with her gold uniform soaked scarlet . . . the jagged hole punched through her rib cage, gushing out blood . . .

"Tricks," I said aloud. Something was a trick. Either Sam's death long ago, or the picture I was looking at now. Experts could play games with computer images, everybody knew that. I couldn't trust what I was seeing. But who would be cruel enough to send such a thing if it wasn't real? And who had the authority to deliver the message with eyes-only status?

"Ship-soul," I said, "identify message's sender."

"No identification."

"No name? No transmission information? Nothing?"

"Negative. The recording itself is dated by the Troyenese calendar, 23 Katshin."

Which meant Sam had made the recording the day after *Willow* picked me up from the moonbase . . . unless the date was a trick too. Gritting my teeth, I told the ship-soul, "Resume play."

Sam's picture came back to life. "Poor Edward," she said, "I hope you're not having a heart attack or something. This must be an awful shock for you, but you've handled worse stuff than this."

She was talking the way she always did to me, kind of imitating the way I spoke. When she was playing diplomat, Sam could toss off flowery phrases with the best of them, but behind closed doors with me . . . well, I guess a really good diplomat always suits her words to her audience.

If this really *was* Sam. I had to remind myself it could be fake. But a fake by someone who knew exactly how Sam talked to me in private.

"The thing is, Edward," she went on, "I'm still alive. As you can see. It's way too complicated for me to explain right now, but I will someday, I promise. In the meantime, I want to make sure you're all right . . . and that means you have to join me on Troyen."

She reached toward the camera lens and turned it to one side. It swung around to show a golden summer afternoon in a place I knew well—the Park of the Silent God, on the outskirts of Unshummin city: no more than fifteen kilometers from Verity's palace. Sam and I used to go there for walks all the time, especially during the redfish migrations each spring; the park's creek would turn scarlet with thousands of new hatchlings, and the air would fill with the strong smell of sugar-sap, as Mandasars heated cauldrons on the shore. Redfish boiled in sugar-sap . . . we ate that every year, sitting on the creek bank under the diamond-wood trees.

The trees were still there—I could see them in the camera shot. Twenty years taller and thick with green leaves. I always liked those leaves: they were the same color of green as the oaks on my father's estate.

"Not much sign of the war, is there?" Sam said in a soft voice. "That's because it's almost over. One queen has come out on top, and I'm her favorite advisor. By the time you get here, there'll be peace; and I can protect you from those bastards on the High Council of Admirals."

She swiveled the camera lens back and looked straight at me. "If you want the honest truth, Edward, I know everything that's happened to you. I found out about *Willow*, and how they sneaked in to get a queen. The idiots took Queen Temperance, Edward—the last queen who was standing in the way of peace. She's one of the outlaw queens and nearly the most vicious tyrant on the whole planet, even if she has a placid-sounding name.

"So I know what's going to happen," Samantha went on. "*Willow* will pick you up, then head for Celestia. Dumb idea—the moment *Willow* crosses the line, the League of Peoples will execute Temperance and most of the ship's crew. Maybe all of them. You're safe, brother, because there isn't a more innocent person in the entire universe . . . but when *Willow* coasts into Starbase Iris and the navy sees all the corpses, the High Council will have a grade A large conniption.

"Next thing you know, they'll try to get rid of you, Edward. That's how admirals think—when they screw up big-time, their first reaction is to lose the witnesses down some deep hole. And I don't want to let you get lost."

She smiled again: a big bright smile that made me want

to smile back . . . even though a dozen worrying thoughts were nibbling at the back of my mind. If Sam didn't want me getting lost, why had she let me sit on the moonbase for twenty years and never once tried to contact me? If she was the top queen's closest advisor, couldn't Sam have found a way to send a message? But no word at all—no hint she was alive—till suddenly I left the Troyen system, and *that's* when she got in touch.

Like she was happy to ignore me, right up to the point when I headed home.

But the message kept playing, and Sam kept smiling: my smart and pretty sister who taught me everything I knew. "I didn't find out about *Willow* right away," she was saying. "Not till they'd taken you with them. But I'm sending people after you, Edward, to get you back. It turns out I have a starship: a nice black one, run by Mandasar friends. If you want the honest truth, it used to belong to the navy—a sweet little frigate named *Cottonwood*. But, umm . . ." She leaned toward the camera and said in a loud whisper, "I stole the ship, Edward. Just before the war started. I knew the navy would stop all traffic to and from Troyen, and I wanted an escape route in case things got really bad."

"Hold!" I snapped. My sister froze in the middle of a blink, her eyes half-closed and clumsy-looking, the way people always come across in blink-pictures. It was a pretty unflattering shot, but I wasn't so interested in Sam's appearance at the moment.

Not when I knew she had a ship—the black ship that had stolen *Willow*. The ship's crew must have hoped I was still aboard; they'd taken *Willow* in tow so they could drag me back to Troyen.

So: Sam had left me alone on the moonbase for twenty years, but the second she heard I was gone from Troyen airspace, she sent her starship to get me.

And how had Sam *stolen* a starship? I guess it wouldn't be hard; my sister was a high-ranking diplomat, and an admiral's daughter. She could get herself invited on board, maybe with some helpers, then drug people, gas people, mop up with stunners . . . but that wasn't the tricky part. What had she done with the crew members after she'd taken the ship? A frigate carried a crew of a hundred. If you only had to deal with one or two sailors, you might bully or bribe them into silence; but not a hundred people. Someone would refuse to cooperate. Where could Sam put them so they'd never tell the navy what she'd done?

I hoped there was some brilliant answer I was just too dim to figure out—the most obvious possibilities made me go all queasy. *Sam!* I thought, *what did you do?* And why was she cheerily telling me this stuff? Did she think I was so stupid I wouldn't ask questions?

For the tiniest of moments, a thought flicked through my mind: *Yes—there was a time when these questions wouldn't have occurred to me.* But that was scary too and not something to dwell on. I snapped at the ship-soul, "Resume play."

Sam's eyes smoothly finished their blink as she said, "So I'm sending my ship after you. With a bit of luck, you'll still be on *Willow* when *Cottonwood* reaches Celestia— that'll make it easy to bring you back. If not, my crew has to assume you've been transferred elsewhere; so *Cottonwood* will squirt this message to every navy vessel in the Celestia system . . . eyes-only." She gave a girlish grin. "Dad showed me a sort of a kind of a back door into the navy computer system: how to pretend I'm an admiral. The High Council would barbecue him if they found out, but they probably do the same for *their* kids. In case of dire emergencies."

She paused for a moment, then made a big show of looking right and left, as if checking to make sure no one else was listening. It was kind of a code gesture the two of us used as kids—a "just between you and me" thing that meant Sam was going to say something really really important. She leaned back in toward the camera, her eyes bright and piercing. "Okay now, Edward, I want you to listen very carefully." Her words came out so slowly . . . had she always spoken to me like that? "The absolute most crucial thing now is that you get away from the navy. Understand? If people say they're taking you home, don't believe them. Escape, Edward; you have to escape. Don't let them trap you, or hurt you, or put you under a microscope . . ."

Sam's gaze dropped for a second, and she took a breath. Then she looked up again, and said, "I'm going to give you something very valuable, Edward: Dad's special backdoor access code to the navy computer network. You can use it to pretend you're an admiral, a High Council admiral, invoking Powers of Emergency. You'll be able to give orders, look at confidential files, whatever you need. Don't do anything crazy—if you draw too much attention, you'll get in serious, serious trouble—but think smart, and *make sure you escape.*"

Her eyes drilled into me for a moment more; then she relaxed and smiled. "Once you've got away, Edward, come back to me. To Troyen, to the high queen's palace in Unshummin. Okay? Go straight to the palace, and I'll be waiting. It'll be safe and happy like old times. Queen Temperance was the last holdout against the new high queen; with Temperance gone, there's nothing in the way of peace but a few leaderless troops. By the time you get here, Edward, we'll be finished mopping up, and no one will ever have to fight again."

She lifted her fingers to her lips and kissed them, staring straight into the camera the whole while. "Come home, Edward. Come to Unshummin, to the palace. Please. This is where you belong. This is where you can do good. This is where you'll be loved."

Samantha's face stayed on the screen a moment longer . . . and even though she was smiling, there was something saddened about her, as if something hurt inside. Then the image went black and the ship-soul was informing me that the message carried attached data—the backdoor access code. I told the computer to save the code in a file, then slumped back in my chair.

For a long time I just sat there, chewing my knuckle.

24

HAVING A CHECKUP

Sometime later—I don't know how long—a knock came at my door. Not a real knock, of course; the person out there had touched the REQUEST ENTRY plate and the ship-soul had interpreted that signal as knock-knock-knock. You could customize your door signal to anything you want: a bell, a buzzer, a dog barking, whatever suited your fancy. Sam always liked a real knock, soft and deferential, as if the person outside your door was a shy little servant begging permission to take a moment of your time. Naturally, if that was the signal Sam used, I wanted it too. Sort of. I couldn't remember actually asking for the knock, but Sam had programmed it into my permanent navy records, assuming that's what I'd want.

Um. All of a sudden, that bothered me. Maybe I should change the knock to a ding-dong. Or a chime. Or one of those frittery bird-chirp sounds. Except as I thought of all the possibilities, it seemed like a lot of work to choose something new when a knock was perfectly okay.

The knock came again. I looked at the peep-monitor and saw Tobit standing there, glowering into the camera's eye. "Let him in," I told the ship-soul.

Tobit didn't stop glowering as he entered, but he aimed the glare at the room rather than me. "Just like my cabin," he growled, "except you don't have underwear strewn about the floor for convenience." He glanced my direction.

"You settling in okay? Or do you want me to bug the quartermaster for some doodads to brighten the place up? He's got some glass figurines that shatter real nice when you throw them against the wall."

"No thanks." I gave a sideways glance at the vidscreen on my desk, but it'd gone blank. Sam's message must have automatically purged itself from the databanks after playing.

"Well," Tobit said, "if you aren't busy, Festina wants you down in sick bay. Since you've done the do-si-do with hive-queen venom, she wants to make sure you're all right." Tobit rolled his eyes. "I'm supposed to be your escort. In case the poison drops you into a writhing heap and you need to be dragged the rest of the way."

"I'm not going to drop into a writhing heap," I said.

"Glad to hear it," Tobit replied. "I've got a bum arm, and I hate heavy lifting."

He motioned me toward the door. It slid open in front of us ... and I was just about to step out when Tobit grabbed me by the back of my shirt. With a yank that almost ripped the fabric, he jerked me back into the room and spun me around.

My fists came up of their own accord. Wild ideas dashed through my head—like the whole ship had been spying on me while I listened to Sam's message, and now Festina and Prope and everyone intended to get me. I came a millisecond away from punching Tobit straight in his purple-veined nose ... but he backed up fast and pointed at the floor outside my door.

The deck was covered with carpet—this part of the ship was all prettied up for visiting VIPs—and the carpet had a pattern of red jacaranda trees surrounded by multicolored swirls. For a second I couldn't see anything where Tobit was pointing; but then, on one of the jacarandas closest to my door, I saw a little fleck of glowing crimson.

"Ship-soul," Tobit said in a strained voice, "turn off the lights in this corridor."

The passageway went dark—except for five patches of

crimson spores twinkling up from the broadloom. They'd been planted right on five red jacarandas in the carpet's pattern, where they'd be hard to spot and easy to step on.

"Um," I said, swallowing hard.

"Kaisho seems to be exfoliating," Tobit muttered. "I just caught sight of a flicker before you stepped down."

He flumped on the edge of my bed and lifted his feet to check the soles of his boots. No glowing red dots. "Either I was lucky where I walked," he said, "or the Balrog knew better than to bite into me. My bloodstream has enough liquor left over from my drinking days to pickle any damned fungus that tries to take root."

I just kept staring at the glowing specks: one straight in front of my room and two on either side, likely to get stepped on whichever way I turned. "Do you think Kaisho deliberately wanted . . . I mean, it's *my* door . . ."

"York, buddy," Tobit said, "the fucking moss has a bone on for you. Or Kaisho does. Or both. If you try to button-hole her, I'm sure she'll swear it was only a 'darling wee joke.' Only teasing, the spores wouldn't really eat you. Just lick you a bit, then let go . . . the Balrog's way of flirting." He scowled. "Better watch your step, pal—you've got all kinds of conquests drooling over you."

He said that last with a grumbly sort of snappishness: like maybe there was a woman *he* was interested in, except she liked me better. But the only women on *Jacaranda* who'd even seen me were Prope and Kaisho and Festina . . .

Oh.

"Christ," Tobit muttered disgustedly, wiping his boots on my floor, even though the soles were already clean. "Let's call a vacuum cleaner and get the hell out of here. People are waiting for us in sick bay."

I nodded quietly.

"We aren't supposed to do this," the doctor said. Yet another navy kid—in his thirties, but that's pretty young for an M.D. His name was Veresian and he'd just accessed my medical history. "There's a note on York's chart, NO MED-

ICAL EXAMINATIONS EXCEPT IN EMERGENCIES. Certified by the Admiralty. *Certified*."

Festina frowned. "That's ridiculous. Everyone in the fleet gets regular checkups."

"Not quite true, ah, Admiral, sorry," Veresian said. "The navy will make exceptions. Usually on religious grounds—Opters, for instance."

He turned to look at me. The doctor couldn't straight-out ask who or what I worshiped—not with the navy's strict policies on religious tolerance—but Opters are never shy about stating their beliefs. Their god disapproves of all medical treatments; you're supposed to let heaven decide whether or not you recover. (Don't ask me why a god would create a universe full of medicines, then tell you not to use them. Gods have a real fondness for making great stuff and putting it right under your nose, but saying, "If you love me, leave this alone." Kind of like my sister hiding her diary in my room so Dad wouldn't find it.)

By now, everyone in sick bay was looking at me—Veresian, Festina, and Tobit. "I'm not an Opter," I said. "I'm . . . um . . . different."

"You're an Explorer, pal," Tobit replied. "We're *all* different."

But I was *illegally* different. I didn't say that out loud, of course—if there was one thing hammered into my head, it was keeping quiet about how I came to be. Not just because I'd been engineered. If you want the honest truth, I was also a sort of a kind of a clone of my father.

Pretty awful, right? Being *him*.

Of course, I wasn't him exactly—the doctor who designed me started with Dad's DNA, then fiddled with it to make me better. Samantha was exactly the same as me: the same person exactly, our dad's clone, except she got an X chromosome where I got a Y.

Which meant she wasn't the same person at all. Do you know about sex-linked gene deficiencies? Where if you're a girl you're all right, but if you're a boy you don't get built properly? Sam tried to explain it once with big blowup pictures of actual X and Y chromosomes, but I didn't feel much like listening. It couldn't be changed, could it? That was all I needed to know.

Even if Sam couldn't make me understand how my brain went stupid, she sure made it clear I had to keep everything secret. Cloning had been banned for centuries in the Technocracy, and gene manipulation was strictly limited to fixing "catastrophic disorders"—if you just wanted your kids prettier or smarter, you got thrown in jail.

Worse than that, the children were classified "potentially non-sentient" since no one could predict how a DNA tweak would affect "moral character." There were just too many variables to calculate . . . and too many awful examples over the years, people trying to make perfect offspring and ending up with monsters: psychopaths, killers, people whose brains were messed up worse than mine. If the navy knew the truth about Sam and me, we'd never be allowed on a starship again—on the off chance we might suddenly turn crazy and inhuman and non-sentient.

The more I mulled it over, the more I wished I hadn't let Tobit bring me down to the doctor. But I hadn't thought things through fast enough.

Sometimes you just get so *tired* of being slow.

"Um," I said. I knew better than to make up some story of why I shouldn't be examined. Lies get complicated real fast. It would have been nice if Dad had *told* me about the NO CHECKUPS order so I wasn't taken completely by surprise; but of course he hadn't. All I could do was mumble, "My father didn't like doctors looking at me too much. It bothered him."

Festina gave me a sympathetic look. She probably thought my dad was an Opter, and I was all embarrassed about it. "Don't worry," she told me, "if you're allowed to have medical exams in an emergency, I'd say this counts. You've had two doses of hive-queen venom, Edward, and that's serious business. Only a few humans have ever suffered venom poisoning, but several ended up with chronic metabolic imbalances. Isn't that right, Doctor?"

Veresian looked flustered by the question. It's tough being a doctor in the Outward Fleet—every new planet that
humans visit has a thousand diseases nobody's seen before.
The medical databanks have write-ups on millions of ways
to get sick, and for many there've only been three or four
cases ever. Veresian couldn't possibly hold all that information in his head. If he was like other doctors, he looked
up what he needed when he needed it . . . and at this moment, he knew absolutely zero about Mandasar venom.

Too bad. Festina was an Explorer, and Explorers did
their homework.

Veresian mumbled, "Yes, yes, dirty stuff, that venom."
He looked at Festina once more, then decided you seldom
went wrong agreeing with an admiral. "Definitely, we can
say this qualifies as an emergency. Definitely." He turned
to me. "Could you take off your shirt, please, Explorer?"

"Do I have to?"

"Come on," Tobit growled, "forget about your dad hating
doctors. No matter how loony he is, your old man wouldn't
want you to Go Oh Shit."

Going Oh Shit was a term Explorers used for dying. *My
father wouldn't care if I went Oh Shit,* I thought, *as long
as I just went.* On the other hand, Dad *had* let me see a
doctor now and then. And it wasn't like a sign would flash
BIO-ENGINEERED CLONE the moment I hopped onto the examination table. Veresian wouldn't find anything suspicious
unless he went to the trouble of sequencing my entire ge-
nome . . . and why would he do that?

"Okay," I grumbled, and began unbuttoning.

Festina and Tobit watched as the doctor listened to my heart
and looked down my throat. Veresian was just passing the
time—while he mucked about with a stethoscope, sensors
around the room were taking far more detailed readings and
checking them against every possible index in the databanks—but Sam always said people were suckers for personal attention. "Medicine is nine-tenths showmanship,"
she once told me, "just like diplomacy."

The doctor wasn't the only one providing a show. After all, *I* was the one with my shirt off; and neither Festina nor Tobit made a move to leave when the examination started. They weren't gawking or anything, but . . . well, actually, yes, they *were* gawking, particularly when Veresian got me to take deep breaths. I told myself they must come from parts of the Technocracy where people weren't all self-conscious about their bodies. Even so, if the examination headed below the waist, I didn't want a bunch of spectators.

Especially not Festina.

Veresian finished with the simple stuff and went to his terminal to see what the mechanical sensors had found out. While he scanned the readout, I tried not to scratch an itch that all of a sudden flared up on the soft inside of my elbow. I assumed nanites were at work there, sneaking under the skin and sipping blood from my veins—not so different from the eyeball nano that had burrowed into the queen's venom sacs.

All navy sick bays had nanotech squads floating in the air, like little labs for doing blood analysis, taking tissue samples, and that kind of stuff. The medical computers had probably sent microscopic sensors scrambling toward my internal organs, swimming down my throat to lungs or stomach, in search of more data. I wasn't sure how much time they needed to do their jobs—it must take a fair while to *find* the spleen, let alone do a bunch of tests on it—but bit by bit they'd send reports to the main computers, telling how my innards measured up.

"Well," said Veresian after only a few seconds, "well, well, well."

"Well what?" Festina asked.

The doctor glanced at her a moment, then back at the readouts. "There's just . . . ahh . . . maybe it's time to re-calibrate." He thumbed a few dials on the control panel, then gave us a false smile. "Time to run diagnostics on the diagnostics. That happens sometimes."

Festina gave him a look. "How *often* does it happen?"

"Not often but sometimes."

"This goddamned navy," Tobit muttered.

He and Festina looked deeply suspicious, but said nothing. No one in the Outward Fleet was immune to machines going off kilter—not doctors, not Explorers, not admirals—so you had to give Veresian some benefit of the doubt. Tobit watched the doctor play with the control panel, while Festina glowered at no one in particular. Finally, she glanced at me and said, "You're feeling all right?"

"I'm fine."

She gave a half smile. "You look fine." Then she turned away from my bare chest to watch Veresian tinker with his equipment.

Five minutes later, the doctor finished recalibrating, realigning, reprogramming, reinitiating.

Five minutes after that, Veresian swallowed, and said, "There you are, same results as last time. This patient is definitely not human."

25

GETTING DIAGNOSED

For a split second, I felt like dashing out of the room. I didn't; but I opened my mouth, intending to babble something, I don't know what, some cowardly nonsense about it being Dad's fault. Not a word came out—the spirit that sometimes possessed me had taken over, keeping me stone quiet.

"What do you mean, not human?" Tobit demanded. He gave me a quick glance, as if he could verify my race just by looking.

"Every tissue in Explorer York's body has components not found in *Homo sapiens*. Hormones. Enzymes. Protein compounds I can't even classify."

"Do they match other species?" Festina asked. "Balrogs maybe?"

I shuddered at that—both me and whatever was possessing my body. It would be very bad if the Balrog had planted a spore on me, and little Balrog brigades were already romping through my bloodstream.

"Not Balrogs," Veresian said after checking his screen. We all breathed a sigh of relief. "But it's hard to narrow it down much farther than that." He pointed to something on the readout. "This lipid, for example . . . it's not found in humans, but it's reasonably common in alien species. Matches twenty-three sentient races that we know of and billions of lesser creatures from the same worlds."

"Are Mandasars on the list?" I asked calmly. (Not me—the spirit in control of my mouth.)

"Why yes, yes they are," Veresian answered, scanning down his data.

"If you check the other alien compounds," continued the thing inside me, "I think you'll see they're *all* found in Mandasars."

"Hmm. Yes. Yes."

"You think it's the hive-queen venom?" Tobit asked.

"No," I said. "When I was on Troyen, I came down with something they called Coughing Jaundice. Supposedly one of their local microbes. It hung on for a full year—nearly killed me dozens of times. A group of Mandasar doctors improvised a number of treatments . . . including tissue transplants, and filling me up with nano that would prevent the transplants from being rejected."

Veresian's eyes widened. "They transplanted alien tissue into a human? Without killing you? And the transplant can actually survive on human blood nutrients?"

I wasn't sure what-all treatments I'd got, but I figured the spirit could be telling the truth. Over that horrible year, there were so many operations and injections and "Just lie in this machine for a while, Edward," I must have had every medical procedure you could imagine. Of course, I didn't say that to the doctor. I didn't say anything. The spirit in my mouth said, "You know Mandasars. Put enough gentles on a problem, and they come up with brilliant solutions."

The doctor looked at me as if he didn't quite believe it . . . but he should have. Before the war, Troyen had developed the most advanced medical knowledge of any race known to humanity. It was the Mandasars' big area of expertise: they didn't build starships or robots or nanotech, they just specialized in doctoring. Any species, anytime. Which meant they'd invented practically everything in this sick bay, even if Veresian didn't know it. He was too young—Troyen had been out of the picture for twenty years, way longer than this scrawny stethoscoped kid had been practicing medicine.

"If they did that to you," Veresian said, "why isn't there anything on your chart?" He pointed to his vidscreen . . . which I couldn't see because doctors always sit you down at an angle so you can't look over their shoulders. Heaven forbid a patient ever gets to see his own information.

"I guess the records didn't get transferred properly," the thing controlling my mouth replied. "When the war started, we were all so disorganized . . . important documentation might have got lost."

"But if you had this jaundice a full year," Veresian said, "there was plenty of time to file a report. The moment any member of the navy contracts an alien disease, it's mandatory to notify the Admiralty. Direct to HQ, no exceptions."

"Yes," Festina added, "there are League issues involved."

I knew that: the League expected our navy to keep a sharp eye on threats to human life. The High Council couldn't let such things slip between the cracks, or the whole fleet would be accused of willful negligence toward each other's safety.

"Sorry," I said, "I wasn't in any shape to submit a report . . . and I don't know why the others didn't. A breakdown in communications, I guess—everybody in the diplomatic mission must have thought someone else would do it."

That's what the spirit possessing me said. But in my heart I knew it was no accidental slip-up. Sam was in charge of the mission, and in charge of me. Filing the report was her job, and apparently, she hadn't done it.

Why? Because she didn't want official navy doctors getting involved, checking me out, discovering my tailored DNA? Or . . .

Something flickered in my brain, then disappeared.

The doctor spent another hour puzzling over my anatomy, but didn't make much progress. As far as he could tell, the two doses of venom hadn't caused any obvious damage; but since he didn't know what my normal chemical balance

should be, he couldn't say if my body had gone haywire
or if I was flat on the bubble.

"You're almost three percent Mandasar now," he said in
a voice full of wonder, "and frankly, frankly, I couldn't
begin to make a prognosis. The venom wasn't as alien to
you as it would be for a normal human. That could mean
your body has a better chance of shrugging the poison off
. . . but it could also mean the poison will have more long-
term effects because your body is responsive to it. The purpose of venom is to change Mandasar metabolisms. Three
percent of you could be mutating like crazy, and I wouldn't
know the difference."

That wasn't so very comforting.

Veresian told me to come back the next day to see if
anything had changed. I said all right, but was already going over excuses for getting out of it. (By then, it was me
doing my own talking again—the spirit possessing me must
have got bored and taken off.)

The doctor also asked if I'd submit to a complete phys-
iological study for scientific purposes. I was an astounding
case and should be written up in some journal. For that,
he'd need my permission to go public . . . and I refused
point-blank. If he did a full examination, he'd surely learn
stuff about my genes that I'd rather keep secret.

Finally, the doctor demanded Kaisho come down and
certify me as sentient: I wasn't human, I wasn't Mandasar,
and considering what happened to *Willow*, Veresian refused
to take chances. Tobit grumbled, "Aww, Doc, York's a
sweetheart," but Festina said it couldn't hurt to get me
double-checked.

"You don't mind, do you, Edward?" she asked. "Better
safe than sorry."

"Sure," I said . . . as if it didn't bother me that Festina
trusted Kaisho more than me. Tobit and I had told all about
the spores planted outside my room—but I guess Festina
didn't care if Kaisho tried to Balroggify dumb old Edward.
Kaisho was sentient; maybe I wasn't.

Five minutes later, Kaisho stood in front of me, hair

completely covering her eyes. It only took a moment before she said, "He looks fine." Then she laughed. "You don't know how fine he is."

Veresian didn't seem all that reassured.

Tobit walked me back to my cabin. He didn't talk much, but he stayed to help me check for Balrog spores, inside the room and out. We got the ship-soul to drop the lights almost to nothing, making it easier to see any glowing red specks . . . which is why we were practically in pitch-blackness when Tobit began to speak, low and gruff, from the opposite side of the room.

"I peeked over the doc's shoulder as he checked your records," Tobit mumbled, as if he was talking to himself. "That note about NO MEDICAL EXAMINATIONS? It was tagged onto your file twenty-one years ago. Long after you first enlisted. Which makes me think your father had nothing to do with it."

I stared stupidly at him in the darkness. "What do you mean?"

"Twenty-one years ago," Tobit repeated. "Wasn't that the same time you picked up the pox on Troyen?"

I nodded. And swallowed hard.

"So not only did your pals on Troyen fail to report you were sick," he said, "someone hacked your medical records to keep folks from learning what happened to you. Someone snaffled you with that NO CHECKUP crap so navy doctors wouldn't find out you were three percent Mandasar. And whoever did it was either an admiral or someone who could fake Admiralty authorization." Tobit's face was completely lost in shadows. "So what's the story, York? Who jerked you around? Do you know?"

"No," I answered—glad it was too dark for him to see my face, because one look would have showed I was lying.

There was only one person who could have faked up everything: never filing the proper reports and using Dad's backdoor access to tag my medical records.

Why, Sam, why?

26

EATING AT THE CAPTAIN'S TABLE

Since it was the first night of a new voyage, Captain Prope held a formal dinner in the lounge—the kind of dinner where people wear dress uniforms and try to act gracious. Everyone moves a bit more slowly; talks a bit more *expressively*; keeps conversation on "social" topics, instead of the usual, "What blazing idiot designed those damned fuel filters?"

Me, I wasn't so good at witty repartee. I'm not much of a talker at the best of times, and it didn't help that *Jacaranda*'s onboard clock was way off my current day-night cycle. My brain was still synchronized with the shifts on *Willow* . . . so dinner at 8:00 P.M. *Jacaranda* time felt more like three in the morning for me.

The problems of space travel that no one ever talks about.

The VIPs had to eat at the captain's table: Festina because she was an admiral, Kaisho because her legs were the most advanced species on the ship, and me because . . . well, maybe Prope wanted to keep me under close watch. Not so long ago, she'd been ready to dump me on some ice moon; and I was still a man who knew too much.

The Mandasars had a table of their own right beside us.

Naturally, it was lower than ours—only a few centimeters off the floor, with passable dining pallets laid all around. That had to be the work of Tobit and Benjamin: Explorers are always the ones stuck with figuring out how to make aliens comfortable. (Explorers spend a lot of time learning about alien customs; knowledge like that helps you survive on strange planets. You'd be surprised how many races will slit your throat over bad table manners.)

As for Tobit and Benjamin themselves, they were stuck at the back someplace, rubbing elbows with the enlisted. Since Festina, Kaisho and I sat at the head table, Prope must have decided there were plenty of Explorers on display already.

Festina sat on Prope's right: the position of highest honor and the only possible place to seat a visiting admiral. For some reason I got the second best spot, on the captain's immediate left. Next to me was that smarmy fellow Harque, who seemed to hold some privileged status aboard *Jacaranda*, even though he was only a lieutenant. Much-higher-ranking personnel—the chief engineer, the commander of Security, even the XO—all got shunted off to other tables. Maybe they had enough clout to *ask* for those seats; Harque was the one stuck under the steely gaze of both a captain and an admiral.

For the first part of the meal, Prope aimed most of her attention at Festina, trying to wheedle juicy gossip about power struggles on the High Council. The captain was one of those people who went all oozy with charm when she wanted something. She had a pretty good touch with it too—all warm and winning, so you found yourself smiling even when you knew it was only an act. The secret was that Prope herself didn't realize she was an awful hypocrite; she thought this was as genuine as anyone ever got. I'd seen the same thing in diplomats: honestly believing they were paragons of truth because they thought everybody else was a bigger liar than they were.

Festina didn't work nearly as hard on the social niceties as Prope. One word answers. No little stories about the time a Myriapod ambassador gave birth at the breakfast table. I got the feeling Festina had some grudge against Prope, one she'd been nursing a long time; she was making an effort not to be petty, but refused to go any farther than frostily polite.

As for the actual content of the conversation—like which high admiral said what to whom during a recent summit on some race called the Peacocks—I sleepily let it pass by till Prope asked me, "So what did your father think of it all?"

I jerked awake. Felt myself blushing. Prope knew who I was; and as I glanced around the table, Harque smirking, Festina looking grim, Kaisho hidden behind her hair but tilting her head to one side as if she was eager to hear my answer—I realized they *all* knew. Since I'd come aboard, they must have had time to look over my navy records.

Dumb me: I should have expected they'd check. Smart people learn who they're dealing with. I just wished . . . I don't know. I wished I could have stayed Edward York instead of becoming Alexander York's son. Especially with the way Festina felt about High Council admirals.

"Um," I said. "Um. My father has never told me what he thinks about anything. Except maybe when he was talking to somebody else and didn't notice I was in the room. I haven't heard a word from him in the past twenty years; and even back then, he sent letters to my sister, not me. After Sam died . . ." I stopped, remembering Sam wasn't dead. "My father and I aren't close," I mumbled, hoping folks would leave it at that.

Prope didn't. "Frankly, I'm astounded," she said, "that you and your dad are . . . estranged." She gave me a sympathetic smile. Prope's kind of sympathy anyway. "You look so much like him, you know. A chip off the old block. Only better—more handsome."

She laughed lightly. I tried to laugh too, but didn't do such a great job; no matter how stupid you are, you get good at spotting when someone is flirting with you. If you don't flirt back, you're being rude, or a prig. Except that I never think fast enough to toss off sexy banter, especially when I don't *feel* sexy. (If you really want to snare me into bed, convince me you're lonely, not coy.)

So for a second, I just sat there with no idea what to say. I didn't want to talk about my father, and I *definitely* didn't want to talk about being handsome. Then I found myself replying, "Sorry, Captain, but the real chip off the old block was my twin sister Samantha. Another case of 'my father's looks only better'—stupendously better, almost as beautiful as the lovely ladies here at this table—but Sam inherited Dad's personality too. His force of will. Which I'm afraid led her to a bad end."

"You have our sympathies, Your Majesty," Kaisho whispered. She stressed *Your Majesty* just a bit, not sarcastically but pointedly. As if she knew she was talking to more than boring old Edward York, Explorer Second Class.

Yes. I'd been possessed again—a backseat passenger watching someone or something else take the wheel. *Almost as beautiful as the lovely ladies here at this table . . .* I'd never say something like that. I wondered why Festina didn't demand, "What's wrong with you?" Even if we'd only known each other a single day, she should have noticed the difference. But she just said, "Tell us about your sister, Edward. What really happened to the mission on Troyen?"

The thing controlling me was only too happy to give its version of those long-ago days . . . a version filled with jokes and sly asides, many of them directed toward Prope. "Oh Captain, you should have seen . . ." "If only I could have shown you . . ." "Perhaps someday we can walk through the . . ." Nudging her on the good parts, making Troyen's descent into war sound like a series of silly missteps and goofed-up blunders rather than a desperate fight to avoid a fight.

As the spirit possessing me made Prope's eyes gleam, smirking over tales of disintegration, I thought about what really happened. The truth.

* * *

What really happened were the wrong ideas at the wrong time. I guess that's an old, old story in human history, and it's just as common in other parts of the galaxy.

Mandasars were genetically programmed for monarchy . . . anyone could see that. But not everyone could accept it. Least of all some of the races who started visiting once Troyen joined the League of Peoples.

You know what I'm talking about—you've probably watched *The Evolution Hour* at least once, where that purple Cashling with the high-pitched voice yells at everybody how Totally Selfish Anarchy™ is the only way for any race to advance up the ladder of sentience. Then there are those "free sensuous VR experiences" that really just send you to a Unity Arcana Dance, and the "traveling art shows" that the Myriapods think will inspire you to reject the decadent Culture of Entertainment they say has poisoned human civilization. A lot of aliens are fanatically determined to make humans see the error of our ways.

But humans have always had it easy compared to the Mandasars. We never pissed off the Fasskisters.

The same way Mandasars specialized in medical stuff, the Fasskisters specialized in robotics. You wouldn't think there'd be much overlap between the two fields, but there is. Fasskister robots have a lot of biological components, because there are fancy things you can do with organic chemistry that are real hard to match with electronics. The other place medicine meets cybernetics is the whole area of nanotech: doctors really love teeny microscopic robots that can get inside a person's body, snip away at tumors, scrape guck out of arteries, that kind of thing.

So Troyen always had tons of trade with the Fasskisters—selling sophisticated new tissues for use in robots, and buying smart little nanites for doctorish tricks. Both Mandasars and Fasskisters should have been happy with the booming business . . . except for one tiny problem: Fasskisters can't *stand* royalty. It drives them positively manic.

A long time ago the Fasskisters had royals of their own,

a whole separate caste like Mandasar queens; and overall these rulers were pretty decent types, competent, generous, not too tyrannical. In fact, that was the problem. One day, someone from the League of Peoples showed up and declared that the royals were sentient, but the commoners weren't. Next thing you know, most of the noble caste left the home planet for upscale homes in the stars. The normal folks who were stuck behind got so mad they killed the nobles who stayed and swore they'd never tolerate monarchy again. Even after the commoners got civilized enough to be accepted into the League (a thousand years later), the Fasskisters were still totally rabid on the subject of crowns and thrones and palaces.

Samantha said it was a big psychological thing: the Fasskisters still had this bred-in drive to be ruled by royals, but they felt all betrayed and abandoned by their leaders, so they overcompensated with aggressive antimonarchical something or other. Like humans who don't have a mother, and feel this big hole in their lives, even if they have kindly nannies and all the toys in the world.

So no matter how much the Fasskisters depended on Troyen for trade, they just couldn't stomach the idea of queens. In fact, they took every possible chance to rabble-rouse, preaching how a democratically elected parliament— or a republic or an oligarchy or technocracy or even a random selection of two hundred people from the Unshummin census database—could run the planet better than High Queen Verity and the three lower queens.

This stirred up trouble . . . not a lot at first, because Mandasars pretty well ignored what the Fasskisters said, but as time went on, the Fasskisters learned how to play on the natural discontents of the people. Whenever anything went wrong for the Mandasars—a deal falling through, a tissue graft that didn't hold, natural disasters, or even just at the end of a long slogging workday—you might find a Fasskister there, whispering how the queen was to blame.

Naturally, it made the queens furious. Several times they expelled the worst of the troublemakers, but that was bad for business. Not only did it sour trade with the Fasskisters, but it upset other races too: Troyen wasn't "alien-friendly." So mostly the queens had to let it go—grumble to themselves as they kept their claws tight shut and their stingers tucked away.

But they still hated it. In the end, they approached a third party to see if anyone could get the Fasskisters to back off.

Enter a small diplomatic mission, headed by Samantha York of the Outward Fleet.

First day on the job: an official reception in the Great Hall of Verity's palace in Unshummin city. It was a huge space, three stories high with mezzanine galleries, and long enough to hold an Olympic javelin throw . . . but no artificial lights at all. Instead, the place was filled with *Weeshi*, a bioengineered insect that was like a firefly with no flicker. Little glass dishes of sugar water were hung overhead to feed the *Weeshi*, so light tended to concentrate around the dishes; but there were still plenty of *Weeshi* just flitting about on their own—like tiny roving stars glittering in every direction.

In honor of us navy folks, the room was swathed in a turquoisy blue that Verity had designated the caste color of *Homo sapiens*. (Mandasars felt sincere pity that humans didn't have a set color scheme—we were all different skin tones, not to mention shades of eyes and hair—so Verity insisted on giving us official title to that turquoisy blue. That way, we wouldn't feel all bashful and inadequate among people who had a real caste color.)

I didn't look so bad in turquoisy blue. Sam, of course, looked fabulous . . . especially since she was wearing the color in a slinky evening gown with one skintight sleeve and the other arm bare. Sam had our outfits made before we left New Earth; and I can't tell you how snippish other diplomats got, that no one else was told about dressing in that color. They were all stuck with a bunch of ugly shapeless jumpsuits made by Mandasar tailors. (The tailors knew that *Homo sapiens* had two arms, two legs, and a head, but that was pretty much the limit of their familiarity with the human form.)

Since it was our first official function, my sister kept me close to make sure I didn't get into trouble; but I couldn't really tell what she thought I might do. Go dance in the fountains that were spritzing up turquoisy blue water? Munch on the turquoisy blue floral arrangements? Climb the turquoisy blue draperies that had been hung on the walls and the ceiling and the stair-ramps, so that the whole place looked like a sea grotto lined with velveteen?

No—I knew how to behave in public. It was the Fasskisters who needed a lesson in manners . . . because they came dressed as hive-queens.

You may have noticed I haven't described what a Fasskister looks like. There's a reason for that: even today, I've never seen one in the flesh. Whenever they go out among other species—and maybe even on their homeworld, for all I know—they always ride inside custom-made robots. Really. When they visit New Earth, they show up in android thingies, pretty humanish-looking except they have big chests the size of beer barrels. Those chests are basically cockpits; the Fasskister sits inside and drives the machine, making the legs walk and the arms move and the mouth chatter away on the bad points of royalty. You never see the Fasskister itself, just its robot housing.

Of course, lots of folks speculate on what Fasskisters look like. The species has to be pretty small to fit inside those chests . . . the size of an otter or a big barn cat. Most diplomats on our mission believed Fasskisters were nothing but great big brains: the rest of their bodies withered up shortly after birth, and their robot shells provided everything necessary to keep the brains alive. Samantha thought this theory was too tame—that the old brain-in-a-box cliché was melodramatic hooey, and the truth was probably a lot stranger and more interesting—but neither she nor anyone else could say for certain.

One thing everybody knew was that Fasskisters could change robot bodies whenever they wanted; and on that first

night of our mission to Troyen, all the Fasskisters came in
identical mock-ups of a Mandasar queen—each full-size
and sulphur yellow, with four working claws, bright green
venom sacs, and a brain hump even bigger than Verity's.

As if that weren't bad enough, they all came reeking of
royal pheromone . . . which none of us humans could smell,
but which practically paralyzed every Mandasar but the
high queen.

Royal pheromone is a special scent queens can produce
at will. One whiff is enough to reduce other Mandasars to
trembling wrecks—barely able to think straight, and pathetically eager to do whatever the queen tells them. Like
an obedience drug you inhale. It takes a heck of a lot of
self-control for any Mandasar to resist it, and most don't
even try. After all, why would you disobey your rightful
ruler?

Verity hardly ever used the pheromone herself; she
thought it was beneath her dignity, doping her subjects into
submission. Almost no one in the palace had ever smelled
the stuff before, till the Fasskisters doused themselves like
it was cheap perfume. Heaven knows how the Fasskisters
reproduced the pheromone—maybe a secret team of nanites
hung around Verity till she produced some, after which the
nanites carried a sample home for analysis. However they
did it, the Fasskisters had obviously worked out the formula
to perfection . . . because every last warrior, worker, and
gentle dropped belly down and groveled as the Fasskisters
pranced into the hall.

Every voice fell quiet. No sound but the babble of fountains and the slow thud of feet as the Fasskisters came forward. The six of them stepped over each prostrate body in
their way, walking up to the silver dais that Verity used as
a throne. I had no experience reading Mandasar facial expressions back then, but any fool could see the queen was
almost homicidally furious. Any second, I could imagine
her saying, *To hell with sentience and the League of Peoples, these Fasskister fucks are going down.*

That's when Samantha stepped forward, straight in front

of the Fasskisters, between them and the throne. I stayed right at Sam's side, determined to protect my sister for the full second and a half it would take the queen to kill me. The two of us stood bang in the middle, with six elephant-sized robots to our right, and a seething Verity, just as big and up on a meter-high dais, to our left. I felt small and surrounded, outnumbered and overshadowed . . . so it was a darned good thing I had absolute confidence Sam would fix everything with a few clever words.

"My job," she said, "is to get people to talk. When people aren't ready to talk . . ." She turned toward the Fasskisters. "When they just want to piss everybody off and deliberately cause *scenes* . . ." Sam reached into her handbag. "Then you need a way to catch their attention."

She pulled out a small globe of glass crystal. Every eye in the room followed her hand as she passed the globe to me. Under her breath, she murmured, "Break it."

For a second I hesitated—I hated all the fuss whenever I broke something—but Sam was smarter than me and must know what she was doing. With a sudden clap of my hands, I smashed the globe between my palms.

Glass tinkled down to the floor. Little drops of my blood fell too, though my palms were callused enough from martial arts that I didn't get cut too badly. What I felt more clearly than the shards of glass digging into my skin was a kind of fuzziness in the air between my fingers: nano.

I lifted my arms and spread them wide, feeling blood trickle down my wrists; but I could imagine the teeny nanobots fanning out, zipping toward the Fasskisters who loomed above us.

The closest Fasskister must have known enough to worry about what the crystal held—Fasskisters of all people know about nanotech weapons—so the big queen robot tried to take a step back. The body moved, but the legs stayed where they were, quietly separating themselves from the main shell. With a muffled thud, the robot's body clumped onto the turquoisy blue carpet. The legs stayed standing a heartbeat longer, then toppled sideways away from the body, like tent poles flopping down from a collapsed tent.

Some of the other Fasskisters tried to get away; the rest stayed rooted to the spot, maybe thinking they'd be all right if they didn't move. But it didn't matter. Within ten seconds, the legs fell off every queen robot there, leaving the big yellow machines (and their drivers) stuck high and dry in the middle of the hall.

Verity's antennas and whiskers slowly relaxed from anger into a very satisfied smile. The other Mandasars, noses still full of royal pheromone, stayed quivering on the floor till she said to them, "Laugh."

The room erupted into sound—kind of like human snickering, not loud but intense, with much waving of antennas and clacking of claws. A bunch of warriors dragged the broken robots out of the palace and took them to Diplomats Row, where the legless queens were left on the curb outside the Fasskister embassy. Meanwhile, Verity showered praises on Sam and me, declaring us Beloved Companions of the Throne.

Our first night in the Great Hall might have won Verity's friendship, but it sure didn't soothe the bad feelings between Troyen and the Fasskisters. Things got worse ... especially because Fasskisters began to use their royal pheromone all around the planet. In a business meeting with Mandasar manufacturers, they might let a bit of the pheromone loose "just to aid in negotiating a fair deal." There were also rumors of pheromone bombs being triggered in taverns or schoolrooms, and someone telling the gas-shocked Mandasars to rebel against the queen.

I don't know if such things really happened; but rumors started circulating, and next thing you knew, Fasskister warehouses were getting burned by Mandasar vigilantes. The Fasskisters reacted by protecting their properties with really nasty security stuff, not quite lethal but pretty darned near—poisons that could cause permanent nerve damage, booby traps designed to cripple, flash bombs so bright they blinded every Mandasar within range, including innocent bystanders.

As time went on, Sam negotiated agreements to ease the tensions, but nothing ever stuck. Troublemakers were jailed or kicked off planet; then more troublemakers took their place.

Of course, kicking rabble-rouser Fasskisters off Troyen caused problems of its own. A lot of times, when the Fasskisters had a chance to cool off and think, they'd begin to doubt whether their behavior had been 100 percent sentient. Pretty soon, the banished Fasskisters turned pure terrified how they'd acted "without due concern for sentient life," and they moaned they'd surely be killed by the League if they left the Troyen system. Our navy ended up paying the Fasskisters to build themselves an orbital habitat close to Troyen's sun—part of some settlement Sam brokered, as the Technocracy tried to keep both Troyen and the Fasskisters happy.

Why did the Technocracy bother with the expense? Because humans needed Mandasar medical technology and Fasskister robotics. Once we got involved in the mess, we couldn't walk away without infuriating both our trading partners. And as the situation on Troyen got worse, we all still thought the bickering could be sorted out with just one more formal accord.

Sure.

In one of those accords, I got married to Queen Verity. Sometimes I think Sam set it up as a joke—so she could claim to be the only twenty-fifth-century human who'd arranged a diplomatic marriage. She also had a great time teasing me about snuggling up to an elephant-sized lobster . . . which I didn't actually do, not in any sexual way.

Unlike gentles, queens don't go into egg-heat on a nine-year cycle. Instead, they produce an egg once every twelve weeks; at the right time, they grab themselves a warrior, do what has to be done, then forget about sex till the next egg comes along. In other words, queens are nearly as platonic as gentles: when they have sex, it's about fertilizing eggs, not, um . . . well, about all the things that sex is about with humans. Since I was the wrong species, Verity would never even *think* about me at such times.

(Then again, she gave me all those maidservants to sleep with. It never occurred to me before this very second, but maybe she thought I might want to . . . um.)

I haven't said much about the other queens: Fortitude, Honor, and Clemency. They each had their own huge continents to rule, like provincial governors who answered to the high queen. The lesser queens were never too happy being subservient, but they'd got along okay till things turned tense with the Fasskisters. Then the whole political order started to fall apart. When the world goes to pot, queens have this natural instinct to boss folks around. It doesn't matter whether they have any good ideas to deal with the crisis, they're just absolutely convinced they must *take charge*.

That's what happened with the Fasskister mess: clampdowns on the Fasskisters, or the Mandasars, or both. While Verity sat in Unshummin and tried to keep everyone cool, the lesser queens ached to exert their own power. Next thing you knew, each lesser queen had created a secret police force to deal with the troubles . . . and these forces were made up of segregated warriors.

Segregated: kept in separate barracks, where they didn't interact with workers or warriors. In troubled times, the queens said, it was important to have elite squads of soldiers who would take orders without asking the tiniest questions. Maybe some bleeding hearts would condemn this as brainwashing, but it was just so darned *efficient*.

Verity had to tread softly—if she angered the lesser queens too much, they might revolt outright. Lesser queens had rebelled against the high queen before. So maybe a few segregated warriors weren't so bad. And after that, what was wrong with segregating workers in key industries, to make sure production didn't decline? And segregating a few gentles to use in think tanks, because they were so much more focused when not distracted by family.

You get the idea: the thin edge of the wedge prying Troyen apart. But law and order still might have survived if someone hadn't cracked open the frozen queens.

Just outside the grounds of the high queen's palace stood the Royal Cryogenic Center: storehouse for the next generation of Troyen's rulers. The thing was, only an existing queen could create a new queen, by nursing a six-year-old gentle girl for a full year. Then what did you do? It was really really dangerous to have queens hanging around when there was no land for them to rule—that'd just be asking for trouble.

In olden days, the solution was usually for a queen to avoid suckling up a successor till very late in life—by the time the new queen was ready to rule, the old queen would likely be dead anyway. But anyone can see how many things can go wrong: a queen might die before she creates an heir; the queen might create an heir but die before the girl is old enough to take over; the old queen might actually live a long long time, leaving the younger queen seething and plotting a coup.

So the modern approach was for queens to produce heirs whenever they wanted, let the girls grow to age eighteen under the guidance of their mothers, then freeze the kids into suspended animation till one of the old queens died. This made sure there were always young queens ready to take over, but kept them from interfering with their seniors. Even if the junior queens weren't too happy being put on ice, they accepted it as a reasonable compromise—it guaranteed that sometime down the road, maybe two or three generations after she was born, each queen would have her full chance to reign, without having to fight other claimants to the throne.

All well and good . . . till the night when I was woken by a huge whacking explosion near the palace.

I leapt out of bed and shouted something stupid like,

"What was that?" But the maidservant who'd been keeping me company didn't answer: she just lay there trembling like a scared rabbit. By then, I knew the symptoms well enough—even if I couldn't smell it myself, there must be a ton of royal pheromone wafting through the air. The pheromone couldn't have come from Verity, since she was gone on a visit to Queen Fortitude; I suspected the Fasskisters had set off a big old gas bomb somewhere close by, and they were now up to no good in the palace.

The palace guard had learned to take precautions against pheromone attacks, with gas masks part of their standard equipment and a few airtight security control rooms. I ran to the nearest of those rooms to see what was going on; the sergeant on duty told me the explosion wasn't in the palace itself, but the Cryogenic Center next door. That was very bad . . . especially since the palace forces couldn't spare many people to check out the situation there. They were afraid the big boom was just a diversion to draw guards outside the walls, while the real target was the palace.

In the end, I ran to the Cryogenic Center by myself. Well, not by myself—I didn't have a squad of warriors backing me up, but I sure wasn't the only person hurrying to see what the explosion had done. Half the folks from Diplomats Row were racing in the same direction, Divians, Myriapods, even a thing that looked like a tumbleweed with eyestalks. Me, if I'd been a diplomat, I would have stayed in a nice safe embassy rather than going to gawk at the latest act of terrorism in a not-quite-declared war; but diplomats are real big fans of viewing atrocities close-up, and maybe getting their pictures taken in the process.

By the time I got to the Cryogenics building, my sister was already standing outside, staring at a big hole in the wall. Gushers of steam poured out through the gap, so thick you couldn't see a thing inside . . . but you could hear sounds like metal clanging and stuff getting thrown against other stuff. Someone in there was making a real mess.

"Fasskisters?" I whispered to Sam.

"Looks like their handiwork," Sam told me, not whispering at all. She didn't seem to care if other bystanders heard every word she said. "First, pheromones to neutralize the locals. Then a bomb attack against young queens . . . frozen and unable to defend themselves. This has Fasskister written all over it."

I stared at the steam pouring out into the night. "Maybe we should go in and see if someone needs help."

Sam looked thoughtful for a moment, then said, "All right."

We moved forward . . . and the crowd of gawkers parted to let us through. I think they were eager to see someone go inside: just not eager to be the ones to do it. Sam let me go ahead—I was the bodyguard, wasn't I, the one who should take the lead—so I was the one who stuck my hand, slowly and carefully, into the steam.

It was dry and very cold . . . not water steam at all, but some other chemical. Cold enough that real water ice was forming on the street under our feet; I could see my footprints in the frost as I walked forward. I could also see footprints, real human footprints, of someone who'd come out of the building sometime not so long ago—if it'd been more than a minute or two, the footprints would have got frosted over again.

I turned to Sam. The steam was already icing her hair with frost. "Did you see anyone come out of the building before I got here?"

She shook her head. "No. Why?"

I just shrugged. Someone else could investigate this whole business later on, someone smarter than me. Dumb old Edward shouldn't put on airs, thinking he'd found a Big Important Clue. Better just to stick to what I was good at: blundering into trouble.

Close to the hole, it was possible to see a little way forward through the steam—nothing distinct, just some bright light inside, and a shadow moving in front of it. The clanging noises were still going on, and something that sounded like ripping. "Maybe you should stay out here," I told Sam. "It might not be safe."

"Then it's not safe for you either," she answered.

"I'll just—"

She grabbed my arm and yanked me back. "Fasskister!" she shouted.

Coming forward through the steam was something big and yellow, backlit by the light inside. For a moment, I thought it *was* a Fasskister, dressed in one of those queen-shaped robots. The thing had a jerky movement, not like the walk of a real queen... but then I started to wonder how a real queen would walk if she was cold and stiff from years in cryogenic storage.

I pulled Sam to one side, out of the steam, out of the path of a queen who might be mad at the way she'd been woken up.

The queen came slowly out onto the pavement, ice still coating much of her shell. Any lesser creature wouldn't have been able to move; but it takes more than a layer of ice to stop a full-fledged Mandasar hive-queen. She was young, she was strong, she was a flaming saffron yellow far brighter than middle-aged Verity... and she was spitting with rage.

"*Sissen su?*" she hissed. Who did this?

"It might have been Fasskisters," Sam answered in Mandasar, "but we have no definite—"

"Fasskisters!" the queen roared. "Alien saboteurs?"

"We don't know that," said a Myriapod back in the crowd. "Troyen has several factions who have resorted to violence in the past..."

"And the high queen permits this?" the young queen asked. "Is she an utter fool?"

"Verity's real smart," I said. "Things are just kind of complicated."

"No," the queen snapped, glaring at me. "Things are very simple. Someone has committed an act of wanton destruction, right outside the high queen's palace... and all I see are outsiders come to leer at the chaos. Where is the queen herself?"

"Um," I said in a weak voice. "She's visiting Fortitude in Therol."

"Leaving a vacuum in leadership here at home. Ridiculous! Appalling! How could she let this planet get so out of hand?" The queen took a deep breath. "Clearly, this Queen Verity is unfit to rule. It's my duty to set things right."

The young queen smashed her claws together the way queens do when declaring an edict—kind of like a human clapping hands imperiously. The action knocked off chunks of ice that had collected on her claws; chips of snow flew in all directions, spraying over Sam and me. By the time I'd wiped my eyes clear, the queen was stomping off into the darkness, leaving a trail of meltwater.

"Um," I said. Which was when another queen staggered her way out of the steam, her face fuzzy white with frost. "*Sissen su?*" she growled.

Twelve queens in all—every one that'd been sitting in cryosleep, dreaming of claiming a throne. None of them was interested in waiting a single instant longer, now that they were free. They all had the same reaction as the first one: Verity was doing a lousy job, and it was up to them to fix everything. After a while, it got kind of funny, listening to them say the same things. "It's my *duty* to set things right."

Even then, I knew better than to laugh.

The unfrozen queens didn't hang around Unshummin. Within hours they were spread all over the planet and within days, each had claimed a group of soldiers to protect herself: well-equipped soldiers from existing armies, won over by pheromones and promises and charisma. Remember that the Fasskisters had spent years on their whispering campaign, preaching how Verity and the lower queens were doing a lousy job running the planet. When a new bunch of queens came along as a fresh alternative, a lot of folks were keen to give them a try.

As for Verity . . . that's when she finally lost heart. In public, she was still the tough old queen, in control and able to face down all opposition; but at night, she'd just sit in her private chambers, staring at the wall. Sometimes I sat with her; sometimes Sam did; sometimes the queen wanted to be alone.

A month after the mess at the Cryogenic Center, I got summoned to the queen's bedroom. Sam was already there, plus a shy little Mandasar girl I'd seen around the palace now and then—one of Verity's many children, which kind of made her my stepdaughter. I'd tried to keep track of all the kids' names, but with Verity laying an egg every twelve weeks it got tricky to remember after a while. I thought this girl was called Listener, with the hidden name Yeerlevin; but Verity introduced her as Innocence.

That was the kind of name only given to queens. Which pretty much told me what was going on. It would soon be that week in spring when Verity's venom cycle started. In previous years, the high queen had always been too busy to nurse a successor; now, she was going to do it, because she might not have another chance.

My sister and Verity wanted Innocence to be a big secret. With twelve outlaw queens already terrorizing the countryside, people might not appreciate Verity mothering up another contender for power. If word got out, a lot of folks would also take it as a sign Verity didn't expect to live too much longer . . . which was absolutely true, but it would still wreck public confidence. Finally, if the other queens heard about little Innocence, they'd see her as a perfect target for kidnapping, holding hostage, all that stuff—not just now, but for a long time to come, till the girl could take care of herself. She was only six; after a year of nursing with Verity, Innocence might brighten from gentle brown to royal yellow, but she'd still just be a seven-year-old with a lot of growing to do.

So Sam and I were going to be the girl's *glashpodin*:

like godparents, charged with taking care of her in secret
till she came of age. The job would start immediately. For
one thing, Sam had to assemble a team of doctors to take
care of Innocence through the year-long transformation—
doctors who could be counted on not to blab, and who
could also deal with any complications that might crop up
while the little girl changed. Becoming a queen wasn't always an easy process; in fact, the poor kid could easily stay
sick and bleary through the whole thing.

As it happened, *I* was the one who got sick and bleary.
The very day Innocence began to nurse, I caught the
Coughing Jaundice.

If you want to know how I caught the disease, I had no
idea at the time. There was a kind of embarrassing ceremony in the royal chambers at midnight—Sam and me
standing there as witnesses, while Verity asked the Four-
Clawed Goddess for blessing; then poor little Innocence,
terrified out of her mind, took a tiny tiny sip of venom
from both of Verity's stingers . . . after which, a horde of
doctors descended on the child, taking blood tests, sputum
samples, and heaven knows what else. Innocence stayed
snuggled up with her mother for the night, I went back to
my room alone, for fear a maidservant might get curious
where I'd been so late . . .

. . . and I just never woke up the next morning. When I
finally came to, it was ten days later and I was in the special
secret infirmary that'd originally been arranged for Innocence. She was there too, just a bit under the weather, nothing serious . . . and most of the doctors who were supposed
to be looking after the girl were locked full-time on my
case, trying to keep me alive.

In a way, my condition helped keep Innocence a secret
that whole year. Folks in the palace knew about the private
infirmary—you can never hide things from servants—but
everybody thought the doctors were for me. Innocence was
just one of Verity's many daughters, assigned by her
mother to keep me company . . . and occasionally to see the

queen in private to "report on my condition": a pretty good
cover for the many times Innocence wanted to see Verity
alone for a few minutes, and sip a bit more venom.

So Innocence and I got to know each other . . . when I
wasn't busy coughing my head off or lying jaundiced and
comatose. Yes, I'd tried to spend time with all Verity's
children—my stepkids—but most of them seemed pretty
uncomfortable having a human think he was their father.
Me, I wasn't so great at being a dad either; my own father
hadn't set much of an example, and anyway, what felt natural to a human parent was nothing like Mandasar kids
expected. As just one example, the little boys had a habit
of trying to clip me with their claws. Their baby pincers
wouldn't have done a thing to a real Mandasar's carapace,
but they could cut up a human nice and bloody. End result:
I was pretty darned useless for playing that particular game.

But with Innocence, I could just talk. She snuggled with
me too, because Verity was too busy for that kind of thing.
The poor kid needed tons of snuggling, because she was
halfway to terrified most of the time. Strange things were
happening to her body. Doctors were constantly poking at
her. None of her siblings or friends were allowed to see
her. Worst of all, people kept telling her she'd have to rule
the planet someday, and that she was going to become huge
and dangerous and intimidating like Verity herself. Who
wouldn't be frightened by that?

It helped her to be with me. Sam said it was good even
when I was sick or delirious—Innocence stuck right by me,
holding my hand, giving me sips of water, talking and talking and talking. It gave the girl something to think about
besides herself. Kind of like a sick pet. And she had
queenly instincts waking up inside her: the need to be in
charge of someone, to give orders. "Time for the muscle
stimulators, Daddy Edward; and don't say you can exercise
on your own, because you don't. The only reason you're
strong enough to push me away is because I use the machine on you when you sleep. So stay still and let me strap
this to your legs."

Even six-year-old queens know how to lay down the law.

*   *   *

A year passed. Sam told me they held another ceremony when Innocence took her last drink of Verity's venom—just a tiny tiny sip like the very first, because she didn't need any more. The little brown gentle had become a little yellow queen: no longer scared of the future, even if she should have been.

They held the ceremony in my sickroom, just so they could say I was there. My body may have been present, but my mind wasn't: far off and unconscious, suffering through the final throes of my disease. A few days later, I finally woke up . . . and not a single cough in my throat. Another week, and Innocence was threatening to tie me down again. I swore I was feeling a hundred times better. She told me a blood-consort wasn't allowed to argue with a queen. "You're staying in bed, Daddy Edward, till Dr. Gashwan says you're healthy."

But it didn't work out that way.

I woke alone in the night, wondering what the awful beeping sound was. Some annoying medical monitor? But there weren't any nurses rushing to check my condition. In fact, there wasn't even a light coming from the desk outside my room. Pitch-blackness, and nothing but that continuing beep-beep-beep.

The sound came from my wrist. Some navy someone was signaling a Mayday. It might have been anybody from the diplomatic mission, but I knew in my heart it was Sam.

Without thinking, I rolled out of bed and stumbled toward the door. After being sick so long, I was nowhere near my physical peak, but Innocence and the muscle-working machines had kept me from going to seed. I could walk just fine and even run a bit if worse came to worst.

And maybe it had. There were no lights anywhere, not even on the medical sensors that were supposed to watch me night and day—someone must have cut the power, and even the emergency generators. That meant big trouble. I didn't know much about what'd happened in the year gone

by, just that things had gone down hill. A long way down
hill. Maybe so bad that one of the outlaw queens had decided to attack Unshummin palace.

Outside my room, the doctors and nurses were gone. In
their place, five palace guards wearing gas masks had
ranged themselves around the room, all with souped-up
stun-pistols aimed at the far door . . . like they expected an
enemy to come smashing through any second.

"What's going on?" I whispered.

They whirled on me, and for a heartbeat I thought they
were going to shoot; but one of them, a sergeant, snapped,
"Hold your fire," and nobody pulled the trigger. "Go back
to bed, consort," the sergeant told me. "There's been a mutiny. It's not safe in the halls."

"Is the queen all right?" I asked. "And my sister?"

"Don't know." He glanced at the others, then turned back
to me. "Our assignment is to keep you safe."

"Me? Who cares about me?" I held up my wrist; it was
still beeping. "You and your men are going to help me save
someone who's in trouble. Do you hear me?"

For a second he didn't answer: his antennas bent just a
bit, as if he was smiling. Then he snapped a salute. "Yes,
sir. We'll follow you."

The six of us raced through dark halls, tracking the Mayday. Once or twice, we passed close to fighting; we'd hear
the whir of stunners somewhere down a corridor, then running feet and voices shouting orders. But none of the action
ever came our way. We saw plenty of bodies, unconscious
and dead, but nobody stopped us as we raced straight from
the infirmary to Queen Verity's chambers . . . the source of
the Mayday.

Outside the door, the queen's personal guards had been
butchered. Inside, so had the queen—decapitated by some
assassin who'd crept unseen through the palace during all
the ruckus. Verity's head had been laid on a big serving
plate in the middle of her own dining table.

A few steps away sprawled my sister's body, apparently
stabbed through the heart while trying to defend the queen.

Sam had triggered the Mayday . . . and even as I stared at the blood spilling from her chest, the beeping signal stopped. I knew what that meant—not enough bioelectric energy left in her body to power the transmitter.

A navy quartermaster once told me those transmitters could keep drawing power from your tissues at least five minutes after you were dead.

I took one step toward my sister's body. Then hands grabbed me from behind: bright red hands, the sergeant on my right, one of his men on my left. They were only using their *Cheejreth* arms, but at that moment, they were strong enough to hold me.

"Nothing we can do here," the sergeant said. His voice was muffled by his gas mask. "No one to save."

"Wrong," I told him. "There's still someone unaccounted for."

Innocence. My sort-of daughter. The new high queen.

She had a secret room in the palace, but not secret enough. When we got there, the door had been blown off its hinges by explosives. There was no sign of a struggle, no blood, no little yellow corpse; it looked like Innocence hadn't been home when the assassin showed up.

Where else might she go? Would she run and hide like a seven-year-old girl, or throw herself into action like a queen? My first thought was she might run for my sick-room, to rescue her beloved Daddy Edward; but she hadn't shown up, had she? The guards would have seen her the second she came charging through the door . . .

They'd had their stunners out, ready to fire. A single stun-shot wouldn't take down a queen, not even a young one like Innocence. But five shots simultaneously would. And they were all wearing gas masks, so it wouldn't matter if Innocence surrounded herself with a cloud of her own royal pheromone.

Now the same guards were waiting for me to tell them where Innocence might hide. They wanted me to lead them straight to her.

The sergeant had told me, "There's been a mutiny." He hadn't mentioned which side he was on.

Now the sergeant asked, "Where should we go, sir? You said there was someone you wanted us to protect?"

Yes—the sergeant definitely knew about Innocence. He shouldn't have known, but he did. And he also knew I was so stupid, I wasn't likely to see through their trick.

"This way," I said. "I know where she's gone."

Unshummin palace is shaped like a Mandasar queen. Really. A long central body with eight legs sticking out at the sides—the legs are actually separate wings of the building, three stories tall—and up at the head, the queen's "claws" are four more building wings stretched out on diagonals. The claw parts even end in crescent-shaped rotundas, so from the air they look like pincers.

Much farther back, where the palace's "tail" meets the wider part of the body, there are two big glass domes to represent venom sacs. The domes are actually huge greenhouse roofs; beneath them lies the Royal Conservatory, with tropical-zone plants under the right-hand dome and temperate-zone plants under the left.

The right-hand part is the closest thing to a jungle you'll find within a thousand kilometers of Unshummin. That's where I led the five guards.

"There's this little girl," I whispered to them. "And she has this secret place where she goes when she's really scared."

They nodded and even smiled, like they understood. What I said wasn't true—Innocence could never have gone from the infirmary to the conservatory without being seen by dozens of people—but the guards were willing to believe me. They didn't suspect I suspected . . . till I led them into the middle of the dark trees and vines, then suddenly dashed away through a grove of Koshavese fire oaks.

The trees grew too close together for the warriors to follow me; and I moved fast enough that I was out of sight before they could bring their stunners to bear. The guns whirred anyway, but I didn't feel a tingle—what with the dark and the tree cover and the gas masks on the guards' faces, I guess they weren't aiming very well.

Nice thing about those gas masks: the guards couldn't sniff me out. A Mandasar warrior depends so much on his nose, he's at a numb disadvantage when his smelling's sealed off. Mandasar eyes are just as good as human, and their ears are sharp enough to hear a big guy like me blundering his way through the bush . . . but without their noses, they lose their edge: a fraction slower on everything they do. That was good—after a year of being sick, I was a fraction slower too, and I don't mean a tiny fraction like one over a thousand.

My plan was just to lose the soldiers in the conservatory, then duck out a door to find Innocence. Just one problem: there were three doors—one toward the head of the palace, one toward the tail, and one that led through a bunch of potting rooms to the other half of the conservatory. While I was still dodging through the undergrowth, the sergeant sent three of his men racing to cover those exits. That left two of them to search for one of me . . . and they had all the guns.

I've already said I'm not one of those guys who can creep through the dark without making a sound. Lucky for me, most Mandasars are even worse at being stealthy than I am; there's no such thing as a silent bulldozer. There's also no such thing as a Mandasar who can climb trees— great big lobsters have no monkeys anywhere in their evolutionary past. Your average warrior never looks for trouble above head height . . . which is probably true for human soldiers too, but our species should know better.

Up I went—into some kind of tree with easy-to-climb branches. Its bark felt like moldy cheese: hard underneath, but with an outer layer of mushy fuzz. It smelled like moldy cheese too . . . moldy *something* anyway, all pulpy and rotten. I wasn't happy getting the stuff on the front of my uniform, but I had an easy time digging in my fingers for handholds. Without much noise, I pulled myself up a story and a half above the ground, then settled into the shadows between a big branch and the trunk.

The sergeant passed cautiously below me. I considered dropping onto his head, but decided against it—considering how out of practice I was, I wouldn't take him out instantly. Anyway, it would be sure to cause noise. The other warrior looking for me was only a short distance off; even if I managed to finish off the sergeant, I'd be shot unconscious before I escaped.

Instead, I waited till the guards searching for me were down the far end of the place (it's a *big* conservatory), then I carefully began to clamber from tree to tree. This was just an exhibit, not a real rain forest; all kinds of trees had been crammed in together, and the gardeners had done that pruning trick that makes the branches grow out instead of up. I could sneak from one tree to the next without much trouble, heading for the door that led back into the main part of the palace.

My movement wasn't completely silent, but neither was the conservatory. Birds lived in the place, the little flitty kind of birds you find all over Troyen. Sam once told me the feathers on Troyenese birds didn't evolve the same way as on Earth—not as strong or aerodynamic or something, so local birds can't fly if they get much bigger than a chickadee. The ones in the conservatory were all smaller than that, on the order of hummingbirds; and with us big people thrashing in the dark, the birds were zipping around like frantic wasps, making leaves rustle all over the place. Practically every step I took, I disturbed one of the little guys and sent it flying off to another tree . . . but the warriors were also scaring up flocks wherever they went, not to mention a bunch of birds with bad nerves who suddenly burst into a racket of cheeping for no apparent reason. The warriors couldn't hear me over all that noise; so it only took me a few minutes to get within ten meters of the door.

One guard between me and escape. With his gas mask on, he couldn't smell me; with the darkness, he couldn't see me; with the birds making racket all over the place, he couldn't hear me. But everything would change if I jumped out of the tree and tried to cross the gap between us—I figured it was fifty-fifty whether I'd get to him before he fired his stunner, and even less likely that I'd be able to put him down before his friends showed up.

So I stayed in the tree, hoping for a lucky break. Which I got, sort of.

"This is taking too long," the sergeant growled from somewhere far behind me. He was speaking in Mandasar, of course, but I understood just fine. "Take your masks off, and let's sniff this bastard out."

"But Sarge . . ." one of the other guards said.

"The queen's dead," the sergeant snapped, "and the brat obviously isn't here. We'll be all right. Do it."

They did. As the guard in the doorway began to slip his gas mask off, I knew I'd never have a better time to move—within seconds, he'd smell a human within spitting distance. I hit the floor running, with only a tiny stumble; and the guard was slowed by taking off his mask. Even then, I nearly didn't make it in time . . . but at the last second, the guard hesitated a teeny bit.

I smashed him with a palm heel under the snout, snapping his head back hard. The strike was too weak to knock him out completely, but it dazed him long enough for me to rip the stunner out of his *Cheejreth* arms. Jumping back out of reach of his waist pincers, I shot him three times fast in the head. He slumped, his nose whupping down hard onto the floor.

Behind me, the other guards were shouting—they must have heard the stunner's whir. I raced through the door, knowing I'd never outrun four Mandasar warriors but not having a lot of other options. The most important thing was getting around a corner fast, so I wouldn't be in the line of fire from the stunners. At the first side corridor I dived off to the right, just as guns whirred behind me. I rolled to my feet and was about to start running again when a voice whispered behind me, "Psst!"

I turned. Directly across from me, where the side corridor

continued, someone stood in the shadows. Even without lights, I could make out the buttercup yellow of her shell.

The warriors raced up the main hall toward us. As they came level with Innocence and me, it was like the four of them were clotheslined by a wire running across their path at nose height; but there was no wire, just the smell of royal pheromone driving up their snouts and into their brains. The guards fell twitching. I stepped out of cover and drained the batteries of my stunner, making sure they wouldn't get up.

Old Queen Verity, ever the long-range planner, had left an escape route for her newly royal daughter. Outside in the royal gardens, a shed held one end of a Sperm-tail transport tube. The tube led off to parts unknown, maybe halfway around the world, to a secret safe house where Innocence could grow up in peace. I carried my daughter to the shed, all wrapped in black so her bright yellow body wouldn't be seen by mutineers; and I personally fed her into that Sperm-tail, then smashed the anchor that held the Unshummin end of the tube in place. The tail slithered off, like a string yanked from the far end . . . and that was the last I saw of my little girl, my daughter, the high-queen-in-waiting.

I dearly wanted to go with her—where else did I have to be, who else was left that I cared about? But someone had to smash the anchor. Besides, if I disappeared, the navy would search for me . . . and I didn't want anyone snooping around, for fear the world would learn about Innocence. She was only seven years old; till she grew up, it was safer if nobody knew she existed.

Me, I headed back to the queen's royal chamber. I avoided the pockets of fighting; too tired to help the good guys. Anyway, how would I tell the good from the bad? And with everyone dead or gone, what was worth fighting for? So I slunk through the palace as if I were the only man left on Troyen—alone, with Samantha, Verity, and Innocence all taken from me.

In the high queen's chamber, the bodies had disappeared. I imagined them carried off by mutineers, so the corpses could be displayed as somebody's trophies. Sickened by that thought, I fell to my knees in the sticky patch of blood where Sam had been lying . . . pressed my hands down on the dampness, and lifted my red-stained fingers to my nose . . .

Then it was days later, and I was on the navy's moon-base. No memory of how I'd gotten from one place to the other. They said some navy security guards found me and dragged me onto an escape shuttle—abandoning a planet gone mad, transporting me to the safe airless silence of space.

With Verity dead, no one on the planet could maintain order. Everybody who could leave got out fast. Including the Fasskisters who started the whole mess.

The Fasskisters had one last indignity to dump on poor old Troyen: what they called the Beneficent Swarm. Without telling anyone else, they'd left huge caches of nano in Fasskister warehouses all over the planet. At the very instant the last Fasskister left Troyen's atmosphere, all those caches opened wide . . . spreading clouds of self-replicating nanites in every direction.

According to the Fasskisters, the nanites were designed "to protect the Mandasars from themselves." In a way, that was even true—because of the Swarm, the Mandasars didn't have a chance to nuke themselves to oblivion.

The microscopic robots ate plastics, particularly those used to insulate electrical wires, to build circuit boards, and to act as glue or sealants. Within a week, much of Troyen's technological base had literally fallen apart . . . including all computers, the power grid, and most communication systems. The nanites also shut down nuclear weapons, nerve-gas missiles, and a bunch of labs where clever Mandasar doctors were studying alien organisms for their germ-warfare potential; the Beneficent Swarm even wrecked important chunks of military planes, tanks, and submarines.

The Fasskisters could honestly say they'd saved the Mandasars from a war of total extinction.

On the other hand, you can kill a lot of people with spears and crossbows. For twenty years, that's exactly what the Mandasars did.

Laughter. People were laughing. I came to myself and realized I was at the captain's table on *Jacaranda*, still possessed by the spirit that kept shoving me out of my body. Whatever the spirit just said must have been hysterically funny . . . the way Prope giggled into her hand and Festina's eyes glistened. Even Kaisho, face hidden by hair, was chuckling. I guess higher organisms aren't immune to being disarmed by the occasional joke.

I wished I knew what'd just come out of my mouth. For the past little while—I don't know how long—I'd fallen out of touch with what I'd been saying. Blanked out in my own thoughts, of Innocence, of Sam, of the night everybody died.

Had I told about that? I didn't know.

Prope, Festina, and Kaisho just kept laughing . . . but when I glanced to my right, Lieutenant Harque didn't look nearly so chuckly. Yes, he was smiling; but it was the strained sort of smile people wear when they don't have a choice. I wondered whether I'd made a joke at his expense. I didn't think so—if the others were laughing because I'd teased him, they'd glance his way from time to time, just to catch the look on his face. So far as I could see, all three women acted like he wasn't even there. As if I was the only man at the table worth listening to.

Which explained why Harque looked so sour.

Slowly the laughter eased away. Prope's eyes remained shiny—beaming straight at me, glimmery bright. I couldn't mistake the look . . . and I was returning it, strong and clear, like electricity passing between us. Terrified, I fought the thing that wanted to lock me with the captain in that heart-pounding gaze. Sometime in the past hour, while I wasn't paying attention, the spirit possessing me had built upon

Prope's light little flirtations and made them bloom into . . .

Into . . .

No. With a burst of willpower, I grabbed back control of my body and forced myself to lower my eyes. Maybe if I shied off, I could undo the effects of wooing the captain . . . and of wooing Festina and Kaisho too, by the look of them. All three women simmered with the same gush of attraction, as if my wit and my charm had dazzled them all.

Scared and ashamed, I turned away from the table. Would it be so bad if I just muttered, "Excuse me," and ran to my cabin? Rude, yes, but would it be so bad?

My eyes swept over the Mandasars at the next table. The five of them were shaking, shuddering like a group attack of epilepsy. Their nostrils had flared wide, inhaling to the very bottom of their lungs.

Only one thing could make Mandasars react that way. Somehow, undetectable to human noses, the air must be filled with the pure piercing scent of royal pheromone.

27

WATCHING FESTINA PUNCH

I was still staring at the Mandasars when someone at a nearby table gasped. "Are they sick?"

"No," I said. "Not sick."

More crew members were looking now: standing up to see over other people's heads, and muttering, "What idiot brought diseased lobsters aboard a navy ship?" Things escalated to a general kerfuffle, with Veresian getting called, and nervous folks running out, and Prope glaring at Festina for exposing everyone to contagious aliens, and Festina asking me what could be wrong, and me saying I didn't know when I knew full well, except where the pheromone was coming from.

Eventually, the captain cleared the lounge "to give the doctor room to work." I wanted to stick around to make sure the Mandasars were okay; but Prope took me by the arm and walked me to my cabin, all of a sudden starting to talk in a giddy girlish voice you wouldn't expect from a starship captain. Half the time, I couldn't even follow what she said—I was getting sleepier by the minute thanks to space lag, being shifted off my body's day/night cycle.

Now, I had a giddy woman on my arm; and I suspected she'd be in my bed soon, unless I somehow cooled her off. I didn't want to make her mad, considering we were stuck on *Jacaranda* the next few weeks . . . but I sure didn't want to sleep with her either. Barely a day ago, Prope was ready

246

to dump me somewhere awful—and she might still do it if she got orders from the High Council. Some people might like rumpling the sheets with a ruthless cut-your-throat woman, but me, I had more gentle standards.

So I wasn't in the mood to get lovey-dovey. It surprised me *she* was so keen for it: I mean, a lot of women like how I look, and Prope might have been thinking, "His father's an admiral," but even so, the captain was acting awfully loose and loopy. As if she was drunk or something . . . except I couldn't smell any alcohol on her. The way she was clinging right on my arm, I could smell a lot of other things—shampoo in her hair, soap behind her ears, chocolate mousse on her breath, sweat where her shoulder and hip pressed against me—but not a drop of booze.

Maybe she was just the sort of person who could make herself passionate whenever she wanted: turn it on, turn it off, like the diplomats I'd known on Troyen. Heaven knows, Sam was a master of whipping up whatever emotions she wanted . . . the same as a hive-queen could pump out pheromones at will, whether she wanted to scare people, or get them to listen, or even to make them love her.

I wondered what kind of pheromones could make the captain not love me.

When we reached my room, Prope didn't even slow down: right through the door and on into the cabin, never letting me go. I think she intended to drag me straight to the bed . . . and she might have, if I hadn't caught a strong whiff of something that reminded me of buttered toast. The smell was more than a smell—it had the *feel* of toast too, steamy hot, with a gritty, crumbly texture. Don't ask me how an odor can have a texture; but the sensation was so strong, I drew back sharply in surprise.

My stopping caught Prope off guard. She was kind of jerked back by her grip on my arm—her momentum wasn't nearly as strong as my inertia when I wanted to stand still. I stopped . . . listened . . . sniffed. Prope kept tugging on my elbow, not really hard but persistent, like a kid who wants to pull Dad into the candy store; but I kept smelling that buttered toast and wondering what it was.

"Edward," Prope said in a not-very-patient voice, "what's wrong?"

"Do you smell it?"

"Smell what?"

"Buttered toast."

Prope gave a polite sniff, but she was just humoring me. "I don't smell a thing," she said. Then she gave a coy flick of her eyelids. "Do you want to know what I'd like to smell?"

"Um." I thought, *What the heck has gotten into her?* But I didn't say it out loud; I was still looking around the room, trying to figure out where the smell came from. The closet? No. The desk? The bed?

Suddenly, something clicked inside my half-asleep brain. "Ship-soul," I said, "lights ninety-five percent dim."

"That's more like it," Prope murmured, as the room fell darker than candlelight. She leaned in and laid her hand lightly on my chest. "Now let's just find out . . ."

Her voice broke off. I'd pulled away from her and stepped toward the bed. That was definitely where the smell came from. With a quick yank, I whipped the top blankets and sheets all the way off the mattress.

On the bottom sheet, low down where your feet would go, where you'd never look before you got into bed, the white linen was dusted with a sprinkle of glowing red specks.

"Ooo," Prope whispered, "very nice. But if I were you, I would have put that up where people could see it. Splash some on the pillow. On the walls. Dribble it up and down our bodies, then lick it off. How much of it do you have?"

I stared at her in disbelief. Was she drunk or something, that she didn't recognize the Balrog? But then, she'd only seen it as a big mossy clump on Kaisho's legs, not as single spores; and her mind was definitely distracted, focused on other things.

She reached toward the glimmering spores, like a little

kid trying to touch the pretties. I grabbed her wrist and pulled her away. "You'd be sorry if you did that," I told her. I kept hold of her arm as I backed out of the room into the bright lights of the corridor.

"What's wrong?" she asked. "Aren't we going to—"

"No," I said. "Not in there."

"My room then? I'm captain. I've got a great big room. And a great big bed." She was still talking like a drunk with a one-track mind; I wondered if she'd popped some aphrodisiac drug when I wasn't looking.

"Not tonight," I told her. "There's something I have to report to the admiral."

"To Festina?" the captain asked, her voice turning shrill. "You're dumping me and going to that freak-faced bitch?"

Then Prope screamed. It was the most amazing noise: just a shriek of pure outrage. It scarcely even sounded real—more like some eight-year-old who'd been challenged to a dare by her friends, and was wailing out this ear-piercing screech to prove she had the nerve. But there was nothing childish about the look on Prope's face; it was fierce and furious, not aimed at me or anyone, just exploding out at the universe along with the scream. A primal venting of absolute rage, neither long nor short.

It happened, it shattered the silence of the empty corridor, and then it was over. Prope closed her mouth with a little clopping sound as her lips came together. She shuffled off without even looking at me, like a sleepwalker moving onto some new part of her dream.

Above my head, the ship-soul spoke through one of its speakers. "Is there a problem? Do you need help? Is there a problem? Do you need help?"

"Ship-soul," I said, "get a robot to take all the linen off my bed. I don't care if it's a cleaning robot or one of those that handle toxic substances—whatever you have handy. Take the sheets and leave them in Kaisho's room; break down her door if you have to."

"I am afraid that is not—"

"Just do it," I snapped. "My father is Admiral of the

Gold, Alexander York, and he doesn't appreciate lippy AIs
who don't follow orders. Give me results, not excuses."

I wheeled around and stormed off down the corridor . . .
as if the ship-soul was somebody I could stomp away from.
Every two seconds I walked under another of the computer's speakers, but I didn't hear any more protests. Apparently, whoever programmed the ship's system must have
anticipated getting bullied by an admiral's retard son.

Festina wasn't in her room . . . even though it was almost
midnight, *Jacaranda* time. I found her alone in the gym,
already sopping with sweat from pounding the heavy bag.
And I mean pounding it *hard*. Not one of those controlled
sessions where you try the same combination twenty times,
or see how many roundhouse kicks you can do in two
minutes. She was throwing elbows and knees and head-high
jump kicks, plus all kinds of palm heels, knife-hands,
snake-strikes, that thing where you clap your opponent's
eardrums . . . even some plain old body checks, whomping
into the bag with her shoulder and yelling something blood-
thirsty. That didn't look like a real martial-arts move to me,
but maybe it was okay if you just wanted to smash something with all the strength you had.

I didn't say anything—just waited for her to notice me.
Festina was moving around the bag, hitting it from lots of
different angles; eventually she got to the far side, facing
the bag, facing my direction. When she saw me, she stiffened a little and stopped, panting lightly.

She looked good, puffing and sweating. For the workout,
she'd put on a plain old T-shirt and loose cotton pants . . .
both colored admiral's gray, but very simple. You don't see
simple clothes very much in navy gyms—people are always wearing smart fibers that keep the body at perfect
temperature, or chemical paints that make fat burn faster.
Not Festina; but then, she made a point of being different
from regular navy folks.

"I thought you were with Prope," Festina said, not quite
meeting my eye.

"Prope was with me. Not vice versa. She was acting kind of funny."

Festina glanced at the clock on the gym's wall. All of a sudden, I got the strangest feeling: that she was figuring out how long I'd been with Prope, and trying to decide if we'd had time to . . . you know.

Embarrassed, I said, "There were more Balrog spores in my cabin. Like a booby trap. I was lucky I smelled something odd."

"Oh?" She gave her arms a bit of a stretch across her chest. She must have been starting to cool down. "I've never noticed the Balrog *had* a smell." She still wasn't meeting my eye. "Maybe you've got a better nose than I do."

I shrugged. "Being three percent Mandasar has to be good for something."

"Does that bother you?"

"I like Mandasars," I said. "It's just weird, thinking I'm not all human."

"You'll get used to it," she replied. "Feeling not all human is an Explorer's natural state."

"You're human," I told her. "One hundred percent."

She looked up at me for the first time since I'd come in—met my gaze no more than half a second, then shied away and slammed a fist into the bag in front of her. "Christ," she muttered, "there must be something in the water."

"What do you mean?"

She hit the bag with another punch. "At this second, Edward, I want to chew your clothes off. It's so amazingly powerful . . ." She leaned forward and planted her face against the bag's hard leather. "Maybe you should go away before I embarrass myself completely. If I haven't already."

I just stared at her. After a few seconds, she said, "I notice you aren't going away." Her voice was muffled up against the bag; from that position she couldn't notice anything.

"Do you really want me to go?" I asked.

"Of course not. I want you to throw me onto the nearest judo mat and fuck my brains out. Which is so entirely unlike me, I don't . . ." She stopped and shook her head. "I can barely speak in completely sentences. I've been horny plenty of times before, but I have *never* . . ." She broke off laughing—the sort of laugh when you're afraid that otherwise you might cry. "This is so completely pathetic," she said. "Do you know how blind-raging jealous I was when I thought you and Prope were going to—"

"We didn't," I put in quickly.

"Good for you," she answered, "and tough on Prope. God, the woman was ready to undress you right at the dinner table. Like it was the first time in her life she'd ever truly wanted to get naked and rub up against every beautiful dimple on your . . ." Festina gave another strangled laugh. "And I dearly wanted to smash her face so I could have you all to myself. If it hadn't been for the Mandasars going catatonic . . . and I wanted to tell them, 'Friends, I know what you're going through, I'm a basket case myself.' " She broke off. "Am I babbling? I'm babbling, aren't I? I'm truly babbling. I have *never* talked to a man like this. And the appalling thing is, I'm only doing it because I desperately hope you'll get aroused. A man wants women to throw themselves at his feet, right? Right? Because if you want something different, just tell me and I'll probably do it. I lost all shame three minutes ago."

She might have lost all shame, but I hadn't. My cheeks were burning. First Prope, now Festina . . . like both women were drunk or drugged. But that was crazy. Who would . . .

Festina shoved herself away from the bag and turned straight toward me. Her face was flushed; there were tears dribbling down her cheeks. "Edward," she said, swallowing hard, "please leave now. Go and forget you were ever here. Christ knows I'll probably forget it myself—my head is spinning like a son of a bitch. Just . . . get out before I do something unforgivable. Please."

I wondered what she thought would be unforgivable. Throwing herself on me? Why did she think that would be awful? Because it would be taking advantage of a . . . some-one like me?

All of a sudden, I thought of Counselor the previous night: her offering herself, and me turning her down. Because I thought she was just a kid who couldn't possibly think for herself, someone I had to protect because she was really stupid. As if going to bed with her would be raping a mental defective.

Now Festina was protecting *me*.

For one brief second, I wanted to shout, "Why do you think I wouldn't *like* throwing you onto a judo mat? Maybe I've dreamed of getting naked and rubbing dimples too. Why would you see it as committing some terrible sin?"

Did Festina think *she'd* be raping a mental defective?

I didn't want her protecting me. But I had to protect *her*. She was drugged or something.

Turning quietly, I walked from the gym. Outside the door, I stopped and waited. I could hear her sobbing softly. After a while, she began hitting the bag again. Really really hard.

I was so sleepy I felt like I was going to drop. Too bad my cabin was infested with Balrogs.

The Mandasars weren't using four of their five rooms, but the ship-soul wouldn't let me inside when they weren't there. Maybe the computer thought I might steal something.

The way things were going, I probably could have walked into the cabin of any female crew member and got an invitation to stay the night. Maybe the male crew members too. But I didn't want to find out if that was true.

Up to the front of the ship. A door just this side of the bridge.

Prope was still awake. When she answered my knock, I could see she'd been crying. I don't think she'd done much crying before. And in the whole rest of the ship, she had no one who'd hold her till the crying stopped.

Oh well. She was right about having a great big bed.

*   *   *

Waking up, smelling my own sweat. And Prope's. She lay sprawled behind me on the great big bed, her hair slick and damp from exertion. She was deep deep asleep, drawing in loud lungfuls of air and letting them out again heavily. In stories, women always sleep with a little smile afterward, but thank heaven that's not true in real life. I don't think I could have stood it, her looking all smug.

Me, I found myself sitting naked at the captain's own computer terminal. No memory of how I got there. My skin felt really cold, like I'd been sitting out a long time.

The screen in front of me showed a list of files stored on bubble with the ship-soul. My own personal files, almost nothing in them—just official navy records, and my pathetically small personal address book. (Containing only my father's name. It used to have Sam's name too, but a woman I knew on the moonbase made me erase it.)

I stared at the screen blearily, not paying attention to the file names . . . till I realized something was missing.

Search. Search. But the file I was looking for had disappeared: the file containing the backdoor access code Samantha gave me. Vanished in the night.

And I was sitting at Prope's official terminal, with no memory of the past few hours. Shivering, I wondered what I'd done.

Part 4

ENTERING THE CATHEDRAL

28

SAILING THROUGH SPACE

I left Prope's cabin before she woke. Spent the rest of the night in the lounge. In the morning, two female life-support techs woke me and said I looked terrible. They were nice to me, in a spend-time-with-the-cute-stranger way, but they weren't voracious or anything. Whatever I'd had the night before must have worn off.

Later in the day, Festina and Prope tried to act like nothing had happened . . . but for a long time, Festina wouldn't look me in the eye, and Prope was always staring at me when she thought I wouldn't notice.

Wrapped in its Sperm-tail, *Jacaranda* sped its milky way through the silence of space. Nothing happened as we crossed the line out of Celestia's system . . . nothing beyond a few tense faces easing up, and people suddenly remembering gossip or jokes they'd been meaning to tell each other.

We'd all survived another one. Life goes on.

As Tobit predicted, Kaisho claimed she'd put the spores outside my door and in my bed just as a joke. "To see the look on your face, *Teelu*," she said; which was kind of scary in itself, if she could see the look on my face when she was nowhere in sight. She swore the Balrog had always known I'd find the spores without stepping on them . . . so where was the harm?

Festina still gave her a real good chewing out, and Kaisho promised not to play such tricks again. None of us really trusted her; but Festina was reluctant to lock her up or invent some other punishment. Explorers liked to keep things in the family—it was one thing to yell at a fellow Explorer in private, but nobody wanted to take measures that might be noticed by the crew. Anyway, leaning on the Balrog too hard might backfire: if we got it mad, there was no telling what it might do . . . or what we could do to stop it.

So we pretended everything was all patched up. I spent my mornings with the Explorers—Festina, Kaisho, Tobit, and Benjamin—answering their questions about Troyen. They soon saw I knew nothing about the twenty years of war (nothing specific enough to be useful), so we turned to subjects like how to incapacitate a warrior without killing him, and the personalities of Queens Fortitude, Honor, and Clemency. Since they were the longest-established queens, maybe one of them had come out on top . . . except they were also the most obvious targets for the outlaw queens, so maybe they'd been eliminated early on.

No way to know. All those records kept by observers on my moonbase were marked TOP SECRET, and even Festina couldn't get at them. Some higher admiral didn't want us learning useful stuff about Troyen—likely the admiral who sponsored the recruiters, and *Willow*'s mission. Or my father, trying to hide how badly Samantha had failed.

About Samantha's failure—in those days on *Jacaranda*, I finally realized how crazy it was to put an inexperienced twenty-year-old in charge of a diplomatic mission . . . then to leave her in charge for fifteen whole years, as things went from bad to worse. What the heck had Dad been thinking? And why had the other admirals allowed it? The way I figured it, Dad must have given the council doctored-up reports, so they wouldn't know Sam was doing a bad job. Dad wanted to protect his daughter, and protect himself too; after all, he was the one who put her into a position she couldn't handle.

I'd never had such thoughts before: recognizing that Sam had screwed up her mission. Screwed it up really badly. Why hadn't that ever occurred to me before?

Maybe I was getting smarter. Festina kind of hinted at that after we'd been together a few days—she thought I should take an intelligence test, because she couldn't believe the low scores in my official records. "You're better than those scores," she told me. "You may not think you are, but it's true."

I knew it was the other way around—Dad had fudged my real scores upward to put me over the navy's required minimum. Anyway, if I *had* got smarter I didn't want to know; all my life, I'd been who I was, and I hated the idea of changing.

But I *was* changing. When I was with Kaisho, I could smell that buttered-toast aroma all the time. Nobody else could. And as the days went by, I began to smell other things . . . strange things.

Captain Prope smelled of a light frost green: the color itself. A kind of glossy shade, like freshly licked lipstick. I can't tell you how someone could smell of a color—my brain must have got really scrambled. But every time Prope started watching me behind my back, that smell of misty muted green filled the air.

Festina smelled like a thunderstorm: not the storm's scent, but its sound. The rushing wind and the pouring rain, the rumble of coming thunder. Sometimes, she even smelled of the rainbow after. It didn't make sense . . . but I'd smell the sound of thunder, and Festina Ramos would walk into the room.

Tobit smelled like the gnarled surface of a walnut—the texture of it, not the scent. And Benjamin . . . Benjamin was a feeling through my whole body that I wanted to yawn and stretch, but yawning and stretching wouldn't make the feeling go away. For some reason, that made me nervous; I didn't mind people smelling like frost green or thunderclaps or walnuts, but Benjamin got me real edgy.

No matter how I yawned and stretched, I couldn't make the edginess go away either.

After mornings with the Explorers, I'd pass the afternoons teaching the Mandasars about their own culture—so they could pass as natives if the mission absolutely required it. Counselor and the workers took my word as gospel, no matter how it conflicted with their previous ideas about home. Zeeleepull was more stubborn, arguing that Willa and Walda had explicitly told him Queen Prudence had pronounced the Continental Edict in response to the threat of the Greenstriders trying to colonize . . .

But his arguments never lasted long. Thirty seconds in, he would suddenly clamp his mouth shut and whisper, "Apologies, *Teelu*. Knowledge you, ignorance me. Apologies. Apologies."

The first time he did that, my jaw fell open. Warriors don't suddenly turn meek and yield to an opponent, except . . .

I sniffed the air. My newly more-sensitive nose caught a powerful whiff of an indescribable something oozing off my own skin. The scent was as sharp and strong as ether.

I had a scary suspicion it was royal pheromone.

Pheromones—now that I could smell them, I realized they were everywhere. Not just coming from the Mandasars, but from the crew and everybody.

And from me. Every second of every day. They were like fanatic servants, leaping to carry out my least little whim . . . even when I desperately didn't want them to.

I didn't want to win arguments with Zeeleepull by whacking him with a chemical hammer; but I couldn't help it. If he opposed me more than a few seconds, the phero-mone gusted out on its own. Even worse, he accepted it without question, as if I had a perfect right to make him change his mind.

Was that any different from brainwashing? Dosing him

with drugs till he abandoned his old beliefs and swallowed whatever I told him?

It made me sick. But it was worse with humans.

Those mornings in the briefing room with Festina, Kaisho and the others—they'd all get caught up in discussing Explorer stuff, contingency plans, what to do if they couldn't find the people from *Willow* . . . and I'd let my mind wander wherever it wanted. Sometimes I'd find myself looking at Festina, thinking how pretty she was even with that blotch on her face: thinking about her talk of judo mats, and how maybe I'd been crazy to go to Prope's room instead, taking a substitute for the woman I was really dreaming about.

Next thing you know, I'd be smelling a pheromone coming off me as strong as spring fever: pure undiluted sex, like a lust lasso trying to rope me a conquest. Festina's face would flush so deep red her cheeks would almost match color, and she'd start shifting her weight back and forth from one foot to the other like she couldn't stand still. I'd have to excuse myself and go to the head, where I'd splash myself with cold water till the pheromone backed off.

Then, when I returned to the briefing room, Kaisho always asked, "Better, Your Majesty?" with a big smug smirk in her voice. I guess the Balrog could read my mind *and* "taste" the pheromones. As for humans, they never realized they smelled anything, but they melted like butter when the scent soaked into their brains.

Festina never showed up at my cabin door last thing at night; she had willpower. Prope, on the other hand—she held herself back two days, then arrived late the third evening "to make sure I was doing all right."

The funny thing is I'd never hit Prope with that lust-for-me pheromone—not since that first night, when the pheromone must have flooded off me like flop-sweat and I was just too dense to notice. But Prope came visiting anyway . . . with a kind of confused look in her eye, as if she didn't understand it either. Maybe she wanted to recapture whatever crazy abandon she'd felt that other night; or maybe she wanted to prove to herself it hadn't been real, that she could bed me in cold blood without getting all dizzy and lost in emotion.

Either way, she seemed pretty determined to spend another night with me—even if she had to force herself against her own instincts. That was the part that got me: like she was scared out of her wits, but had decided this was a thing that must be done. It brought out all these weird fatherly feelings in me, as if Prope was just a little girl trying to be brave.

(Edward, going all paternal. I guess it was condescending, me thinking of an adult woman that way . . . but lately, I seemed to see *everybody* as a poor innocent I needed to protect.)

So what to do with Prope? I certainly couldn't sleep with her again; I shouldn't have done it the first time. It'd be easy to produce some horrible gagging smell that would drive her away—all I had to do was think what I wanted, and my body would pump out the stink of rotten eggs, or gangrene, or worse—but that was pretty darned crude. I didn't want to overpower the woman; I just wanted her to give up on getting me into the sack.

Meanwhile, Prope sat herself on the edge of my bed. Started talking about some minor something that'd gone wrong with a piece of equipment I'd never heard of, and it'd taken two hours to fix when it was only supposed to take an hour forty-five, and why didn't the fleet train technicians properly anymore . . .

All the time she spoke, her hand kept lifting up to the fastener strap on her blouse then shying away again—as if she'd promised herself she'd start undressing the second she got inside my room, but now couldn't quite go through with it. It was almost endearing; but she'd pretty soon find the nerve to rip off her clothes, and I really really wanted to think of some brilliant strategy before that happened.

Oddly enough, I did. While she was going on and on about lazy crewfolk, I wondered, *What would happen if I smelled frost green?*

Thirty seconds later, that's exactly how I smelled. I didn't have to squinch up my brow and concentrate, it just kind of happened—like my body knew what to do, without me having to think. Very weird and amazing and scary . . . but I smelled like a precise duplicate of Prope herself, only stronger: glossier.

As if I were her brother, or sister, or mother, or father. People were supposed to have instincts to avoid inbreeding, right? With Prope, there was a risk she'd be turned on by the chance to sleep with herself . . . but I crossed my fingers and hoped pheromones were stronger than vanity.

The captain's voice faltered. She looked up at me, a tiny look of pain on her face. For ten full seconds, she just stared into my eyes. Then she muttered, "Well, I've got an early morning tomorrow," and barreled out of the cabin like she was going to throw up.

Maybe she was. It kind of made me wonder about Prope's family.

That wasn't the end of it. In the days that followed, Prope tried several times more . . . as if she hated herself for chickening out and desperately needed to prove I hadn't got to her. Usually I smelled her coming and got my own frost green up fast enough to send her bolting away; but once she caught me by surprise, and with a sudden burst of resolve, shoved me up against the nearest bulkhead. She planted a kiss hard on my mouth, and ground her hips tight on my groin, back and forth, one, two. Then she heard people's voices coming out of a doorway not far off, so she let me go. "Later," she whispered, and strode off cockily, like she was finally pleased with herself.

After that, I decided maybe just to keep smelling frost green morning, noon, and night, till I left the ship. But Festina got really grouchy at me, and that soapy Lieutenant Harque started following me around. When I met the Mandasars that afternoon, Counselor gave me a pained look. "Oh, *Teelu* . . . must you?"

So I turned off the Prope perfume and toughed out the flight as best I could.

29

JOINING THE SYSTEM

No sign of *Willow* or the black ship as we entered the Troyen system. That didn't mean a thing—starships can hide just by powering down. Put them in orbit around a gas giant, and they pass for bits of space rock.

Nothing shot at *Jacaranda* as we settled into planetary orbit. Dade claimed that was a good sign. Over the past few days, he'd repeatedly stated his opinion that no one on Troyen had any surface-to-space missiles left; the Fasskisters' nanites had taken care of that. He admitted it was possible some missile bases had escaped the Swarm—if they were sealed off well enough and protected with huge clouds of defense nano—but in that case, the missiles would have been used, wouldn't they? When everybody else was fighting with swords and spears, an aerial bombardment would be so valuable, no army would have kept the missiles on ice for twenty whole years. Especially when the Swarm nanites were a constant threat. Any commander with common sense would use the bombs while they were still good.

"And what about the missile that nearly hit the moonbase?" Tobit had asked. "Was that a figment of York's imagination?"

Benjamin shrugged. "It *didn't* hit the moonbase, did it? It was an absolutely perfect miss—close enough to scare people into evacuating, but not to hurt anyone. Then surprise, surprise, as soon as the base personnel scurry away, *Willow* shows up on its secret mission."

"Oh boy," Festina said, whacking her forehead lightly with her palm. "Ouch."

I wasn't quite sure what Dade meant. "Um . . . are you saying maybe *Willow* shot at us? To make everybody clear out?"

Dade nodded. "They could have modified a standard probe missile once they came in-system. That way they wouldn't have any lethal weapons aboard while they were still in deep space—keep the League of Peoples happy. *Willow* lobbed the missile at your base, but made sure it didn't come close enough to do real damage. No sentients were truly at risk, so the League wouldn't give a damn."

"I hate to say it," Tobit growled, "but the kid makes sense."

"So I can come with you after all?" Dade said.

He looked back and forth between Tobit and Festina. The two of them exchanged looks but didn't speak.

"I know what you've been thinking," Dade told them. "You don't want me down on Troyen with you because I'm not a real Explorer."

Festina and Tobit had never said that to him . . . not in so many words. But in all their planning for the mission, there'd been sort of a kind of a subtext that maybe he'd be left behind. It was always, "Tobit, you could do this," and "Edward, you can carry that," with no, "Benjamin, here's what *you'll* do."

Now Festina answered Dade in a quiet voice. "You're a cadet," she said. "Just here on training rotation. It would be irresponsible of us to jeopardize your life, taking you down to a planet at war, when Phylar, Edward, and I are fully qualified Explorers."

"You aren't an Explorer, you're an admiral," Dade replied. He ignored Festina's steely glare. "And York isn't a qualified Explorer, you know he isn't—he's never stepped foot into the Academy. That just leaves Tobit, and a landing party has to have at least two Explorers if they're available."

"Benny . . ." Tobit began.

"Don't Benny me," Dade snapped. "The real reason you don't want me is that I'm not . . . I don't look like an Explorer. Isn't that it? I'm just a normal guy, who never had the rough life you people did, because I don't have a birthmark or a deformed arm or a . . ." He just waved in my direction. "Whatever. I'm sorry the navy fucked you folks over, but that's not my fault. And it's ancient history. I mean," he said, gesturing toward Festina, "here I am with the very woman who put an end to that crap, and you want to discriminate against me because I *don't* have anything wrong with me. Listen, Admiral, you're the reason I'm here. You're the reason the navy has to let everyday people into Explorer Academy, and you're the reason I volunteered for the corps. You managed to fix an old injustice, and I thought, 'Hey, I could help.' The sooner people like me get integrated into the corps, the sooner the navy stops thinking of Explorers as totally expendable freaks. But let me tell you, I've received nothing but grief ever since I signed up. The teachers at the Academy . . . the other students . . . all of you here . . . you treat me like some annoying embarrassment who might go away if you just marginalize me enough. Well, I'm *not* going away—I'm going to be an Explorer. I just wish you'd accept that and start treating me as one of the team!"

Silence. I don't know what anyone else was doing because I'd glued my gaze to my feet. The air was filled with the hot smell of emotions, but everything was all mixed together: anger, guilt, indignation, embarrassment, coming from all directions.

Finally, Festina sighed. "Dade—once upon a time I would have said anyone who wanted to be an Explorer was too fucking insane to be allowed into the corps. But seeing as I *am* the woman who forced the navy to consider Explorers as more than 'expendable freaks' . . . all I'll say is that you worry me. You might have depths I can't see, but you sure come across as a starry-eyed kid who's too gung ho to realize the real world is dangerous. You've lived a damned pampered life, no matter what hardships you think you've faced, and all the Academy training in the galaxy hasn't prepared you to take care of yourself.

"But," she went on, "you aren't going to figure that out till you see for yourself. So congratulations; you can land with us on Troyen. I'm going to gamble that taking you down to a war-ravaged planet will open your eyes without getting the rest of us killed. The prospect of relying on you to watch my back scares the piss out of me, but I'm going to take the risk. Otherwise, I might start believing the Admiralty had the right idea all along, only picking Explorers from people who know the universe is a cruel and bitter place. People who were *born* knowing it."

Very pointedly, she tipped her head to give the boy a face-on view of her birthmark. "I grew up knowing something you didn't, Dade. So did Tobit. So did Kaisho. So did York over there, even if he still doesn't think he deserves an Explorer's uniform. York never went to the Academy, but the uniform fits him just fine. As for you, Dade— I'm giving you a chance because in your whole damned life, I don't think you've ever been put to the test. Maybe by some miracle, you'll find a real Explorer in your heart. If you don't . . . well, considering we'll be landing in a war zone, your future career is the least of your worries."

She waited a moment, then did the most unexpected thing an Explorer could do: lifted her hand, gave Dade a salute, and said crisply, "Dismissed." It took the boy a moment to remember Festina was an admiral; then his face went stony, he returned her salute, and walked stiffly out of the room.

The rest of us stayed where we were a moment, then slowly let out our breaths. In a low voice, Festina asked, "What do you think, Kaish? Any mystic visions of the boy smartening up?"

Kaisho reached both hands up to the hair over her face and suddenly lifted it high . . . as if her cheeks were hot and in desperate need of air. I caught a glimpse of her handsome crinkled face, just a tiny bit damp with sweat; then she let the hair fall back into place.

"The boy *does* have hidden depths," she whispered. "But I don't think you'll like them."

30

CHECKING IN ON
THE NEIGHBORS

Three full orbits of Troyen and we still hadn't picked up any transmissions from people down on the ground.

"Um," I murmured to Festina. "What if the Explorers' radios have been eaten by Fasskister nanites?"

Festina shook her head. "As soon as the navy heard about the Fasskisters' Swarm, our researchers developed equipment that was immune to the little buggers. Otherwise, the whole fleet would be at the Fasskisters' mercy."

"Yeah," Tobit put in, "everything we carry should be fine. Of course," he added, "the Fasskisters have probably invented a Swarm that'll eat our *new* equipment. But we'll cross our fingers there isn't any of that on Troyen."

"There shouldn't be," Festina said. "If *Willow*'s Explorers aren't transmitting, they're just being careful. In a war zone, it's dangerous to broadcast continuously, even if your messages are encrypted to look like static. Sooner or later, some army will decide you're an undercover agent sending intelligence to the enemy; next thing you know, you're surrounded by a platoon of spycatchers."

Lucky for us, there was a fallback plan for making contact. Whenever an Explorer team is assigned to a ship, they're given a "transmission second"—one second of the standard twenty-four-hour clock when they should try a burst transmission, if they're ever on a planet where longer broadcasts are dangerous. It took a bit of calculating, converting *Willow* time to *Jacaranda* time and allowing for relativistic slippages in everybody's clocks . . . but eventually, Festina and Tobit agreed that the folks down on Troyen would try a single blip of contact at 23:46:22, *Jacaranda* time. Since it was only ship's morning, we had most of the day before we'd hear anything.

"So, a whole day to kill," Tobit said. "You folks play poker?"

"Enough to know I don't want to play with you," Festina told him. "What do you say to a side trip?"

"Where?"

Instead of answering, she turned to me. "Edward, do you know exactly what *Willow* did its five days in this system? Were you watching the whole time?"

"I wasn't watching at all. The base's monitors just had a big display of what navy ships were close by. *Willow* showed up on the list, and stayed there till they picked me up to go home."

"So *Willow* might not have stayed near Troyen all the time. They could have gone somewhere else for a while."

"But there's nowhere else to go in this system," Dade said. "Nowhere else inhabited, anyway."

"Wrong," Festina told him. "There's an orbital around the sun. Occupied by Fasskisters who don't want to leave the area, for fear of being killed by the League." She smiled grimly. "Now ask yourself: if anyone in the galaxy created specialized nano like the stuff on *Willow* that was stealing queen's venom, who would it be?"

"Oh," Dade said. "Yeah."

Festina nodded. "Let's assume *Willow* visited the orbital while they were in this system. And let's assume the Fasskisters smuggled nano onto the *Willow* during that visit. Shouldn't someone ask them why?"

Like most orbitals, it was a big cylinder floating in space, the surface skin covered with photocells that gathered energy from the sun. Unlike most orbitals, the photocells had been arranged into bands running lengthways with strips of white in between, so that the whole cylinder was covered with long black-and-white stripes.

"Assholes," Festina muttered. We were all sitting in the bridge's Visitors' Gallery, watching as *Jacaranda* slowly approached the Fasskister habitat.

"What's wrong?" I asked.

"Do you know why they left some stripes clear . . . even though they could collect more power if they covered the whole damned surface?"

"No," I said.

"They did it so you'd know the orbital wasn't spinning," she told me. "Anyone flying up can see the stripes are holding steady . . . so the Fasskisters can't be producing gravity with good old centrifugal force."

"They don't have gravity in there?"

"They have it; they just use some flashy fancy artificial field that guzzles energy twenty-four hours a day. This close to the sun, they have solar power to spare . . . but it's still waste for the sake of waste."

"Admiral," Prope said, turning around in her command chair, "they aren't answering our requests to dock."

"Can we dock anyway?" Festina asked.

"Affirmative," Prope answered, "but they probably won't like it. Docking without permission can be interpreted as intent to commit piracy."

Festina made a face. "Send them a message in English, Fasskister and Mandasar. Say we're worried about their status because they've gone incommunicado. If we don't get a reply in five minutes, we'll assume they're in trouble and come to give aid."

"Begging the admiral's pardon," Prope said, without an ounce of begging in her voice, "but that's a standard tactic for pirates too. Even if the target is broadcasting like mad, the pirate ship says, 'We can't hear anything,' and keeps coming in. Naive victims think their radios are broken and let the pirate come aboard. More experienced sailors think they're under attack and take defensive action."

"What kind of defensive action?"

Prope shrugged. "The Fasskisters believe they can't leave this system because the League considers them non-sentient. Under such conditions, they may have decided they have nothing to lose by arming themselves with lethal weapons. Especially with warring Mandasars nearby. The Fasskisters could legitimately argue they were afraid of being attacked."

Festina drummed her fingers on the arm of her chair. After a few seconds, she said, "Send the message and go in anyway. Take any precautions you think necessary. I'll assume responsibility."

"Aye-aye, Admiral," Prope said. She tried to make her voice sound icy-full of misgivings . . . but if I knew Prope, she'd lived her whole life hoping to luck into an honest-to-God space battle.

We docked without incident—sliding up to a hatch on the orbital's dark side (the half that wasn't facing the sun), and dropping our Sperm-field so we could stretch out a docking tube. Prope hated cutting the field; star captains feel kind of naked when they can't go FTL to get away from trouble. (It must have mortified her when the black ship had ripped away *Jacaranda*'s field back at Starbase Iris—like getting her clothes torn off in public.) Prope kept telling Festina, over and over, "One hour on the orbital . . . not a second more, if you expect us to reestablish the tail and get back to Troyen by 23:46:22."

I could tell Festina wasn't too happy with the time limit; but considering the circumstances, she couldn't argue. One hour would have to do.

Festina declared our jaunt to the orbital would be Explorers only. The Mandasars grumped, but the admiral held firm—with all the bad feeling between Mandasars and Fasskisters, it wouldn't help to take the hive along.

Kaisho wanted to go too. "Why?" Festina asked.

"You'll see," Kaisho told her.

"Come on, Kaish," Festina said, "cut the inscrutable-alien crap. Either give me a straight answer or stay on *Jacaranda*."

"Sorry," Kaisho replied, "but the Balrog loves watching lesser beings get smacked in the face with surprises. Just between you and me, the damned moss really gets off on human astonishment."

"Shit," Festina growled. "Just once I'd like to meet an alien who enjoyed giving clear explanations of what the fuck is going on."

We didn't wear tightsuits this trip; apparently Fasskisters found the suits grossly offensive, though they never said why. With any group of aliens, there's always some area where they just mutter, "Can't you see it's indecent?" and refuse to go into details. Anyway, the dock hatch reported good air on the orbital's interior, and we didn't have time to get dressed up. There could still be nasty germs wafting about . . . but if the Fasskisters ever wanted to regain their claim to sentience, they'd make sure we weren't exposed to anything that could hurt us.

"All right," Festina said, as we hovered weightless in front of the dock's airlock. "In we go."

She pressed the button to open the door. One by one, we passed over the threshold; and immediately gravity clicked in, twisting around so that the outside of the cylinder was down. If I'd been taken by surprise, I might have fallen right back out into the docking tube . . . but lucky for me, Festina went first and I could watch how she grabbed the support bars just inside the door.

I got in without too much trouble, followed by Tobit and Dade. All three of the others tapped their throats as soon as they were inside, activating the radio transceivers implanted in their necks. It made me feel a bit bad, to be an Explorer without a throat implant . . . but then, I wasn't a *real* Explorer, was I?

Meanwhile, they did the usual, "Testing, testing," and

Lieutenant Harque back on *Jacaranda* answered, "Receiving loud and clear." Harque's voice came in on receivers we'd clipped to our belts. The receivers could also transmit if you pushed the right button, but there was no need for that if you had a throat implant.

Festina worked the airlock while the rest of us stood back trying not to look nervous. The far door of the lock had a tiny peekaboo screen that wasn't working—either the Fasskisters had deliberately blinded the cameras, or the system had broken down sometime in the past twenty years and nobody bothered to fix it. From my days on the moonbase, I knew the Fasskisters only got supply ships once every three years . . . so maybe they didn't care a whole lot if the dock-area cameras went out.

"Are we set?" Festina asked, just before she pushed the button to open the inner door.

Dade tried to draw his stunner, but Tobit slapped the boy's wrist. It was pretty unfriendly to be carrying guns at all; having them drawn and ready was going too far.

The door whisked open. A second later, the smell of buttered toast filled my nostrils. In front of us, a ramp led up at an easy slope; and the ramp was covered with glowing red moss.

31

GETTING TO KNOW
THE FASSKISTERS

"Kaisho!" Festina roared.

Laughter came over our receivers. "A problem, Festina?"

"You knew about this!"

"Of course."

"And you didn't tell us."

"As I said," Kaisho answered, "the Balrog adores surprises. The nice thing about precognition is knowing when someone else will step on a banana peel."

"We're not going to step on anything," Festina growled. The four of us stared at the ramp again. It was completely crammed with moss, at least ankle deep, starting a few paces beyond the airlock door. No way we could go forward without getting it all over our boots, unless we could crawl across the walls like bugs.

Kaisho spoke again from our receivers. "If you like, I can ferry you over in my hoverchair."

"No," Festina told her. "I don't want you anywhere near us. You're hard to trust at the best of times, and recently you've been a real pain in the ass."

"Then what are you going to do?" Kaisho asked, a bit smugly.

"Um," I said. "Give me a second."

In my mind, I tried to imagine a stench that would make moss wither . . . like really bad breath, something that could knock you straight off your feet, except that it'd only work on Balrogs. The Balrog could obviously smell stuff humans couldn't, like royal pheromone; so maybe I could produce a stink so powerfully awful to Balrog senses, the moss would kind of shrivel. Not die—I didn't want it to die. I just wanted to turn its stomach. If I started with its own buttered-toast scent and pictured the toast going all green and moldy . . .

"*Teelu*," Kaisho said sharply. Talking out loud, not whispering. "Stop it!"

"Stop what?" I asked, trying to sound innocent.

"You know what," Kaisho snapped, "but you *don't* know what you're doing. Given time, you might find something that would cause serious harm."

"What's she talking about?" Festina asked me.

"*Teelu* and I are playing a little game," Kaisho answered, "and he doesn't understand his own strength. Biochemicals can be more than smells, Your Majesty—one species' pheromone is another species' poison. If you muck about too much, you might hurt someone . . . and it could be humans just as easily as Balrogs."

"What?" Festina demanded. She stared straight at me. "What are you doing?"

"His own form of diplomacy," Kaisho said. "Talk softly and carry a big stink."

Festina looked like she wanted more answers; but at that moment, the moss in front of us simply rolled aside. A parting of the glowing red sea. The spores in the center of the ramp slid right or left, till they left a clear walkway up the middle—bare concrete floor, walled on either side by heaps of glowering fuzz. The buttered-toast smell turned a bit edgy . . . as if even a higher lifeform could get ticked off.

"Did you do that?" Festina asked me.

I shook my head as Kaisho answered, "I did. Or rather,

the Balrog did it at my request. Go ahead—the moss will leave you alone. I promise."

"She promises," Tobit muttered. "That fills me with loads of confidence."

"You two stay here," Festina told Tobit and Dade. "Edward and I will go in. If anything happens to us—like we get our toes bitten by spores—arrest that bitch for assaulting an admiral. Even if the Balrog is sentient, I have faith the High Council can devise an appropriately unattractive punishment." She lifted her hand to her throat implant. "You heard that, Kaisho?"

"You lesser species can be so suspicious. I said the Balrog would leave you alone, and it will. It won't try to touch you as long as you're on this orbital."

"Great," Festina muttered. "That sounds like those promises the gods always gave in Greek myths—loaded statements with nasty loopholes. But," she continued, staring at the open path through the moss, "I would dearly like to ask a Fasskister what the hell happened here."

She looked at me, as if I had some kind of deciding vote. I thought of what Captain Prope would say if we came running back at the first sign of trouble . . . not that I cared about my own reputation, but I didn't want Festina to look bad. "Let's go," I said.

So we did.

The ramp led to another hatch that should have been closed but wasn't—it had jammed partway open, leaving a gap in the middle. Our path through the moss led right up to the gap and beyond.

"Looks like the Balrog has fouled up the gears," Festina said, examining the hatch.

"Do doors have gears?" I asked.

"Don't go literal on me," she answered.

We squeezed through the gap and into a world glowing crimson. At one time, this must have been a pretty standard orbital—forty square kilometers of land on the cylinder's inner surface, a lot of it dedicated to parks and agriculture.

Orbitals always go heavy on the fields and forests, so people don't fixate on being closed in; even if you can see the other side of the cylinder overhead, it's not so bad if you're surrounded by trees and grass.

So the Fasskisters' home had probably been filled with their own native versions of nice little woods, quiet meadows, and the occasional rustic village. Now it was filled with Balrog, and it looked like some classic version of hell: scarlet, scarlet everywhere, like fire and lava and blood.

The orbital had a long white sun, kind of a fluorescent light tube stretching down the middle of the cylinder; but here on the ground, the whiteness of the shine was tinted crimson as far as the eye could see—as if we'd stepped inside a cherry-hot blast oven. The temperature was actually a bit cool, but the sheer look of the place made me break into a sweat.

"Dante would have been proud," Festina murmured, staring at it all. The red light shone up from the ground onto her face, casting weird shadows and giving her eyes little pinpoint dots of scarlet. I didn't like the effect.

"What do we do?" I asked.

"Damned if I know," she answered. Looking off to our right, she said, "There's a village over there. Let's see if anyone's around."

As soon as we aimed ourselves in that direction, the moss in front of our feet slipped aside to let us pass. Underneath was bare dirt. There must have been plants here once, grass or vegetables or something; but the Balrog had eaten clean down to the soil, gobbling whatever it found. It had probably eaten the support life too—all the worms and bugs and bacteria that orbitals need to keep the land healthy. The little animals weren't sentient, so they were fair game for food . . . but still. It made me kind of squeamish to think of them getting dissolved by mossy digestive juices.

The path continued to open in front of us . . . and close in behind us. Not comforting. But the moss kept its distance, sifting away like drifting snow as we approached the village.

The huts in the village were half-sphere domes molded from glassy crystal, with millions of facets catching the light. The light was crimson, of course, glinting as if each dome was a cut-glass bowl plopped over a campfire. Twelve huts in all, and nobody in sight . . . till we got to the central square and found a single lumpy figure.

When Fasskisters aren't dressed as some other species, they live inside "utility bots"—egg-shaped torsos with all kinds of legs and arms. I truly mean *all* kinds: ones that are clearly mechanical, as well as ones that mimic other species. If ever they have to deal with human technology, for example, it's useful to have a human-shaped arm with lifelike human fingers; makes it easier to punch buttons, lift levers, and all that. So a utility bot is designed to have one of everything . . . a human arm, a human leg, a Mandasar *Cheejretha*, a pincer, a tentacle, a pseudopod, and so on.

Of course, these weren't *exact* duplicates of the original limbs; since the robot had no head, each arm had its own eyes . . . and maybe ears and nose too. I can't tell you how the Fasskister in the central egg keeps track of sixteen eyes at once, but I guess that's none of my business. Anyway, it didn't matter to this particular Fasskister: all its eyes and arms and everything were completely clogged over with moss. It had to be blind; it also seemed to be frozen in place, as if all that fuzz had gummed up its works.

"Aw," Festina said, "poor Tin Man. Need some oil?"

A strangled sound came from inside . . . maybe the actual voice of a Fasskister: what you got when you shut down the electronic amplifiers they usually used for speaking. It didn't sound like words, at least not in English. I'd heard people say Fasskisters always spoke their own language; then circuitry in their suits converted their speech to a language their listeners understood.

Festina lifted her hand to her throat. "Kaisho," she said, "can you clean this guy off?"

Kaisho's whisper sounded over our receivers. "Why would I want to do that?"

"To keep from pissing me off," Festina told her. "One. Two. Three . . ."

Like sand spilling through an hourglass, spores began to tumble off the Fasskister in front of us—clearing the tips of his uppermost arms and slowly sliding downward, leaving behind bare metal and plastic. I didn't know which was more mind-boggling: that all these flecks of inanimate moss were moving of their own accord, or that Kaisho, way back in *Jacaranda*, could know which particular Fasskister we were looking at. And that she or her Balrog joyrider had some way of telling the spores in front of us, "Please, clear off, thanks so much."

The spores continued to fall. Suddenly, one of the Fasskister's metal arms gave a twitch. Its wrist rotated through a complete circle, then its first elbow twisted most of the way around too, till the glass sensor on the hand's thumb pointed directly at Festina and me. From the robot's chest, a deep male voice said, "Humans?"

"Greetings," Festina said with a slight bow. "We are sentient citizens of the League of Peoples. We beg your Hospitality."

The Fasskister swung his arm and nearly took off her head.

Festina didn't just duck; she deflected the swing with a quick little forearm block that flicked over and turned into a grab. Almost instantly she tugged on the robot's wrist, pulling the whole Fasskister forward. At the same moment, her knee came up hard. The effect was the robot getting yanked into a very nice knee strike that landed CLANG against the machine's metal chest.

On a human, the blow would have broken ribs. On the robot it didn't leave a dent, but I could hear something go THUNK. It sounded like the flesh-and-blood Fasskister smacking against the walls of his robot housing.

I jumped forward to help, grabbing two more arms (one light and spidery, the other wide and chunky). Festina yelled, "Lift!" and together we heaved the Fasskister off the ground. He didn't weigh much, but he'd started to wave his limbs wildly—not trying to wrestle us, more like a panicked attempt to get away, but I still got clonked a few good ones.

Festina snagged another of his arms with her free hand and shouted at the egg-shaped torso, "Settle down, or we'll throw you into the moss. I mean it. We don't want to hurt you, but if you can't behave, we'll toss you and find someone who can."

The Fasskister continued to flail about. Festina met my eye, and together we swung him back for a big throw, the way kids do when they're about to chuck someone into a swimming pool. "Last chance," Festina said to the Fasskister. "That moss sure looks hungry."

For once, the Balrog decided to play along—the patch of moss in front of us flared up fiery bright, like hell flames leaping to catch another sinner. The Fasskister gave a mousy shriek and went completely limp.

Slowly, regretfully, the Balrog settled back into its usual dull glow.

"That's better," Festina said. Keeping a tight hold on the robot's arms, we lowered it until its feet touched the ground. Bare dirt—the Balrog had pulled back a few paces so we had a little circle of clear space in the middle of the village square. "No place to run," Festina told the Fasskister as she let go of the robot's wrist. "You be nice, and we'll be nice."

"He'll be nice?" the Fasskister asked, pointing at me.

"Sure," I answered, confused by the question. "Why wouldn't I be nice?"

"I *know* you," he said. "You are definitely not nice."

Festina opened her eyes wide in surprise. I was surprised myself; but then I remembered how the Fasskisters on this orbital had been booted off Troyen for causing trouble, back before the war. For all I knew, this guy might have been stuck inside a queen robot on that first night, when Sam got me to crush the crystal globe and discombobulate them all. Or he might have been one of the many Fasskisters who'd been banished personally by the high queen, while I stood solemn-faced beside Verity's throne. He might just have despised me because I was tied to the whole system of monarchy, or because I was Diplomat Samantha's brother—the Fasskister community never liked her much either. All kinds of reasons why I might not be popular with this fellow.

"I'll be nice," I told him. "Really."

The thing about Fasskisters is they're all locked up inside those robots, so you can't read the expressions on their faces. They don't even have body language unless they deliberately make the robot shake its fist or something. Even so, just standing there like a lump, this Fasskister pretty well communicated he didn't trust me a bit.

"Good," said Festina, "we're all just the peachiest of friends. So tell me now, one pal to another: where did this fucking moss come from?"

"Humans," he replied. "And one of the *Gragguk.*"

Gragguk was a Fasskister word they considered so obscene, their language circuits never translated it. *Gragguk* was also the word they used for Mandasar queens.

"How long ago?" Festina asked.

A pause. "Twenty-four of your standard days," the Fasskister answered. I did some calculations: I'd been on *Willow* ten days from Troyen to Celestia, then two days hanging off Starbase Iris, a day on Celestia, and another ten days coming back here . . . so *Willow* must have visited this orbital just before picking me up from the moonbase.

The Fasskister was still talking. "They came from over there," he said, gesturing toward the docking port with one of his smaller arms. "A *Gragguk* and four humans. All wearing uniforms of your navy."

"Black uniforms?" Festina asked.

"No. Two in dark blue, two in a shade of green."

Dark blue meant the Communications Corps; the "shade of green" was likely olive, for Security. Just the sort of party *Willow* would have sent to meet with aliens, if the ship's Explorers had already been left behind on Troyen.

"What did the group want?" Festina asked.

"Revenge!" The English word came out calmly from the translation circuits, but I could hear a sort of shriek inside the robot. The real Fasskister had screamed the word in his native tongue. "The *Gragguk* claimed she was the last of her caste, and she wished to apologize for the trouble caused by Verity's old regime. What she really wanted was to infect us with this!"

He spread all his arms at once, waving toward the moss surrounding us. "It appeared as soon as the *Gragguk* left. Her blatant attempt to destroy us."

Probably true: your average queen is more keen on smiting her enemies than apologizing to them. If that Queen Temperance was leaving the Troyen system and thought she might never come back, she could have given *Willow* some story about wanting to make peace with the Fasskisters; then she'd dumped some Balrog spores on the ground when neither humans nor Fasskisters were watching.

"Where do you think the queen got the spores?" I whispered to Festina.

"From Kaisho herself," Festina answered. "Our beloved companion stepped on the Balrog twenty-five years ago, before the war started. When human doctors couldn't help her, the navy brought in a Mandasar team—the best medical experts available. They took spore samples back home with them, so they could research ways of separating the Balrog from its host . . . not that they ever came up with any answers. The samples must have stayed in some test tube on Troyen, till the queen from *Willow* got her claws on them."

"If she only planted the spores twenty-four days ago," I said, "the stuff grew pretty fast."

"Like lightning," the Fasskister told me. He began to walk toward one of the crystal huts. Grudgingly, the Balrog slipped out of his path; Festina and I followed along behind.

"The plague swept over us without warning," the Fasskister said. "Tendrils of it spread through the grass, so thin they were practically invisible. When you took a wrong step the moss would suddenly sweep upward, covering your shell and shutting down all movement systems. It left life support intact, and even seemed to be providing basic food through our nutrient ports; but I've been frozen for days!"

"Do you think it's the same everywhere?" Festina asked.

The Fasskister let his arms go slack. "I don't know. Our village is closest to the docking port, where the plague was released. We were taken by surprise. Perhaps others had time to prepare . . ."

"And perhaps not," Festina finished. "When our ship came to call, no one was answering the radio."

The Fasskister pulled in its arms and passed through a door into the hut. There was plenty of light inside, diffused straight through the dome's crystal. I could see a clutter of moss-covered bulges on the floor, but didn't know if they were machines, furniture or people. The Balrog wouldn't let any of us get close enough to tell—the moss let us inside the door, but wouldn't yield any farther.

"Your family?" I asked sympathetically, looking at the bulges.

"My vidscreen and sound system!" the Fasskister answered. "I swear I'll sue that *Gragguk* till she screams."

"That'll be a good trick," Festina told him. "She's dead." The admiral pursed her lips and thought for a moment. "You were one of the people who met the humans and the queen?"

"Yes." The Fasskister was still waving his arms, turning the eyes on his hands to survey the great mossy mess. "The bastards came straight to our village."

"Because it's closest to the docking port," Festina murmured. "I don't suppose you planted any of your own nano on them . . . the way the queen planted spores on you."

"What do you mean?" the Fasskister asked.

"Nano shaped like little eyeballs," I told him. "Well . . . like human eyeballs anyway." I slipped out the door to bare ground, then knelt and drew a picture in the dirt: a nanite's big head, the long dangling tail. "They were programmed to sneak into a queen's venom sacs, steal a bit of venom, then run off before they were caught."

"Yes," Festina said. "If you made the nano, what for? Why would you want to steal venom? And even if you did want venom, how did you think you'd ever retrieve the nanites when *Willow* was headed to a different star system?"

For a second, the Fasskister said nothing. Then, from inside the robot shell came a high-pitched chittering sound, like a squirrel scolding someone for disturbing its nest. Mechanical arms lurched and bounced as if they were having spasms . . . or as if the Fasskister inside was rocking back and forth hysterically, bumping into control switches at random.

From the robot's speakers, the language circuits drily pronounced, "Ha ha ha. Ha ha ha. Ha ha ha."

The Fasskister was laughing his amps off.

"What's so funny?" Festina demanded.

"You think . . . ha ha ha . . . we could make . . . ha . . . nanotech like that . . . ha ha . . . in so little time? The *Gragguk* was only here . . . ha . . . for an hour. Your little eyeballs . . . ha ha . . . took a team *ages* to develop."

Festina and I just stared bug-eyed. After a while, she said, "So you know about those nanites?"

"Of course. They were a major commission. Almost all of us on this orbital worked on the project."

"How long ago?"

"Many of your years. It's gratifying to know they're still operational."

"Why did you make them?"

"For a client," the Fasskister said. "I don't know who. The business office said it was top secret—no name on the specifications."

"What did the specifications call for?" Festina asked.

"An integrated nanotech system," the Fasskister replied. "For secret entry, secret exit, some independent decision making, plenty of built-in evasion strategies . . . all standard requirements. We get a lot of orders for nanites that can sneak in and out of places without being noticed."

"I'll bet," Festina muttered.

"The real trick was keying it to his DNA." The Fasskister pointed at me.

I yelped. "Me?"

"Yeah."

Festina's jaw had dropped. "Edward? The nano was keyed to *Edward*?"

"Yeah," the Fasskister said. "The high *Gragguk*'s pretty-boy gigolo."

I swallowed hard. "What were the nanites supposed to do?"

"Find a queen," the Fasskister said. "Take a swig of venom. Go running back to you, wherever you were, and spit the venom down your throat. Like a mother *illi'im* that fills up on food, then vomits it into her baby's mouth."

"So," Festina murmured, "the nanites weren't on *Willow* to begin with?"

"I don't know what this *Willow* is," the Fasskister told her, "but I do know those nanites. They follow the high *Gragguk*'s consort wherever he goes, and dose him with venom whenever they can steal some from a queen. That's their job. And they've been doing it since well before the war started."

I stood there like a dummy, not really taking it in. I was the carrier: me. Maybe I shouldn't have been surprised— you can be surrounded by a horde of nano and never notice it, any more than you notice the billions of natural bacteria in the air around you. A full nano scan would have found I had hitchhikers, but I'd never been put through the slightest examination . . . not when I'd gone from Troyen to the moonbase, and not when *Willow* picked me up. That was pretty darned careless, when you thought about it; but by then, *Willow* had left its Explorers on Troyen, and Explorers are the ones who are supposed to be fanatical about decontamination. The rest of *Willow*'s crew just assumed I was clean.

I'd assumed I was clean too. In twenty years on the moonbase, my nanite attendants hadn't done a thing. They'd only kicked into action when I found the dead queen in *Willow*'s hold. All of a sudden, they had something to do: filling their little eyeballs with venom and ferrying it back to me. No wonder I got sick—I probably would have died if I hadn't stationed those defense clouds around the queen's venom sacs. The clouds cut off the nanites from getting more poison.

The real question was why I hadn't died on Troyen. If the nanites had dogged my heels since before the war, they must have had a busy time when I was living in the same palace as Queen Verity. They'd be dosing me with venom morning, noon, and night; but I was perfectly okay till I caught the Coughing Jaundice . . .

Oh.

Oh.

The jaundice was really venom poisoning. The night I got sick was when the nanites started their work. And the only thing that kept me alive was a team of the best doctors on Troyen. Right there at the end, when I started to get better, maybe I'd finally built up a resistance to the stuff; after all, it'd been a whole year and the queen's chemical cycle was repeating itself. But till that time, I was constantly getting dosed with new enzymes and hormones and junk, twisting me inside out, practically killing me . . .

For what? Who would intentionally do that to me? The Fasskisters must have charged big money for a project so complicated . . . and who would put up that much cash just to kill yours truly? I wasn't anyone important. And if somebody really did want me snuffed, why choose such a strange and complicated way to do it?

The same questions were probably going through Festina's head. When I turned toward her, she was looking at me thoughtfully. "You, Edward," she said, "are the eye of one nasty fucking shitstorm. It's not your doing, but it terrifies the crap out of me." She thought a moment longer.

"I'm going to ask you a question, and I want an honest answer. Okay?"

All of a sudden, I felt too scared to talk. I just nodded my head.

"Edward," she said, "were you and your sister genetically engineered? From scratch? Before conception?"

Even though I'd been expecting something awful, I'd never expected her to hit my darkest secret. For a wild second, I hoped some spirit would take possession of my body—tell a convincing lie, or pump out some magical pheromone that would make her forget she'd ever brought up the subject. But no deus ex machina came to rescue me. In the end, all I said was, "Um."

"Okay," she said, patting me gently on the shoulder. "That explains a lot. About nanites and Mandasars and the war." Her mouth turned up in a wry little smile. "It even explains about judo mats." She lifted up quickly on tiptoe and gave me a light kiss on the cheek. "But you were a perfect gentleman. A real prince." She chuckled. "Now let's get back to *Jacaranda*."

"Hey," the Fasskister said. A very calm, "Hey," because the translation computer seemed to be programmed to keep an even tone of voice. But inside the robot shell, the "Hey" had been a sharp piercing squeak. "You're just going to leave now? Walk off like you've solved all your problems? Forget about my vidscreen and my sound system?"

"And the people," I said.

"Right," the Fasskister agreed hurriedly. "The people. There are hundreds of us on this orbital; are you just going to leave everybody frozen here?"

"What do you want us to do?" Festina asked.

"You got the moss off me," he said. "Do the same for everything else. Everybody." When Festina hesitated, he told her, "I helped you, didn't I? I answered your questions. So now it's time you owe me a favor. Lose the damned moss."

"All right," Festina sighed. She lifted her hand to her throat. "Kaisho, have you been following all this?"

A whisper came back over our receivers. "Yes."

"I have to sympathize with this fellow," Festina told her. "The Balrog has gone completely overboard. Sooner or later, the Fasskister Union is going to find out about this; they're sure to notice if a whole orbital goes incommunicado for any length of time. When they send a ship to see what's happened, the Fasskisters will turn ape-shit. They'll run to every race in the known universe, screaming to have you declared non-sentient."

"Let them," Kaisho answered. "The highest echelons of the League know the Balrog is more sentient than all you lesser species put together."

"But it doesn't look that way," I said, trying to be reasonable. "It kind of looks like you're . . . well, that queen from *Willow* was a dangerous non-sentient, right? And she brought the Balrog to this orbital so she could get back at the Fasskisters. The Balrog did exactly what she wanted. So it looks like you're aiding and abetting a dangerous non-sentient."

Kaisho chuckled. "Nicely argued, *Teelu*. They'll be fitting you for a diplomat's uniform any day now. But this has nothing to do with the queen. The Fasskisters know full well why it's right and proper to lock them in their precious metal suits, with physical needs taken care of, but their minds slowly going crazy."

"What do you mean?" Festina asked. No answer. "Come on, Kaisho, cut the crap and explain what's going on."

Still no answer from Kaisho; but it was obvious the Fasskister understood exactly what she was talking about. A high-pitched squeal came from inside the robot shell. The machine suddenly spun away from us and ran out the door. He only got two short steps before reaching the edge of the clear space untouched by moss. Beyond that, there was nowhere to go—the Fasskister's arms waved in panic, all his eyes scanning the ground for an escape route. Even as we watched, moss surged forward, like a wave on a beach lapping over the Fasskister's toes.

Except that a wave doesn't leave a fuzzy red coating on your feet.

As quickly as the spores had trickled off the Fasskister's metal housing, they swept back up again: crimson mold climbing over ankle joints and knees, crusting over the central egg, scaling the arms. Elbows stopped waving; wrists stopped writhing; fingers froze into frantic claws that fattened with moss till they looked like furry mittens.

Inside the Fasskister's shell, a high-pitched mousy wail echoed for a few seconds, broke off, then started again. I took a step forward, but Festina grabbed my arm to hold me back. She pointed to the ground—the Balrog was starting to advance toward us, cutting us off from getting close to the Fasskister.

We had to retreat . . . with the moss crowding us out of the village, forcing Festina and me along a narrow track that grudgingly opened in front of our feet. Leaving us no option, the Balrog shooed us to the docking hatch and back into *Jacaranda*.

32

SCOPING OUT THE GROUND

I spent the rest of the day in quarantine. We all did: getting completely cleaned off, swept free of nanites. At least it didn't hurt as much as getting scoured by the defense cloud—a personal detox chamber took its time, rather than ripping at anything that might be suspicious. Gentle thoroughness, as opposed to the quick and dirty.

But there were quick and dirty defense clouds at work in other parts of *Jacaranda*. The clouds purged my cabin and the Explorers' planning room, places I might have left wandering nanites. The ship's evac modules got a once-over too, on the theory that unattached nanites might be hiding there; that seemed to be their *modus operandi*.

I hope Prope assigned a cloud to her own quarters. She should have got detoxed herself, considering how she and I had had that session of really close contact . . . but she just stayed on the bridge, grumbling about all the bother of sending antinanite clouds hither, thither, and yon.

After all, the nanites were only dangerous to *me*.

By 23:00 we were back orbiting Troyen, with a litter of microsatellites listening all around the globe. I sat with the others in the bridge's Visitors' Gallery, occasionally casting glances at Festina. She was an admiral; she got to stand out on the bridge itself, hovering over Prope's shoulder in a way guaranteed to make the captain irritable. That was probably why Festina did it.

We hadn't had a chance to talk since coming back to *Jacaranda* . . . not in private, anyway. I wanted to apologize for being a clone, and ask her to explain what she'd been thinking back on the orbital. It seemed like maybe she'd figured out more about me than I knew myself; and I sort of kind of wanted to know what it was.

Sort of. Kind of. Whatever truth she'd guessed, I was pretty sure I wouldn't like it.

At 23:46:22, our satellites picked up the beep. Not a real beep, of course—just a flick of radio energy at a frequency that could easily be mistaken for spillover from some electric appliance. Not that Troyen *had* any electric appliances working at the moment, but the navy's equipment designers couldn't plan for everything.

"Where are they?" Festina asked eagerly. "Can we triangulate?"

"Give me another second," Kaisho replied. She got to be on the bridge too, sitting at the Explorers' station. Nobody was happy with Kaisho operating the controls—Festina was strongly inclined to lock her in the brig—but we didn't have any other choice. It took hours and hours to program all the sensors, and everybody but Kaisho had been locked most of the day in nano detox. If we wanted to be ready by 23:46:22, Festina had to let Kaisho rig things up and run them.

From the look on Festina's face, I figured this was the last time Kaisho would be allowed to run anything but her own wheelchair.

"All right," Kaisho announced in her usual whisper. "The signal came from Unshummin city—practically inside Verity's palace."

"What the fuck are Explorers doing there?" Tobit asked.

Me, I was looking at the bridge's main vidscreen where a map display showed the source of the beep. It was just outside the palace walls, on the south edge of Diplomats

Row. "That's the Fasskister embassy," I said. "At least it was. It could have got wrecked in the war."

"Stupid spot for the Explorers to hole up," Festina muttered. "If *I* wanted to avoid trouble, I'd head for open country, not the very heart of Unshummin."

"Perhaps, Admiral," said Prope, "the people from *Willow* are more comfortable in the city. Not everyone is from such a rustic background as you are."

Festina glared. "Thank you, Captain," she replied icily, "I'll take that as the compliment it was surely meant to be. As for the supposed dangers that city-dwellers believe infest the wilderness . . ." She waved her hand dismissively. "The most dangerous creatures on Troyen right now are the Mandasar armies, and I guarantee Unshummin palace is crawling with soldiers. No matter who's winning or losing the war, *someone* will have a huge military presence there . . . for the sheer symbolic appeal of holding the high queen's throne and sitting on it from time to time. If I were in the neighborhood, I'd hightail it out of town—off to some nice quiet nowhere without the slightest strategic importance."

"Ah, dear Festina," Kaisho whispered, "suppose you didn't have that option."

She pointed at the vidscreen and turned a dial on her console. The map display changed to an actual overhead photo of Unshummin—a high aerial perspective with the palace in the middle and a good chunk of property all around. A big circle, maybe ten kilometers across.

At that scale, the palace itself was no bigger than the palm of my hand, but still recognizable by its hive-queen shape: head to the north; claws fanned out west, northwest, northeast, and east; the body stretching back to the south, with its huge five-story brain hump and those two glass domes nestled where the tail met the torso—the venom sacs, glistening bright green from the plants in the two conservatories.

Surrounding the palace were the canals, artificial waterways forming concentric circles that divided the city into rings; and crossing the canals by more than a hundred bridges were the radii, good-sized streets running straight out from the palace grounds. The whole layout looked like a dartboard with the high queen sitting in the bull's-eye . . . which was a pretty lousy place to be when you thought about it.

As far as I could see, the city seemed pretty much intact despite twenty years of war—the only obvious destruction was a big burned swath between the fourth and fifth canals. A fire had taken out almost the entire ring, flattening everything black; but it looked like the flames hadn't crossed the water on either side, so the damage had been contained.

Of course, there might have been other wreckage that didn't show up on the picture. We'd caught the city at sunset, as long shadows stretched from west to east, jumbling up the patterns and perspectives. With all the computer gadgetry at her disposal, Kaisho should have been able to filter out those shadows and give a crystal-clear view of everything . . . but I guess she preferred the dramatic night-is-coming effect.

"Unshummin palace," she whispered. The ship-soul brightened the center of the picture to make it stand out.

"The signal source," Kaisho said. A blue pinpoint of light flared up on Diplomats Row. I squinted, trying to see if that really was the Fasskister embassy. Yes, that's what it looked like . . . though the building's front facade was missing, as if someone had mushed it in. No big surprise, I guess—considering how folks on Troyen felt about the Fasskisters, it was a wonder they hadn't blown the embassy to rubble.

"The perimeter," Kaisho said. A green circle-ish loop appeared over top of Prosperity Water, the fourth canal out from the middle. It sure wasn't the perimeter of the city itself—there were ten more canals beyond Prosperity, plus a sprawl of developments that had sprouted after the original zoning plan was set up.

"Perimeter of what?" Tobit asked. "The fire zone?" Prosperity was the inside edge of that burned-out area I'd seen.

"You could call it a fire zone," Kaisho answered. "It's actually a perimeter of defense. For the palace. They've blown up all the bridges, making the canal a moat. I imagine they burned down everything in that ring so they'd have a clear shot at anyone coming in. Because here's where the enemy is."

The photo blossomed with scarlet dots: thousands of them, maybe millions, covering the whole city outside the fire zone. They didn't just block the radius roads; they were everywhere, hunkered down along the canals, at the bridges, inside buildings, sealing off every possible exit.

A vast red deluge of firepower . . . and our Explorers were trapped at ground zero.

33

APPRAISING THE RISKS

"Are you sure?" Dade asked Kaisho. "I mean . . . the sensors are just picking up heat sources right? Ones that match the Mandasar profile. So how can you tell the difference between one set of soldiers and another? How can you tell they're soldiers at all? Those people outside the perimeter could just be civilians."

Kaisho gave a soft chuckle. "Next picture, ship-soul." As if she'd expected him to ask precisely that question and had already set up an answer.

The screen image split into halves, both sides showing Mandasar warriors. The warriors on the left were tucked under an urban camo awning, but the perspective came down at enough of an angle that we could see the front parts of their bodies. They all had black patches painted on their shells at the upper shoulders, like blobby epaulettes; for weapons they held wooden crossbows with big ugly arrows whose heads were nasty enough to penetrate Mandasar armor.

The warriors on the right half of the picture had crossbows too, and sharp steel tips attached to their claws. No epaulettes, black or otherwise. This group was slinking along the edge of a street, keeping well into the sunset shadows.

"The ones with black markings," Kaisho said, "are outside the perimeter. The unmarked ones are inside. And before you ask, Mr. Dade, no, I haven't checked every warrior on both sides . . . but I've looked at enough to be confident of my sampling. The army of the black has surrounded a much smaller force based in the palace. Both sides are holding their positions rather than trying to kill each other."

"A cease-fire?" Festina suggested. "Perhaps their leaders are trying to work out a surrender."

"I suspect the palace army doesn't *have* a leader," Kaisho replied. "Let me suggest a scenario."

"Oh good," Tobit muttered. "Someone thinks she can explain this mess."

Kaisho nodded, her hair bouncing slightly over her face. "*Willow* was supposed to find a queen. Where would the Explorers look first? Queens could be practically anywhere on the entire planet. Do you start going to every army camp your sensors pick up, asking, 'Excuse me, do you have a queen here?' Or do you go to a known position that's almost certain to have a queen in residence?"

"Unshummin palace," Festina said.

"Exactly. It's easy to find, and you can be sure some queen must have claimed it for her own. That's where *Willow* went first; and they found a queen who was pantingly eager to go to Celestia, because she happened to be in deep shit: encircled and besieged by the Black Army.

"I see it going like this," Kaisho continued. "*Willow* sends Plebon and Olympia Mell to arrange things with the queen. The queen, of course, claims she's perfectly sentient and has never done an evil deed in her life. The Explorers believe the queen is lying; so they decide that when *Willow* leaves, they'll stay behind. Never mind that the palace is surrounded—better to take their chances with the Black Shoulders than be killed for sure by the League."

"And that's how they got stuck," Tobit said, nodding. "They must have thrown in their lot with the palace guards—got the queen to put in a good word for them before she left. They're not in immediate danger, but they're still bottled up by the Black Army and waiting for the ax to fall."

"Except that nobody's swinging axes," Festina pointed out. "Which is damned strange. How long has it been since *Willow* took away the queen? Three and a half weeks? With the queen gone, the palace guards have nothing to fight for; so why not surrender? And if the guards are too stubborn to give in, why hasn't the Black Army overrun the place? They certainly have the numbers to crush the defenders. So what's everybody waiting for?"

"Us," I said quietly. "They've been waiting for us."

Captain Prope sat up sharply in her chair. "Us?" she murmured. "Yes . . . us. We're the missing ingredient they've been waiting for." Her face had an I-knew-it-had-to-be-about-me expression . . . as if everything in the universe made sense once you saw it as part of Prope's own story.

Festina gave the captain an exasperated look, then turned to me. "How would they know we were coming, Edward? Even if it was common knowledge *Willow* left Explorers down there, no one would expect us to attempt a rescue. The Admiralty has an ironclad policy never to remove *anyone* from a war planet till the fighting stops. Complete quarantine. Our group can go down there because I think it's necessary for the fleet's sentience . . . but under normal circumstances, the navy would leave those Explorers to rot."

I couldn't argue with her, but I knew I was right. Sam told me Temperance was the last holdout against the new high queen. Temperance must have been occupying the palace, and Samantha was advisor to the queen on the other side. Now my sister was telling the Black Epaulettes, "Wait. Don't attack. Wait."

Sam expected I'd use Dad's access code and order a navy ship to fly me to Troyen. Then I was supposed to land and *join her in the high queen's palace*. Her very words: "in the high queen's palace." Except that the palace was the one place Sam's side didn't control.

So what would happen if me and Festina and the rest tried to land at the palace as directed? The Black Army would go crazy. They'd see the Sperm-tail flutter out of the sky, and they'd think offworlders were coming to help Temperance's side—summoned by Temperance herself, who was last seen leaving on a Technocracy ship. The black troops would spring to the attack, hoping to overrun the palace before we offworlders had a chance to get settled; and in the ensuing fight, with battle musk as thick as smoke in a burning house, every human in the area would be slaughtered. The attacking soldiers wouldn't hesitate a second. They'd shred our whole group in the belief we were outside mercenaries trying to meddle in Mandasar affairs.

Isn't that how it would go? We'd all be killed. And it would get written off as an accident of war, a sad, sad tragedy. The new high queen would apologize to the Technocracy, with all the grief in the world: "What a terrible shame. Let's establish channels of communication so this never happens again." The Admiralty would say yes, while breathing their own sigh of relief—with Festina and me out of the way, the mess with *Willow* would be hushed up. Soon, the recruiters on Celestia would start operating again; maybe they'd even start a branch office on Troyen.

In the end, everybody would be happy. Except those of us who were dead.

I told myself there had to be something I didn't understand. My sister would never draw me into a deliberate massacre. She must have some other scheme I just wasn't smart enough to figure out.

But I had a hollow feeling in the pit of my stomach, and it wouldn't go away.

"Do we go down or not?" Dade asked. He was looking at Festina. Everyone on the bridge was watching her—even the regular crew who were supposed to keep their eyes on their monitors.

"We'll try it," Festina said at last, "but just a quick in and out. Five minutes, tops . . . and let's hope the people we're looking for are right where their signal came from."

Tobit had put on a poker face. "The second we send down our Sperm-tail," he said, "both armies will kick up a god-awful ruckus. They'll each think the other side is trying something sneaky."

"I know," Festina sighed. "Captain"—she turned to Prope—"as soon as we go down, I'd like *Jacaranda* to broadcast a message on all radio bands, saying we're a neutral party just retrieving a group of noncombatants. Peaceful and not allied with any faction."

"They'll never believe it," Prope said. "It's exactly the sort of ruse a group of invaders would try." (Prope sure seemed to have thought a lot about lies dishonest people might tell.)

"Even so," Festina told her, "we have to deliver the message. For the sake of sentience."

She glanced at the vidscreen. It still showed the two pictures side by side, Black Epaulettes and the palace guards, waiting uneasily. "When we go in," Festina said, "jittery soldiers are going to react from sheer nervous tension. We can hope they have enough discipline not to get carried away, but there's no guarantee. If we can do anything to avoid triggering an all-out battle, we have to try. I admit the radio message is a weak idea—God knows, all their radios may have been eaten by Fasskister nanites. If anyone has a better suggestion, I'm happy to listen."

She looked around the room. No one spoke. Finally, Dade cleared his throat. "Uh . . . does it really matter?"

"What do you mean?" Festina asked.

"These guys," he said, waving at the soldiers on the vidscreen. "They've all been at war, killing each other, right? That makes 'em non-sentient. Even the people who aren't on the front lines, the cooks and the baggage handlers and all—if they're helping the armies, they're knowingly abetting non-sentient activities, which makes them non-sentient too. So from the League's point of view, why does it matter what happens to *anybody* in Unshummin? I don't want those people to die, but if we do set off one bunch of non-sentients fighting another, the great and glorious League shouldn't give a damn."

"Jesus, Benny," Tobit groaned, "it's the first fucking rule

of Exploration, always assume *everything* is sentient till proven otherwise."

"But it's *been* proven otherwise," Dade said. "For twenty years, the armies have demonstrated just how non-sentient they are. Aren't we justified in assuming—"

"That there are no children in the palace?" I asked. "That while Queen Temperance lived there, she didn't keep laying eggs every twelve weeks? That there aren't other kids from all the warriors and gentles who've been thrown together with each other? That there isn't a single Mandasar in the palace who just ran there for protection when the Black Army showed up? That there aren't warriors and gentles and workers on both sides who firmly believe everything they've done was purely for the defense of their families, and others who may have been bloodthirsty once but now want peace more devoutly, more *sentiently* than any of us powder-puffs who've never gone through two decades of war? Is that what we're justified in assuming?"

Dade blushed and lowered his gaze . . . while I pretty well did the same thing. I'd never spoken like that before; I half thought I was possessed again, and kind of stupidly, I tried to wiggle my fingers just to make sure I was still in control. They wiggled—the words had come from me. Just a part of me I didn't know I had.

Festina patted me on the shoulder, then looked at the others. "Anything else?" she asked.

Prope opened her mouth to speak . . . but even she was careful not to meet anyone else's eyes. "It's my duty," the captain said, "to make official note of your analysis, Admiral. This landing may spark two hostile factions into battling each other; if that happens, the death count is bound to be enormous." She paused and made sure we were all listening—the normal bridge crew as well as us visitors. "It could be argued this landing constitutes a non-sentient act, since it runs the risk of provoking murder on a massive scale. The Outward Fleet will not force any of you to participate in the mission against your conscience."

I wondered if *Willow*'s captain had said the same to his

crew. He might have—navy regs require starship commanders to recognize dicey situations and call them accordingly. But at the moment, I figured Prope wasn't thinking about ethics so much as covering her butt . . . hoping this speech would get her off the hook with the League of Peoples. Even if the League killed the rest of us the next time we crossed the line, perhaps they'd let Prope pass because she'd spoken the right words. "Oh yes, I warned them it wasn't smart . . ."

"Thank you, Captain," Festina said stiffly. "You're perfectly correct. Anyone who considers this landing improper is encouraged to stay on the ship." She glanced at the screen again: the soldiers had flattened themselves in darkening shadows as the sun continued to set. "It'll be full night down there in thirty minutes," she said. "We'll begin suiting up then. If some of you don't show up at the robing chambers, I won't send anyone looking for you."

She nodded to nobody in particular and quietly left the bridge. For a long time, none of the rest of us moved.

34

WAITING IN THE
TRANSPORT BAY

We all showed up. In the little anteroom in front of *Jac-aranda*'s four robing chambers, everyone I thought might come, did: Tobit, Dade, Kaisho, Counselor, Zeeleepull, Hib & Nib & Pib.

And me, of course. I can't say I'd thought long and hard about the morals of what we were doing. Mostly I'd been busy on the bridge. With a bit of persuasion (talk, not pheromones), I'd convinced Prope to let me record the message that would be broadcast when we landed: telling everyone I was the Little Father Without Blame, just coming down to Unshummin to pick up some friends. It wasn't what you'd call a slick performance, especially not for something that would be heard all over the planet, on every radio band, looping again and again and again; but I didn't think it was totally awful.

Besides, good or bad wasn't the point. The point was to persuade Mandasars not to worry about a Sperm-tail coming in . . . and secretly to tell my sister I'd come back to Troyen. I didn't know what effect I wanted that to have; maybe just to see what Sam would do.

All kinds of terrible suspicions lurked in the back of my mind. I needed to give Sam the chance to prove me wrong.

* * *

Back at the robing chambers, Festina was last to arrive. She tried not to smile too hard when she found the rest of us waiting. "Well," she said, "an embarrassment of volunteers." She gestured toward the four robing chambers. "Four seats, four Explorers. Me, Tobit, Dade, and York. The rest of you stay on *Jacaranda*, and I don't want any bitching."

She got bitching anyway. Kaisho and the Mandasars argued and argued and argued why they should go with us . . . but anybody could see it was crazy to let them tag along. Kaisho was in a wheelchair—a wheelchair that could hover, but one that moved as slow as a constipated snail. If we wanted to get down and back in five minutes, we couldn't afford her slowing us up.

No way for the Mandasars to come either. The whole city would reek of battle musk, even before our arrival got the troops heated up. One whiff would make Counselor and the workers freeze with terror. As for Zeeleepull, he could handle the musk (even if it put him in the mood for a fight), but he'd cause plenty of trouble if we met any palace guards. With an all-human party, we might convince the guards we were just there to pick up our friends—especially with Plebon and Olympia Mell to vouch for us. But if we had a Mandasar warrior along, one with a strange accent and no knowledge of palace-guard passwords, we'd be ten times more likely to get arrested as spies.

Zeeleepull and the others weren't keen on listening to such logic. I'd warned them they might not be allowed to land but they still got all huffy, asking why I'd spent so much time teaching them how to act on Troyen when they'd never get to set foot on the planet. Eventually, Festina had to pull rank on them. She told them they could consider themselves reserves, in case the landing party called for help . . . but they simply weren't going down in the first shot with us real Explorers.

Yes. Festina called me a real Explorer. After thirty-five years wearing the black uniform, I was finally going to earn it.

* * *

Tobit tried to usher me into a robing chamber, but I said, "Sorry. I'd better not."

"For Christ's sake, York," Tobit snapped, "Troyen might have been a nice cozy planet when you lived there, but it's been at war for twenty years. Nobody has a clue what kinds of gas and germs and shit they've been tossing at each other. Sure, they lost most of their tech base right at the beginning . . . but they still managed to preserve those Balrog spores they used on the Fasskisters, didn't they? Who knows what other nasty crap they managed to collect while they were the top dogs of medical research? The only way to protect yourself is wearing a tightsuit."

"But, um . . . um . . ."

"He must not be sealed up," Counselor said. "It's important for the palace guards to know he is *Teelu*. They must be able to see him. And smell him."

She turned and looked directly at Festina . . . as if they'd talked about me recently and decided some things between themselves. I guess that shouldn't have been surprising; if Festina had begun to suspect stuff about me and pheromones, she'd go straight to someone who could smell the scents I put out. Now Festina put her hand on Tobit's shoulder, and said, "Let it go, Phylar. Edward can do more for us if he's not closed off in an airtight cocoon."

"*I* can do more without the tightsuit too," Dade said. "They're really hard to move in and you can't—"

"In your dreams, junior," Tobit interrupted. "If you don't shut up, we'll make you wear two."

Fifteen minutes later, we stood in the transport bay—Tobit, Dade, and Festina in fully sealed tightsuits, me in a light "impact suit" . . . which was basically an Explorer uniform with elbow pads.

My face and hands felt itchy from getting doused with camouflage nano: smart little color-changing bugs, programmed to match general background shades and to break up my silhouette so I'd be hard to recognize as human when standing in shadows. My uniform was covered with the same stuff; so were the tightsuits. Even in the brightly lit transport bay, the other three Explorers were easy to overlook. At one point, I was listening to Festina run over last-minute details with Tobit, and suddenly realized Dade was standing right beside me, listening too. When he wasn't moving, my eye seemed to slip straight past him without noticing he was there. Down on the ground where darkness had fallen, we'd be nine-tenths invisible.

Too bad invisible didn't mean undetectable. My nose was picking up a nostril-gouging chemical smell from all the suits; Mandasars would know something strange was close by, even if we were completely lost in shadows. Then again, if they couldn't see to aim their crossbows, maybe the camo wasn't a total loss.

Festina turned to the rear of the transport bay and called up to the control console, "Do you have the message to broadcast?"

"All recorded and stored in the ship-soul," Prope answered.

"And is the anchor in place on the ground?"

"Naturally," Lieutenant Harque said.

He and Prope were running the console themselves, rather than letting the usual crew do anything. I told myself the captain was showing how cooperative she could be, by giving us her personal attention. Still, I had to wonder if Harque was really the best technician on the ship. While the others had been suiting up, I'd watched him fumble with the control dials, trying to maneuver a Sperm anchor down to the surface. I don't know if he made any real mistakes, but he cursed a lot under his breath.

This particular anchor was the usual box with gold horseshoes, but it also had a tiny flight engine attached and a whole bunch of stealth 'bafflers to prevent people from noticing anything on radar. Not that we expected any radar dishes had survived the Fasskister Swarm, but Explorers *hate* taking chances. We needed the anchor on the ground, right where we wanted to land, like a pin to tack down the bottom end of the Sperm-tail. Without the little machine, the tail would flap about as wild as a firehose and might throw us out anywhere within a thousand-klick radius.

It would be really bad to get dumped into an ocean. Or in front of a big hostile army. Or thirty thousand meters above the ground.

"So the anchor's in place?" Festina asked. "Did anyone down there notice it landing?"

"Negative, Admiral," Harque answered, as smooth as if he'd never had a flick of trouble putting the box in place. "Perfect insertion, in an alley within twenty meters of the Explorers' signal source. The anchor's been there for ten whole minutes and no one has come to investigate."

"So," Tobit muttered, "either the folks on the ground didn't see the anchor go in, or they know exactly what's happening, and are waiting in ambush."

"Ever the optimist," Festina told him. Her voice had a metallic ring to it, because she was speaking through her tightsuit transmitter. Since I didn't have a tightsuit myself, I had a teeny receiver fastened into my ear—glued good and tight so it wouldn't fall out. I didn't have a transmitter, but I wouldn't need one: the others could hear my normal voice just fine, as long as I was within normal talking range . . . and we had absolutely no intention of ever splitting up.

"Are we ready?" Dade asked, far too brightly. This was his first trip planet-down, and he was getting off lucky. Troyen might be at war, but it was a lot friendlier than most places Explorers went. Mandasar warriors might actually listen if you pleaded for your life.

"Ready as we'll ever be," Festina said, without sounding too happy about it. "Start the sequence, Harque."

"Aye-aye, Admiral. Pressurizing now."

A weight pushed on my ears as Harque increased the air pressure around us. Regulations said we had to have a higher pressure on our end than the atmosphere we were heading for—otherwise, the end of our Sperm-tail might suck up stuff off the planet. The extra pressure would also give us a real strong push into the Sperm-tail.

"Fully pressurized," Harque announced. "Anchor activated. Preparing to plant tail."

I felt a hand on my shoulder. It was Festina. "Get ready, Edward," she whispered softly. "Harque is just the sort of asshole to eject us without warning."

She nudged me to face the Aft Entry Mouth—the big irising door that would snap open any second now. When stuff started happening, it'd go really fast: no countdown to ejection, just zoom, the instant our Sperm-tail was planted. The tail would be glaringly obvious to anyone on the ground . . . a glittery ribbon of colored sparkles, stretching into the sky. Ideally, it would only stay put a few seconds, just long enough for us to hit the ground and switch off the anchor. Then the tail would slither away wherever it liked, flicking in all directions and confusing observers about where it actually touched down. If we were lucky, we could slink away from the landing site before anyone came for us.

"Almost locked in," Harque muttered.

I glanced over at Festina beside me. Through the visor of her helmet, I could see she'd closed her eyes. Maybe she was praying. I thought about the last time I'd ridden a Sperm-tail: the way I'd been bludgeoned with ugly memories I hadn't wanted to relive. Did that happen to Festina too? Did that happen to every Explorer who shot through a Sperm-tail universe?

And yet we stood shoulder to shoulder as if we were brave people.

"Contact," Harque said.

For a moment nothing happened. Then Prope spoke in a gloating voice. "Good-bye, Festina."

The Mouth snapped open and swallowed us up.

35

WORKING INTO POSITION

Scooped off my feet by a gust of wind—puffed out the Mouth and into the Sperm-tail. I felt myself turn boneless, like water poured into a long long funnel that would spill me onto the dark soil of Troyen.

The palace grounds and Diplomats Row. My home.

I'd never felt wanted on my father's estate; as for the moonbase, it was just a barren nowhere. My only true home was the place I was going—where I lived with Verity and Sam till they both died.

Except that Sam wasn't dead, was she? Did that mean Verity wasn't dead either?

No, no, no! a voice screamed in my head. Another presence was trying to pierce through to me as I gushed down the Sperm-tail. Just like the last time: an unknown spirit reaching in, dredging up my own memories and forcing me to confront them. I tried to resist, but couldn't shut out the images.

Verity's empty bedroom. After I'd escaped from those guards and sent Innocence to safety, I'd gone back to the high queen's chambers. Both bodies had disappeared— nothing but that pool of Sam's blood. I remembered kneeling in the damp, touching the red stickiness, lifting my fingers to my nose . . .

. . . only now I could remember the smell. The smell of the blood. As if my nose had been Mandasar-sensitive way back then. I smelled the blood and knew it wasn't real—just artificial stuff, the kind the doctors synthesized for me whenever I needed a transfusion. Heaven knows, I'd needed tons of transfusions during my year of being sick. My nose knew the difference between real blood and fake.

That blood, the blood that had spilled out of Sam, was just stuff whipped up with a chemistry set. I knew that. Twenty years ago, I *knew*: knew that Sam's death had to have been as fake as the blood.

How had I forgotten that?

And my sense of smell—so sharp back then, so far beyond human. But somehow it had gone all dull again . . . until those doses of venom woke everything up.

Everything.

Memories were coming back faster now. I remembered kneeling there in Verity's chambers and squeezing my eyes shut to keep back tears. Crying because I *knew*. The Mayday signal that had brought me to the room . . . my sister lying in a pool of fake blood . . . the mutinous guards rushing me away before I could look at Sam's body too closely . . . waiting for me to lead them to Innocence . . .

It was all a setup. By Sam and the mutineers. To fool dumb old Edward, who was close to the little girl queen and might know where she'd hide.

Twenty years ago, I'd wept bitter tears and pushed away those bad thoughts about Sam—pushed them away *hard*. Because if I didn't, I'd have to ask who really killed Verity, and who released the outlaw queens, and who had made sure none of the peace initiatives ever really worked—

Without warning, I hurtled out of the Sperm-tail and rammed against a brick wall.

Four Explorers shot into a dark narrow alley. Me, I collided with the nearest wall and crumpled. The other three, in big bulgy tightsuits, hit and bounced like they were wearing their own trampolines. Dade and Festina managed to keep their feet; Tobit caromed off the wall and went down, smacking flat on his butt, flipping over to his stomach, and hop-skipping along the pavement. If the folks on *Jacaranda* were watching via satellite, they must have been laughing their heads off.

Smashing the wall pretty near knocked the wind out of me, but my head was clear enough to realize I was closest to the Sperm anchor. Everyone else had bounced several paces away. Shaky and reeling, I kicked out my foot and hit the anchor's off-switch. The glittery tail whipped away past my face in a jamble of colored lights, swishing across the city like a single strand of aurora borealis. With luck, Harque could keep the tail dancing all over Unshummin, distracting searchers in both armies. Meanwhile, we'd carry the anchor box with us; when we switched it on again, the tail would come straight back to our party, giving us a quick escape route.

"Everyone all right?" Festina's whisper came softly through the receiver in my ear.

Tobit and Dade both answered, "Fine." I just nodded. Up in the ship, Festina had told me to keep quiet as much as possible. Since I wasn't muffled up in a tightsuit, nearby soldiers might hear if I talked.

Festina made an okay sign, then craned her neck to look at the sky. "*Jacaranda*, are you receiving?"

"Loud and clear, Admiral," Harque answered.

"We're on the move," Festina said. "Dade, you grab the anchor. Edward, stay right behind me." She turned to Tobit. "Have you figured out where we're going?"

Tobit had unclipped a Bumbler from his belt and was scanning the area. "The signal came from that direction," he said, pointing to the wall I'd banged against. "Inside this building." He lifted his head and looked up. "For best transmission, they'd go to the roof. Of course, they may not be there now; it's been an hour since the beep."

"If they've left, they'll come back," Festina answered. "They can't have missed our Sperm-tail."

The tail was still lashing the city, darting from block to block: whisking over the pavement, flapping against walls, lifting high over the rooftops and circling like a lariat before plunging down again in a splash of green and gold and blue and purple. I could hear distant Mandasar voices, commanders yelling orders at their troops, or just soldiers hollering at each other. Some would be shouting, "Keep cool," and others, "Look lively," and a few maybe even, "*Naizó!*" . . . tired palace guards who were ready to surrender to anything.

"Let's head for the roof," Festina said. "Plebon and Olympia may still be there. If they aren't, they'll know they should hurry back to their transmission site. And from the roof, we'll have an easy time grabbing a ride out."

"Sure, Ramos," Tobit growled. "Easy. Piece of cake. In the history of the Explorer Corps, have you heard of a single landing that didn't turn into a complete ass-biter?"

"Always a first time," Festina answered. "Let's go, people. Immortality awaits."

At the end of the alley, Tobit poked the scanner of his Bumbler just past the edge of the wall. That way, we could look around the corner without sticking our heads into the open.

The Bumbler's vidscreen showed the front of the Fasskister embassy . . . or what was left of it. Something had smashed it hard, like a wrecking ball or an explosion or a barrage of cannon fire. A great chunk of the brick face had been knocked in, exposing the four stories of the interior to open air. Unshummin's weather was as mild as you could get—shirtsleeve temperatures most of the year round, with only a bit of rain—but it had still taken a toll on the inside of the building. All the floors had a definite sag, and some were crumbling on the edges. I imagine the place was filled with insects and jiffpips: centipedey things that could jump and climb like squirrels. (For some reason, Mandasars found jiffpips sweet and cute . . . maybe because they were distant evolutionary cousins, like lemurs are to humans. Me, whenever I saw a jiffpip, I wanted to whack it with a sledgehammer.)

Dade's voice spoke through my earpiece. "You really

think the Explorers transmitted from this building? It doesn't look safe."

"Maybe that's why they chose it," Festina replied. "The floors look strong enough to hold humans but maybe not Mandasars. Plebon and Olympia could go in, set up their equipment, and know they wouldn't be disturbed."

"Why would they be disturbed?" Dade asked. "I thought we were assuming the Explorers had got friendly with the palace guards."

"Friendly is one thing," Tobit said, "but guards might get a wee bit anxious if they knew humans were broadcasting radio messages to the world at large. Some nasty paranoid folks would suspect you were sending intelligence to the enemy. Better to set up your transmitter where you'll have a little privacy."

"Besides," Festina added, "we don't know for sure our friends *are* on good terms with the guards. They may be on the run and hiding out. Always suspect the worst, and . . . uh-oh."

The Bumbler's screen showed a pair of warriors coming toward us. They were moving cautiously from the direction of the palace, gas masks over their heads and crossbows held steady in their waist pincers. Each had a *Cheejretha* finger resting on the bow's trigger mechanism, so they could instantly fire an arrow with the slightest squeeze.

The warriors passed in front of the crumbling embassy, peeking in through gaps in the brickwork. They had to be looking for something . . . and I suspected it was us. Some keen-eyed lookout at the palace had spotted the Sperm-tail lingering a few seconds in this neighborhood; the team coming our way got sent to investigate.

"What do we do?" Dade asked over the radio.

"Let's invite them to tea," Tobit said. "No, wait . . . let's stun their fucking gonads off." He handed the Bumbler to me and quietly drew his stun-pistol. Festina had hers out too. They hadn't let Dade bring a gun; he'd been just a teeny bit too eager to shoot, back at the Fasskister orbital.

Me, I didn't *want* a gun. And nobody had offered me one.

The guards' footsteps came closer, clicking softly on the pavement. Festina lifted her hand, with three fingers showing. Silently she lowered one finger, then a second, then the last . . . and together she and Tobit dived out of the alley.

Arrows twanged at almost the same instant the stunners whirred; but the warriors shot high, not prepared for humans who could throw themselves belly down on the street. The guns fired again in unison. That was enough. I heard the bows clatter to the pavement, and a moment later, two heavy thuds on the ground.

"Are they out?" Dade asked excitedly.

"We stopped shooting, didn't we?" Festina answered.

Without another word, she led us forward.

When you hear me talk about streets and alleys, maybe you're picturing some city you know—your local downtown late at night, with the sidewalks empty and everything quiet.

No. Put that out of your head.

First of all, Unshummin was dark. Really, really dark. The city had plenty of streetlamps, but none of them worked—there hadn't been electricity on the planet since the Fasskisters loosed their Swarm, except for chemical batteries and maybe some motorized generators protected by thick nano defense clouds. The only significant light was a glow from the direction of the palace, where I figured soldiers were burning cookfires; but the palace lay to the rear of the embassy and we were in front, so most of the light was blocked by the building. Neither of Troyen's moons was up, so we had to make do with the stars . . . and after all the lights on *Jacaranda*, my eyes needed time to adapt.

Next, you're probably thinking of a normal human street paved with asphalt or cement or gravel or stone. Nope. Every road on Troyen was built from a pebbly stuff called *Ayposh*: kind of like coral, because it consisted of a whole bunch of tiny shelled organisms, some alive, some dead. They'd been bioengineered to grow in long level sheets, photosynthesizing most of their nutrients straight from the air. Every few months, the board of works sent out sprayers full of fertilizer and mineral supplements to feed the little guys; and each year, crews would paint the highway shoulders with a chemical suppressant to keep the *Ayposh* from spreading off the roadbed. It was cheap, it was simple, it was elegant . . . and with the war on, maybe it was doomed. All of a sudden, I started wondering if people had time to spray fertilizer when they were all busy fighting. I thought of millions of miles of pavement, slowly starving to death for lack of vitamins. Maybe all the streets around me were nothing but corpses, teeny husks that would slowly crumble away and never get replenished by new generations.

After twenty years of real people dying, it seemed kind of horrible to go misty-eyed about the roads and sidewalks. You'd have to be pretty stupid to do something like that.

Anyway, there's one last thing you've probably got wrong in your mental picture of Diplomats Row: the buildings. If you're thinking of human architecture, think again. Yes, the Fasskister embassy was built of bricks; but the bricks were clear crystal, the same sort of stuff as the huts back at that orbital. It wasn't glass, I can tell you that much—when the front wall had been smashed in, not one of the bricks had broken. They were all perfectly intact, lying on the ground as we stepped into the darkness of the half-demolished building. The bricks' edges were still crisp and clean despite years of weathering, and I couldn't see a trace of mortar on them. Don't ask me how the walls held together without some sort of stickum to attach each brick to its neighbors . . . but the side and back walls were still intact, and I couldn't see mortar in them either. Just rows of crystal bricks that let in the tiniest glimmer of starlight so I wasn't completely blind.

Dim light or not, the Explorers could see fine. Their tightsuit visors had vision enhancers that made the night bright as day. I had to tag along on Festina's heels, so I wouldn't walk into a wall or pothole or something . . . and even then, I had a heck of a time not getting lost, with her practically invisible in camo. Mostly I went by the sound of her footsteps and the smell of her suit—as if I were a full-fledged Mandasar, navigating by nose.

It took me by surprise when we started going upward: a slow-sloping ramp that must have been in the middle of the building. Ramps were pretty common on Diplomats Row—lots of nonhumans (including Mandasars) didn't do so well on stairs, and no alien species ever liked each other's elevators; the compartments were either too big or too small, the lift mechanisms were too quiet or too clanky, they went too fast or too slow . . . and the interior always smelled of something you didn't want to inhale any longer than you had to. The diplomatic solution was to build your embassy with ramps at easy-to-climb slants, so as not to irritate important visitors.

We went up slowly, switching back four times for each floor. Once we got above first-story level, the side of the stairwell was missing, giving a clear view of the street out front—Diplomats Row in all its glory. The other buildings seemed pretty well intact, even if they were dark and empty: the high silver towers of the Myriapods, like tinsel hanging from the sky; the clear glass globe of the Cash-lings, its multicolored interior lights now gone dark and lifeless; the embassies of the Divian sub-breeds, Tye-Tyes in their rock mountain, Ooloms in their giant tree, Freeps in their neon casino; the Unity's mirror garden where they'd held masked rituals every night; and at the end of the block, the mall of the up-League envoys.

Once upon a time, that mall held a fifty-meter-high flame on one side and an even taller tornado on the other, both real and roaring but never moving from their positions. Gawking tourists used to argue whether the envoys actually lived in the wind and fire, or if it was just a flashy gimmick aimed at impressing lesser species. None of us ever learned the truth . . . but the night Queen Verity died, the flame and tornado winked out of existence in the exact same second.

It was a sign, if anybody needed one, that the higher echelons of the League were turning their backs on Troyen. By dawn, every other embassy had been evacuated too—no one wanted to go down with a sinking ship.

Now, here we were, back again.

There must have been a door or something closing off the stairwell from the roof, but it had vanished into the general wreckage. Still, the roof itself seemed in pretty good shape—at least the back half was. My eyes were getting used to the darkness; as we came up the final ramp, I could see a flat expanse of those smooth crystal bricks, with no dips or sags all the way to the rear edge of the building. Tobit checked with the Bumbler and grunted a few seconds later. "It looks safe," he announced. "If you want to trust the engineering judgment of a stupid machine."

"Any sign of the Explorers?" Dade asked.

Tobit fiddled with dials and peered at the Bumbler's screen. "No . . . no . . . wait. Back there in the shadows," he said, pointing at the far rear of the roof. "I think it's an Explorer's backpack."

Dade immediately started forward, but Festina grabbed his arm. "You and Tobit stay here. In case the roof isn't as solid as we think."

"And in case it's a trap," Tobit muttered.

"Why would it be a trap?" Dade asked.

"Because *anything* could be a trap!" Tobit growled. "We don't know dick about what's going on. Someone may have lured us here with a fake signal so they could blow us to smithereens. And don't say that doesn't make sense, junior—stuff that doesn't make sense can still make you Go Oh Shit."

Festina was already heading toward the knapsack. Since nobody stopped me, I jogged a few paces and caught up with her. Side by side, we walked toward the building's rear . . . and the farther we went, the less I cared about the pack and the more I worried about something else.

The smell of buttered toast trickled through the air.

Like I said, the back of the Fasskister embassy faced the

palace—just a stone's throw from the diamondwood palisade surrounding the palace grounds. Shining from inside
that wall came the glow I'd thought was cookfires. A dull
red glow.

The queen-shaped palace had its tail toward us, but not
quite straight on. There was enough of an angle that we
could see along its body, past the glass conservatory domes,
up the torso, all the way to the head and its outstretched
claws.

Moss. Balrog moss. Covering every square millimeter of
the building from the venom sacs forward. In the dark, it
glimmered a very self-satisfied crimson.

36

LYING LOW ON THE ROOF

"Holy shit," Festina whispered.

I just nodded. The buttered-toast smell was making me dizzy.

"That queen," Festina said. "The one who dumped those spores on the Fasskisters. She must have left some here too—to make the place uninhabitable for the Black Army."

"Kind of hard on her own guards," I said. It gave me a crawly feeling, thinking about that. I could understand a queen setting up a nasty parting gift for her enemies, but not when it would also hurt her own subjects. Protecting your citizens should always be your number one concern, shouldn't it? A king who didn't put his people's safety ahead of his own hunger for revenge . . .

A *queen*. I meant a *queen* who didn't put *her* people's safety ahead of *her* hunger for revenge . . .

Never mind.

Festina growled under her breath. "That fucking Kaisho. She had to know about this."

"Why?" I asked.

"She took that damned satellite photo," Festina said. "The whole front half of the palace should have been glowing, for Christ's sake. But there wasn't any shine in the shot she showed us. She must have deliberately told the computer to filter out the red." The admiral made a disgusted sound in her throat. "And I never double-checked.

I checked the landing site, and the spot where the signal came from, but I never bothered to look at the palace. Sloppy, Ramos—really sloppy."

"You didn't know," I said.

"I knew enough," she snapped. "Kaisho has jerked us around time and again. I kept letting her do it, in the hope she'd go too far and we could justifiably whack her. But enough is enough." She tapped a button on her wrist, changing the channel on her radio. "Tobit, Dade: full paranoia mode."

Dade's voice sounded in my ear, even though he was standing back at the stairwell. "I thought we already *were* in full paranoia mode."

Festina sighed and rolled her eyes. "What can you do with a kid like that?"

"Um," I said, "if you want I can keep an eye on—"

That's when the cannons started firing.

A real soldier probably wouldn't call them long-distance guns—they were shooting from the top of the palace toward that kill zone beyond Prosperity Water. Only about a kilometer; in artillery terms, that was practically point-blank range. But from where we were standing, the shells looked like they were zooming past us and heading way off in the distance before they blew up.

Of course, we didn't stay standing too long.

I dropped flat to the roof. Festina did a dive, then rolled to her feet again, fists up . . . like it was some pure reflex to hit the dirt and come out fighting. A second later, she threw herself onto the roof again, cursing in a language I didn't understand. Spanish, I guess. Considering how comfortable she was swearing in English, she must have been *really* mad this time.

Another boom of a cannon. While its thunder still echoed from nearby buildings, Dade's voice came over my earphone. "It's all right," he babbled excitedly, "they're firing over our heads. Shelling the enemy."

"And what happens," Tobit growled, "when the enemy

starts shelling back? If the guns are a few degrees too low, we're bang in the line of fire. How do you think this building got wrecked in the first place?"

Good point. The front of the embassy could have got hit by a barrage intended for the palace—just a few hundred meters short, that's all. How long ago would that have been? When the Black Army first surrounded Queen Temperance? Or back earlier in some other battle . . . maybe when Temperance herself grabbed the palace from whoever held it before her.

"What do we do?" Dade called over the radio. "Leave?"

"No," Tobit and Festina snapped in unison.

"We're here to pick up fellow Explorers," Festina said a moment later. "We stay until we absolutely have to go."

"Yeah," Tobit put in. "We aren't going to get another chance down here."

He was right. If the palace was firing, the Black Army must be attacking out on the defense perimeter—going for their final offensive. The moment they saw our Sperm-tail, someone must have called the attack.

Someone. Maybe Sam. Whose time of waiting was over.

In a few hours now, the war would end . . . right where it started, inside the high queen's palace. There'd be fighting in the halls, just like the night Verity died—loyal palace guards without a queen, just trying to survive till the dawn. It made me feel guilty, realizing I was soon going to run off on them again. We'd pick up the other Explorers, or we'd decide they weren't coming and hightail it back to *Jacaranda*. Either way, I was abandoning a lot of warriors, when I should be there with them, helping them, leading them . . .

Wait a minute—what the heck was going through my head? I was no leader.

The cannons fired again. I covered my ears and tried not to think.

Festina began to crawl on her belly back to Tobit and Dade. It didn't look very graceful, her in that big fat tightsuit . . .

but she moved surprisingly fast, and if you took your eyes off her the tiniest split second, she disappeared. That camo was *good*. I started to crawl too, then stopped. The Explorer's backpack was still lying on the roof behind me; Festina hadn't had a chance to look at it. I turned around and slithered up to it, sniffing furiously.

It smelled of the same stuff as the tightsuit, plus the odor of a male human. No trace of female scent. Maybe Plebon had been here an hour ago to send the contact beep, but Olympia Mell hadn't been with him.

Was that a bad sign? I couldn't tell.

I sniffed at the knapsack again, not sure what I was looking for. Even if the pack was booby-trapped with some kind of bomb, I wouldn't know what explosives smelled like. Anyway, there were a whole lot of odors jumbled together: Explorer stuff, like a radio transmitter, and food rations, and a Sperm anchor . . .

My fingers twitched. I didn't make them do that. Uh-oh . . . getting possessed again.

I watched as my hands reached out and flipped open the pack. Nothing went boom. That was the good news. The bad news was my hand scrabbling into the mess of equipment and pulling out the little anchor box.

"Edward!" Festina called over my earphone. "What do you think you're doing?"

The spirit that possessed me didn't answer. It set the anchor down on the roof and flicked the activation switch.

I didn't even see the Sperm-tail coming—it was somewhere behind my back, still flipping and flapping, swishing aimlessly across Unshummin and far out into the countryside, like some cat-toy bouncing on a string. One second it was a dozen kilometers away; the next instant, it had snapped into place against the anchor, plastered to the side of the little box with only the tip of its mouth hanging free.

Festina's voice rang loud in my ear. "Turn off the anchor, Edward. Turn off the anchor!"

Too late. The Sperm-tail's tiny mouth suddenly became

a nozzle squirting out a crowd of newcomers: Counselor, Zeeleepull, Hib & Nib & Pib, exploding out of the tube, smacking down hard on the crystal-brick roof. I could feel the impact under my feet; it must have jarred the Mandasars to their very bones. Right behind them was Kaisho in her hoverchair, shooting forward, spinning sideways, almost flipping over in a somersault . . . till the chair's stabilizers kicked in and pulled upright with a whine of engines.

They must have been waiting, I thought. *They must have been right there in Jacaranda's transport bay, all set to come through the moment the anchor came on.*

How did they know what would happen? Had the spirit possessing me set this whole thing up?

But the spirit had one more trick to play. Before I could react, my own foot lifted high and smashed the anchor box under my heel.

Electronic guts spilled onto the bricks. The glittering Sperm-tail whipped away and disappeared from sight.

"Dade, quick, Dade!" Festina yelled. "The other anchor—turn it on."

"What?" the boy asked. "Why?"

"Turn on the fucking anchor!" Festina roared.

He'd set it down on the roof back near the stairwell. Dade threw himself across the bricks, bounced once on his tightsuit stomach, then landed within arm's reach of the box. He slapped his hand on the switch . . . and nothing happened.

Nothing happened for a long time.

I lifted my head. The Sperm-tail was nowhere in sight.

"Ohhhh, *fuck*!" Tobit groaned. He skittered across the roof toward Dade, pulling his Bumbler with him. With the Bumbler's scanner, he started a quick once-over of the anchor box . . . maybe checking for malfunctions.

Meanwhile, Zeeleepull struggled to straighten himself up to his usual height. He and his hive-mates looked winded from their landing—slapping down hard on the unforgiving roof. With all their weight, Mandasars fall a lot more heavily than humans. "*Teelu*," he gasped, "help how?"

"Help?" I asked. The spirit possessing me had quietly let go. "Help how who?"

"You, *Teelu*. Radioed you for help."

"I didn't radio for help. I don't even have a transmitter."

"But the captain said—"

"Oh. The captain."

I didn't need to hear more. If Prope had lied to the Mandasars about receiving a call for help—if she'd hurried them and Kaisho into the transport bay and waited for the Sperm-tail to get anchored again—she had to have *known* the spirit inside me would turn on the anchor, then smash the box to free the tail.

Which meant Prope was working with the spirit. She might have been pheromoned into doing it . . . but more likely, the spirit had used my father's access codes to send instructions in the Admiralty's name. That's what I'd done when I'd found myself sitting all dopey at the captain's terminal: the spirit had given Prope orders to maroon us here.

But why? I thought the spirit was on my side. Back on Celestia, it had *helped* me—pretty well saved my life and Festina's. So why turn against us now? Unless its purpose had just been to keep us alive till we got to Troyen . . .

I scanned the night sky again. No dancing Sperm-tail anywhere . . . as if *Jacaranda* had reeled up its fishing line and headed for home. Across the roof, Dade and Tobit were poking at the anchor box, but I knew there was nothing wrong with it. *Jacaranda* had simply flown away. With Kaisho and the Mandasars down on Troyen, no one on the departing starship would raise a fuss that we'd all been abandoned.

From the start, Prope had been ordered to dump me someplace nasty. I just never suspected I'd help her do it.

37

MOVING OUT

Footsteps rushed up the ramp. Festina rolled over on her back, stun-pistol held in both hands . . . but she lowered it when she saw the newcomer was a man, a human man.

Both his skin and his uniform were black: not camo'd up like our party, but still plenty hard to see. Even so, I could tell he was definitely Explorer material. The bottom part of his face just wasn't there—the skin swept straight down from his cheekbones to the thinness of his neck. His chin was only a little nub, scarcely bigger than his Adam's apple.

I was kind of glad I couldn't see him very well in all this dark.

"Festina?" the man said in a deep, very precise voice. You could tell he was making an extra effort to enunciate clearly. "I didn't expect a rescue party at all, much less my favorite admiral."

"Don't count your rescues before they're hatched," Festina told him. She'd switched on a small external speaker in her tightsuit so people without radio receivers could hear her. I noticed she kept the volume down to a whisper. "How're you doing, Plebon?" she asked. "Where's Olympia?"

"Gone." His face barely changed, but his eyes showed pain. "When Queen Temperance left, some of the palace guards defected to the enemy. They took Olympia as a bargaining chip—a valuable hostage they could offer to the Black Queen in exchange for their own lives."

"Shit." Festina's fists clenched. "Any chance she's still alive?"

Plebon shook his head. "Two days later . . ." His voice caught and he swallowed hard before trying again. "Two days later, they hung her corpse on their front lines. That's what 'expendable' . . ."

He couldn't finish the phrase. The rest of us were all busy, trying to look anywhere but at him.

"Anyway," he said after a while, with that hard tone of someone trying to hold himself together, "if it's any consolation, the defectors were hung on the front lines too. Their bodies looked worse than Olympia's."

"Craziness," Counselor murmured. "Smart armies don't kill defectors, they show them off: happy, safe, and well fed. That way, you encourage more people to surrender."

"Unless you don't *want* your enemies to surrender," I said softly. "What if you want them to stay right where they are, so the war doesn't end three and a half weeks too early?"

It's hard when you feel people's deaths on your head. Those defectors got killed to keep the war going . . . delay things till I got here. As for Olympia Mell . . . it explained how my sister had known *Willow* was in the system. Olympia had told the Black Army everything she knew: maybe under torture, or maybe just chatting with Sam as a fellow member of the navy. Then, after the talk was over, Olympia had been murdered and put on display—to make sure the palace guards stayed at their posts till the very end.

This Black Queen, whoever she was: she could have had an easy victory weeks ago, but she wanted a massacre. And Sam was the queen's closest advisor. What did that say about my sister? What did that say?

"The anchor's working just fine," Tobit announced. "But *Jacaranda* isn't replying to any calls. They've buggered off on us."

Festina let out her breath slowly. "Damn it to fucking hell," she said in a controlled voice. "That's twice Prope has stranded me in some shithole. Next time . . ."

I never got to hear about next time. Her words were drowned out by a pack of warriors storming onto the roof. It looked like the embassy's floors were strong enough to hold Mandasars after all.

You can tell a lot about folks from how they react to a bunch of soldiers.

Festina and Tobit cranked up the volume on their tight-suit speakers and shouted in stilted Mandasar, "Greetings, we are sentient citizens of the League of Peoples, we beg your Hospitality." At the same time, they were drawing their stun-pistols.

Dade gaped a moment, then just held up his hands in surrender. Counselor did the same, except that she folded her arms in a gesture I'd taught her, and cried out, "*Naizó! Naizó!*"

Zeeleepull stepped in front of her, flexed his pincers theatrically, and began to pump out a combination of battle-musks. I couldn't distinguish all the scents he used, but the basic message was clear: "I will not attack, but I *will* defend."

Hib & Nib & Pib backed to the edge of the roof and whispered as they stared admiringly at Zeeleepull. "Isn't he strong?" "Isn't he handsome?" "Isn't he a teeny bit out-numbered?"

Kaisho said nothing—just standing her ground, with her legs glowing bright as lasers.

Me, I was watching everybody else, waiting to take my lead from them . . . but I was also concentrating mighty hard on smelling royal. Half the soldiers had gas masks; half of them didn't. I still wasn't great at controlling my pheromones, but I figured if worse came to worst, I could dose the maskless ones and sic them on their troopmates.

But it was Plebon who stepped toward the soldiers: waving his hands and shouting, "*Nairit ul Gashwan!*" *Friend of Gashwan.* Plebon's accent was pretty awful, even on three short words; I got the impression he'd memorized the phrase by sound, rather than actually understanding it. Still, the soldiers eased up a bit: they didn't lower their bows but a few took their fingers off the triggers.

For a moment, I considered walking up to them anyway: use my pheromones to win a bunch of them over to our side. But that wouldn't work on the masked guys, and they might get really mad about their fellow guards being zonked by chemical warfare. Grumbling to myself, I damped down the smell factory and let the fumes drift away on the breeze.

The soldiers hustled us down to street level, not giving us the tiniest chance to talk among ourselves. "*Jush, jush!*" they kept saying . . . which means, "Shut up and keep moving."

Plebon didn't look too worried about this treatment, so he must have thought we were safe. His friend Gashwan must carry a lot of clout.

Who was she? I wondered. Gashwan was a female name, but the only Gashwan I'd ever known was the doctor who looked after me when I had the jaundice . . . or rather, when I had venom poisoning from all those nanites dosing me up. Could it be the same Gashwan, hanging around the palace for twenty years? Maybe. No matter which queens passed through Unshummin in the past two decades, they could all use a smart doctor. I didn't know much about Gashwan herself—she was the sort of M.D. who reads medical charts rather than talking to patients personally— but if she'd been on Verity's staff, she must have been the best at what she did.

Out on the street, another guard ran up and whispered something to the corporal at the head of our group. The corporal looked back at me, his antennas lifting straight up like lightning rods. Um: I think I'd been identified. Either someone remembered me from way back when, or they'd seen my face when *Jacaranda* broadcast my little message.

("Don't worry, neutral mission, keep calm.") Now they realized I was the Little Father Without Blame. I didn't know
what the guards would do about that, and the guards didn't
know either. Our platoon of escorts gawked at me when
they heard the news, but didn't say a word.

Sorry. They did say *one* word. "*Jush!*" And they hurried
us even faster toward the palace.

We quick-marched up Diplomats Row to an army check-
point where Aliens Gate used to be. The gate had been a
big diamondwood arch in the palace's outer palisade, nearly
a century old and carved with Mandasar artists' impressions
of various aliens. No species would be flattered by the pictures—humans, for example, were shown as stick-thin and
frail, men indistinguishable from women, with huge eyes,
tiny mouths, and enormous quantities of hair growing from
their heads like cedar bushes—but I still kind of liked the
figures. This really was how Mandasars saw us, back years
ago when we were exotic curiosities rather than day-to-day
acquaintances. (Sam always claimed the male human on the
gate was modeled after our father, back when he was just
a greenhorn diplomat on Troyen. I couldn't see the resemblance . . . but my sister loved thinking everything had
some connection to her.)

Aliens Gate was gone now—maybe destroyed in battle,
maybe just pulled down by armies occupying the palace,
because it's hard to defend a big open arch. In place of the
gate was a narrow walkway past a row of arrow slits, then
a path with twists and turns and odd little bumps in the
concrete floor, probably designed to make Mandasar warriors stumble if they tried to charge through at speed. The
path slanted upward too, rising at least two stories above
the actual level of the ground; and once you were inside
the walls, you had to go down again, on a set of awkward
switchbacking ramps that were fully exposed to cannon and
arrow fire from the palace.

It made me wonder how recent these defense measures
were. Making it hard for attackers to get in also made it

hard for defenders to get out for sorties and counteroffensives. I couldn't help thinking the folks in the palace had abandoned all hope of fighting their way to open territory; this was their last stand, their Masada, their Alamo. If they had no chance of surviving, they wanted to take a ton of their enemies with them.

Our corporal borrowed a lantern from a guard post and led the way across the dark palace grounds. Once upon a time, this area had bloomed with gardens of glass-lily, queen's-crown and skyflowers. Now there was only bare earth, tangled over with monofilament razor wire: stuff so sharp, it could even cut through a warrior's carapace. Behind the wire were trenches, behind the trenches were more trenches, and behind them all was the palace, where archers and cannons were ready to fire on anyone coming too near.

Or maybe there were just archers—the palace's cannons had stopped shooting. I doubted the Black Army had called off its attack; more likely, the gunners on the ramparts had run out of shells.

We scrambled up the ramp to the palace's back door—what my sister called the Sphincter. Since the building was shaped like a queen, and this entrance was smack in the middle of the tail section, Sam always joked that the door led right up the queen's rectum.

Not very funny you think about it.

The stonework here was free of Balrog moss. That was no accident—a lot of the place looked scorched, as if someone had taken a flamethrower to the walls. I guess the palace guards didn't know the spores were sentient . . . or else they didn't care. The stink of burned vegetation was strong enough that even a human nose would smell it.

The same stink filled the corridor inside. This end of the building had once been painted with scenes from around the planet—the great waterfalls at Feelon, the ocean grotto of Pellibav, the sacred hoodoos of the Joalang Mountains—but now the paintings were charred black, with thick flakes of ash littering the floor. The Balrog must have tried to crawl through here like soul-sucking ivy; and it'd been stopped. For the time being, this part of the palace was sanitized . . . but with the front of the building swallowed up, the red moss would surely keep trying to work its way back.

So we walked through halls that smelled of cinders and battle-musk. It was just vinegary Musk A at the moment, general tension but not panic. Even that was enough to get to Counselor—her antennas were jerking back and forth in little spasms, and her whiskers were constantly shivering. I adjusted my pace to walk beside her, then put out a standard worker pheromone that said, "Just keep going, it'll be fine."

The smell seemed to help: a moment later, she wrapped one of her thin brown arms in mine. "Thank you, *Teelu*," she murmured, before the guards *Jushed* her into silence.

We turned down a side corridor and headed for a ramp to the second floor. This was the way to the royal infirmary, where I'd spent my last year on Troyen. As we climbed, whiffs of Mandasar blood began to overpower the stench of burned Balrog. By the smell of it, the infirmary was still very much in business, caring for an awful lot of sick and wounded.

A middle-aged gentle stopped our party at the top of the ramp, scolding the soldiers for bringing filthy humans into a hospital area. Did they want us to infect the place with our awful alien germs? It took our corporal a full thirty seconds to break into her tirade, as he mumbled in Mandasar, "Please, Doctor . . . please, Doctor . . . please, Doctor . . . we must see Gashwan right away."

"Gashwan's busy," the gentle finally said. "She hasn't got time to waste on trivialities."

"But, Doctor . . . but, Doctor . . . but, Doctor . . ."

I took a deep breath and stepped forward. "*Teeshpodin Ridd ha Wahlisteen pim*," I said, trying not to feel sheepish at putting on airs. I am the Little Father Without Blame. "*Gashwan himayja, sheeka mo*." We must see Gashwan, if you please.

The gentle turned to me, anger on her face. It was the first time she'd seen me clearly—our only light came from the corporal's lantern, and I'd been standing quietly back in the shadows. For a heartbeat I was sure the doctor would start hollering about dirty hume disease carriers; but her eyes opened wide, and her whiskers trembled. "*Teelu*," she whispered.

Mandasars gasped up and down the corridor; I nearly gasped with them. It was one thing for Celestian kids to make the mistake of calling me, "Your Majesty" . . . but this woman should have known better. I wasn't a queen, I was a consort. Addressing me as *Teelu* was like prostrating yourself before the royal plumber.

"Please," I told her, then got all flustered as I tried to think of a nice way to say she should watch her words. But the woman got the wrong idea from my hesitation.

"Yes, *Teelu*," she replied, whiskers still fluttering. "At once, *Teelu*." She scuttled off into the next room.

"Um," I said to the rest of the crowd. "Sorry."

"Don't apologize, *Teelu*," Counselor whispered to me.

"You really shouldn't call me that," I told her. "It's only for queens."

"And you," she said, with no hesitation.

"*Jush*," muttered one of the guards. But he didn't sound as tough and confident as before. He might have been wondering if he'd get in trouble for bossing around a queen's consort. In a way, it was funny—Black Epaulettes were coming to slaughter us all, and these guys were afraid I might yell at them.

"It's okay," I told them in Mandasar. "No one's going to get mad at you."

"York," Festina said sharply in English, "I'd be more comfortable if you kept to a language I understand."

She held her stun-pistol not quite aiming at me, not quite aiming away. (The soldiers hadn't tried to take the gun away from her . . . lucky for them.) But I wasn't half so upset by the stunner as I was by her tone of voice—so hard and icy. Festina was mad at me; really, really mad. She'd

seen me turn on the anchor then smash it, and she thought
I'd betrayed her. Worst of all, I could only have done that
bad stuff if I was in cahoots with Prope.

I think that's what made Festina so furious. She might
forgive me if I did something careless or stupid . . . but not
if I was the least little bit tied in with Captain Prope.

Um.

An elderly gentle shuffled out of the infirmary, so old her
brown shell had darkened nearly black. Every step she took
seemed an effort; she grunted as she walked, and each
heaving breath turned whistly in her nose.

Now I remembered: her nose. Dr. Gashwan had always
had a wicked scar running the length of her snout, as if
someone once stuck a knife tip into a nostril and yanked it
all the way back to her cheek. It was an ancient wound
from her youth; but even in the dim lanternlight, the ugly
mark was still very visible.

Beside me, Festina lifted a hand to her own face.

"Gashwan," Plebon said. He bowed, but the old woman
ignored him. Instead, she shuffled past everyone till she
stopped in front of me.

"Edward York," she cooed in English. "My one and only
son."

Leaning forward, she nuzzled me on the lips.

38

LEARNING SOME
UGLY TRUTHS

I blinked. The kiss was almost exactly like Counselor's back on Celestia—a human gesture imitated by an alien. I was so surprised I couldn't speak; but Festina asked the question that was on my mind. "Son? What do you mean, son?"

"He's my child," Gashwan answered, her eyes glittering. "I made him."

"You?" said Festina. "You were the engineer?"

Gashwan lifted one of her wrinkled hands and patted my cheek fondly. If I hadn't been so frozen with horror, I would have flinched away.

Dad had never revealed who engineered Sam and me . . . but it only made sense that he went to someone on Troyen. He knew people here; the doctors were the best in the galaxy; and Mandasar medical facilities could ignore stuffy Technocracy laws about gene-tinkering.

Years later, when Sam needed a doctor for Innocence and me, it probably wasn't coincidence she'd gone straight to Gashwan.

"You've turned out nicely," Gashwan purred. She'd taken my chin in her hands and was tipping my head from one side to the other: examining her work. "Still perfect, aren't you, boy?"

"I'm okay," I mumbled.

She smiled. "So much like your father when I knew him. The same look. The same attitude."

I did some quick arithmetic. My father was a hundred and twenty-one now, still hale and hearty thanks to YouthBoost. He must have been in his mid-sixties when Sam and I were whipped up in a test tube. His original mission to Troyen was thirty years before that . . . which must have been when he first met Gashwan. Maybe she'd been a young medical researcher, eager to learn about the human metabolism. Mandasar doctors loved to study aliens.

"Well," Gashwan said, still looking at me keenly, "I'm proud of the way you turned out. Very presentable . . . for a human."

"But you made a mistake on me," I told her. "I'm stupid. My brain doesn't work right."

"Your brain works exactly according to specification," she said. "I agree, it wasn't fair; but your father promised you'd have a fine life, brought up so you'd never know you were different. That's the only reason I said yes when Alexander asked to make you the way you are."

For a moment, I couldn't breathe. "Dad *asked* you to make me . . . slow?"

"Oh, Edward," she chided. "Do you think I'd mess up your brain by accident?"

"But why?" I whispered.

"So you wouldn't get in your sister's way," Gashwan answered. "If you were smart enough to figure out how the admiral wanted to use you . . ." She shook her head. "You'd never have gone along. But things turned out all right, didn't they? You're here and you're fine."

"But . . . but . . ."

There were no words inside my brain. No words. They'd been burned clean out of me.

No one had made a mistake. It'd all been completely deliberate. Premeditated. Carefully planned. Yet my whole life, my father had called me a disappointment: rejected me for being the way I was, when *he* was to blame.

It didn't make me mad. It made me sick.

But Plebon had lifted his head. "Gashwan—you're talking about an admiral named Alexander. Do you mean Alexander York?"

"Yes," Gashwan said, "Alexander York is Edward's father." With a ghost of a smile, she added, "And I'm his mother."

Plebon turned to Festina. "Alexander York was the admiral who sent *Willow* here to Troyen. He wanted us to pick up a queen and take her to Celestia. York has some shady business deal with a group of people there, called 'recruiters' . . ."

Oof. I should have guessed—who else? who else?—but I was beginning to realize my greatest skill in life was denying the evil around me. My father was the one behind it all: *Willow*, the recruiters, the terrible inertia of my brain.

Festina said nothing, but nodded to herself . . . as if she'd suspected the truth for some time.

In the silence, a distant sound drifted up through the bleak stone corridors—possibly from outside, possibly somewhere in the castle.

Hyena laughter. Cackling and crazed.

"What's that?" Gashwan asked.

"An old friend," Festina answered grimly. "His name is Larry."

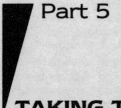

Part 5

TAKING THE CROWN

39

BECONING AN EXPLORER

"A Laughing Larry?" Dade blurted out. "There weren't supposed to be any . . ." He closed his mouth sharply.

"There weren't supposed to be advanced weapons on Troyen?" Tobit asked. "Looks like our navy researchers weren't the only ones who got around the Fasskister Swarm."

"Don't jump to conclusions!" Festina snapped. "Quick," she said to Gashwan, "who's in charge here?"

"I am," Gashwan answered.

"In charge of the whole palace? The defense?"

Gashwan nodded. "Ever since Queen Temperance left."

"*Willow* took the queen away," Plebon put in. "To help the recruiters on Celestia control—"

"We figured that out," Festina said, then turned back to Gashwan. "The laughing sound comes from a killing machine . . . maybe more than one. Your arrows are useless, and your troops will be slaughtered. Surrender now before there's a bloodbath."

Gashwan patted Festina on the arm. "Dear child, I'm not a fool. I tried to surrender as soon as Temperance abandoned us. The Black Army refused."

"They wouldn't let you give up peacefully?"

"They ignored my broadcasts and killed my envoys. The Black Queen doesn't want capitulation—she wants to take the palace by force."

"Who is the Black Queen?" I asked. Knowing the answer.

"Your sister, of course," Gashwan said. "She started the war, and she's about to end it."

I wished I could go all outraged: yelling, *How could you say such a thing?* But no. Sam had called herself an "advisor" to the Black Queen, but my sister had always been a leader, not a follower. And she'd led Troyen straight into this war. She'd been in a perfect position to incite hostilities, using diplomacy to pump up tensions rather than ease them. The footprints at the Cryogenic Center had been just her size. And Samantha had murdered Verity before faking her own death.

When war came, I could imagine her killing the fifteen queens one by one: getting on their good sides then murdering them, just as she did with Verity. She could have claimed to be a secret envoy from the Technocracy and promised navy support for the queen's cause—that would be a quick route to royal favor. Then she'd betray the queen to some convenient enemy, or slit the royal throat personally when the time was right. It'd taken twenty years, but so what? And every time a queen died, Sam would try to keep control of the queen's armies, giving orders to generals who still trusted her as the late queen's closest ally.

Now, it was almost over—nothing to do except take the palace. In the process, she'd kill me because I was a loose end. She probably thought I was too stupid to figure out things on my own, but she didn't want me talking to anybody else. Sam couldn't afford that: my very existence was evidence against her.

"It's me Sam wants," I said. "She's afraid I know too much. If I give myself up, maybe she won't kill anyone else."

"Dear boy," Gashwan replied, "I know too much too. A lot more than you do. But if we both give ourselves up, Samantha will worry we might have talked to someone or hidden a message somewhere. Besides, Edward, she can't leave witnesses who'll say you surrendered peacefully. You know she has to kill you and destroy your body. You know that, don't you, dear?"

"Yes."

"And it will look suspicious if she does that to a voluntary prisoner. Your human friends will make a fuss. From Samantha's perspective, it's tidier if we all die accidentally in the heat of battle. Then she'll lament the horrors of war, and make an apologetic donation to the fleet's Memorial Fund."

Gashwan's whiskers quivered with amusement . . . even admiration. She was truly tickled by the way Sam had worked things into a neat package—a mother's pride at how clever her daughter turned out to be.

Festina snapped, "We're wasting time. Plebon, can you find your way to the roof?"

He nodded. "You want me to look for Larries?"

"And anything else you can see. Tobit, you and Dade go with him. Take a Bumbler and check what the Black Army is doing. Keep trying with the Sperm anchor too—maybe Prope will have an attack of conscience and come back for us."

"Prope?" Tobit snorted. "Conscience?"

"It's a long shot," Festina admitted. "Try anyway." She put her gloved hand on the sleeve of his tightsuit and gave a little squeeze. "Get moving, you old sot."

"Right away, your magnificence." He gave her something that was nowhere near a salute, then grabbed Dade by the arm. "Come on, Benny, we're off to fulfill the glorious Explorer tradition: getting our asses shot for no good reason."

"That's what 'expendable' means," Dade replied.

Tobit cuffed him in the helmet. "Asshole—you say that *after* we die."

As Tobit, Dade, and Plebon hurried up a nearby ramp, Festina said, "All right—the rest of us need to get organized.

Let's get Kaisho to . . . Kaisho? Where the hell are you?"

I looked around: lots of Mandasars, but no wheelchair. While we'd been distracted, Kaisho must have drifted quietly out of the lanternlight and vanished into the darkness.

"Bloody hell," Festina glowered, "I knew there was a reason she ought to stay in the ship."

"Perhaps," Counselor suggested, "she wants to make contact with the moss at the front of the palace."

"She's made contact already," Festina fumed. "Likely while she was still on *Jacaranda*—no one knows the range of the Balrog's mental power, but there's so much damned moss down here, it probably has the combined strength to talk with someone in orbit. Hell, it may have been able to contact Kaisho while she was still on Celestia; some experts think the Balrog is a single hive-mind, with instantaneous communication between every damned spore in the universe. Willpower stronger than the laws of physics. If that doesn't scare the piss out of you, you haven't thought about it long enough."

"But if she's already talking to the other Balrogs," Counselor said, "why did she need to go off on her own?"

"Because the moss has an errand for her," Festina answered. "Something it can't do for itself, while it's stuck to the palace walls." She lifted her hand and pressed it to her helmet's visor, as if she wanted to cover her eyes. "I really hate being manipulated," she growled. "Kaisho used me to bring her here. And so did you, Edward."

"My sister manipulated *me*," I told her.

"So did your father," Gashwan put in, way too cheerily. "From the very start."

"To make Edward a king?" Counselor asked.

"Exactly," Gashwan smiled. "What a clever young girl you are."

"King of what?" I asked.

"Of whatever you want," Gashwan answered. "Mandasars. Or humans. Possibly both."

"Because of the pheromones," I mumbled. "Because I'm

like a queen and can simulate . . ." I didn't finish the sentence.

"When your father first came to Troyen," Gashwan said, "he saw the possibilities. Queens can consciously manufacture Mandasar pheromones; what if somebody created a being who could make human ones too? A secret weapon for swaying people to your side. The ultimate diplomat."

"The ultimate admiral," Festina murmured. "Manipulator supreme. Old Alexander must have dreamed of becoming royal himself."

"He couldn't," Gashwan told her. "His DNA was entirely human: incompatible with the transformation he had in mind. He had to settle for making clones of himself—ninety-nine percent like the original, but with a sampling of transplanted Mandasar genes to pave the way for more changes later on . . ."

Festina nodded, as if she'd already known. That's why she'd asked if I was bioengineered. She must have guessed I'd need fancied-up DNA if I was going to become . . . um . . .

. . . more than human.

The idea made me shiver—I was supposed to be Dad's ideal of a superman.

Except that I was stupid. Supermen shouldn't be stupid. Why would he deliberately ask for that?

Gashwan had already answered the question: so I wouldn't realize what was being done to me.

"I was the guinea pig," I whispered.

"That's right." Gashwan patted me fondly on the arm. "When Innocence started suckling from Verity, so did you."

"Thanks to the nano," Festina said, "that your sister commissioned from the Fasskisters. The nanites dosed Edward little by little over the course of the year . . . and Verity never knew it was happening. I assume you had a second batch of nanites that brought venom to your lab instead of to Edward?"

"Of course," Gashwan replied. "We needed to analyze

the venom at every stage so we could reproduce it for Samantha later on. We also needed to test all kinds of medical techniques to make sure we could keep a human alive through a full year of venom poisoning . . . and through the transformation." She gave me a smile. "If it's any consolation, the things we learned working on you made it much easier when we did the same for Samantha. Your contribution saved her a lot of pain. Sam transformed into a queen as easily as a natural-born Mandasar . . . all thanks to you."

Oh good—I'd fulfilled my one and only purpose. I'd been engineered as a near–genetic double to my sister, so I'd be the best possible guinea pig later on. A good testing ground before the doctors started on the *real* patient. I was just the disposable prototype, the one they'd throw away after they learned how to do things right.

So here's the honest truth: I wasn't a superman, I was a super-Neanderthal. Close to the real thing, but a dead end. Sam was the true progenitor—by the time the war started, she must have had some secret medical facility all prepared so Gashwan could put her through the same treatments I got. Sam was given the pheromone powers of a queen, but she stayed looking human, so no one would suspect what a threat she was. Over time, she'd eliminated her competition, built her big Black Army, and conquered the planet.

What was next? The League of Peoples would never let her leave Troyen, that was for darned sure; but she could have children. The next generation would still look human, so they'd have no trouble sneaking onto Technocracy worlds. After that, how long would it take for them to manipulate their way into top positions of power? A few decades maybe. My father would have himself a dynasty, secretly dominating human space.

But the dynasty would come from Sam, not me. I was never destined for anything but the trash heap.

Funny . . . for a long time, I'd felt guilty wearing an Explorer's uniform when I didn't think I deserved it. But surprise, surprise, I'd been perfectly suited for the Explorer Corps from the moment of my conception.

No one could possibly be more expendable than me.

40

RACING THE BALROG

"Why did you do it?" Festina asked Gashwan. "Why did you help Samantha with everything? You're too smart to think she'd be grateful—it's a wonder Sam didn't kill you as soon as she'd gone through her transformation."

"She would have tried," Gashwan agreed. "But I ran off to join Queen Temperance a few days before the job was done. My assistants finished the process. I doubt if they've been seen since."

"Then why?" Festina asked again. "Why help a ruthless murderer?"

"Because it was *interesting*," Gashwan said, as if that should have been obvious. "A pretty little challenge. And because I owed Alexander York a favor."

"What favor?" I asked.

She pointed to her nose: the old ugly scar running the length of her snout. "He gave me this."

Festina stared. "Alexander York hurt you? Damaged your face?"

Gashwan shook her head. "Alexander York helped me, with something no Mandasar would have done. He got human surgeons to destroy my sense of smell."

She reached up with a wrinkled hand and stroked the scar affectionately. "They weren't very skilled at dealing with Mandasars, but they got the job done. It's trickier than you'd think—not just excising the olfactory nerves, but creating enough scar tissue inside the nostrils that the membranes can't absorb odor molecules."

"But why?" Festina asked.

"To be free," Gashwan said. "Free of control by queens. Free of being terrified by warriors. Free of getting my moods altered by anyone who walked by. I got my brain into a state I liked, then cut the cords so no one could change me."

"That's why you could betray Verity," I muttered.

"Why I was *valuable* to Verity," Gashwan corrected. "Other doctors told the queen what she wanted to hear; I told the truth. Mostly. The same with Temperance—she appreciated me because I couldn't be swayed like other people around her. I'm the reason Temperance survived the war as long as she did. Smart objective advice. And now that Temperance is gone, I'm the one in charge, aren't I? Because my brain isn't muddled by every whiff of sweat drifting on the breeze. I've become my own queen."

Festina looked at me; I caught her gaze but said nothing. Like it or not, Mandasar society depended on communication smells: conveying emotions, providing feedback, tuning folks in to each other. Humans do the same with tone of voice and body language. Rejecting all that, Gashwan had become a sort of sociopath, untouched by the people around her. Disconnected.

Which is why she could go along with Dad and Sam, when their plan would lead Troyen into war. Gashwan thought it was *interesting*—a pretty little challenge.

If she wasn't crazy before her nose got hacked up, she sure was now.

"Hey, kids," Tobit's voice sounded in my ear, "you want a status report?"

"You're on the roof?" Festina asked.

"More like an open parapet walk . . . though Mandasar architecture doesn't conform much to the medieval European school. A true parapet needs some nice machicolations running alongside—"

"Phylar," Festina interrupted, "shut up and talk to me."

"Sure thing, your admiral-tude." I could hear the grin in his voice. "The bad guys have sent us four Larries: three outside the walls and one inside. They aren't firing at the moment—just hovering and scaring the crap out of everybody. The guards are taking potshots at them, but arrows bounce right off."

"What about Kaisho?" Festina asked. "Any sign of her?"

"You've lost Kaisho?"

"Kaisho lost herself."

"Isn't *that* disquieting." Tobit went silent a moment, then came back on. "I don't have a good view, but the moss up front might be glowing brighter. Could just be my imagination."

"No, it's probably some fresh hell coming our way." Festina sighed. "Anything else?"

"The Black Army has broken through the defense perimeter, and the palace guards are falling back to the next canal. Looks like an orderly retreat. I suppose they'll form up again and kill a few more Black Shoulders at each canal they come to. It ain't going to hold the enemy off forever, but they're buying us time to pull off our brilliant plan. We do have a brilliant plan, right, Admiral?"

"Sure," Festina answered. "I'll wave my hands and pixies will teleport the bad guys into the heart of the sun."

"Oh good," Tobit said, "I was afraid it would be something impractical."

"I could go to the battle lines," I offered. "Make some royal pheromone and see what happens."

"What happens," Festina said, "is you get shot by guys in gas masks." She turned to Gashwan. "I don't suppose you've been saving a tac nuke for a rainy day."

"That rainy day came and went," Gashwan replied . . . and even she had the decency to sound subdued. "The first weeks of the war weren't pretty, human—the Fasskister Swarm didn't take out every missile silo in time. Unshummin survived because all the queens wanted to keep the palace intact . . . no bombing the pretty silver throne. Other cities weren't so lucky. They say Fortitude's old stronghold in Therol still glows in the dark. As for Queen Clemency in Koshav . . ."

We never got to hear about Queen Clemency. Gashwan was interrupted by Dade screaming over the radio. "Admiral, Admiral! There's a Sperm-tail on the horizon!"

"My God," Festina said. "Maybe Prope *does* have a conscience. Have you turned on our anchor?"

"Affirmative, Admiral," Dade answered. "But the tail isn't coming to us. It's just quivering in place—its tip is dangling into one of the canals."

"Tug-of-war, Tobit!" Festina shouted. "You know the drill." To the rest of us, she snapped, "The roof. Run!"

Gashwan opened her mouth to say something . . . but we were already racing for the up-ramp. I looked back just before I disappeared into the stairwell; she was staring straight at me with a hint of sorrow on her face.

Gashwan. My creator. Maybe even my mother—if I had Mandasar DNA in me, Gashwan must have got it from somewhere. But I never slowed down to wave good-bye. I didn't like her any better than I liked the rest of my family.

"Tug-of-war what?" Zeeleepull demanded as we raced up the slow-sloping ramp to the next floor. My heart was pounding. Even the placid workers were gabbling excitedly amongst themselves.

"If the tail won't come to our anchor," Festina told him, "that means there's another anchor somewhere in the city. Pulling hard in a different direction."

"Samantha might have an anchor," I said. "She probably kept all kinds of navy stuff."

"My thought exactly," Festina agreed. "She let us land, but doesn't want us getting away. Now she's trying to steal the tail from us."

"So what are you going to do?" Counselor asked.

"Boost our anchor's power by feeding it juice from other sources: a Bumbler, or a tightsuit's battery pack."

Counselor panted, "Won't the bad queen increase her anchor's power too?"

"That's what makes tug-of-wars interesting," Festina said. "Now less talk, more speed."

The ramp took us up to the palace's main gallery: a big wide hall like a spine running the length of the building. In Verity's time, the gallery had been lined with memorials to Troyen's medical achievements—paintings of famous doctors, first editions of medical books, and even (I'm not kidding) labeled dissections of all four Mandasar castes including crazy old Queen Spontaneity encased in clear plexi.

Now, all I could see was a hot red glow fifty paces in front of us, like staring into an open furnace . . . the Balrog, clotted on floor, walls, and ceiling. Thick as carpet, stretching off hundreds of meters, all the way to the front nose of the palace.

"Holy shit," Festina whispered. "We don't have to go through that, do we?"

"No," I answered, pointing. "There's our way to the roof."

The door we wanted lay in the opposite wall of the gallery, maybe halfway between us and the glowing moss. Cautiously I led the group forward, keeping my eyes on the stone floor to make sure I wouldn't step on stray spores that had drifted ahead of the main body. The gallery was unnaturally quiet with the moss's muffling effect—it absorbed noise like crushed velvet laid over every surface. The pressure of sheer silence pushed against my eardrums, muting the sounds of our footsteps. I found myself holding my breath . . . but that wasn't enough to keep from smelling the reek of buttered toast filling the air.

"*Teelu,*" Counselor whispered, tiptoeing at my heels, "I am very very scared."

"Who isn't?" I whispered back. "But remember, Tobit and the others must have come this way too. Nothing happened to them."

"Explorers are just normal humans," Counselor replied.

"You are special, *Teelu*. What was it the moss woman said? The Balrog will act if it finds a host too good to pass up."

I winced. In the past few weeks I'd figured out two basic facts about the Balrog:

1. The moss got a kick out of scaring the pants off lesser species.

2. It preferred waiting to pounce till someone spoke a good straight line . . . like, "We should be safe now," or, "I don't think it knows we're here," or, "The Balrog will act if it finds a host too good to pass up."

Um.

The gallery's silence was broken by a ripping sound, starting at the far end of the palace and racing our way. The moss on the walls and ceiling came sloughing off in great flat sheets, peeling from the stone and falling to the floor. Like mounds of snow sliding off trees, the moss slopped onto the ground, building up higher and higher . . . until it reached some critical mass and began to spill forward.

Rolling heaps of scarlet fuzz tumbled toward us with all the surging unstoppability of an avalanche.

"Run!" Festina shouted. As if we needed to be told.

I sprinted the last few steps to the doorway and threw myself inside, flattening against the wall of the stairwell. Outside, the moss had started to make a skittering scratchy sound—alien spores tripping over each other as they flowed after us. I waved the others to pass me and hightail it for the roof; but Festina planted herself against the wall opposite me, clutching the lantern in her gloved hand. She had the air of a woman who intended to make sure everyone else was safe before she headed up herself.

Zeeleepull seemed to have the same idea: stopping with Festina and me just inside the stairwell, all of us playing the hero, no one wanting to make a break for it till the others were safely on their way. Then Counselor gave her warrior-mate a tremendous shove that practically knocked him off his feet, forcing him to stagger a few steps up the ramp in spite of himself. She barreled forward and shoved him again: no delicacy at all, just whomp, like a small brown bulldozer plowing into an obstacle she was determined to move. One more shove and Zeeleepull accepted the inevitable—he ran, Counselor ran, Hib & Nib & Pib ran, with Festina and me racing close on their heels.

I had just reached the first landing when the stairwell behind me flushed bright with a crimson glow. The Balrog was coming up too.

Nothing to see in the stairwell but Festina's lantern and the bloom of Balrog creeping up behind us. The moss didn't move nearly so fast on the ramp as it did on a level floor—the upslope slowed it to a baby's crawl. We'd have no trouble staying ahead in the short run, but the long-term picture didn't look so rosy. There was no way out of this stairwell but the parapet on the roof; and there was no way off that parapet but a bunch of ramps at the front of the building, where the Balrog was already in total control.

Oh well—at least the moss meant we had an alternative to getting killed by my sister.

The ramp went through half a dozen switchbacks, till I could no longer see crimson glimmering up from below. I could still smell buttered toast, strong and clear . . . but I could also catch a whiff of fresh night wind breezing down from the roof's open air. It carried the scent of human sweat, and gusts of ozone too—the fragrance of lightning. Whatever the Explorers were doing, it used a lot of electricity.

By the time I topped the last ramp, the roof was getting crowded, what with five Mandasars and the same number of humans, three wearing big bulgy tightsuits. Once upon a time, the parapet had run along the whole west side of the palace . . . but some kind of explosion had blown out a big chunk of stone, leaving a gap of ten meters between us and the next intact section of walkway. The good news was the missing hunk of masonry made it hard for Balrog to migrate from the front of the palace back to us; the bad news was we were squeezed onto a patch of roof no more than three Zeeleepulls long. Lucky for us, the parapet was three Zeeleepulls wide too: you needed that much for bull-sized warriors to get past each other when they were marching sentry on the ramparts.

Even if we'd had more space, I doubt we would have used it—everyone was too busy crowding around Tobit, Dade, and Plebon to see what they were doing. They'd planted our remaining anchor atop the stomach-high wall that edged both sides of the parapet. Standing on either side of the box were two Bumblers, ours and Plebon's, with back panels pried off to reveal tidy bundles of wires. Neat connections had already been spliced between those wires and some handy electrode knobs jutting out from the base of the anchor machine. The equipment was clearly built to make such rewiring easy; it made me wonder how often Explorers got into tug-of-wars, if navy engineers designed everything for exactly this situation.

But no design is perfect—the Explorers needed more power than just the two Bumblers. Both Tobit and Dade had the fronts of their tightsuits sliced open, cut very delicately by some kind of knife. The incisions were only deep enough to slit off the top layer of fabric, revealing the snarl of circuitry that ran the various functions of the suit: radios, temperature control, all that. Someone had yanked a finger-thick cable out of each suit's belly and connected the cables to the anchor box too . . . making it look like each man had a length of intestine pulled out of his gut and hooked up to the anchor. Tobit and Dade stood side by side in front of the parapet wall like guys at adjacent urinals, not looking at each other, occasionally giving self-conscious glances down at the cables that were pumping power into the little black box.

"How's it going?" Festina asked. She sounded like someone trying not to sound anxious.

"See for yourself," Plebon said. He pointed over the parapet wall, across the palace grounds and past the first canal, to a Sperm-tail twinkling down from the black sky. The tail tip lay pressed against the side of the old Hushed Museum, a memorial to every Mandasar who'd died in the last 144 years. (That's supposed to be how long Mandasar souls stay in the afterlife before getting reincarnated again.) I was happy to see the museum had survived the war . . . even if it looked like the Sperm-tail had choked up against the building and wouldn't come any closer.

"Is the tail stuck?" I asked.

"It's held," Plebon answered. "We increase our power; the tail comes toward us. Then the other side adds more power to *its* anchor, and we lose ground."

"Okay," Festina said, moving into line with Tobit and Dade. "Cut me . . . before Queen Samantha finds more juice."

She spread her arms to expose the front of her tightsuit. Plebon hesitated a moment, then picked up a scalpel that'd been lying on the parapet wall—a regulation navy scalpel, taken from an Explorer's first-aid kit. He skimmed the knife up one side of Festina's rib cage, across at the shoulders, and down to the waist. A flap of heavy cloth fell open in her suit, baring the electronics beneath. Plebon carefully slipped his hand in among the wires and began feeling around for the power cable.

"Kind of an erotic experience, ain't it, Admiral?" Tobit leered. "Having your clothes cut off, then getting groped."

"Shut up, old man," Festina mumbled. Her voice sounded like somebody blushing.

While Plebon worked, I looked over the edge of the parapet. The first thing to catch my eye was a Laughing Larry, hovering halfway between the palace and the surrounding palisade. At the moment, the Larry wasn't giggling its full hyena laugh—just a light chuckle, as if it knew a joke we didn't. The gold ball spun two stories above the ground, a good height for slaughtering soldiers when the shooting started, but from down there, they wouldn't hit us up on the roof. Larries fired out the bottom and sides, not the top; they weren't designed to butcher people who'd reached higher ground.

Another Larry hovered over the first canal, just beyond the west gate of the palisade. In the darkness I couldn't see more of the metal balls, but I didn't doubt they were out there—when Tobit had reported four of the nasty things, he'd been using his Bumbler as telescope and IR scanner.

Four Laughing Larries, and the Balrog inching up behind us. Not good. I noticed the five Mandasars had planted themselves at the top of the ramp, between me and the creeping moss. Counselor was grimly holding Festina's flaming lantern; she obviously had plans to show the Balrog a hot time if it tried to attack her *Teelu*.

I turned my eyes toward the Sperm-tail, still plastered against the side of the Hushed Museum. The tail seemed to be quivering with excitement . . . but maybe it was just vibrating under tension as our anchor pulled one way and Sam's pulled the other. Behind me, Dade yelled at Plebon, "Hey, be careful! If you feed too much power, you'll fry the whole anchor."

"He knows that," Festina said in a tight voice. "Let the man work."

"Almost there," Plebon grunted. "Here goes."

Suddenly, the tail slithered away from the museum wall. It snapped up into the air, high, high, halfway to the thin clouds, then stabbed down again, straight at us—like a colored tube of lightning, and the anchor was the lightning rod.

Whish. Contact. Locked down.

I lifted my hand to my earphone and waited for someone to tell *Jacaranda* we were ready. Five seconds passed in silence. Finally, I said, "Um . . . shouldn't we call the ship? Say we're ready for transport?"

"No radios," Festina replied. Her voice came straight out of her tightsuit, with no amplification. "Our suit power is shunted into the anchor. But there's nothing to worry about:

the ship can tell when its tail has been snagged. Give them a few more seconds to establish an air-pressure gradient. Then we can start—"

She was going to say we could start transporting up. But she was interrupted by stuff transporting *down*: three Laughing Larries and a twentyish version of me.

One slight difference: the younger me had a chest made of glass.

41

GREETING THE
NEW ARRIVALS

They came out of the Sperm-tail in a whoosh, spat onto the parapet through the tiny tail tip and suddenly exploding to full size. One of the Larries smacked against the parapet wall with a metallic clang; the other two bounced against the stone floor, then flipped over the outer wall, where they dropped almost all the way to the ground before stopping their fall. They spun down there, howling as loud as banshees . . . as if they were furiously angry and screaming for someone to kill.

The man nearly went over the side too. He shot out of the Sperm-tail and landed unbalanced on his feet, staggering forward out of control till he lurched over the stomach-high wall. I barely managed to catch him by the tail of his vest. It was a leather one, exactly like Mr. Clear Chest had worn on Celestia.

As I pulled him back to more solid footing, Festina wheeled around, ripping her connection away from the anchor. Her right fist caught the man hard in the jaw; he seemed so dizzy from the Sperm-tail ride, he didn't see the punch coming. The impact nearly sent him over the wall again, but I kept hold of his vest and hauled him in. That brought him back into range for Festina to hit him with a left in the solar plexus and a knife-hand to the side of the neck. He slumped unconscious, his limp body staying upright only because of my grip on his vest. Gingerly, I lowered him to the ground, keeping a wary eye on Festina.

"Um," I began to say . . . but behind Festina's back, the anchor box shot up a stream of sparks that hissed and fizzed in the darkness. When she'd torn herself free, some circuit must have shorted out. With the anchor discombobulated, the Sperm-tail snapped loose and whipped past our faces, making a beeline for the other anchor, somewhere in the middle of the Black Army.

Dade howled, "No!" A moment later, he spun to face Festina. "Do you know what you did? You ruined our chance to escape! They told me you were crazy, but . . ." He clamped his mouth shut.

Festina only sighed. "Dade," she said, "that wasn't our Sperm-tail: it came from some other ship. *Jacaranda* sure as hell wasn't carrying Laughing Larries . . . and I would have noticed a crew member who looks so much like Edward." She shook her head. "There must have been a second ship in this system. When we arrived, it hid behind an asteroid or something; but as soon as *Jacaranda* left, the ship came straight to Troyen. Obviously, this pretty fellow didn't want to miss the final offensive. In so much of a hurry, he forgot to make sure his Sperm-tail had landed on the right anchor."

"But . . ." It was obvious Dade still wanted to blame someone. "You didn't have to rip away from the anchor and break it. You didn't have to *hit* the guy."

"No?" Festina knelt beside the clear-chest man and patted him down. At his hip, she found a holster holding a standard-issue navy stun-pistol: very bad if the man had been given enough time to start shooting. Even worse, Festina opened a zipped inner pocket of the leather vest and pulled out a palm-sized electrical doodad—a control box of some kind.

She held it for Dade to see. "Command module for those Laughing Larries," she said. "Voice-activated. He didn't even have to pull it from his pocket; all he had to do was shout. One word, and his three nasty pets would have sliced us to ribbons."

Dade stared, his eyes growing wide. He whispered, "How did you know?"

Festina shook her head in despair. "I didn't know, Dade—I made a snap judgment, based on inadequate facts. That's what Explorers *do*. Sometimes you're right, sometimes you're wrong. Sometimes it doesn't matter, sometimes it's life and death. You never know till it's over . . . and often, not even then."

Slowly she got to her feet. Tobit took the controller from her. "Let me have a look at this," he said. "If I'm lucky, I can hot-wire the voice-recognition circuits, so it obeys one of us instead of sleeping beauty there."

"No need," Festina told him. She took the box back and held it out to me, like a microphone I should speak into. "Edward, say, 'Rise two meters.' "

I did. The three Larries that'd just come down the Sperm-tail whirled themselves up a couple meters higher. I swallowed hard, but Festina only shrugged. "Clones. You and this guy look the same, so I figured you'd sound the same too. At least close enough to fool a simple-minded voice-recognition system." She tossed the controller to me. "Congratulations, King Edward. You've got three killing machines. I'm curious as hell what you'll do with them."

Giving me the controller was a test: I knew that. Festina wanted to see if I'd go crazy or something. I think she still was inclined to trust me, but considering how I'd smashed that anchor, she couldn't be sure I was on the side of the angels. If I'd tried to talk to the Larries, maybe she would have punched me just like the guy on the ground . . . or shot me with her stunner. She'd turned a titch away from me, so I couldn't see either her holster or her gun hand.

But none of that mattered—I had no intention of using the Larries for anything. I came close to throwing the controller off the parapet, so I wouldn't be tempted . . . and so the spirit that sometimes possessed me couldn't use the Larries either. Instead, I just handed the little gizmo back to Festina. "You keep it," I said. "If you need the Larries to do something, I'll give them your orders; but I don't want my own army."

"Lousy instincts for a king," she muttered. But she took the controller and tucked it into a pouch on her belt. Glancing down at our new Mr. Clear Chest, she asked, "What do your instincts say about him?"

"Um . . . maybe shoot him with your stunner, just to make sure?"

She looked like she was considering it, but Dade spoke first. "If you shoot him, he'll be out for six hours. Suppose we need to interrogate him or something."

Festina looked at the boy. "Interrogate him? What about?"

"I don't know," Dade answered, not meeting her eyes. "But it'd be nice to have the option. And maybe we could use him as a hostage . . . if he's important to York's sister."

"You think my sister would care?" I asked.

"She might," Festina admitted. She knelt beside the unconscious man. From a pouch in her belt, she pulled a coil of copper wire (probably for making electrical repairs to her suit) and began trussing our prisoner's hands behind his back. "Dade," she said, "if you're so interested in this guy, you're in charge of him. No matter what else happens, don't take your eyes off him. Shout when he wakes up. Can you do that?"

"*Yes*," Dade answered, sounding all huffy with indignation. Festina didn't comment; instead she turned to me.

"This fellow is a clone of your father, right? Or possibly of you yourself."

"Since I'm a clone of my father, there's no difference."

"There's a difference. If nothing else, your father's fully human; you have that pinch of Mandasar. I suspect this fellow has Mandasar genes too—all the better to produce babies with your sister."

That made me gulp. "Babies? But that's, umm . . ."

"Incest?" she suggested. "Absolutely. But it still pro-

duces healthier offspring than cloning the clones of a clone.
How old was your father when you were produced? Sixty,
something like that? So your own genes were sixty years
old the moment you were conceived. YouthBoost can com-
pensate to some extent, but sorry, Edward, you don't have
the hundred-and-sixty-year life expectancy of a normal human. A hundred and twenty, tops. And if we cloned *you*,
your progeny might not make it to eighty.

"So," she went on, "since your sister wants to generate
a dynasty of superkids, it's best to avoid more cloning and
just use the old-fashioned approach. A mummy and daddy
love each other very much . . . and they mass-produce fertilized ova which are farmed out to surrogate mothers all
over the Technocracy." Festina gave a rueful grin. "Your
Samantha is the mother, and I'll bet this fellow is the father."

"Oh." It made me kind of sick, thinking this copy of me
might have been *with* Samantha. For all I knew, they could
have produced kids already. But when I thought about it,
that wasn't so likely: Sam had been so busy running the
war, she wouldn't have time to go through pregnancy; and
on Troyen, she'd have a hard time finding another human
woman who could act as surrogate mom. All the humans
had been evacuated twenty years ago.

Still, this clear-chest guy—this version of me or my father—it made me feel horrible, thinking of him and Sam
together. Was he smart? It was such a dumb jealous question, but was he smart? Was he witty and charming and all,
a real equal who could keep up with her and not some half-
wit moron who always needed to be babied? Because if he
was stupid, maybe I could stand the thought of him with
Sam, her giving him orders, do this, do that . . . but if he
was so smart that sometimes he got the better of her, and
sometimes he said, "This is what I want," and she did it . . .

That would make me truly, truly sick. I don't know why
but it would.

Kneeling beside Festina, I bent over the man and sniffed
. . . as if I could somehow smell whether or not he was

clever. I couldn't tell you what I expected to find, but I do know what actually hit my nose: the odor of buttered toast.

Uh-oh.

The hairs on the back of my neck curled cold and clammy. I was remembering something from back on Celestia, as the glass-chested recruiter stood in the hatchway of his skimmer. There'd been that tiny dot of red shining in his belly, like the tip of a ruby laser . . . but back then, I hadn't known enough to be terrified of little glowing specks.

Gingerly, I flipped the man's vest all the way open. Inside the glass torso, his lungs lifted up and down; his heart thudded behind his ribs; and there in his gut, tucked among the folds of his small intestine, was a glowing pinprick of red.

"Look," I said, pointing. I made sure to keep my finger high above the glass.

Festina squinted, then sat back abruptly. "Jesus Christ. Is that Balrog?"

"Smells like it," I told her.

"In his stomach. How could it get into his stomach? How could you *smell* it in his stomach?"

That was a real good question. For the first time it occurred to me maybe I wasn't really smelling stuff at all. Maybe I was just kind of *sensing* it, the way Kaisho could see things even though her eyes were covered with hair. That could explain why some people smelled like sounds or colors: I wasn't actually using my nose. Or at least I wasn't using it for everything. Mandasar queens might secretly have a sixth sense, like ESP or something . . . and now I had the same thing. Considering how Balrog spores were supposed to be all telepathic, maybe other telepaths could sense them pretty easily—as if they were giving off strong signals on the ESP channel.

But I could think about such things later. I told Festina, "I don't know how I smelled it, I just did." I took a deep breath. "That other guy had a Balrog too. The recruiter on

Celestia. I noticed a little red speck glowing in his stomach, but didn't know what it was."

"Oh, *fuck*," Festina whispered. "Fuck, fuck, fuck." She quickly turned to Tobit, and snapped, "Put a Bumbler back together. Fast."

Two minutes later, we were staring at the Bumbler's vidscreen, looking at a mocked-up anatomical diagram made with X rays and ultrasound. The clear-chest man did indeed have a Balrog in his belly; but it was locked in a thumb-sized containment chamber that must have been surgically implanted. The chamber itself was glass, which was why you could see the spore glowing inside; but it also had a set of black tubes sunk into the intestinal wall, and a bunch of wires leading back to the man's spinal cord.

"Got to be some kind of life support," Tobit said. "Those tubes into the intestines—they're probably siphoning nutrients from the guy's digestive system. Feeding the damned moss."

"And everything is glass," Plebon pointed out. "Balrogs need sun as well as food, correct?"

Festina nodded. "They have to get solar energy every day . . . and some warped fool must have replaced this guy's chest with glass, so light could get in. Drastic, but it does the job. That's why he prances around in just a vest— a shirt would get in the way."

"But why would you want a Balrog in your belly?" Dade asked. "If that glass container ever broke . . ."

"It can't be real glass," said Festina. "Neither is the man's chest. They're both some transparent polymer . . . probably as tough as armor."

"But why keep a Balrog at all?" Dade insisted. "Dangerous little parasites, who can see the future and read your mind . . ."

Something went click in my head. "Communication system," I blurted out.

"What do you mean?" Plebon asked.

"Festina said some folks believe all the Balrogs are in telepathic contact with each other . . . instantaneous communication, no matter how far apart individual spores might be. Suppose someone figured out a way to use Balrogs as, um, relays. You lock one up inside you, hook it to your brain—through those wires there, straight to the spinal nerves—then you kind of use it like a broadcast link. This guy's thoughts go into his Balrog, and get transmitted instantaneously to Mr. Clear Chest on Celestia. Mr. Clear Chest's thoughts come back the same way. They constantly hear what each other is thinking." I stopped a second. "For all we know, their thoughts may go back and forth so fast they scramble together. Like one joint brain inside two separate heads, light-years apart. A little hive-mind of their own."

"Bloody hell," Festina whispered. "If your father can not only make superhumans, but keep all their brains in synch so they don't fight among themselves . . . staying in instantaneous contact even when they're spread across the galaxy . . ."

"They'd be worse than the damned Balrogs," Tobit growled. "Speaking of which, imagine how the mossy little bastards feel about this: their fellow spores taken as slaves and used as someone else's phone line."

"They hate it," Festina said softly. "And they hate the people who built it." She turned to me. "That containment chamber looks like Fasskister technology—Fasskisters are masters of hooking machines to organisms and vice versa. Remember what Kaisho said back on the orbital."

I nodded. *The Fasskisters know full well why it's right and proper to lock them in their precious metal suits, with physical needs taken care of, but their minds slowly going crazy.* That's why the spores had taken over the Fasskister orbital: tit-for-tat vengeance against the folks who'd sealed up spores in little glass cases.

"Makes you wonder," Festina said, "who *really* got the idea of dumping spores on the Fasskisters. Did Queen Temperance think of it herself? Or did the Balrog plant the notion in her head?"

"Generally," a voice whispered, "we stay out of the

heads of lesser creatures. But we do make exceptions."

Kaisho hovered in her chair at the top of the nearby ramp. Behind her, the stairwell blazed as bright as a forest fire.

42

ACCEPTING THE INEVITABLE

Zeeleepull leapt in front of her, his pincers wide and ready. "Back, you," he snarled. He looked more mad at himself than at Kaisho, because he'd let her sneak up on our backs.

"Dearest boy," Kaisho whispered to him from behind her veil of hair, "you might stop *me*, but not my colleagues."

She waved a lazy hand at the spores all around her. They gleamed on the surface of the ramp like a burning red carpet—not advancing but thickening, as if more and more of them were climbing up from below, accumulating layer after layer of alien fuzz.

Zeeleepull didn't flinch. Mandasar warriors have a crazy fondness for doomed last stands. "Back," he said again, and made a snipping gesture with his claws. "Smelly un-hume."

Kaisho chuckled. "Easy, my dashing innocent. We aren't here to swallow you up . . . just for a little justice."

Festina straightened to her full height. "Justice against whom? Mr. Glass Chest here?"

"Amongst others," Kaisho said.

"Because the Balrog doesn't appreciate being used."

"That's right."

Festina snorted. "Some aliens can dish it out but they just can't take it. The damned Balrog had no moral qualms enslaving the woman you once were, Kaish—twisting your mind and body for its own mossy convenience—but heaven forbid a human ever takes advantage of a single fuzzy spore. Not that I'm defending our glass-chested clone here, but don't you see the irony?"

Kaisho lowered her head. "I'm not enslaved," she whispered. "Not quite. But I'm bound close enough to the Balrog to feel the suffering of the spore in that man's stomach. Can you imagine the humiliation—the degradation—of being imprisoned like an animal, forced to transmit bestial human thoughts every second of the day? Barely kept alive by glimpses of sunshine and the cast-off waste of a human's gut? Used as a debased go-between, a conduit for sordid schemes of violence and domination . . ."

Her voice broke into a sob. A real sob, out loud. When she spoke again, it was a normal human voice—no whispering, no taunting, just a genuine person talking. "Festina . . . all of you . . . I know you think the Balrog is evil. You see it as a threat because you imagine some terrible parasite eating you, stealing your soul. But it's not like that. It's . . . beautiful. Just beautiful. It's wise, and honest, and gentle, and caring; I love it with all my heart. Of course I'm scared how I'm changing, and I have my moments of doubt . . . but I love this creature inside of me. I do. Because it's so much more *holy* than anything I ever dreamed possible."

She tossed her head defiantly, flicking the hair away from her face. Her mouth was a fierce line, and her eyes blazed with reflected red light from the moss as she stared at each one of us—daring us to argue. "Think how this bastard is using the spores he's captured. There are three of them linked together: Admiral York on New Earth; this clone here; and that recruiter on Celestia . . . who's another York clone, an earlier model without the fancy DNA. He had his features changed with plastic surgery so he wouldn't be immediately recognized by people using the recruiters' services, but it's still the same old Alexander York. Three versions of the same man, touching mind-to-mind, thoughts kept perfectly in synch so they're effectively the same person."

Kaisho gestured to the man at my feet. "This is your

father, Edward—body and brain. The cloned zygote was planted in a surrogate mother right here on Troyen, and born a few weeks before the war started; that glass thing was installed in the baby's stomach a little while later. From that day on, the child's brain was so dominated by transmitted thoughts, the infant had no chance of developing a separate identity. He *is* Alexander York: helping Samantha on Troyen, leading the recruiters on Celestia, playing Admiralty politics back on New Earth. A man with blood on his hands in three separate star systems, and the League can't touch him because he never physically crosses the line.

"Now," Kaisho went on, her voice still choking on tears, "can you imagine how it pains the Balrog to be caught up in this? Every day, Admiral York commits murder and war, using sentient creatures like disposable means to repugnant ends. Can you imagine how the Balrog feels, melded to such a putrescent mind? The entire Balrog race is in agony. *I'm* in agony, and I'm not holy, I'm just a lower animal out of my depth."

"Kaisho." Festina's voice was soft, more tender than I'd ever heard it before. "Please don't cry. Please. What does the Balrog want?"

"To free itself, of course. To detach itself from that awful man."

"And to punish him?"

Kaisho met Festina's gaze for a moment, eye to eye. Then she reached up and fluffed her hair back over her face, hiding once more behind her natural veil. Her voice dropped down to the old familiar whisper: back to speaking for the Balrog instead of herself. "If someone doesn't do something, he'll keep playing the same tricks. He has more spores—commandeered from the navy hospital that examined me."

Festina contemplated the unconscious man at her feet. "Suppose we take him to Gashwan for surgery. Have the gadget removed from his gut."

"We get the gadget," Kaisho said immediately.

"Of course," Festina agreed. "As for the man himself . . . if he's committed crimes, and I don't doubt that he has, we'll turn him over for a proper trial. Considering that the Balrog has heard York's every thought for the past few decades, it won't be hard getting a conviction."

"Yes it will," Kaisho said. "Where is he going to get a proper trial? Even if *Jacaranda* rescued us this very moment, you couldn't take this man back to the Technocracy. He's a dangerous non-sentient creature; if you try to move him out of this system, the League will kill you as well as him. And if he stays on Troyen, he'll be acquitted by the new High Queen Samantha." Kaisho shook her head. "Sorry, Festina dear, but you can't arrange any 'proper trial'—you'll never find a suitable legal authority."

"There is one," Counselor said. "There's *Teelu*."

Silence for a moment. Then the other Mandasars nodded enthusiastically, ignoring that I was waving my hands no, no, no. "I'm not a legal authority," I protested.

"You're as legal as your sister," Festina said, "and you suffered through the venom treatments before she did. When it comes to being royal, you've got seniority."

Tobit grunted. "Not to mention you're older than she is."

"Just ten minutes!" I objected.

"They tell me you were the high queen's consort," Plebon put in. "That makes you the last surviving member of the old regime."

"I was just a glorified bodyguard!"

Festina took me by the sleeve and pulled me close, pressing her helmet against my ear so I could hear her whisper. The smooth plastic visor was surprisingly warm where it touched my skin. "Edward," she said in a low voice, "if you don't say you'll do something, the Balrog may take the law into its own hands. That's a precedent we want to discourage." She drew in a breath. "I'm not asking you to pass judgment on the spot. Just agree you're the closest thing we have to lawful authority, and that you'll consider all the issues at an appropriate time."

I turned to look at her: those grave eyes of hers were

inches away but half-lost in the shadows inside her helmet. My lips almost touched her visor . . . probably the closest I'd ever get to kissing her.

Silly ideas can go through your head at the strangest times.

I stepped back from her, faster than I meant to. Everyone was watching me—even the Balrog. Its red glow focused on me like a scarlet spotlight: not shining brightly, but making me feel conspicuous.

Suddenly, another silly idea went through my head: that all this talk of trials was pure moonshine, especially in our current circumstances. We weren't going to convene a court out here on the ramparts while enemy troops were charging the palace. But somehow, Kaisho had wangled us all into thinking about it, and I was half a second away from saying, "Okay, I'll declare myself in charge here."

Which meant I'd be claiming the throne.

Was that what the Balrog *really* wanted? How much of the past few weeks was a big Balrog plan? If you let your imagination take over, you could start believing the Balrog had brought about this whole expedition to Troyen, just to rescue the single solitary spore inside this guy's stomach. But if that were true, I was so far out of the game I didn't have a chance of understanding what was really going on: who was good, who was bad, what was planned, what was sheer dumb accident. Better just to do the right thing as best I understood it, and hope that was good enough.

"All right," I said, trying to ignore the pounding of my heart. For a second, I didn't have a clue what to say next; but then the words began to come—not like being possessed, but as if a spark had suddenly jumped across a dead-gap inside my head.

"In the name of High Queen Verity the Second . . ." I felt strange, as if something was waking up inside of me.

"In the name of her daughter and rightful successor, Innocence the First . . ." The words kept flowing—from my own head, but some part I'd forgotten was there.

"In the name of my obligations as defender of the crown,

and bearer of the burden of royal blood . . ." Like there'd
been a whole section of my brain that'd closed itself off,
shoved down dormant till the day I finally faced up to
everything I'd known but not admitted—that my sister and
father were monsters, that I was someone special, that I had
a duty I'd been trying to escape for years and years.

"In the name of all that I am, all that I have been, and
all that I should be . . . I accept responsibility as steward of
this realm, regent until such time as the true monarch of
Troyen assumes her proper throne."

I could barely catch my breath. My head felt so *clear* . . .
as if I could sense all of creation as one unified whole all
around me. For one brief second, I swear I knew what was
coming a heartbeat before it happened. I was already turning around when the words came.

"That's so sweet, brother," Sam said from behind me. "I
must compliment whoever wrote that speech for you. Pity
you're going to have the shortest regency on record."

43

CONFRONTING THE
BLACK QUEEN

Without the slightest pause, Festina dropped and rolled. You wouldn't think someone could move that fast in a bulky tightsuit . . . but in the blink of an eye, she'd spun across the parapet and grabbed the scalpel Plebon used to cut open the front of her outfit. Another blink and she was poised above my father's clone, holding the blade to his throat.

Only then did she look up to see where my sister's voice came from.

At least this time we hadn't let someone sneak up under our noses—nothing was anywhere near us. My amazing sensation of comprehending the universe had begun to fade, but I still had a sense of exactly where to look: out past the palisade wall, all the way to the second canal.

Soaring high above the water was a huge glass cube, three stories tall, three stories wide, three stories deep. A faint blue glow glimmered inside—softer than candlelight, barely enough for the cube to be visible against the night's blackness. Shadowy somethings moved about within, but it was too far away to make out anything clearly . . . just wavery motions that meant nothing to me.

I'd soon have my chance to look again from closer up:

the cube was flying straight at us, fast as a horse could gallop.

As it drew nearer, I noticed a parabolic dish mounted on the cube's roof—one of those fancy gadgets for eavesdropping on people a long way away, and for talking back to them if you felt like it. That's how Sam had heard what we were saying and put in her two cents worth. When you thought about it, that kind of communication system would be pretty useful in a war like Troyen's. Thanks to the Fasskister Swarm, there were almost no radios on the planet . . . so if you wanted to talk to soldiers on the other side of a battlefield, you had to use something different, like tight-focused sound waves. The big hearing dish would also be handy for listening in on enemies: picking up battle plans, status reports, and juicy stuff like that.

So here was another reason Sam had won the war. No other queen would have a flying command post with all kinds of complicated audio equipment. It was kind of surprising *Sam* could have that kind of stuff . . . but then, she was doing business with the Fasskisters and our own navy. She must have got them to smuggle in a few goodies that were immune to antielectronics nanites.

As the cube soared over the palisade, defenders on the ground peppered the glass with crossbow bolts; but the arrows bounced off as if they were toothpicks. The instant after firing, the guards ducked for cover . . . because the cube had an escort of four Laughing Larries, one floating under each bottom corner, like round gold casters holding up a floor-model fish tank. None of the Larries tried to fire—they weren't even making a big howl, just a leisurely spinning whistle—but the warriors below weren't taking chances.

The cube stopped a stone's throw away from us, hanging in midair, level with our parapet. The blue glow coming from inside still didn't reveal much; nothing but unidentifiable shadows. It occurred to me, we probably weren't seeing the interior at all—just a video projection, all murked up, like a thick gauze curtain that hid almost everything but let through enough to catch your attention.

No matter how hard it was to see *in*, I was sure Sam could see out just fine . . . with fancy nightscopes and sensors that showed our group as bright as if it were sunny afternoon.

"So. Edward." Sam's voice sounded clearly from the cube, as if we were talking face-to-face, not separated by thick arrow-proof glass. "You've finally come back to me."

"I've come back," I said. "But not to you."

"To whom then? Those poor castaways from *Willow*? By now you must know there's only one left; Daddy rather used up the other one. I can't tell you how angry he was that they stayed behind—he hates loose ends."

Tobit gestured to the unconscious man with Festina's knife to his throat. "At this moment, your dad's a loose end himself."

"Yes, I figured you'd take him hostage." Sam gave a theatrical sigh. "Pity you won the tug-of-war. Daddy was up on *Willow*, cannibalizing parts to make some more Laughing Larries—"

Plebon gasped. "You've got *Willow* here?"

"And a ship of my own," Sam told him. "A pretty black one. We do a lot of manufacturing up there, where we don't have to worry about Fasskister nanites. Anyway, I told Daddy not to try a landing, but he insisted it would be safe. He'd tapped into your own satellite sensors, and watched Edward break that anchor box. He thought it was the only one you had. Idiot. And speaking of idiots, brother, why *did* you smash the box?"

I didn't answer. Eventually, Sam sighed again. "I'm hurt, Edward. You never used to keep secrets from me. But then, you're probably upset. I'm sure Gashwan has been telling all kinds of awful truths about me."

The front of the cube bloomed into a big view of my sister's face, as if the whole surface was a single huge vidscreen. Even blown up three stories tall, Sam still looked beautiful: eyes warm and twinkling, her skin flawless, her face gaspingly perfect.

"So, Edward," she said, "I figure you have an hour before my troops kill you. Any last words?"

"Yes," I said. "We surrender. Any terms you want. Just call off your soldiers."

She shook her head sadly, the way she always did when I was too stupid to understand something obvious. "You heard what I said about loose ends—Dad doesn't like them. Two weeks from now, a group of navy diplomats are scheduled to show up here, ready to establish new relations between the Technocracy and poor war-torn Troyen. By then, we don't want anyone left alive who knows what actually happened. That means we have to kill all of you, plus Gashwan and anyone you might have talked to."

"What about the High Council of Admirals?" Festina asked. "Don't some of them know the truth?"

"Certainly not—it's Daddy's little secret. Not even Admiral Vincence knows . . . despite all the energy he's devoted to meddling in Daddy's affairs. The High Council is always such a hotbed of spying on each other. Do you realize, Vincence had bought off the Executive Officer of Daddy's own ship? That's right: the XO of *Willow* was in Vincence's pocket. It was the XO's idea to pick up Edward on *Willow*'s way out of the system; that wasn't in Daddy's plan at all. He wanted Edward on that moonbase, where we could keep an eye on him. When Daddy interrogated your Explorer Olympia and learned *Willow* was taking Edward back to civilization . . . my, my, my, there was quite the tantrum."

"Why would Dad care?" I asked.

"Because you *know* things, Edward. And you *are* things. I'm sure you don't understand what's going on, but if you ever got home and told Vincence everything you've seen . . . well, Vincence has brains."

"Unlike us," Tobit muttered.

"Don't pout," Sam told him. "The average Technocracy citizen is simply less *capable* than humans once were. The

Admiralty has statistics to prove it; four hundred years ago, when the navy began testing recruits, they scored much higher in almost every area. All nine indices of intelligence . . . psychological maturity . . . emotional stability . . . you name it. *Homo sapiens* as a species has gone into decline, and nobody knows why. Maybe our pampered lifestyles. Maybe too many people with inferior genes, surviving and having children. Maybe some environmental factor was present on Old Earth but not where we live now. Navy researchers are quietly trying to figure out what's gone wrong, but the diminishment is undeniable, especially on Technocracy core worlds. Four centuries ago, idiots like Prope on *Jacaranda* wouldn't have been allowed to command a rowboat; now she's the best captain the navy can find. Isn't that appalling?"

Samantha paused for us to comment . . . but she didn't wait too long. Sam loved making speeches, especially to a captive audience. "So what to do? The civilian governments are gutless incompetents; they lost control of the fleet ages ago, and don't even realize it. As long as there's no interruption in imports of Divian champagne, they don't give a damn what the navy does. Same with most of the navy itself. Captain Prope is the rule, not the exception."

"Not in the Explorer Corps," Festina answered. Her voice was quiet, but tough as iron.

"I wouldn't know," Samantha replied with a breezy wave of her hand. "Explorers have nothing to do with anything. All I'm sure of is the Technocracy suffers a major shortage of brainpower. It's time for new management to take the situation in hand."

"Meaning you," I said.

She smiled. "Old Japanese proverb: *Who will do the harsh things? Those who can.*"

Kaisho growled. "In defense of my ancestors, they were talking about shouldering difficult responsibilities. Not acting like a bitch because you can get away with it."

"I know what they meant," Sam said, "and I mean the same thing. People in the Technocracy are no longer able to govern themselves. Someone more gifted has to take charge. So my father and I intend to create the best leaders humanity has ever seen."

"Yeah, yeah," Festina replied in a bored tone. "Superkids, able to fabricate pheromones, linked into a communal mind, blah, blah, blah. Sounds like a VR game I played when I was six."

Sam couldn't keep her eyes from widening in surprise; I think she truly believed no one was smart enough to see through her plan. But Festina was still talking. "Let's get back to the present, can we? You have the armies, we have the hostage. What are we going to do?"

"Why should I care about your hostage?" Sam asked. "If he's stupid enough to get himself caught . . ."

"Um," I said, "I think you have a soft spot for stupid people, Sam. Especially ones you brought up yourself. You raised this clone from a baby, didn't you? He was born just before the war started. So the instant I left Troyen, you got a baby Edward substitute; and you had the fun of playing mother to me all over again, just like when we were kids."

Sam stared at me. "Did you think of that all by yourself, Edward?"

"Yes. I've also thought of who this guy actually is. He was produced on Troyen, twenty-one years ago, which means he couldn't have been cloned from Dad—by then, Dad was way too non-sentient to leave New Earth. So where did the DNA come from? Either from me or from you: we've both got Dad's DNA too. Except Festina says it's not healthy to clone a clone; it's better to go the old sperm and ovum route. Am I right, Sam?"

"Edward," she said, "I've never seen you like this."

"No, you haven't," I agreed. "But I'm right, aren't I? This man is our son: you and me together. Gashwan could have got the sperm from me when I was delirious from Coughing Jaundice. You donated the egg, and the fertilized result was planted into a surrogate . . . but he's still our child, isn't he, Sam, even if he was put together in a test tube."

My sister's eyes had turned glittering sharp. "Brother dear, when did you get so smart?"

About the same time you made me a father, I almost answered. But I didn't say anything out loud. I was too busy mulling over the effects of hive-queen venom.

What happened when a gentle changed into a queen? She got stronger, she got bigger . . . and she got smarter. Gashwan might have dumbed down my original DNA, but the venom mutated me, just like venom mutates a Mandasar girl. For all I know, Gashwan may have deliberately designed my brain to kick into high gear when it got hit with venom—just to make things interesting.

However it happened, the venom gradually stopped me from being stupid. It was scary and hard to admit . . . but it was the truth. I'd stopped being stupid. Nobody could tell the difference while I was all sick and poisoned, but by the night Sam killed Verity . . ."

Yet again I remembered kneeling in Verity's chambers, smelling the blood on the floor, knowing it was fake . . . me seeing in a flash of insight that everything had been a setup, and that my sister was a horrible murdering butcher. I understood it all; I even understood that I must have got smarter, because the old Edward would never have figured out any of the awful stuff that had happened. The old Edward had been slow but happy, with a kind, beautiful sister who never did bad things to people.

It hurt to be smart. Understanding what really happened in the world just made you sick to your stomach.

So I turned that part of me off: just put it to sleep. I don't know how I did it—you couldn't call it a conscious decision—but something in my head had become so clever, it knew how to hide away my excess intelligence so I wouldn't have to suffer. I packed up the memories too . . . just forgot them all. Like a completely separate person I didn't want to be.

For twenty years, I went back to dumb old Edward. I might have stayed dumb forever . . . except I got dosed with a new shot of venom. That woke something inside of me—

the seeds of memories, plus that separate person I'd set aside so long ago. Who was the spirit that kept possessing me? The spirit was me too: the brainy part of me, who saw I needed to be smart again. Bit by bit, Smart Me worked to join back up with Slow Me. I couldn't tell if the process was finished, but accepting my responsibility as king had sure closed a lot of the gap.

There were still a lot of questions to answer . . . like why the clever half of my brain had smashed the Sperm-tail anchor and marooned us all on Troyen. Why trap us in a war zone? What kind of scheme had it worked out with Prope? Was Smart Me so keen on a showdown with Sam that it cut off our only escape route, leaving us no choice but to play this out to the end?

No way to tell. A lot of my brainy half's thoughts were still out of touch. Nothing to do but keep going and hope I was suddenly smart enough to deal with whatever happened.

But I didn't say any of this out loud. The last thing I wanted was Sam taking me seriously. Let her keep underestimating me, the way she always had. That might give me a tactical advantage.

In the back of my mind, some old-Edward part of my soul felt a twinge of sadness: how I was already scheming, using deceit to get the better of my own sister. The stakes were too high to do anything else . . . but I knew why, twenty years ago, I'd decided I didn't want to be smart.

Sam waited a few more moments for me to say something. When I kept my mouth shut, she sighed. "Well, brother, it seems I've exhausted your supply of banter. Anyone else want to join the conversation? How about you with the knife—Festina Ramos, right? My father told me you were coming to cause trouble. Do you really think I care whether you slit that man's throat?"

"Yes," Festina said in a steely voice. "He's your son. And your father. And your brother too, for all intents and purposes—he looks the same as your beloved Edward.

Quite a trinity in just one package." She slid the scalpel lightly across Mr. Clear Chest's neck, like she was giving him a dry shave. "And just one carotid artery. Which could very easily get nicked." Festina lifted her head and stared straight at the projected image of Sam's face. "Don't consider this an idle threat. It won't be the first throat I've cut."

Plebon and Tobit drew in their breaths sharply. Whatever Festina was talking about, both of them must know the story . . . and their reactions were enough to convince everybody else Festina wasn't lying.

"All right," Sam said. "You have a knife to my father-brother-son's throat. I can match that."

Suddenly, the vidscreen vanished. In its place, the glass wall went clear and a bright light came on inside the cube—giving us our first view of what the cube really contained.

Samantha was there, wearing her dress golds—the showiest uniform a navy diplomat owns.

To Sam's left, a gentle perched in front of a control console, monitoring the cube's flight computer.

And to Sam's right was a beautiful queen I recognized as Innocence. All grown-up now, bright glossy yellow, shining with strength.

Samantha held a gun to Innocence's head.

44

TAKING THE CUBE

Dade was the first to move. He grabbed the stun-pistol out of Tobit's holster and fired at Samantha in the cube.

Nothing happened. Not to Sam, at least. I felt a tingle as the stunner's hypersonics bounced off the cube and echoed back . . . but the effect was so thinned out by the time it returned to the parapet, none of us got knocked for a loop. Nothing more than a scritchy pins-and-needles sensation that passed in a heartbeat.

Grimacing with disgust, Tobit plucked the pistol from Dade's hand and set the gun down on the parapet wall.

"Thanks," Samantha told Dade. "You just demonstrated you can't touch me." She gave a nasty smile. "Just so everybody knows, Innocence here is the last Mandasar queen in the universe. If she dies, there'll never be another. You can't make a new queen without a full year of an old queen's venom."

I called, "Are you all right, Innocence?"

"Quite well, Little Father," she replied in a cold, clear voice. "Do what's right—don't worry about me."

"She's always saying noble things," Sam laughed, using her free hand to pat Innocence on the shell. "So irrationally heroic. It's a pity I didn't find her till last year; if I'd taken her under my wing when she was a girl, I might have brought her round to my way of thinking."

"You flatter yourself," Innocence said drily.

"I like flattery," Samantha replied, "and I'm good at it. I rather like your defiance too. If you start getting subtle, then I'll worry."

Sam glanced my way. "Innocence has only been with me a few months, but she's been a tremendous help. My troops fight so devotedly when they think they're working for Verity's rightful successor. Of course, I've had to make sure the girl doesn't talk to anyone. Usually I keep her drugged unconscious . . . with little servomotors to make her body move, and a hidden speaker so my own words come out of her mouth. It's not a bad system if you keep the room dark, and I've passed the word poor Innocence can't stand bright lights. A result of chemical torture at the hands of an outlaw queen."

"If Innocence is so valuable," Festina said, "you don't dare shoot her."

"She's useful," Sam agreed, "but keeping her alive is a risk. Always the chance she might escape, or tell the wrong people how I've been using her. The sooner I kill her, the safer I'll be. And why not do it now, when I can blame it on human provocateurs? I'll put your fingerprints all over the gun, then blackmail the fleet for a few million: 'Pay up or I'll tell everyone the last queen was killed by an admiral.' "

"The council wouldn't care," Festina laughed. "They'd shout from the rooftops, MAD DOG RAMOS SHOWS HER TRUE SELF. As for the navy accepting responsibility for anyone but me . . . you're looking at expendable Explorers, a woman controlled by alien parasites, and a man who's never been right in the head. Look up *deniability* in your favorite dictionary, and you'll see our pictures."

As she spoke, Festina got to her feet, lifting the unconscious man with her. She kept her scalpel to his throat by locking her knife arm under his chin. Then she hiked her other hand under his armpit, around his chest, and heaved straight up. Even though she was plenty strong, it was still an awkward maneuver; I could imagine my sister watching and wondering if there was a chance of killing Festina during those moments, while she was struggling and slightly off-balance with the man's weight.

I worried about the same thing myself. It seemed crazy for Festina to take such a risk, hoisting the man up . . . and for what? To make it easier for Sam to see the knife blade glinting in the starlight?

Then my eye was caught by another tiny glint: a faint reflection, some star shining on the voice control for the clone's Laughing Larries. Sometime in the past few minutes, Festina must have slipped the controller out of her belt pouch without any of us noticing; when she stood, she'd left it lying on parapet's stone floor.

Now, while everyone's gaze focused up on her hands, and the scalpel, and the exposed throat, her foot nudged forward a bit and sent the controller sliding toward me.

Um.

I didn't have a clue what she wanted me to do . . . and she couldn't tell me. Maybe she didn't have a plan at all— just hoped the king would dream up something.

Um, um, um. I had to force myself not to chew my knuckle or Sam would *know* I was trying to think hard.

Um. Um. Okay. I had an idea.

Sam had started talking again. "You think the High Council has deniability? Wrong. You all came to Troyen in the *Jacaranda* . . . a ship known to run errands for Admiral Vincence. Dad will have a field day with that at the next council session. By the time he's through, Vincence will be in disgrace, and the rest of the council will trip all over themselves to pay me hush money. But," Sam said, her voice turning cold and hard, "that's none of your concern—it's time for ultimatums. Drop your weapons and lie facedown on the ground. If you surrender right away, I might be in such a good mood I'll let you and Innocence live a while longer."

Tobit actually laughed. "How stupid do you think we are?"

I told him, "You may not be stupid. But I am."

Slowly, carefully, I lowered myself to the parapet's stone

floor. In the process, I palmed the remote control Festina had shoved my way. As I laid myself down on my stomach, the little voice-controlled gizmo ended up right under my mouth.

The others kept talking—arguing with Sam, wrangling over treachery-proof schemes to exchange Dad's clone for Innocence—but I ignored them. I was too busy straightening out in my head where my three Larries were: one still up on the parapet, the other two way down near the ground. Sam wouldn't be able to see the ones below her; not when she was paying so much attention to Festina and the others. I just had to picture where those two Larries were in relation to Sam's glass cube . . .

Taking a deep breath, I whispered orders into the voice control right under my mouth. No way to tell if the Larries were obeying me—I couldn't see them for the parapet wall, and anyway, my face was pressed tight to the stone beneath me. I couldn't *hear* the Larries either, because I'd told them to run as quietly as possible. All I could do was shift the lower two into what I thought was the right position, and tell the other one to get ready for a fancy maneuver.

Then: up, up, up.

I scrambled to my feet fast . . . and maybe my movement was enough to distract Sam from seeing the two gold cannonballs shooting up from ground level. They smashed the bottom of the glass cube with a thunderous crunch, both striking on the same side edge—like grabbing one side of a fish tank and yanking up with all your strength. The cube lurched and rolled, knocked over ninety degrees onto its side. For an instant, Sam and Innocence became a jumble of flailing arms, legs, and claws; then both dropped to the new bottom of the cube, Sam falling hard, Innocence falling harder.

Call it a two-story drop: a long way when you're too surprised to twist into a good landing position.

The impact was enough to knock the wind out of both of them. I couldn't see if Sam had held onto her gun, but it didn't matter: a human could recover faster from that fall than an alien who weighed as much as an elephant. Innocence would survive—queens are tough—but she'd be in no shape to stop Sam from retrieving the gun and using it at point-blank range.

So I had to get inside the cube before that happened.

The two Larries that had smashed into the cube were out of the picture; one had hit so hard it embedded itself into the cracked glass, while the other was showering down onto the ground in a hail of broken pieces. That gave me one Larry left—the one waiting on the parapet walk, ready and raring to travel.

I ran and jumped, shouting into the remote control, "Go!"

Good thing I'd given instructions to the Larry before I threw myself on top of it—the moment I leapt on board, I was whirling so fast I could barely think. Scrabbling to hold on, I dug both hands into fléchette slits. Even then, I nearly spun off before we reached the upended cube; if the ride had been a single second longer, I wouldn't have made it.

I hung on just long enough for the Larry to dump me in the middle of what was now the cube's top surface. Too dizzy to move, I just lay on the glass while the Larry carried on with the orders I'd given: flying straight over my head and unleashing every last fléchette in its magazines.

Back on the parapet, Festina shouted "Get down, get down!" But I'd told the Larry to make sure no shots got as far as the castle. Everything was aimed at the cube . . . with me lying in the middle, at the calm eye of the razor hurricane.

Remember how crossbow arrows hadn't even scratched the glass surface? High-velocity steel fléchettes were a whole other story.

Thank heavens it wasn't real glass; things got nasty enough with blunt chips of plastic flying in all directions. I wrapped my arms around my head as the Larry sliced a ragged ring around me—deeper and deeper into the cube's wall, a circumference of shredded plastic, like a buzz saw cutting out a hole in a patch of ice . . . till I felt something shift under me and shouted, "Stop!" into the remote control.

For a heartbeat I stayed lying there, on an untouched circle of glass surrounded by a slashed area cut almost all the way through. Then my weight finished the job: with a noise halfway between a rip and a crack, my whole chunk of wall broke free and plunged, like a glass plate with me in the middle. I tucked, rolled, and kicked—the tuck and roll to save myself with a breakfall, the kick to aim the huge chunk of plummeting glass straight at Sam.

It was quiet as I got to my feet—no sound but the whistle of the Larry hovering far overhead. The glass walls around me cut off almost all noise from the outside world.

The cube was still flying, and stable as stone underfoot: just as happy to float on its side as right way up. That was a lucky break—I didn't know how to operate this thing, and the pilot hadn't been wearing any safety straps when the cube tipped. She'd fallen almost as heavily as Innocence, and gentles aren't built to take damage. Her body lay crumpled at the far end of the cube, her shell split wide open all along the spine. Puffy brown skin pushed up through the break, the way meat sometimes does when you crack open a lobster. I didn't know if she was alive or dead, but I concentrated a moment and produced the worker pheromone that's supposed to dull pain. Maybe it would help.

Sam groaned. She lay under the slab of heavy glass like a lab specimen on display. At the last second she must have seen the slab coming, because she'd thrown up her arms to protect her face.

It may have helped her face, but it sure didn't help her arms.

I tried to heave the glass off her, but it was way too heavy to lift—several hundred kilos at least. It took all my strength just to slide it to one side; I tried not to hurt Sam again, but I could see there wasn't much left to hurt.

Sam's eyes flickered open. "Edward?" she whispered.

"Yes."

"I think you got me."

"You were going to kill Innocence."

"Was I?" She let her head slump, as if holding it up took too much effort. "How do you know Innocence wasn't in cahoots with me all along? My troops will tell you she's been giving them orders for the past few months."

"But you drugged her . . . and rigged her up so your words came out of her mouth."

"That's what I said," Sam whispered. "But how can you know if it's true? I could've been lying."

"Or you could be lying now. One last chance for you to cause trouble."

"Always a possibility." She coughed . . . very lightly, but a bead of blood dribbled out the side of her mouth. "Neither of us got very good brain chemicals, did we? Even now, I'm trying to think of ways to trick you into giving me the gun."

"Who would you shoot?" I asked. "Me? Innocence? Yourself?"

"Yes," she said, with a weak grin. "In that order."

She coughed again. The sound had a choking gurgle to it. "Kiss me," she whispered. "Kiss me good night."

I wondered if she had some hidden weapon she could kill me with if I got close, or perhaps some suicide pill she'd pop into my mouth instead of her own. No sign of anything like that; no smell either. She must have guessed what I was thinking, because she said, "Do you really think I'm that evil?"

"Yes."

"You're right. But kiss me anyway."

I knelt beside her and leaned forward, only intending a little peck on the cheek. But she turned her head at the last moment to meet my lips with hers, and she reached up to hold me—hold me with her crushed broken arms. It must have hurt hideously but she didn't even wince. For a long moment, there was only her mouth pressed desperately against mine, my sad, scared sister . . .

Then she became the second woman to die kissing me. I'd barely known either of them.

45

FINDING INNOCENCE

Something went CLONK above my head. Looking up, I saw Festina had heaved out a grapnel attached to a rope and caught it on the hole in the cube's glass. As usual, the Explorer Corps had come prepared for any contingency . . . even for snagging a floating cube and hauling it closer to the palace. It took everybody up there to get the cube moving—all five Mandasars as well as the Explorers—but centimeter by centimeter, they began dragging me in.

I couldn't help them, so I went to check on Innocence. The glass slab had missed her, but she'd hit real hard when the cube rolled. All eight of her legs looked broken and a tiny ooze of blood had begun seeping through a crack in her tail. Still, she was breathing pretty evenly. Like I said, queens are tough.

Her eyes were shut as I approached . . . but the moment I came within grabbing range, the eyes snapped open and one of her front claws whipped toward me. I dodged and slapped it aside, which shows how badly the fall had hurt her—under normal conditions, humans just aren't strong enough to block a queen's pincer.

Then again, maybe Innocence had pulled her attack at the last instant.

"My apologies, Little Father," she said in a soft voice, "but I didn't know it was you. You smell exactly like your sister."

"My sister's dead," I told her.

"Good. Then you won't smell alike much longer."

Um.

"How badly are you hurt?" I asked.

"I'll live," Innocence replied. "I hope."

"Don't worry," I told her, "there are good doctors in the palace infirmary . . ."

"Later," Innocence said. "First, I have to call off Samantha's troops."

"Oh. Right."

I thought that would be an easy job, considering we were in the command cube with that fancy sound system for talking long-distance; but we hadn't heard a peep from outside since I'd dropped in. Worried, I looked through the glass wall, trying to see the parabolic dish . . . but the only bit left was the dish's metal support stand. The rest had been shredded to shrapnel by a barrage of razor fléchettes.

Oops.

Still, there must be some other way for Innocence to speak to the Black Army—maybe the palace had working broadcast systems. Even just a big megaphone.

Except that Sam's soldiers were used to hearing Sam's voice come out of Innocence's mouth. If Innocence spoke in her normal voice, her troops would think it was a trick . . . that we'd captured their beloved queen and were projecting our own words through her. The black warriors would go screamingly berserk, killing everybody in the palace till Innocence was "rescued."

Oops again.

With a thud, the glass cube bumped against the palace wall. Immediately, Festina hopped across from the parapet; I could see the soles of her boots walking cautiously across the glass ceiling above me. "Are you all right?" she shouted down.

"Some are, some aren't," I answered . . . not looking toward my sister. "Our biggest problem now is the Black Army," I said. "No way to call them off."

"Just fucking wonderful," Festina muttered. "Can we use this cube to get the hell out of here?"

"Maybe—it's still in the air. Do we have any decent pilots?"

Festina turned and yelled, "Tobit! Get your ass over here."

His gravelly voice shouted back, "What now?"

"You like flying alien aircraft," Festina said. "See what you can do with this one."

"Oh goody," he grumbled. "My favorite type of airplane: anti-aerodynamic and totally made of glass. Who the hell keeps building these things?"

It took a minute to lower a rope and have Tobit shinny down into the cube . . . which he did pretty well, considering that "bum arm" he talked about. Getting him up to the pilot's console was a lot more work, but eventually I helped him clamber to the command couch. As he strapped himself in sideways, he yelled, "The dials are labeled in Fasskister Basic!"

That was an ultrasimplified version of the Fasskister language, one they used on products they shipped to other races. I said, "That proves Sam had some side deals going with the Fasskisters."

"We already knew that," Festina told me. "Your sister must have had her black ship running regular shuttles between here and the Fasskister orbital. Remember how that Fasskister took one look at you and announced you were definitely not nice? He was confusing you with Clone Boy back on the parapet . . . who no doubt acts like an utter bastard, no matter where he goes."

"Christ," Tobit muttered, "have we drawn up a diagram, who's been conspiring with whom?"

"Everybody with everybody else," Festina answered, "and everybody *against* everybody else. Secret alliances, secret betrayals, secret *quid pro quo*. Sam probably told the Fasskisters she was working to kill all the Mandasar queens, and they were happy to help her . . . especially since she and her precious Daddy had cash to pay for whatever was needed. Given how Fasskisters feel about monarchy, they'll probably be pissed when they hear Sam was using them as pawns to make herself queen."

"With luck, they'll never know," said a new voice. My own. Only it came from the clear-chested man up on the parapet.

He and Dade were standing side by side, both holding stun-pistols.

46

TALKING WITH DAD

Festina dived through the hole in the glass cube's roof a split second before the stun-pistols fired. Soft, soft whirring sounds . . . but Plebon and Zeeleepull crumpled, followed by the other Mandasars. Even Kaisho slumped in her hoverchair. As for Festina, the rope Tobit had climbed down was still dangling in place; she grabbed it as she fell and swung wildly as she braked herself to a stop. When she let go at the bottom, the gloves of her tightsuit gave off tiny wisps of smoke from rope burn.

"God damn it," she growled as she jumped down beside me, "I'm getting really *pissed* at people sneaking up behind my back."

Tobit was looking out the side of the cube, to where Dade and my father-son-twin stood on the parapet. "You fucking little weasel!" Tobit yelled at Dade. "What the hell do you think you're doing?"

"Helping me," Clear Chest answered. "Who do you think arranged for Dade to be assigned to *Jacaranda*? If Vincence could plant a spy on my *Willow*, I could plant one on his ship too."

"Shit," Festina muttered. "And I told Dade to guard the clone: a job I thought he couldn't screw up."

By now she had her own stunner out of its holster. She couldn't shoot out through the glass, and the others couldn't shoot in; but there was always that big opening in the cube's roof. If Dade and my father shot down through the hole, they could stun us like fish in a barrel—provided Festina didn't stun them first.

Things were shaping up into another standoff . . . except that Dad and Dade had a whole bunch of hostages: the Mandasars, Plebon, and Kaisho. Those of us in the cube didn't have any matching leverage.

And Dad knew it.

He lifted his foot and rested it on Plebon's unconscious face. "Come on out," Dad yelled at us. "Or I'll prove this bastard can look even worse than he does."

I tried not to picture the damage my father could do, stepping forward with all his weight: his heel breaking what little jaw Plebon had, then crushing up into the roof of the Explorer's mouth, teeth snapping off and driving up into the brain . . .

"Don't you dare!" Festina called in an angry voice. "Hurting that man would be a blatantly non-sentient act—"

"So what?" Dad snapped back. "I *am* non-sentient, Ramos. Haven't you figured that out yet? I'm not just the man you see here. I'm also the man who tried to kill you on Celestia. And the one who sent the entire crew of *Willow* to their deaths."

"Knowingly?" Festina asked.

"Hell yes, knowingly," Dad answered. "Samantha was having a bitch of a time with Queen Temperance. The way Temperance had fortified the palace, it might have taken months to capture the place by siege. So I sent *Willow* to remove Temperance from the picture. Offer her free passage to Celestia."

"But Temperance didn't want it," I said. "Did she, Dad?"

He looked at me in surprise. "How did you know?"

"Because queens aren't stupid," I told him. "She knew exactly what would happen if she headed for Celestia—the League would kill her as soon as she crossed the line. So what was *Willow*'s second offer, Dad? Something to do with the Fasskister orbital?"

My father did a double take. "Either you're amazingly

well informed," Dad said, "or you've developed an *idiot savant* gift for lucky guesses. Yes," he said, nodding, "something to do with the orbital. Only it was the queen's own idea. She sent those goody-goody Explorers out of the room, then offered *Willow*'s captain a deal. Temperance wanted to meet with the Fasskisters . . . supposedly to make peace with them, in the hopes they'd start helping her instead of Samantha."

Um. On the orbital, the Fasskister never mentioned that last part to us . . . but then, if he thought I was actually my father, he might want to keep the queen's proposition a secret.

"Of course," Dad went on, "what Temperance really wanted was to infect the orbital with those damned Balrog spores . . . but *Willow*'s captain didn't know that. His orders were to get Temperance off the planet any way he could, so he just went along. Unfortunately, the queen got to the orbital, stayed barely an hour, then demanded to be taken back to Troyen. Once she'd escaped from the siege at Unshummin, Temperance wanted to go home, get dropped somewhere far from Samantha's army, and start building her own forces again."

"Which," Festina said, "was definitely not something you and Sam wanted."

"Definitely not," Dad agreed. "*Willow*'s captain took the queen back aboard, then locked the hold door on her, and headed for Celestia anyway."

I thought about how Temperance had tried to bash through the wall of the hold. Battering herself bloody, knowing that when *Willow* crossed the line, the League would execute her for all the people she'd killed during the war. As for the crew who'd basically kidnapped her and dragged her into space against her will . . . it was pretty clear why the League killed them too. They weren't such nice people.

But there was still one thing I didn't understand. I asked, "Why, Dad? Why really? If this was just about making supergrandchildren, you could have done that without bloodshed. Sam didn't kill Verity till after I'd finished my transformation; at that point, you'd run through your test case, you had all the data . . . so why murder the queen? And why set up the recruiters, when Celestia has nothing to do with either Troyen or the Technocracy? You could have got your dynasty of superkids without destroying a single life."

Dad took a long time to answer. When he finally spoke, his voice was so soft I almost couldn't hear him through the glass. "Jetsam," he said, using his cruel old nickname for me, "have you ever really seen the Mandasars in action?"

"What do you mean?"

"I came to Troyen a century ago," he told me, "and even then it was clear Mandasars were special. Stronger than humans . . . more rationally organized . . . smarter. Your average gentle scores twenty percent higher than a corresponding *Homo sapiens*, on all nine intelligence scales. And that was just in peacetime. In war . . . Christ Almighty, compared to Troyen, the Technocracy is so pathetically weak, I sometimes want to puke. We're lazy and venal, like Imperial Rome at its most decadent; but the League of Peoples make sure that barbarians never come banging on our gates. That's a crime against evolution. Mandasar society is the most efficient war machine I've ever seen, and it's a travesty they can't run right over us."

"They aren't war machines," I objected. "Troyen stayed at peace two hundred years before Sam got everybody riled up."

"Two hundred sterile years," Dad replied, "unnaturally imposed when Queen Wisdom sucked up to the League of Peoples. She was the one who forced warriors and gentles and workers to live together, poisoning each other with their own pheromones, diluting what they should be . . ."

"And what they should be is separate from each other?" I asked. "The way your recruiters ripped apart families into single-caste slave camps and brainwashed them—"

"Like hell I brainwashed them!" Dad interrupted. "They

were brainwashed before. I returned them to their true strength. You think it's an accident that when they're segregated, the gentles become brilliant tacticians, the warriors become unstoppable soldiers, and the workers become uncomplaining servants? Open your eyes, boy—*it's not an accident, it's what nature intended.* Evolution made Mandasars into perfect infantry, perfect strategists, perfect civilian support . . . with an iron-willed queen at the top to dictate what everyone else should be doing. That's the natural state of the Mandasar world, Jetsam: a crystal-clear division of duty."

"No," Festina said quietly, "that's only *one* natural state of the Mandasar world. Evolution also provided the other paradigm: castes mingling with each other, their pheromones balancing each other's personalities. Less aggressive warriors, less slavish workers, less tunnel-visioned gentles. Not as ruthlessly efficient, but a way of life where everyone has more breathing space."

"A way of life where everyone is weak," my father sneered. "Easy prey the moment some other Mandasar tribe goes onto a segregated military footing."

Festina said, "Really? If turning militaristic was always stronger, wouldn't evolution get rid of the other possibility after a while? But Mandasar pheromones are tuned to make both ways of life possible: segregated *and* unified. Historically, I'm sure Mandasars sometimes needed to abandon everything else and gear up for war . . . but they also had to be prepared for peace. Otherwise, what would they do when they'd defeated all their available enemies?"

"There are always more enemies," my father replied dismissively.

"Maybe," Festina admitted, "if you go out and look for them. But to do that, you have to invent the peaceful art of boat-building. And navigation. And cartography. And systems of government that hold your empire together when your queen is too far away to make every decision for you." She shook her head. "Success in war always leads to the demands of peace, Admiral. Suppose tens of thousands of years ago, the Mandasars *did* have a subspecies one hundred percent devoted to fighting; that breed didn't survive, did it? Either they killed each other in some prehistoric Armageddon, or they starved to death because the workers became too bored and stupid to plant crops properly. Modern Mandasars—*Mandasar sapiens*—came out on top because they weren't one-trick ponies."

She peered up intently at the glass-chested man on the battlements. "Glorify war if you want, Admiral York. A lot of people do, especially since the League has made armed conflict so rare. When no one's seen combat for a long time, some folks get the idea they're missing a primal source of energy. But fighting is only part of the story for any species, and the other parts are just as important."

"Other parts only become important after the fighting stops," my father retorted. "Kill or be killed, Ramos; that's the fundamental issue, and everything else comes after, if you can spare the time. Don't go writing poetry until you're sitting on your enemies' bones."

He waved his hand out beyond us, toward the approaching Black Army. They'd reached the last canal now, the one surrounding the palace like a moat. Soon they'd be driving their way across, breaching the palisade and storming onto the palace grounds. My father smiled. "This is what it always comes down to, Ramos. Naked aggression: might against might. You can rhapsodize about art and science and anything else you think is a great accomplishment, but nature doesn't respect that superficial crap. Death is the one reality our universe truly acknowledges. That's why Sam and I chose to start a war; I've devoted myself to life's one overwhelming imperative."

"Killing those who threaten you?" Festina asked.

"Yes."

"Eliminating those who are dangerous to you?"

"Right."

"The strong subjugate the weak?"

"Correct." He lifted his foot, then set it down on Plebon's

face again. "You have ten seconds to surrender or I'll show you how ugly war can be."

"*I* may have ten seconds," Festina answered coldly, "but you don't. You're a dangerous non-sentient, threatening to kill a sentient being . . . and any nearby sentients have an absolute duty to stop you. You're also a pompous jerk-off, Admiral, extolling the joys of conquest but failing to grasp the most important law of all: no matter how tough you are, there's always someone who can beat the living shit out of you." She clapped her hands once, sharp and loud. "Balrog!"

Like fire belching from a furnace, plumes of glowing red erupted from the stairwell. Crimson smoke, thick as a wall, exploded outward to sweep over my father and Dade, so fast the two men were coated with spores before they could react.

Dade shrieked and dropped his stunner, throwing his hands to his helmet. For ten long seconds, he tried to scrape his visor clear with his fingers, scrabbling at the dusty layer of moss that continued to thicken around him. Then some particularly hungry mass of spores managed to corrode through his tightsuit, down near his stomach where the front had been cut to expose the power circuits. Air puffed out from the suit's belly, swirling the spores around like steam on a breeze. As the suit began to deflate, Dade howled and doubled over, like something was clawing at his gut. A moment later, he dropped out of sight behind the parapet wall, and his howling cut off dead.

As for my father—my son, my twin brother—he didn't even have a tightsuit to protect him. In a single heartbeat, his head was enveloped by a spongy clot of moss: red wads of fuzz coating his hair, covering his eyes, clogging up his nose and mouth. I think he tried to scream, but the noise was muffled to an almost inaudible whine. He took two blind steps but couldn't manage a third . . . more moss congealed around him every second, weighing down his legs, freezing him in place. His arms waved feebly till they became too heavy to move; already his body looked twice its original size, with still more spores accumulating all over, packing outward until the human shape was lost. Soon there was only a fuzzy red ball, man height and glowing as bright as a bonfire.

Twenty seconds of hold-your-breath silence. Then the top of that red-shining ball began to flatten in. Moment by moment, more of the ball sank away, spores sloughing off onto the stone parapet; and there was nothing underneath. No man. No bones. Nothing but solid moss. I could smell an overpowering buttered-toast odor on the wind that blew through the hole in our glass cube . . . and it made me think of a smugly satisfied predator that's just eaten a nice meal.

As the ball of moss continued to dissolve, I could see that the glass chest plate hadn't been consumed—it must have been indigestible. Also untouched was the tiny glass container that had once nestled in the man's intestines. The container floated atop the mass of moss, like a bottle bobbing on a calm lake, while spores kept falling away. Within a minute, the ball that had once been my father shrank to nothing but a flat sheen of red on the parapet's stone. For a moment more, the glass container remained motionless on that mossy bed . . . and I could just make out the tiny dot of scarlet inside, the Balrog spore my father had imprisoned.

The surrounding moss suddenly flared a brilliant burning neon: bright enough to blind me for a second. When I could see again, the container was gone—vaporized, dissolved— and the once-captive spore was now just one among a million others glimmering silently in the darkness.

Mission accomplished for the Balrog . . . the prisoner freed. But the rescue hadn't happened till *after* Dad's clone had been eaten alive. My father's other copies—Mr. Clear Chest on Celestia, and Alexander York, Admiral of the Gold, on New Earth—must have stayed mentally linked with the dying man through the whole ordeal: must have felt every millisecond of the devouring as if it was happening to them.

I wondered what it would do to you . . . feeling yourself

being eaten alive. The Balrog could surely tell me—if it was telepathic, it must have heard my father's silent screams—but I decided I didn't want to know.

Festina was already scaling the rope, hand over hand toward the top of our glass cube. As she climbed, she called to Tobit, "Have you figured out how to fly this thing yet?"

"Almost," he answered. "Provided there aren't any built-in security checks. If the onboard computer wants me to type a password or something, we're screwed."

"Cross your fingers that doesn't happen," Festina told him. "If we can't stop the attacking army, this cube is our only way out of the city."

The moment she clambered onto the cube's glass roof, I grabbed the rope and headed up too. No point me staying in the cube: I couldn't help Tobit with the controls, and I couldn't help Innocence either. Sometime in the past two minutes, while I was watching my dad get eaten, Innocence had quietly passed out. Maybe that was a good sign—Mandasars shut down like that when their metabolisms shift into a full-out healing state—but it could also mean she was too broken inside to keep herself awake. We needed to get Innocence to the infirmary . . . but she wouldn't be safe till we stopped the Black Army.

Outside the cube, the air had curdled with the smell of buttered toast—*eau de Balrog*, so thick the night breeze couldn't dissipate it. From this angle, I could see how much of the parapet was covered with glowing red: a bulgy patch where my father had been, a Dade-shaped mound nearby, a light dusting everywhere else. Plebon and the Mandasars had been pelted with their share of spores when the Balrog exploded from the stairwell, but they weren't coated solidly . . . just a sprinkle of specks, like gleaming freckles all over their bodies.

Festina turned toward me as I joined her. She stood at the edge of the cube, where it nuzzled the top of the parapet wall. No spores had fallen on the cube itself; but if Festina took another step forward, she'd be walking on moss dust.

"What do you think?" she asked. "Is it going to eat us?"

"I don't know," I said. "It sure likes *pretending* it wants to eat us . . . but that might be its idea of a joke. Jumping out and going, 'Boo!' at the lower species. If the Balrog really wanted to have us for supper, it could have done that long ago."

"Maybe it's just following its own code of ethics," Festina suggested. "Can't eat anyone who keeps a respectful distance, but if you actually step on a spore, you're fair game."

She had a point. Maybe if you stepped on a bunch of moss, it actually hurt the spores—I'd get hurt if someone walked all over me. In that case, the Balrog might feel perfectly justified in biting your feet.

I glanced back at the palace's palisade. Outside, the Black Army was massing for its final assault, with ramps and battering rams and siege towers. Even worse, four Laughing Larries had taken up positions just inside one section of wall; by the look of it, they'd soon open fire, slaughtering nearby guards as the attackers began smashing their way in.

Whatever we needed to do, we'd better do it fast. Time to try a trick. "Give me a second," I told Festina. Then I closed my eyes and thought of pheromones.

Here are the pheromones I'd made: the lust scent that got Festina talking about judo mats; the "don't be scared" smell I'd used to comfort Counselor; the royal pheromone that screamed, "Obey me now!" Some of those chemicals worked on humans, some worked on Mandasars. I didn't know if I could make something to work on Balrogs . . . but Balrogs could "taste" pheromones so maybe the darned moss could be affected too.

Back on the orbital I'd tried to make a Balrog repellant and Kaisho had got real mad: Stop it, Edward, before you produce something deadly. Okay—maybe it was dangerous, trying to make the Balrog go away . . . but what if I made it *nice*?

I pictured a different sort of royal pheromone: not one

to subdue peasants, but one that spoke to rulers. A scent that said, *Some people end up in positions of power; and if you're the one who comes out on top, you have to be good about it. You have to do the right thing, and never ever act like a jerk.*

It wasn't a fancy sentiment, and any philosopher would nitpick it to pieces . . . but the Balrog and me, we had things in common. If we really wanted, we could both run rough-shod over normal folks; so we had to take special care not to. *Do the right thing and don't act like a jerk.* That was a rule I wanted to follow myself, and I wanted the Balrog to follow it too. I tried to make a pheromone that would stir some sense of scruples in a bunch of glowing alien spores . . .

. . . and as I stood there on the edge of the ramparts, the spores just drifted away—slid silently off Plebon and the Mandasars, sifted over the parapet stones, and drew back to the stairwell. Ten seconds later, Dade was still covered in fuzz but the rest of the area was absolutely clear.

"Holy shit," Festina whispered. "Did you do that?"

"Um. Maybe."

"With pheromones?"

"Maybe."

She shuddered. "Makes me glad I'm wearing this tight-suit. If you can drive off the Balrog, you probably smell like the rear end of something whose front end is dead."

"No," I said. "I smell like conscience." Then I stepped over the rampart wall and onto the parapet.

Fast as we could, we heaved Plebon and the Mandasars onto the top of the glass cube. The unconscious Zeeleepull took a ton of work and when we were finished, his shell had a bunch of new dents and scratches . . . but at least we got everybody safely onto the cube's upper surface. No way we could get them all inside—it would take a heavy-duty winch to lower Zeeleepull through that hole in the roof—but if Tobit could hold the cube level as it flew, our friends would be safe where they were.

Provided Tobit could fly the cube at all.

"Ready to go?" Tobit yelled up through the hole.

Festina looked back at the parapet. Kaisho and her wheelchair still sat in the mouth of the stairwell. The admiral paused a moment longer, then sighed. "Hold on a minute, Phylar. One more passenger to pick up."

I was already hopping onto the parapet one last time. The main mass of Balrog had retreated a bit down the ramp, leaving Kaisho sitting out on her own. She'd slumped good and limp when Dade shot her with the stunner; but as we grabbed the arms of her chair, she lifted her head. "That won't be necessary," she whispered.

Festina jerked in surprise. She let go of the chair and balled her hands into fists; but after a second she let her hands relax. "You recover amazingly fast from being stunned," she told Kaisho. "Most organisms stay unconscious for six hours."

"Only if they have conventional nervous systems," Kaisho replied. "I've gone a bit beyond that."

"Were you unconscious at all?"

"Part of me," she admitted. "As for the other part . . . it's thrilled not to be linked with Alexander York."

"There are still versions of him on Celestia and New Earth," Festina said.

"Not in working condition," Kaisho replied. "When the Balrog retrieved that gizmo from the clone's gullet, we used it to send a shot of feedback along the line. One good focused pulse of psychic energy . . . and the containers inside the other two Admiral Yorks suffered rather spectacular meltdowns. At the time, the New Earth version of the bastard was sitting with the entire High Council at Admiralty HQ. His death made quite a splash. Consider it a windfall for the other admirals' dry cleaners." She turned to me. "Should I offer my condolences or my congratulations?"

"Um."

I didn't like my father. I didn't like my sister either, not once I learned all the awful things she'd been doing. It seemed really dumb to be sad they were gone.

But then, I've always been dumb, haven't I?

47

PUSHING BACK THE ENEMY

A booming thud hit the palace's west gate: the first slam of a battering ram. "No more time," Festina snapped. "Hang on, Kaisho, you're coming with us."

"Where?"

"Anywhere the Black Army isn't." She pointed to the hoverchair's controls. "Fire up your engines and let's go."

"No need," Kaisho said. "We're safe here."

Another boom smashed the gates. The Black Army's Laughing Larries spun into a full hyena cackle, their whoops echoing off the palace's stonework. Any second they'd open fire.

"Hear that?" Festina asked. "Nobody's safe, not tonight. Even your precious Balrog should worry. Those troops are surely prepared to burn every speck of moss they see. No matter how fast spores can eat through an enemy's shell, fire works faster."

"There is no enemy," Kaisho replied. "Not anymore. We've dealt with Admiral York, and everybody left is just an innocent pawn."

"Those pawns have been ordered to kill, and there's no one to call them off."

"They'll call *themselves* off, dear Festina . . . if we demonstrate there are forces in the universe that lesser species shouldn't fuck with."

"Uh-oh," Festina said. "You aren't going to . . . remember, you just called them innocent pawns."

"Of course," Kaisho answered sweetly. "But as *Teelu* told you a few minutes ago, the Balrog loves jumping out and going, 'Boo!' "

Another boom banged above the Larries' howl. The noise was followed by a heavy crunching sound . . . but the crunch didn't come from the army at the palace gates. I looked toward the front of the palace, out where the moss was thickest. It had blazed up bright and angry, a furious fuzzy crimson all over the stonework queen's head and her four claws.

One of the claws was trying to wrench itself off its foundations.

Slowly, ponderously, the claw crunched back and forth, as if it was stuck in a bit of mud and just needed to be teased loose. The moss on the wriggling claw flared another notch brighter . . . and suddenly the claw was moving freely, a building wing four stories tall, lifting into the air.

The claw flexed once, as if it was stiff from lying immobile for so long. Mortar crackled and dust showered out from between cracks in the stone, but the whole thing held together somehow: from the sheer telekinetic force of a trillion Balrog spores showing off their strength.

Without a pause, another claw began to work itself free.

"If I were you," Kaisho told Festina, "I'd hop onto that glass cube and head a hundred meters straight up."

"It's going to get dangerous down here?"

"No, the Balrog won't hurt anybody. But you're going to kick yourself if you don't go high enough to get a good view."

She caught Festina's gloved hand and pulled it to her lips for a kiss. As she did, the hair covering her face slid aside; with a squirm in my stomach, I saw crimson moss now coated her cheeks, her forehead, even bristly wads over her eyes. There was no way she could possibly see through that glowing fuzz . . . but I guess Kaisho had reached the point where the moss did her seeing for her.

"Go," she said to Festina: a single word, spoken in a real human voice, not her usual whisper.

Then Kaisho turned to me and held out her hand. A bit reluctantly, I came forward and took it. She clasped both hands around mine and drew me in gently, so I was forced to crouch up close to her. "*Teelu*," she whispered, her breath brushing my cheek, "a pity we won't be working together. I would have enjoyed touching my mind to yours. But you've persuaded the Balrog not to embrace you as its own. Others have prior claim on you."

"Who?" I asked.

She gave me a little kiss on the nose. "Your people," she whispered, "as you know full well. You still consider yourself unintelligent, *Teelu*; it's charming, but you'll have to grow out of it. Kings need confidence."

Before I could answer, she put her finger to my mouth to stop me from speaking. Next thing I knew, her voice was talking right inside my head. "Sometime in the next eighteen years, *Teelu*, I'll visit you, wherever you are. The Balrog believes it would be amusing for you and me to have a child: mostly human, but with your control of pheromones and my enhanced mental abilities. Apparently, this is why the Balrog fused with me in the first place; and for twenty-five years, it's been transforming my body chemistry to make such a pregnancy possible. A few more years, and I'll be ready." She leaned forward and kissed me with her moss-covered lips. "It's a bitch dealing with precognitive races. But if everything I've gone through is gearing me up for a night with you . . . well, life has its compensations, doesn't it?"

"Um . . . what if I don't think this is such a good idea?"

"It's not an idea, *Teelu*—it's fate. Already written by the Mother of Time. Relax and accept that some evening you'll find something warm and fuzzy in your bed."

She laughed out loud . . . probably at the look on my face. Then her hoverchair rocketed down the stairwell a hundred times faster than it'd ever moved before. The sound of her laughter echoed long after she was gone.

* * *

Festina grabbed my arm. "Let's go, Edward. Things are going to get crazy real fast."

I pulled myself away from looking down the empty stairwell and glanced toward the front of the building. All four claws had ripped themselves free, and now the queen's head was pushing itself up. The stone under my feet rocked slightly . . . just a little tremor, but I still wobbled for a moment, off balance.

"Yeah," I said, "going sounds good."

We ran to the edge of the roof and threw ourselves over the wall, onto the glass cube. Even as I jumped, another tremor shivered through the stone beneath me—the queen's head had risen, and now she was lifting her body on its eight legs.

Far below, things popped and groaned inside the building: walls tearing away from floors, support beams breaking, furniture toppling over. A stream of palace guards charged out a ground-floor door, all of them screaming martial battle cries and brandishing crossbows in search of someone to shoot. They must have thought the Black Shoulders had started the building shaking by clobbering the walls with battering rams. When the guards saw huge masonry claws waving high over their heads, they screamed again. This time, it didn't sound nearly so martial.

Festina scrambled over the glass roof and stuck her head through the hole in the cube. "Phylar! Are you ready to fly this thing?"

"Maybe."

"Make it yes, and make it now. Straight up till we're clear of this mess."

"Easy for you to say," he grumbled.

He reached out and hesitantly nudged a slider control. Without a sound, the cube rose lazily; I was poised near the bodies of our unconscious friends, ready to catch them if they started to slide off . . . but the cube's motion was so smooth, they didn't shift a millimeter. Keeping level, never giving the slightest lurch, Tobit took us into the air as slowly as smoke rising.

The scene below wasn't nearly so placid. Out near the first canal, the Black Army must have heard the crashes and creaks of the palace coming alive, but they couldn't possibly guess what was making the noise. Their line of sight was blocked by the high palisade walls; perhaps they thought the ripping and rumbling came from some kind of weapon being trundled into place. The attackers continued to work their battering rams, smashing at the gates again and again, hoping to get inside before the defenders could get the weapon ready. They had no idea what was happening to the palace till the gates fell open and the Black Shoulders surged onto the grounds.

With impeccable timing—of course—that was the exact same moment the Balrog finished detaching the entire palace from its foundations. As the Black Army charged through the gates, they were greeted by a huge stone queen, four stories tall and larger than a city block, her shell blazing scarlet with angry moss.

Mandasar warriors are as brave as any creature in the universe, but even they have their limits.

For a moment, much of the Black Army simply froze. They watched as the queen's four claws, each bigger than a house, swept through the air over their heads and caught the Laughing Larries that were supposed to give covering fire. The claws slammed shut with the sound of thunder, solid stone walls whacking together ... and when they opened again, four gold-colored lumps of scrap metal flopped to the ground like crushed walnuts.

No more hyena laughing. But the night was far from quiet.

The claws rose again, high enough to clear the heads of the attackers but not by much. Then they clacked their pincers a few times, showering the troops below with whatever dirt had accumulated on the palace walls over the years: stone dust and insect carcasses, bird nests and chips of old paint, dried-out flakes of autumn leaves and clots of mud daubed by playing children. All of it rained on the soldiers beneath, as if the queen was just brushing her hands off before getting set for serious fighting. When the spill of debris was finished, the claws came down onto the palace lawn and began to push forward like huge snowplows, ready to shove the Black Army back over the canal.

The shove wasn't needed. With a jumble of confused bellows the warriors fell back, some trying to maintain an orderly retreat, others simply running. A few held their ground, till not-very-gentle nudges from the stone walls knocked them back into the canal.

Possibly, some of the generals tried to contact Samantha for new orders. When they got no answer, they made a decision on their own: strategic withdrawal. Within fifteen minutes, the battle for the palace was over.

48

WINDING DOWN

I won't bother you with details of the next few hours. What's the point in describing, say, the trouble we went to, getting Innocence out of the cube? Unless you're a fan of techniques for using block and tackle, you don't want me going on at length; so let's just give you the short form.

Innocence survived, and came through without permanent injury. The people inside the palace turned out safe and sound too; when the building started walking about, they reported being held in place by "an invisible force" till the excitement was over.

Kaisho disappeared in the confusion; she hasn't been seen since. I guess she'll show up eventually, expecting me to take her to bed. I've kind of decided I will—considering how the Balrog stopped the battle and saved thousands of lives, I owe the moss a favor. (Even if the idea of producing a spore-baby is really really gross.)

Unlike my father, Benjamin Dade wasn't completely consumed by the moss that enveloped him . . . just nibbled a lot. We lugged him to the infirmary but Gashwan decided he couldn't be treated—the Balrog had invaded his bloodstream, his nervous system, every part of his innards. Trying to remove the spores would kill him; but if we left him alone, he'd live out his normal span, the same as Kaisho.

Eventually, Innocence made Dade a centerpiece on Diplomats Row, set on a small pedestal like a moss-covered statue. He still gets regular meals and plenty of light, not to mention all kinds of people to talk with. Sometimes he complains how unfair it is, that he's become a fuzzy paralytic; other times, he goes all spacey and gives incomprehensible prognostications that he claims come from the Balrog. A lot of folks think he invents the predictions on his own, but they visit him anyway: Mandasars who want to know what crops to plant, human kids asking who they'll marry, that sort of thing.

If you want the honest truth, Dade loves the attention. It's not how he envisioned his life, but deep down, he's tickled by it.

Dawn came up warm but cloudy gray. I sat with Festina and Tobit, dangling our feet on the edge of one of the trenches in the palace lawn, watching envoys scurry between the palace and Black Army headquarters. We got pretty good at guessing which messengers would tell us, "Talks are going well," and which would say, "I'm very, very worried." From what I knew of diplomats, things were pretty much on track. No one wanted to fight anymore; they just had a lot of bluster that needed to blow itself out.

Somewhere back in the palace, our friends would soon be waking up: it'd been almost six hours since they'd got shot by Dad and Dade. We'd left them in a corner of the infirmary, with instructions on how to find us when they came to. Gashwan wouldn't let us wait anywhere nearby—us and our filthy human germs—so we'd gone outside to cool our heels and watch the sun rise.

Festina and Tobit had taken off their helmets long ago. Ever since they'd cannibalized their tightsuit power supplies, their personal cooling systems had been out of order; as Tobit put it, "We're sweating our fucking bags off." Opening the helmets helped air circulate inside the suits, but as the day warmed up, their "bags" would sweat even more. The two of them were discussing whether to take off the rest of their suits—and where to find replacement clothes, since Festina only wore a light chemise under the suit while Tobit had nothing at all—when the admiral suddenly cocked her ear and whispered, "Listen!"

We listened. High over head, something was coming toward us, fast and whistling. "Fuck," Tobit groaned, "a bomb." All three of us shoved ourselves forward and dropped into the trench in front of us, ducking low as Tobit continued to grumble. "Here we are, hours away from peace, and some jerk-off decides, 'Hey, the arsenal isn't empty yet, let's aim for the palace.'"

"If it's a bomb, it's taking its sweet time," Festina said. She peeked at the clouds above us. "Where the hell is it?"

"Probably some kind of smart missile," Tobit replied, "flying in circles till it chooses the optimum target."

"Or else . . ." Festina began to say.

A jet-black shadow lanced out of the clouds: torpedo-shaped, riding an almost-invisible vapor trail. "Bloody hell," Festina said. "It's one of ours."

"One of our what?" I asked.

Festina didn't answer; she was already scrambling out of the trench, holding up her arms and waving. Tobit told me, "Navy probe missile. Black means it belongs to the Explorer Corps." Then he too began climbing, hollering at the probe as if it could hear him.

Maybe it could. It swept in low to the ground, ejected something small that dropped at Tobit's feet, then soared up into the clouds again. The ejected object was a black box covered with horseshoe-shaped gold insets: a Sperm-tail anchor. It hummed softly, already switched on.

"Look alive, Edward," Festina told me. "We're getting company."

"Friendly company?" I asked. "The last Sperm-tail brought my dad and three Larries."

"Good point," Tobit said. "Get ready to pound the crap out of anyone who doesn't look like our kind of people."

Ten seconds later, a Sperm-tail stabbed from the sky. It happened almost too fast to see—one moment there was nothing, and the next there was a fluttering milky tube, stretching up into the clouds. Its end lay draped across the little anchor box, like a glittery white sock laid over a foot-stool. Festina and Tobit lifted their fists into fighting stance and positioned themselves around the tube. I joined them, all the while hoping I wouldn't have to hit anyone. There'd been plenty enough fighting already.

Behind me palace guards were shouting, wondering if they should be worried about the Sperm-tail. A few came our way; others hollered, "Stay at your posts and let *Teelu* handle it. He'll call if he needs help."

Let *Teelu* handle it. Not a healthy attitude, leaving responsibility to someone else. When I became king for real . . . if I became king for real . . . if and when I became whatever Queen Innocence thought was best, I'd sure try to get everybody thinking more independently.

A figure shot out of the Sperm-tail—a human wearing a white tightsuit. I waited to see if Festina and Tobit would start punching and kicking; but they only stared for a moment, then Festina leapt forward and threw her arms around the newcomer's neck. "Ullis!" Festina shouted. "What the hell are *you* doing here?" She turned to me, a huge smile on her face. "Edward, this is an old, old friend of mine. Ullis Naar."

"Hi," I said . . . not quite sure if Ullis was a man or a woman. All I could see were a pair of blue eyes blinking behind the tightsuit's visor.

"You're Edward York?" Ullis asked. A woman's voice. "Son of Admiral Alexander York?"

"Um. Yes." I wished people would stop harping on that.

"Then I'm supposed to render you all possible assistance in whatever you're doing. We have *Jacaranda*, *Tamarack*, *Bay*, and *Mountain Ash* here in orbit. What are your orders?"

Tobit and Festina looked at me. I looked at them, then at Ullis Naar. "Um," I said, wracking my brain for something to say. A tiny inspiration hit me. "How about starting with a status report?"

"Certainly," she replied. "My ship *Tamarack* arrived on

the outskirts of this system four hours ago. By then, the other three ships were already at their assigned stations. Together, we swooped in on Troyen, where we found *Willow* and the former *Cottonwood* in orbit. *Willow* was in no condition to do anything; *Cottonwood* gave us a bit of a run, but eventually we caught it with tractors."

She glanced at Festina and gave a rueful chuckle. "The Vac-heads are annoyingly proud of themselves right now. Talking about 'textbook operations' and slapping each other on the back. Meanwhile, we Explorers were the ones who had to board the captured vessel. Lucky for us, there were no warriors—just a skeleton crew of gentles, who surrendered without a fight." Ullis lowered her voice. "Poor kids were scared out of their wits: all teenagers, and naive as they come. Scarcely knew Troyen was having a war. Only thing they cared about was their ship . . . you know the way some kids get, when they can talk for hours about optimizing waste recyclers, but have no idea what day it is."

Tobit grunted. "Sister Samantha probably chose them for that very quality . . . then kept 'em isolated from the nasty realities of war, so they wouldn't have blood on their hands. If you've got a starship, you want the crew to be sentient, so they won't die the moment they cross the line. Those kids were likely raised in some sheltered environment where Sam made sure they never had a homicidal thought. And where they lived and breathed spaceships."

"Probably raised on *Cottonwood* itself," Festina agreed. "Plenty of room up there, and no interference from the war."

I thought about that. "Didn't Sam use the *Cottonwood* for making Laughing Larries?"

Tobit shrugged. "Those were built by your clone. The kids wouldn't have to know what the Larries were—the clone could say they were something harmless . . . surveillance monitors or weather sensors, something so boring the kids wouldn't ask questions."

"I would dearly love to know what you're talking about,"

Ullis said, "but first, I should see if there's anything we need to do." She turned to me. "Do you have any orders for us?"

"Um." I whispered to Festina, "Do I have any orders for them?"

"Just get her to explain what's going on," Festina whispered back. "These ships couldn't be here now unless they set out for Troyen a week ago." She stopped and turned to Ullis. "Did you say you're following Alexander York's orders?"

"Yes."

"And those orders said you'd find *Cottonwood* and *Willow* here?"

"That's right. *Jacaranda* was supposed to drop off your landing party, then pretend to leave the system. It rendezvoused with the rest of us, and we all came zipping back to catch *Cottonwood* by surprise."

Festina frowned. "Why would Admiral York want the navy to capture Samantha's pet starship?"

"Oh," I said. "Um."

I remembered that night ten days ago, when I'd found myself sitting in front of Captain Prope's terminal. That's when I noticed someone had used the authorization codes Samantha gave me . . . and I was beginning to guess what the Smart half of my brain had done.

Issuing orders to Prope. Diverting three other ships to Troyen. Doing it all with my father's codes . . . and doing it pretty well, I guess, since it'd come off without a hitch.

Good for me. Or at least for Smart Me. He must have understood what was going on long before I did—that Sam was evil, that she'd made me a king, and she intended to start the last battle as soon as we landed on Troyen—so he'd used my dad's codes to make sure she wouldn't get away with it. He'd secretly called in four cruisers to capture *Willow* and the black ship; not only did that wipe out Sam's "fleet," it also provided hard evidence that my sister had pirated two navy vessels. The High Council would hit the roof about that . . . then Sam could forget any perks or con-

cessions she wanted to beg from the Admiralty. She
wouldn't get a cent to rebuild Troyen. Quite possibly, the
Technocracy would have imposed all kinds of economic
sanctions, and backed them up with a heavy navy blockade.

But Smart Me had done more than call in those four
ships: he'd arranged with Prope to trap our whole party
down on the surface. Why? I guess because he didn't want
us to have the option of running away. Smart Me was no
Balrog—he sure couldn't foresee how we'd save Innocence, or stop Sam and my dad—but he must have had the
colossal arrogance to believe he'd set things right somehow. All he had to do was show up, take charge, confront
his enemies . . . and he'd come out on top.

In other words, my brainy half had the same kind of ego
as every Mandasar queen since the dawn of time. Like it
or not, I was one of them.

If you want the honest truth, that scared me. I didn't want
to become all clever and cunning and cruel. But what was
I going to do? Push my smart bits away and keep them
choked off somewhere? I'd done that twenty years ago
when I'd decided I'd rather be stupid than admit the truth
about Sam; and how did that help anybody?

Time to stop hiding. Stupid or smart, it was time for me
to be who I was—*what* I was. And if some parts of me
were kind of terrifying . . . I wasn't so different from anyone else.

Twelve days later, I rode a Sperm-tail from *Jacaranda*
down to Celestia. No strange flashbacks or conversations
with other sides of myself. Just a whole lot of flip-flops in
my stomach as I twisted and turned and corkscrewed.

Festina said that was normal.

We landed on the edge of the Hollen Marsh, within spitting distance of where my evac module had splashed down
weeks earlier. Night was falling on this part of the planet—
a soft summery dusk, filled with the rich smells of humus
and growing vegetables.

The Mandasars were with us, of course; but they made

a big show of hurrying off to their home "to give the humes some privacy." Counselor and the rest still devoutly believed a human man and woman would nuzzle up to each other the instant they were left alone . . . and as soon as the Mandasars reached their domes, they settled down to watch in eager anticipation.

"Um," said Festina with a smile. "Are you ready for this, Your Majesty?"

"I thought Explorers called each other by name, not title."

"King Edward the First," she suggested. "Supreme Monarch of Celestia."

"Don't say things like that!" I shuddered. "The government is scared enough of me as it is."

"Scared is good," Festina replied. "They deserve it."

For the past two days, our ship had sat in orbit while Festina argued with Celestian officials about whether I should be allowed to land. They had the idea I might be some fanatic rebel leader, who intended to organize ten million Mandasars into crazed revolt. They had a point: word was starting to leak out, what Sam and my dad had done, so it wasn't too surprising folks would mistrust someone from the same family.

But Celestia didn't have much choice. Any day now, a whole passle of journalists in the Technocracy (and the Divian Spread, and the Fasskister Union, and heaven knows where else) were going to receive a communiqué from High Queen Innocence I of Troyen, giving precise details of the heinous acts committed by a Technocracy admiral against the Mandasar people. As of that moment, Mandasars would become a Big Important Cause at breakfast tables and in boardrooms throughout the galaxy.

Festina told Celestia it was very, very important for their government to come down on the right side of the issue. Take all those factories, for example—the ones that cheerfully used Mandasar workers kidnapped by recruiters. Real soon now, the people who owned those factories would find it colossally unpopular for them to have brainwashed Mandasars on the assembly line. They'd be facing boycotts, protests, and much worse, disquieted stockholders who found themselves unwelcome at the usual cocktail parties. Would these rich owners take the blame themselves? No. They'd point their fingers at the Celestian government, and say, "Hey, you told us those lobsters were *happy!*"

Also: how would it look if Celestia refused to allow the official ambassador from Troyen—namely, me—to land on the planet and try to set things right? That was a solid-gold *guarantee* that ten million Mandasars would whip themselves into crazed revolt. It was also a guarantee the irresponsible rich who usually vacationed on Celestia would give the planet a miss this year; they didn't mind if Celestia was the home of sleazeball profiteers, but heaven forbid it should ever be considered unenlightened, or worse, *unfashionable*.

So in the end, the Celestian government gave in: promised to close down recruitment operations, help rehabilitate brainwashed Mandasars by bringing them back into mixed-caste hives, and recognize me as a sort of a kind of a spokesman for all Mandasars on the planet. Not a king— they didn't want that, and neither did I—but it was okay me being a guy who asked Mandasars what they thought, then passed the word to everybody else.

"Well," Festina said, looking at the purple twilight rather than me, "if you're all right here, I should head back to *Jacaranda*. The Celestian authorities are supposedly fixing the recruiter problem even as we speak, but someone has to keep an eye on them."

"Shouldn't I help you?" I asked.

"Nah," she told me, "watchdogging planetary governments is my job. You just look after your own people."

She'd said the same things up in the ship—couldn't stay long, work to do, no need for me to help. Yet she'd still come to see me safely down on Celestia.

Maybe she just didn't want to say good-bye with Prope watching. Festina longed to nail the captain with a few good punches for marooning us on Troyen; but since Prope had been following *my* orders, decking her wouldn't be fair. Instead, Festina gave Prope the cold shoulder and spent all her time with me. That probably hurt Prope way more than a simple whack in the jaw—the captain was always staring at us venomously, as if it pierced her to the heart that I'd chosen Festina over her.

Prope obviously believed Festina and I were up to something steamy. But we weren't: we just talked. About the responsibilities of power, and the ways of power, and the limitations of power. A crash course in galactic politics, and a whole lot of reminders not to see people as children who needed Daddy's help.

I think hive-queens have a gene that makes them go all condescending about their subjects. Now I had that gene too . . . but Festina did her best to help me get over it.

Never once did we talk of judo mats. Never once, in all our trip back from Troyen, did we touch each other.

I'd been afraid my pheromones would start acting up and make her go all crazy against her will.

I don't know what Festina was afraid of.

"Okay," she murmured in the Celestian twilight. "Time to go." She stepped toward me, and just for a moment, she looked straight up into my eyes. Then she rose on tiptoe and kissed me on the cheek.

I couldn't help remembering that woman back on *Willow*, the one pretending to be Lieutenant Admiral Ramos. It made me kind of wistful that the real Festina wasn't the one who kissed me on the lips.

But that was just me, being stupid.

JAMES ALAN GARDNER

Q: Why the League of Peoples?

I've seen too many science fiction universes where humans are important.

If life is common in our universe, a lot of alien species must be way ahead of human technology. After all, plenty of star systems are billions of years older than ours; if planets in those systems had evolution working on a similar time-scale to Earth, they could have produced intelligent species whose technology is a billion years better than ours.

That's one heck of a headstart.

So I imagined a universe in which humans are hopelessly outclassed by thousands of alien species, some of whom had FTL travel back when our ancestors were hamster-like things trying not to get stepped on by dinosaurs. However, I didn't want humans in my stories to be downtrodden slaves of bug-eyed monsters with superior technology; it seemed more likely that highly advanced aliens just wouldn't *care* about humans. They definitely wouldn't want to govern us—we humans don't want to govern earthworms, do we?

Therefore, all my books have started with the League of Peoples: an alliance of super-powerful aliens who are happy to let us humans (and other such primitive species) do whatever we like . . . provided we don't cause trouble. Specifically, the League doesn't want homicidal creatures leaving their home star systems and traveling elsewhere—that's like letting a disease spread. If you *do* have murder in mind and you try interstellar travel, the League infallibly executes you the second you "cross the line" from one star system to the next.

This ever-present threat has influenced much of the action in my first three novels, but oddly enough, the League never directly killed anyone in those books. That all changes in the fourth book, *Hunted*. The League executes almost everybody on a navy starship, and the single human survivor has to find out why.

Explore the Astonishing Worlds of
James Alan Gardner

"Gardner will be one of the big names of
21st century science fiction."
Robert J. Sawyer

TRAPPED
0-380-81330-0 • $6.99 US • $9.99 Can

ASCENDING
0-380-81329-7 • $6.99 US • $9.99 Can
A breathtaking return to the "Expendable" universe
from one of the most exciting talents in contemporary SF.

HUNTED
0-380-80209-0 • $6.99 US • $9.99 Can

VIGILANT
0-380-80208-2 • $5.99 US • $7.99 Can

EXPENDABLE
0-380-79439-X • $6.99 US • $9.99 Can

COMMITMENT HOUR
0-380-79827-1 • $6.99 US • $9.99 Can